And What D...

Sarah Long worked for several years in publishing before giving it all up to move to Paris with her husband and three children. Following several years of the Parisian experience, they now live back in London. *And What Do You Do?* is her first novel.

And What Do You Do?

—⚹—

Sarah Long

C
Century · London

Published by Century in 2003

1 3 5 7 9 10 8 6 4 2

Copyright © Sarah Long 2003

Sarah Long has asserted her right under the Copyright, Designs and Patents Act,
1988 to be identified as the author of this work

First published in the United Kingdom in 2003 by Century

Random House Group Limited
20 Vauxhall Bridge Road, London SW1V 2SA

Random House Australia (Pty) Limited
20 Alfred Street, Milsons Point, Sydney,
New South Wales 2061, Australia

Random House New Zealand Limited
18 Poland Road, Glenfield
Auckland 10, New Zealand

Random House (Pty) Limited
Endulini, 5a Jubilee Road, Parktown 2193, South Africa

Random House Group Limited Reg. No. 954009

www.randomhouse.co.uk

A CIP catalogue record for this book is available
from the British Library

Papers used by Random House
are natural, recyclable products made from wood grown in
sustainable forests. The manufacturing processes conform to
the environmental regulations of the country of origin

ISBN 1 8441 3168 8

Typeset by Palimpsest Book Production Limited,
Polmont, Stirlingshire
Printed and bound in Great Britain by
Mackays of Chatham PLC, Chatham, Kent

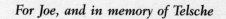

For Joe, and in memory of Telsche

'Don't be disappointed by overestimating happiness in marriage. Remember that nightingales only sing in spring time, but are generally silent once they've laid their eggs.'

Thomas Fuller (1608–1661), *The Holy State and The Profane State: On Marriage*

ONE

'What time is it, Mum? Oh no, I know we're going to be late. If we're late I'm not going to school. It's all your fault.'

Charles-Edouard slumped back into his seat while Laura attempted to carve a route through the anarchic traffic that criss-crossed the Trocadero. It was rather depressing, she thought, that at the age of seven, Charles-Edouard had already developed some of the more disagreeable French traits: hysteria, a filthy temper and a tendency to blame.

'It's 8.42, we've got plenty of time, and it's not my fault if some arsehole is blocking the road,' she replied, honking the horn of the Renault Espace at the driver of the car in front, who had considered it quite normal to hold up rush-hour traffic for five minutes while he double-parked in front of a *tabac* to get his daily fix of cigarettes.

'You said a rude word, Mum,' remarked her other son, helpfully, 'Arsehole, that's where your poo comes out.'

'It's not *that* rude,' said Laura. 'I can think of plenty that are ruder.'

'Well, it's still not very nice to say arsehole, I don't know any other mummies who say arsehole.' He pronounced it daintily with a clear division between the syllables.

Charles-Edouard saw further opportunity to fuel his tide of self-righteousness.

'Yeah, you're disgusting, Mum. Why can't you be nice like Mary Poppins?'

Laura screeched to a halt outside the school and, as every proper chauffeur should, leapt out of the car to open the door for her children.

'Here you are my darlings, have a nice day.'

She watched them run across the playground, Charles-Edouard leading the way, doubled up beneath the weight of his swot-sized satchel. Pierre-Louis, whose stocky figure at the age of five still carried the last traces of baby roundness, followed behind, his gloves sewn slapdash on to an overlong cord which trailed along the ground. She waited until they turned to wave as they reached the door. The headmistress, looking less like an educationalist than an investment banker in her snappy two-piece, slammed the door behind the last stragglers, leaving the parents free to turn away to pursue their busy lives. Laura climbed back into her car. Time for a coffee, she thought.

Laura de Saint Léger, aged thirty-seven, retired executive and mother of two, took up her usual seat by the window of the café. A waiter approached the table. He had the grey skin of those who spend their entire life indoors and clearly hadn't had any fresh air for about fifteen years.

'*Un grand crème et une tartine, s'il vous plaît,*' said Laura.

She knew better than to waste a smile on him as he

took her order without the slightest hint of recognition, even though she regularly wasted the first half-hour of her uneventful day there. She also knew better than to ask for a *café au lait*, having lived in Paris long enough to know this was terribly naff. Tourists called it *café au lait*; for natives it was *crème*.

She glanced round at the company – old people, mostly alone, and a couple of business people poring over computer print-outs. Two American students, pretending to be Bohemian Left Bank poets, were scribbling self-consciously in notebooks. There was little conversation, and no one was smiling. An atmosphere of depressed resignation hung about the dinky tables as heavily as the cloud of tobacco smoke. The new regulations meant that every café had to have a properly ventilated no-smoking area, but this usually took the form of a small '*non-fumeur*' sign tossed on to the least appealing table. That was the French for you. A load of legislation that everyone ignored.

When she first came to live in Paris, Laura used to feel guilty about blowing the equivalent of £3.50 on a cup of coffee and a buttered piece of baguette every morning when she could have more cheaply gone back to the apartment for her breakfast. Now she regarded it as her right, just as her many visitors from England considered it their right to spend as little money as possible. They would come for three or four days to enjoy the free board and lodging which Laura, as homemaker, was happy to provide, but became resentful at having to fork out for the odd refreshment. 'How was your day?' Laura would ask as they returned from their sightseeing trips at five o'clock and fell ravenously upon the contents of her fridge. 'Oh, all right, but you know, we stopped at this café on the Champs Elysées, and do you know how much it was for four coffees? Ten pounds! Outrageous, isn't it?'

Laura stirred her coffee and contemplated the day ahead. The children were off her hands until four-thirty, the longest school day in Europe, a dream for working women. It meant that the home help could spend all day slaving in the apartment before picking up the children and bringing them home for their *goûter*. You saw them at the school gates – mostly African or Philippine women, who called their employers *madame* and knew their place.

There were none of those bossy English nannies that her friends at home competed to employ – spoilt girls who expected their own cars and TVs, and even then you had to get in from work and do your own housework because they were too busy with the Play-doh to give a thought to the ironing. No, French women definitely had the right idea. Sit in an office all day while your home and children are serviced by your grateful employee. No wonder there was a higher percentage of working women in France than nearly any other European country. *Femmes actives*, as they were known socio-demographically.

Laura, on the other hand, was a *femme inactive*. Or a *femme au foyer*. A *ménagère*. Or even – and this was her preferred term – a *mère de famille*, which had nice dynastic overtones and sounded less depressing than Full-Time Mother. It was her choice and she was happy with it, in spite of the glazed response it provoked at dinner parties when she apologetically explained that no, she didn't work, and yes, apart from shopping – and God knows that could fill the hours – she was pretty much her own agent until the children came home. Nine till four-thirty; it wasn't bad. It was the kind of freedom she used to fantasise about in the days when she worked. Look at her now, for instance. She could be locked up in some dull meeting, feigning enthusiasm for another mediocre pet food campaign, instead of which she was hanging out in a Bohemian Parisian café with a copy of the *Daily Mail* and *Libération* – she was so well integrated that she read both.

She flicked briefly through *Libé*. Not much to interest her there, to be honest – she only bought it for the TV guide and so as not to look like a tourist. She put it down and picked up the *Mail*, a paper she wouldn't be seen dead with in England, where it was the fodder of Sloaney secretaries and suburban housewives, but here in Paris she found it a great comfort to conjure up a world of instant coffee and Danish pastries, where women trapped in dull routines were sustained by tales of other, more glittering lives.

Laura, former career girl, now downgraded to housewife, picked over titbits of the rich and famous. Entertaining, provided you didn't know them. But as she turned the pages she came across an unpleasant shock on the Femail pages.

What was this? A picture of her old college friend Penny Porter, posing in the mock fairy grotto of her Surrey mansion, perfectly dressed, and holding a baby!

Laura read the caption: 'Not content with smashing the glass ceiling with her appointment as MD of Interfacts, Penny Porter shows you really can have it all. Little Thaddeus can be proud of his Supermum!' Feeling nauseous, she read on: '"With proper back-up, it is perfectly possible to combine a career with motherhood", says Penny. "I am very surprised that so many of my friends have chosen to throw away everything they have achieved just because they want a family. It seems such a waste.'"

Well, well, thought Laura, bitterly acknowledging the truism that every time a friend succeeds a little something inside you dies. Good old Penny, you had to hand it to her. Practical, capable Penny, always first in with her essay. Efficient, but in Laura's opinion not really that bright.

You couldn't envy her her success: she deserved it. She was single-minded and worked hard for what she wanted. You could tell that she had stepped into the top income bracket from her last Christmas card. It weighed three times as much as all the others and came in a padded envelope. Inside there was a printed message: 'Wishing you a merry Christmas and a successful New Year from Penny Porter and Mark Townsend.' Neither of them had taken the time to sign it – far too busy building their golden future. Laura and Jean-Laurent had had a laugh about it at the time. So now there was a baby as well. The pooling of genes would no doubt ensure that Thaddeus was born with the requisite trio of bulges – pecs, wallet and groin.

Laura stuffed the paper into her bag, overtipped the sullen waiter, and stepped out into the avenue Mozart in a state of confused dissatisfaction. She had always enjoyed laughing at Penny Porter, with her Head-Girl demeanour and clear-eyed certainty that she knew where she was going career-wise. But that was when they were on similar paths; every year they would meet and congratulate each other on their recent promotions, on how they were succeeding in a man's world. And when they parted, Laura would think smugly that at least she knew it was only a game, whereas poor old Penny took it all so deathly seriously.

Then, when Laura gave birth to Charles-Edouard and was riding high on the pinnacle of new motherhood, striking the perfect work-life balance in a glorious juggling act, she could see the envy in Penny's eyes and it had made her glad. Penny had been meticulous about taking her temperature every month and jockeying Mark into action at the propitious moment, but it had always been without result. It was early days, anyway, Penny had reasoned, she really would prefer to be at board level before taking maternity leave.

Laura remembered precisely the moment when she had told Penny that she had decided to jack in her career in order to follow her husband to Paris. It was over lunch at a wholefood café in Covent Garden. Penny was drinking Perrier and eating only green vegetables to improve her chances of conceiving a male child. Laura had delivered her news in a rush of reckless excitement and looked eagerly at Penny, wanting to see some more of that envy, waiting for her to say 'You lucky cow, I wish it was me'. Instead of which, Penny had put down her forkful of broccoli and looked concerned.

'Are you sure you've thought this through, Laura?' she had said. 'You know, I think you're really going to miss working.'

Laura had been decidedly put out.

'Oh yeah,' she had sneered, 'like I'm really going to miss those lovely calls from clients insisting on slapping a pack shot of their crappy cleaning product at the end of every ad. I'm really going to miss dealing with invoice queries. I'm really going to miss having lunch at the Caprice with that pitiful brand manager wetting himself because Trevor

Eve's sitting at the next table, then humiliating me by getting up and asking for his autograph! Come on, Penny, it's going to be fantastic. You can't say you're not jealous!'

Penny had pushed the broccoli round her plate.

'Of course I'm happy for you, Laura, if that's your decision. But I can't help wondering what you'll do all day.'

'Penny, I'm not going to live on some dreary old Welsh mountain, I'm going to Paris, for God's sake. Think about it: soirées and salons, afternoons in the jardin de Luxembourg, *and* I finally get to spend proper quality time with the kids. I can't wait!'

She had mentally written off Penny Porter after that conversation. If Penny was so wrapped up in her delusions of professional fulfilment that she couldn't imagine the potential of a different way of life, then frankly she didn't deserve her entry in Laura's Palm Pilot. And apart from the routine exchange of Christmas cards (she had responded to the quarter-pounder quilted number with the cheapest and nastiest she could find), they hadn't been in touch for three years. So why was it that Laura now felt so aggrieved to read about Penny's baby?

A generous friend – albeit now a distant one – would be glad for her, and happy to see that she was scoring another goal for the sisterhood by managing to combine career and motherhood, striking the same balance that Laura had once successfully achieved before she decided to give it all up. A generous friend would go rushing off to Bonpoint now to buy a layette for little Thaddeus, or, more sensibly, a pair of age two dungarees that he could look forward to growing into.

By the time she had reached the rue de Passy, Laura

had cooled down. Jealous of Penny Porter: was she mad? Here she was with her fantastic life, a husband who adored her, two gorgeous boys, plenty of money, the intellectual excitement of living in the most sophisticated of cities and the freedom to spend her days as she chose. Speaking of which, she had promised herself that she would call in at Kenzo to see what they had.

She sidestepped a West Highland terrier crouched in fouling position bang in the middle of the pavement. Holding his lead was a sour-looking fur-coated woman of the type known in Paris as a *seizième* – belonging to the sixteenth arrondissement: well heeled, conventional, reader of *Madame Figaro*, chilly, of indeterminate age, disapproving of most things except for smart clothes and an elegantly laid table. Give me a few more years and that'll be me, thought Laura.

It took a suit in Kenzo, a couple of silky 'bodies' in Franck et Fils and three pairs of shoes from Carel to help restore her equilibrium, after which there was barely time to pop into Cyrillus for a half-price set of vests for Thaddeus before she had to rush off and fetch the children. Really, she didn't know where the time went.

Laura and her family lived in a fifth-floor apartment in a quiet street behind the Trocadero in the type of building that French estate agents described with Napoleonic puff as *grand standing*, a terminology that reflected the importance of social status. Little people might live in scabby little buildings with scruffy entrance halls and no lifts, but those who stood tall in society would consider it horribly vulgar to live in something that wasn't *pierre de taille*

– constructed from noble blocks of stone to reflect the gravitas of the venerable occupants.

The status of the residents was further determined by how high up they were in the apartment block. The ground floor was of no interest to anyone, since this was the territory of the concierge, now more respectfully spoken of as the *gardien*. The top floor was also disregarded since it was made up of a warren of tiny maids' rooms, occupied these days by immigrant cleaning ladies or unhappy au pair girls, or teenagers escaping the rigorous bourgeois life of their parents living below. Apart from that, the higher up you were the better since you got more light, but in older buildings the second and third floors were often the grandest, with high ceilings and elaborate mouldings, since this was where the richest occupants of the building lived before lifts were introduced.

Returning from school, Laura managed to find a parking space just outside her home, which gave her a small thrill of satisfaction. It irritated her that she had to meet the children from school every single day. After all, she had taken on an au pair girl for the sole purpose of relieving herself of such tiresome chores. But Asa the Finn, their current live-in nightmare, had put her foot down early on about the school run.

Apparently there was a father who had taken a shine to her – unlikely, but apparently true – who was always hanging round the school gates and pestering her for a date. Laura had advised her to take no notice, or else to try dressing a bit less like a harlot, but Asa said that it was too stressful and having a negative impact on her attempts to overcome her eating disorder. So Laura had caved in, as she always did, and now fetched the boys each afternoon, while Asa lay on her sofa and drew up charts for her fourteen-day eating plan.

Laura parked the car, badly as usual, and unloaded children and plastic bags of groceries on to the pavement. She made Charles-Edouard hold the heavy doors open while she ferried the bags through the art nouveau hallway to the coffin-sized lift. There was a plaque at eye level warning visitors that the lift carried two people only – maximum 150 kg. Laura had spent many a tense ride up to the fifth floor pressed up against the flanks of a neighbour while holding her breath and carefully avoiding eye contact after the initial brusque '*Bonjour*'.

Today, the lift was out of order. Someone must have disobeyed the two-person rule, or else two fat people – rare in Paris – had tipped the scales beyond the 150 kg limit. It was going to have to be the *escalier*. Huffing her way up the stairs, weighed down by her shopping, Laura passed the blank double doors of her neighbours' apartments, so unwelcoming with their undistinguishable façades and uniform rectangular mats. You had no idea what you might find inside. Someone had told her that the French deliberately keep the exteriors of their apartments austere to hide their vast riches from the taxman.

The boys reached the fifth floor first, Pierre-Louis wheezing slightly from his asthma. The weather report had given the air quality as *mauvais* today, another excuse for the Parisians to be grumpy, as if they needed one. Laura dropped her bags and fumbled for her keys.

The boys pushed ahead of her into the apartment. Shedding their coats on the hall floor, they burst into the salon, switched on the television and took up their positions on the sofa.

'*Goûter*, please, Mum', said Charles-Edouard, his eyes fixed on the screen where warlike Japanese cartoon figures were attacking each other in a series of crudely macho poses.

'Coming.'

Laura picked up the coats and followed the windowless corridor that led from the grand 'front-of-house' reception rooms to a dark, poky kitchen which afforded little light and an uninterrupted view of the dustbins. This was the price they paid for their *grand standing*. Even though they had a fabulous '*triple living*' – another piece of tortured franglais denoting three high-ceilinged reception rooms with tall windows opening boastfully on to a view of the Eiffel Tower – the room they really spent time in was pitifully inadequate. 'Who cares about the kitchen when we've got those marvellous rooms to entertain in?' Jean-Laurent had wanted to know when they had first visited the apartment. Laura had agreed, swept up in a wave of excitement, imagining herself at the centre of a buzzing salon.

They entertained less than they had envisaged, though. It was such a long way to carry the food from the kitchen to the dining room, and anyway, Jean-Laurent worked so late. Laura spent more time picking up morsels of fish finger from the kitchen floor than dishing out witty ripostes from the chaise longue.

Asa was perched at the kitchen table, picking over an unappetising plate-load of chickpeas and raw cauliflower. She looked up with a reproachful smile.

'Hi, Laura. We've run out of Evian.'

'I know, I've just killed myself dragging six bottles up the stairs. The lift's not working again.'

Asa's consumption of mineral water was a daily source of irritation for Laura. Everyone else drank from the tap, but not Miss Nordic Purity, oh no, she had to flush out her Scandinavian insides with melted snow. Asa had once spent half an hour explaining how other spring waters were no good, as they came from the polluted earth, whereas Evian came from the uncontaminated mountain tops that were depicted on each arm-stretchingly heavy two-litre bottle.

Asa helped herself to a bottle and watched Laura put away the shopping.

'Oh good, you got some more carrots. Are they organic?'

'No idea.'

Laura couldn't understand why Asa was so interested in the provenance of her food, since everything she ate was discreetly regurgitated in the bathroom shortly afterwards.

'I was wondering if you might babysit tonight, Asa. I thought we might go to the cinema.'

'Sorry, I've got a meeting. It's Tuesday.'

'Oh, of course, it's Tuesday, silly me.'

Silly me, thought Laura, for thinking there might be some point in having you here, hogging the kitchen table, eating my food and drinking my mountain water and passing your superior remarks about nutritional balance.

'How's it going, anyway, the programme?'

'Oh, Devon is very happy with me. I managed to eat two rice cakes at lunchtime, but he would have preferred three.'

Laura was not sure about Devon. A fifty-something American who claimed to be happily married, he spent a lot of time offering fatherly support to the vulnerable young girls he met at the Overeaters Anonymous meetings in the basement of the American church. Laura had never met him, but he rang every day to speak to Asa. Apparently he was her programme sponsor so it was all supposed to be above board.

'Well, you're certainly making up for it now,' said Laura as Asa set about cutting up half the contents of the fruit bowl, which she carefully mixed into a generous dish of fat-free yoghurt. 'Would you mind leaving a couple of pears for the boys' tea?'

'Mum! Come on, *goûter!*' Charles-Edouard's command rang down the corridor. 'Coming.' Laura rescued the pears from the depleted fruit bowl and opened a packet of biscuits.

'Do you want orange juice or apple juice?' she shouted, raising her voice to be heard above *Power Rangers*. Really, children just had too many choices these days.

A moment's consultation, then, 'I'll take orange and Pierre-Louis will take apple.'

As if they were in a restaurant. Which they were, really. A hotel-restaurant with a staff of one. You couldn't count Asa's sulky contributions to the domestic household effort.

'OK, coming.'

Laura loaded two glasses and two plates on to the tray and carried it down the corridor to set before her sons.

'Here you are. Would you like omelette or chicken nuggets for tea?'

'Chicken nuggets. Could you move out the way, please, I can't see.'

Charles-Edouard frowned as he craned his neck. Laura decided, as she did most days and with negligible effect, that it was time to assert herself.

'I think we'll have the telly off now. Why don't you do your homework straight away, then it's done?'

Charles-Edouard looked at her with a contemptuous sneer that wouldn't disgrace an adolescent. 'It's much too early, we haven't even had tea yet.'

'So? You don't always have to leave it until the last minute.'

'Are you going out tonight?'

'No. Asa is.'

'Good. I don't like Asa. She doesn't let us watch TV. I hate it when Asa babysits.'

'Don't be horrible about Asa,' said Laura, wondering if her dislike of the girl had been subconsciously transmitted to her son, or whether he had simply inherited her own keen judgement of character.

Laura contemplated the tea/bath/homework/bed routine stretching ahead in all its dreary predictability. At least, she thought, there was some compensation for being confined to quarters. She and Jean-Laurent would be able to spend an intimate evening in on their own without the omnipresent Asa. She would make sure the children were safely tucked up in bed before he got back, so she could give him her full and undivided attention. She would change into one of those flimsy pieces of lingerie she had bought this morning, and maybe wear the jacket from the Kenzo suit. Unfortunately the skirt needed altering – she

had left it with the shop for them to let out an extra inch
or two around the waistband – but her old elasticated
Ghost peasant number would go perfectly well. She would
go to town on the food, too, something nice and rich from
this month's *Cuisine et Vins de France*, with a proper
pudding, maybe a pressed chocolate cake. They would
dine at the formal table, looking out on to the Eiffel Tower,
and Jean-Laurent would talk her through his day.

It was marvellous that she had so little stress now in her
daily life that she was free to give full attention to her
husband. So much better than the old days in London when
she was caught up in her own career and barely had time
to listen to him. Poor love, it had been so tough for him:
he used to complain that he was the forgotten member of
the family, lurking at the bottom of her busy list of priori-
ties along with putting the rubbish out twice a week.

Thank God those days were well and truly over; now
she had become the perfect French wife. And tonight Jean-
Laurent would be enthroned in his rightful place as her
Number One Priority. She would make sure they were
safely cuddled up in bed before the heart-sinking sound
of Asa's key in the lock announced her return to the fold
and the end of their glorious intimacy.

She went back to the kitchen and took a packet of
chicken nuggets and a *magret de canard* from the freezer.

'Rice or pasta?' she bellowed back to her boys. Why did
she always offer them choices? Why not just put it in
front of them? Why try to please them all the time? The
unhelpful answer came ringing back.

'Pierre-Louis will take rice and I will take pasta.'

It served her right for asking.

Two

Three hours later, Laura's master plan for a seductive *dîner à deux* was running perfectly to plan. The children were in bed and she was snipping the ends off the *haricots verts*, while listening to the *Archers* crackling faintly from the radio that was placed against the window to minimise interference. Radio 4 played a larger part in her life now that she lived abroad. She had never had time to listen to it much in London, when the *Archers* coincided with handover time with the nanny and the phone was always ringing.

Jean-Laurent used to get home earlier in those days, when he was studying for his MBA. Her younger man. He was usually back before her, and she would come home from the office to find him bouncing Charles-Edouard on his knees, a picture of carefree youthfulness, his student files tossed carelessly on the kitchen counter while the nanny smiled indulgently as she prepared the baby's bottle. He liked the way she dressed then, in tight powerful clothes. 'I love to be your kept man,' he would say as he slipped his hand up her short skirt. 'You know, I just have this thing about older women. Especially businesswomen in tiny little suits.'

He had been her lodger before he became her husband. Her girlfriends had been quite jealous when her advertisement in *Loot* turned up the good-looking Frenchman – he was certainly a cut above the sad cases that usually came crawling out of the woodwork in response to her demand for a single professional male. Not that she had been advertising for a boyfriend, of course. She did have friends who had gone down that route: finding themselves single at the age of thirty, they had commendably set about doing something about it and joined discreet dating agencies called things like Drawing Down the Moon or Reining In a Man. Her old school friend Caroline Murray had tried placing an ad – she called it an advert, though Laura kept telling her this was old hat and immediately marked her out as unmarriageable – in *Time Out*'s lonely hearts, then read out the replies to an assembled committee of girlfriends who helped her sift them into two piles: Too Sad to Contemplate and Worth a Sniff.

Laura, however, had been perfectly happy with her single status. She had already had one live-in boyfriend, so she knew she was capable of maintaining a happy relationship. She had reacted well when Simon had ended it, explaining that he wasn't really ready to settle down and therefore it just wasn't fair on her for them to carry on. She had thanked him for his honesty and agreed that they must remember the good times, that in no way did it represent five years down the pan. When he became engaged to someone else three months later, she had spent a weekend weeping under the duvet, but then emerged, calm and resolute, to count her blessings and remind herself that thirty was hardly the end of the line, that spinster was a joke word from another century and that the notion of being on the shelf was a cruel legacy from an age before sisters were doing it for themselves.

So when she advertised for a professional male house-mate, it was simply a matter of seeking a balance in the house she owned in Stockwell. She already had one girl lodger and she didn't want to turn the household into a seething pit of female hormones, all thin skin, empathy and synchronised cycles. She imagined she might get a sensible chartered accountant who ate square meals and played football at weekends; she liked the idea of his sports kit hanging up to dry alongside the lacy G-strings.

But when Jean-Laurent turned up on the doorstep she was, frankly, bowled over. He was so young, just twenty-two, and spoke English with a halting French accent you felt had been designed for the sole purpose of seducing recently dumped romantic Englishwomen. He was study-ing, he said without irony, to become a Big Businessman, and he had a copy of Porter's *Competitive Advantage* tucked under his perfectly muscled arm as if to prove it.

She took him upstairs to show him the bedroom and stood back to let him in. He brushed against her as he passed, and as he walked over to look out of the window – at a rather frightening sink estate; she hoped to God it wouldn't put him off – she took in his jeans, the way they hung around his hips with a louche insouciance that only really works on bodies not long out of adolescence.

He turned to her and smiled. Dark hair, blue eyes, a

miraculous fusion of Celtic fringe and hot Latin lover.

'I like it,' he said. 'And I like you, too.'

Laura tried to hold his steady gaze but was overcome by an old maidish flutter and quickly led him down to the kitchen for a mug of tea so they could continue the interview in less intimate surroundings.

'I've got two more people coming to see it tonight, so I'll call you after that,' she said, trying to appear impartial.

He raised his eyebrows in mock dismay.

'You mean you don't want me?'

Don't be ridiculous, she thought. The idea of not wanting him was so ludicrous it was beyond the realms of possibility. Not wanting him was about as likely as fancying Neil Kinnock.

'Well, you might like to think about it,' she said. 'Stockwell isn't exactly South Kensington, after all. Although it's only five stops on the tube,' she added quickly. Was she crazy, trying to put him off?

He twisted his beautiful face into a pout of disagreement.

'No, South Kensington is full of French people. While I am here I want to live in the real London, with real English people. Like you.'

'How long is your course?' she asked, already in a panic in case he said six months.

'Two years.'

Two whole years. With him under her roof. What bliss. She hoped he couldn't see how much pleasure his answer had given her, and switched the conversation to the safe and general.

'And what do you make of us over here? Us *"rosbifs"*? Do we live down to your expectations?'

'Oh, I like the people here. Very nice, very friendly. But you know, I think the English men are strange.'

'Strange?'

'Yes,' he said, looking at her meaningfully over his Princess Diana mug. 'I think they do not look after their women.'

Laura knew he would look after her. He would cherish her. He would worship the ground she walked on. He wouldn't say he wasn't ready to settle down and then get engaged to somebody else three months later.

He moved into her house the following week, and into her bed a month later. Laura was ecstatic. On Saturday mornings they lay entwined together while he read her passages from Sun Tzu's *The Art of War for Executives*.

It was extraordinary, he said, how the battle plans of some old Chinaman who was a contemporary of Confucius held such relevance in today's business world. 'Conquerors estimate in their temple before the war begins,' he would proclaim as she came back to the bedroom with two cups of coffee. 'The great general entraps the enemy but retains his own freedom.'

Then, as she took off her dressing gown and slipped under the covers, he would pull her towards him and get straight down to business. 'The best military strategy is to use superior positioning,' he would murmur as he took up his own vantage point. 'Cross the mountains by following the valleys,' he would add, with a light and thrilling caress, then, slightly less erotically, 'When crossing a swamp, move quickly . . . keep away from gorges, hollows and crevices which form natural traps and snares.'

They would get up some time in the afternoon and go shopping to Sainsbury's at Nine Elms. He always pushed the trolley, pausing at every shelf to study packaging for evidence of brand advantage. 'You know, Laura, the troops of a skilled leader are like the simultaneously responding serpent that lived in the mountains of Chang. If its head is threatened, its tail attacks, if its tail is threatened, its head attacks. And if the body is threatened, both head and tail attack together. Brilliant.'

Sometimes, to be honest, she did get a bit tired of Sun Tzu.

'I can't see any snakes in here, though, Jean-Laurent, only ready meals, luckily. Do you want Goan fish curry or Chicken Tikka Masala?'

'I don't mind. But not that moussaka you got last time. One day, Laura, you will learn to cook. I will take you to live in France, we will go to the market and you will be ashamed to think of those days when you used to insult your French lover by giving him frozen food only fit for a dog.'

But he didn't really care. He agreed with her that an hour wasted in the kitchen was an hour that could be spent in the bedroom, and the bedroom was where they liked to be.

Laura's friends were gratifyingly jealous when she arrived at parties with her new French boyfriend. The women found him charming; his foreignness set him apart and added value to his already striking looks. The men ganged up defensively, agreeing that his failure to enjoy sinking six pints of bitter was clear evidence of his dodginess. Her gay friend Christopher hoped they were right, and didn't bother to disguise the fact that he was green with envy.

'God, that boy's hot,' he said one night, watching Jean-Laurent jiving to REM's 'Shiny Happy People' (like all French people, he always danced *'le rock'*, 1950s style, no matter how inappropriate the music). 'Do pass him on to me when you've finished with him. He's obviously a woof. No offence, Laura, but when a girl gets a boyfriend who's so much more attractive than her, it's always a sure sign.'

Dinner parties were a little more difficult. Jean-Laurent's English was fast improving but the quick-fire references over the dinner table left him feeling mute and foreign.

'What did Clovis mean?' he would ask, 'about his boss being a bitter little *redbrick* person?'

'Oh, it's just a load of snobbish old nonsense,' Laura reassured him. 'I can't tell you how happy I am to have you as an escape from all that stuff.'

When he became her lover, he still carried on paying the rent; she didn't want it to seem that she was paying for his services. But of course she financed his lifestyle. He was only a student, albeit one with appetising prospects, whereas she was coining it in at the agency. Clients loved her – she was smart and a bit posh, but not so much as to make them feel inferior. Other people at the agency might smirk when the marketing director of Bartons bakery boasted that he probably had the best TV set in Orpington, but Laura would nod appreciatively and ask how wide the screen was, and whether he had integral speakers with Dolby surround-sound.

Jean-Laurent was fascinated by her tales from the

office. She represented the world that awaited him, an arena where all his carefully learned business precepts would be put into action, where he would Learn to Fight, Do it Right, Burn the Bridges and Seize the Day as instructed by Sun Tzu. Until he arrived at that great day, he was happy to rely on Laura for providing food and wine and the company of those who were really starting to make a difference in their chosen careers. As a Frenchman he understood the importance of knowing the right people, and realised his employment prospects could only be enhanced by living with the youngest group account director of Soul, Baring and Fuchs.

When Laura fell pregnant with Charles-Edouard, it was to Jean-Laurent's credit that he didn't turn a hair. Other young men of his age might have been a little less calm, might even have harboured dark thoughts of fleeing on the next plane back to Paris, but Jean-Laurent had expressed his sincere joy, proposed marriage and suggested that the house should now be put in their joint names since they were effectively to become an economic unit.

The female lodger tactfully departed and was in time replaced by a solidly built Slovakian nanny whose unswerving interest in Jean-Laurent's business studies might have presented a threat had she not looked like the back of a bus. 'My employers are a wonderful couple,' she would boom out to anyone who crossed the threshold. 'I respect and admire them enormously.'

After completing his course, Jean-Laurent was snapped up by one of those conglomerates that you always associate with soap powder but who also make ice cream and instant custard. When his lithe torso slipped effortlessly out of his student jeans and into a navy blue suit, Laura felt reassured that the age gap between them had suddenly narrowed, and celebrated by conceiving a second child. By the time Pierre-Louis was born, they were just like any other married couple. Everyone said you would never think she was so much older, they looked so good together.

And now, several years down the line, it was payback time and Laura had been served up the perfect Parisian life of leisure. The student had become the serious earner, the career woman was now the kept woman. As an investment, Jean-Laurent had proved to be a sound bet, Laura thought smugly, inserting slivers of garlic into the dark red flesh of the duck breast as the jaunty theme tune of the *Archers* faded into the self-righteous urgency of Robin Cook preparing to *Face the Facts*.

She switched off the radio and poured a generous measure of extra virgin olive oil into a cup. It was funny how all olive oil claimed to be extra virgin. You couldn't get the raddled old slightly soiled variety, which presumably must exist somewhere, probably in Italy where olive-growing peasants sacrificed all the virginal stuff to the export market and made do with the dregs.

She must look out for it next time they were in Umbria – it could make an interesting addition to her storecupboard. She was getting bored to death with extra virgin olive oil, to be honest. Not like vinegar, where you had infinite choice. Raspberry, balsamic, cider, sherry, white wine with a sprig of dried-up tarragon hanging down inside the bottle. She could remember a time when all you got was malt vinegar. Delicious on chips, but unthinkable on salad.

Uncorking a bottle of chilled Bourgogne Aligoté, Laura prepared herself a Kir. The thick blackcurrant syrup swirled into the wine, creating a deliciously adult version of Ribena. Quality of life – that was what they had, and now, with dinner prepared, she was free to enjoy her aperitif.

How different this was from when she worked. She thought back to that terrible time when she had returned to work from maternity leave after Pierre-Louis was born. Exhausted by night feeds and with a trying toddler competing for her attention, she had been looking forward to reclaiming the order of a structured adult world. But she hadn't reckoned on her emotional fragility, and found herself wounded by snide remarks from colleagues like, Here she was again after a nice rest, and, How long before she popped out another one and took a few more months off?

Her boss, though legally obliged to appear supportive, had let slip that he found her rather less on the ball than she used to be. Once, during the Coffee and Networking session at a conference, she had forgotten a senior client's name and had been gauche enough to ask him to remind her of it. 'Buck up, Laura,' her boss had said. 'You're not at the mother and baby group now, you know!'

She had toughened up after that and battled on, but like a trapped animal she began obsessing about finding a way out. It took two years for the opportunity to present itself. Two more years of hard grind until Jean-Laurent was offered a big job in Paris and his wife the chance to become the passive Trailing Spouse. Laura had thrown in the towel with unrestrained rejoicing and jumped on the long slide to domestic happiness. She remembered the relief, how thrilled she had been when she had told her friends. 'Do you realise,' one stressed-out working mother had said, 'that you are the envy of every woman in this room?'

She carried her glass into the *triple living* and contemplated the perfection of her current life. While her friends in London were stuck on the treadmill, grinding up another rung on the oh-so-illusionary career ladder, here she was with nothing to do except look forward to a civilised evening with her gorgeous young husband who at this very moment was working his socks off to support his devoted family.

They usually ate in the kitchen, but tonight she was showing her gratitude by setting the table in the dining room with the fussy clutter of crockery, glasses and *serviettes* that Jean-Laurent liked to sit down to. He had a very French respect for the importance of *les arts de la table*, and she had even put out the shell-encrusted centrepiece that he had bought her for Christmas, although she privately thought it rather ugly and not worth the space it took up. It was specially designed to support a plate of coquilles Saint-Jacques, and came with a set of eight gold-sprayed giant shells containing clusters of imitation pearls that you were supposed to put in front of each guest's place setting.

Laura moved into the salon and settled into an armchair to watch the flashing lights of the lift slowly climbing its way up the Eiffel Tower. A view that people would die for, the stuff of a million postcards, and a far cry from the problem estate which was all you could see from her sitting room in Stockwell. Strange to think that they had wanted to pull down the Eiffel Tower after the Great Exhibition. Aesthetes found that its metal lines defaced the city skyline. No danger of that now. A few years ago they had hired a team of mountaineers to paint it. She used to watch them from her window, dangling off their cords, holding paintbrushes instead of ice picks.

Laura was on her second Kir when the phone rang. She walked through the grandiose double door to the third room of the *triple living*, which served as an office. Or a study. They couldn't decide what to call it, both functions being unnecessary to their home life. She picked up the receiver.

'Allo?' She answered with the standard French salutation which always made her friends from England laugh. "Allo, 'allo,' they would reply jokily, getting into continental mode in anticipation of the nice free trip to Paris they were usually calling to fix up.

This time, though, it was her friend Francine.

'*Salut, Laura. Je te dérange?*' In spite of their reputation for rudeness, the French were always terribly apologetic on the phone, anxious in case they were disturbing some intimate moment. They certainly never called during mealtimes; that would be an unspeakable invasion of privacy.

'No, not at all, how are you, Francine?'

'Oh, *ça va*. I am just ringing to confirm dinner on Thursday.'

'Yes, that's fine, we're looking forward to it.'

'*Bien*. You have our address? So here is the code: AB 596. *Ciao.*'

Laura jotted the numbers down in her diary. After nightfall, most apartment buildings became impenetrable fortresses, accessible only to those equipped with the secret code. Gone were the days of the nosy concierge who knew exactly who was invited where. As a vigilante she had been supplanted by an electronic panel, which left her only the unglamorous tasks of cleaning the porch and dragging out the wheelie-bins each evening. No wonder the French considered it a job best left to the Portuguese.

Jean-Laurent de Saint Léger, twenty-nine and gorgeous, was reading a business book in his office. He spent quite a lot of time reading business books. He kept a pile beside his side of the bed, and a back-up supply at work, where he was earmarked as the bright young hope of marketing. He couldn't get on a plane these days without picking up two or three slim manuals at the airport bookshop, books carefully targeted at jet-setters like himself who put them on their expenses.

Today he was flicking through *Stress and Counterstress – Guidelines for Executives and High Achievers*. He liked the message that stress was necessary. Giant sloths and koalas hung from trees and had no stress, and were now endangered through their loss of natural defences. That couldn't happen to him. The point about being a big shot was that your stress level lifted you above the little people. Big shots did not creep home for a quiet night in with overweight older wives. No sir. Big shots met their girl-friends in buzzy happening places where they could be admired.

He reached for the phone and fiddled with his pen while he waited for Laura to answer. He was surprised how adept he had become at lying.

'Hallo, it's me. Look, I'm sorry, but something's come up, and I'm going to have to have dinner with François to sort it out.'

Laura's heart sank. Her careful preparations were all for nothing then.

Jean-Laurent heard the disappointment in her silence.

'Hallo? Laura?'

She pulled herself together. She shouldn't be ungrateful – it was hardly his fault that he had to make sacrifices for his high-powered job. She tried to lighten up.

'Dinner with François, as opposed to dinner with André?' she said brightly.

'What?'

'Nothing, just an allusion to a masterpiece of the French cinema. Don't worry, you're French, you wouldn't know it.'

'I'm sorry, it's a real bore. I wish I could come home instead.'

'It *is* a bore actually. I've done a *magret de canard*.'

'Oh no, I thought maybe you would have eaten with the children. Are they OK?'

'They're all right. Pierre-Louis got eight out of ten for dictation. Not that that can be of any real interest to you, in your great office crisis.'

'It's much more interesting to me, actually, but you know what François is like, he gets very stressed out before these big conferences, so I just need to run through a few things with him.'

'Well, he's the boss. Oh, Francine rang. Are you still all right for Thursday?'

'Oh . . . yes . . .'

He sounded evasive.

'I might be a bit late, though. Probably better to meet you there?'

'All right. I'll see you later then.'

But she couldn't entirely resist piling on the self-pity.

'Don't worry about me, sitting quietly alone in front of the telly.'

'But you like watching telly, and you always say you like to have time on your own. Go and have a bath and make yourself beautiful.'

'More beautiful, I think you mean.'

'More beautiful. *Au revoir, chérie.*'

'What time will you be back?'

'I'm not sure. Don't wait up for me.'

'OK. Bye then.'

'*Ciao.*'

Alone in his office, Jean-Laurent sat back in relief. A slight twinge of guilt only served to add an edge to his excitement at the evening ahead. And anyway, he knew that he did not need to feel guilty. Flavia had made that quite clear. Their falling in love was not his fault, it had just happened. He was a highly charged person who needed to live life on a higher plane, not being dragged down by the suffocating domesticity that seemed to suit Laura so well.

When he had promised to be faithful to her, she had been as sharp-witted in the boardroom as she was hot in the bedroom. It was she, not he, who had changed. What had he done to deserve someone whose conversation these days rarely got beyond play dates, marks out of ten for dictation and cunning ways with polenta? Not to mention the fact that she was now a good two stone heavier than when he had first met her. Flavia had explained that in a previous age Laura would probably have died in childbirth anyway, so it was quite normal that he, an alpha male, would have gone on to other, better things, such as a twenty-eight-year-old Jungian psychologist with a fabulous arse.

He glanced back down at his book and studied the arousal-performance curve. It seemed you performed best when under some stress, just enough to get the heart and blood sugar up to a reasonable level of excitement. He picked up the phone to leave his message.

'Flavia, I'll meet you at Barfly, nine o'clock.'

Laura hung up and went into the kitchen, forcing herself to be positive. She enjoyed her own company and this was an opportunity for a lovely, quiet evening in on her own. But she would have preferred to spend it with Jean-Laurent. She loved to hear his stories of office life, who said what to whom, to applaud his moments of triumph and commiserate on the minor setbacks he encountered on his road to international business glory.

She shoved the *magret de canard* back into the fridge. Pity, she had been looking forward to that, but she certainly wasn't going to cook it just for herself. How tragic could you get? For her birthday, Jean-Laurent had once given her a copy of a cookbook by Delia Smith called *One Is Fun*. For when he was away on business, he said. As if anyone would bother to go to all that trouble so they could sit down for a lonely three-course dinner on their own. Is that what Delia did, carefully measuring out a solitary ounce of flour to create that memorable meal which she could then congratulate herself on in the echoing silence of her dining room? Laura thought of all the people she could give a copy of the book to: her recently widowed uncle, perhaps, or her still-single friends. A marvellously tactless gift for a fortieth birthday. Still unattached? Not much chance now – here, have a copy of *One Is Fun*.

She slid a frozen pizza into the microwave and refilled her glass. Carrying her downgraded meal through into the salon, she sank on to the sofa and switched on the television. The only thing that *Libération* had recommended was a documentary on Channel 5 about a high school in a suburb of Paris. Saint Denis was the suburb in question: it always was on these slice-of-real-life programmes. You saw it signposted off the A1 running north to the airport; the sign ought to read 'Saint Denis, favoured location of gritty documentary makers'. The suburbs had a different connotation here in Paris. In London it suggested dull people mowing their lawns. In France, *'la banlieue'* was high-rise territory where the social problems were.

Instead of brewing criminal tensions in the inner city, they were all banished to the no-man's-land beyond the *périphérique*, to places like Saint Denis. This was what gave Paris its bourgeois, toy-town flavour.

She flicked channels. A tedious studio discussion on Channel 3 with thirty people having their say on the thirty-five-hour week. She changed to Channel 1 and found *Sacrée Soirée*, where the usual crew of French stars were having a conspicuously good time together, clapping their hands as best they could whilst holding large microphones and looking quite out of tune with the morose demeanour of most of their compatriots. That left her to choose between a dubbed American TV movie and something with people glowering at each other in a vineyard that she thought she might have seen before.

If she were in England now, there was bound to be some juicy detective thing on that she could really wallow in. Or she could ring a girlfriend for a chat. Or catch up on some paperwork that she had brought home from the office. Fill in her expenses.

She switched off the TV and was suddenly panicked by the strange silence of the apartment. Those gleaming parquet floors depressed her sometimes, and there was something cold and impersonal about the high windows with their ornate iron bars. Alone in her beautiful prison, what wouldn't she give to be back amidst the chintz curtains and fitted carpets of her cosy house in Stockwell?

But this was stupid and negative. Most people would give their eye teeth to be in her position. She went into the bathroom and performed her *toilette*, as she now called it, wondering whether to keep on the silky lingerie to surprise Jean-Laurent on his return from his business dinner.

In the end her need for comfort was stronger, and she settled on the winceyette nightshirt and went to bed with the memoirs of Brigitte Bardot. Brigitte was recalling her amazement that the concierge of a Spanish hotel where she was staying seemed unwilling to sleep with her. Him a nothing, given the chance of a lifetime to sleep with Brigitte Bardot, and all he could do was weep and say that his grandmother had just died. It was, she said, the first and last time that anyone had ever refused her. Laura yawned and switched off the light.

Much later, she heard the bedroom door and was aware of Jean-Laurent undressing surreptitiously in the darkened room, taking care not to wake her. As he slipped beneath his side of the duvet and hunched his back against her, she turned towards him and wrapped herself into his warm, familiar shape. After the hurly-burly of the chaise longue, she thought, the deep, deep peace of the double bed. Thank goodness she was married.

Thank goodness I'm not married, thought Asa, replacing her toothbrush and taking a swig of breath freshener. Poor old Laura must have spent hours last night preparing that disgusting looking duck, but Jean-Laurent had obviously let her down again. Asa knew this because when she got in from her meeting, she had gone in search of a late night snack and found two breast fillets festering on a plate in the fridge.

And now Laura was at it again. She'd fished out the same bit of meat and was once more trying to please her husband by cooking him up an old carcass. How sad was that? But at least it left Asa free to go out again tonight. On a rather special date.

She spat out the Listerine and looked at herself in the mirror. Twenty-four years old and fifty-five kilos heavy but you couldn't see the fat bits in this mirror and she was not displeased with what she saw from the neck up. Fresh complexion, blonde hair hanging limply to the chin in the straggly style recently reclaimed from the 1970s. Delicate gold nose-ring which in her darker moments made her think of a fat bull being pulled into the market to be prodded and bartered over by rough farmers. Luckily there was no full-length glass in her bathroom. She needed to go into Laura's bedroom to be confronted by the bloated reality of her silhouette, which mocked her with its obdurate folds of whale flesh, as cold and heavy as the northern seas of her native Finland.

She felt better now, purified by the expulsion of those empty calories she had so greedily wolfed down. Two family-size bars of Côte d'Or chocolate and a whole baguette now safely despatched to the Paris sewer system where they could do no harm. Leaving her free to plan a reasonable, vegetable-based meal in accordance with her fourteen-day meal plan.

Asa from Finland. She didn't need a surname, since au pairs lived like cuckoos in the nests of their employers. Her mail was sent *chez* de Saint Léger, which was all anyone needed to know. Asa, the Finnish au pair, temporarily attached to Laura and Jean-Laurent and their two tiresome children. At least she could get up and leave whenever she wanted. Unlike poor Laura, trapped there for ever to watch her sons grow and flourish while she faded into obscurity. God forbid Asa would ever find herself in that position.

As au pair jobs went, hers wasn't bad. At least she was allowed to live in the apartment, and had her own luxurious bathroom and a decent-sized room. Most of the *jeunes filles* were banished to the top of the building to tiny *chambres de bonne* with one shared toilet. That could be very embarrassing in view of her present problems, though she was making good progress thanks to Devon, her sponsor at Overeaters Anonymous. She thought fondly of his hand squeezing hers at the last meeting. The way he looked into her eyes. He felt her pain. Which made her feel doubly guilty about the bingeing session she had just indulged in.

Still, she would be able to put on a good performance for him now. They were to meet in one of the few vegetarian restaurants the city had to offer. He said it was good for her to eat in public. He would go through her meal plans with her, make sure her goals were realistic. Just the two of them. She put on a last coat of mascara and headed for the door.

Laura called to her from the kitchen.

'Are you off out, Asa?'

There was no mistaking the pleasure in her voice.

'Yes. I'm meeting some friends.'

'Good for you. Have a nice time.'

Don't patronise me, thought Asa.

'Thank you, see you later,' she said.

'Well, there's an unexpected treat,' announced Laura as she flounced into the living room with two champagne flutes. 'I was going to be nice to her and give her a glass, but now we'll just have to finish the bottle ourselves. Here we are, my darling, let's drink to a gloriously intimate evening.'

Jean-Laurent put down *Le Point* magazine and held the glass up to the light.

'Is it the vintage? We're not celebrating anything, are we?'

'Yes we are. We are celebrating our perfect life, our happy marriage and the best decision I ever made, which was to follow you to Paris.'

Jean-Laurent looked at her suspiciously.

'I hope this is not a case of the lady doth protest too much.'

'You see, you're not even English but you can still quote Shakespeare. What a catch you are, how blessed I am.'

'What has brought this on? Not planning to leave me, are you?'

'Ah, but always the underlying distrustfulness of the Frenchman. No, of course not. Why, are you planning to leave me?'

'Not until I have eaten that *magret de canard*. I must say that from a low base you have achieved a culinary prowess that would satisfy even the most demanding mother-in-law. In fact, you might say you have become the perfect French housewife.'

'Jean-Laurent, you know I don't like that word.'

'What's wrong with it? It's what you are, isn't it?'

'No, it's not what I am. I am a rather talented account director who has decided to take some time out for the sake of her family. My mum is a housewife. She wears Ecco shoes, irons my dad's underpants and goes to coffee mornings, bless her.'

He laughed.

'Whereas you go to the café for your coffee, wear Manolo Blahnik stilettos and get the au pair to see to the laundry. Quite different.'

'Please, just don't refer to me as a housewife.'

'All right then, how about household manager?'

'Jean-Laurent!'

'OK, OK, as far as I'm concerned, you're just my lovely lady wife. *Santé!*'

They clinked their glasses.

'Do you remember Penny Porter?' said Laura.

'Of course. Very intelligent woman, very focused. Quite sexy, too.'

'Don't say that! You're meant to say hard-bitten and self-obsessed. And with all the sex appeal of a male chartered accountant.'

'Actually, I do recall she had rather large feet.'

'Thank you. Well, she's had a baby.'

'So what?'

'I know, so what. People do. But there was a picture of her in the *Daily Mail*.'

'That rag! I thought you never read it.'

'I don't. But there she was. In a lifestyle piece. Boring old Penny Porter the subject of a lifestyle piece! I couldn't believe it. Banging on about the joys of combining career and motherhood.'

'You're not jealous, are you?'

'No, of course not. She chose her career, I chose lifestyle. But now she's got both, damn her.'

Jean-Laurent sighed and sank back into the sofa.

'Laura, stop it, this is getting boring. It was your choice. I didn't have to take this job, we could have stayed in London, but you seemed only too keen to chuck in your career. You can't blame her for doing what you might have done. Choices, it all boils down to choices!'

'I know, I know, you make your bed and you lie in it. And at least I get to lie with you.'

'At least you do.'

'How was François?'

'François?'

'Your dinner date last night.'

'Oh, François. Sorry, I was on another tangent. Yes, well
. . . François was François, you know what he's like.'

'No I don't, I've never met him.'

'We'll have to invite him round, then,' said Jean-Laurent.

Though not too soon, he thought. It wouldn't do to
have Laura tripping up his favourite alibi.

THREE

Like any other urban couple with a modicum of social ambition, Laura and Jean-Laurent did dinner parties. It was essential if you wanted to count yourself part of Paris society. It was only the famous and successful who could throw up their hands in horror at the idea of sitting around a table with eight other couples. Laura thought it must be wonderful to be like those featured in *Gala* magazine who didn't have to bother. '*Je ne suis pas mondaine,*' was the claim of every famous actress who could afford to chuck an endless stream of invitation cards into the bin in favour of a quiet night in. But when you were a faceless housewife, you needed to take every opportunity you could.

Tonight they would be the guests of Francine and Dominique Duvall, who had also promised to invite Sylvie Marceau, a singer who had shot to stardom in the sixties with a song about a lollipop that she used to lick suggestively on stage beneath the leering gaze of one of those hoary old French singer-songwriters. In the UK she would have been a one-hit wonder, speedily forgotten, but the

French were remarkably loyal to their celebrities and decades later she remained a fixture on the showbiz circuit, though she still managed to find time for her one-time school friend Francine. Her doctor husband was also expected, a renowned anti-ageing specialist who was thought to have performed miracles on his wife.

Laura had met Francine at an afternoon class in painting on porcelain, the hobby of choice of Parisian women with time on their hands. It was vaguely creative but didn't require any talent, the modern equivalent of petit point. Laura had given up after a few sessions – there was something depressing about defacing perfectly decent plain china with nervously applied floral motifs.

Francine, on the other hand, was an enthusiast, and every time she entertained, her guests were confronted by yet another set of dinner plates embellished with swirls and dots. She had even opened a little shop to sell her work, but most of her business came from private sales, where friends were invited to part with their money in exchange for a few bits of china and the knowledge that they were making a sisterly contribution to the cause of new careers for middle-aged women.

A dinner party midweek was always a bonus for Laura, since it gave a focus to her day and allowed her plenty of time to prepare. In her previous life she would have gone straight from work in her office clothes, but now she could spend all morning thinking about her look, and all afternoon laying out the options on the bed. She had learned from Parisian women that the success of an outfit was all in the detail, and selecting the right bag and shoes was absolutely critical.

There was another very good reason for Laura taking more care over her appearance now than she ever had before. She had discovered that clothes were an armour, and the more elegant you appeared, the better equipped you were to deal with that terrible question. The question that Laura dreaded as much as every other non-working person. The question that hung in the air whenever strangers exchanged small talk across a bourgeois dining table. It was only a matter of time before someone would throw it at her in all its innocence:

'And what do you do?'

Or, in French:

'*Qu'est-ce que vous faîtes dans la vie?*'

When they first moved to Paris, Laura had read a book on French etiquette that said it was terribly bad form to ask people what they did. It just wasn't done. Well, clearly she was moving in the wrong circles, because she couldn't think of a Parisian party when she hadn't needed to make her grotesque apology, harking back to what she *used* to do, and explaining about lifestyle change and the stimulating experience of living abroad.

To boost her confidence tonight, she was intending to wear the new Kenzo suit she had bought on Monday. Flattering, nipped-in jacket, size twelve, and long flowing skirt, size fourteen, that she had picked up this morning on the way back from the school run. The extra inch they had built in meant it fitted her like a glove, skimming forgivingly over her tummy and hips. It was black, like most of her clothes. More specifically, to correspond to the dictates of this season, it was Surface Black, which meant it had a bobbly texture that prevented it from being just Plain Black.

Personally, she would have chosen the cigarette trousers that went with the jacket, but she could tell from the wince on the sales assistant's face that even with a few alterations she would still have looked like a tub of lard shoehorned into an ice cream cornet. Parisian women all looked fantastic in trousers, of course. Damn them and their tiny little bums.

They worked at it, though; every pharmacy in the city had big posters in the window promoting anti-cellulite medication. *Peau d'orange* was how they described cellulite – skin of an orange; or, even more unflatteringly, *culotte de cheval* – riding breeches, suggesting the bulging thighs of an English horsewoman, gripping the flanks of her mount as she hurtled round the point-to-point. She thought of those size ten French sticks twisting their thin lips into a *moue* of horror at the thought of developing horsey thighs. It was enough to keep you off the *pains au chocolat* for the rest of your life.

To offset the severity of the surface black, Laura had chosen a silver scarf with a red trim detail that very nearly matched her scarlet shoes. Taken with the slightly battered twinkly clutch-bag that had stood her in good stead since her college ball days, she felt it made a very satisfactory ensemble.

At six-thirty she locked herself into the bathroom, away from the noisy clatter of the children's teatime, to begin her beauty ritual. She had bought a new lipstick from Sephora in rue de Passy, a cavernous emporium of colourful beauty products, like Body Shop but five times bigger and without the self-righteous overtones. You could bet that no French woman would risk applying a product to

her precious skin that hadn't first been tested on a pale
rat in some laboratory cage.

Laura had been on a special two-day course recently
to learn how to apply make-up, so she understood the
importance of drawing a white line down the centre of
her nose. Once you had smudged it into the surround-
ing foundation, you really didn't look one bit like a Red
Indian. She then took a dark brown pencil to outline
her lips, and set about filling in with the new Chanel
lipstick.

She stared moodily at her reflection from beneath her
eyelashes, heavily blackened in the style of Princess Diana
in the *Panorama* interview. Not too bad for a woman of
her age. It was just a shame that she had to go to the
dinner alone. But then it was sometimes quite sexy to
arrive separately. Jean-Laurent would catch sight of her
across the room and be struck by how attractive she
looked. '*Bonsoir*,' he would say, '*on se connaît, je crois*,' I
believe we've met.

She emerged, phoenix-like, from the steam of the bathroom and picked up her coat from the cupboard in the
corridor. On her way out, she stuck her head round the
kitchen door to say goodbye. Charles-Edouard waved his
hand in a bored, mechanical impersonation of a greeting.
So young and yet so cool. Could you be postmodern at
the age of seven? Pierre-Louis stuck his lower lip out and
looked injured at her leaving. Asa glanced up from the
chicken nuggets she was disdainfully flipping on to two
plates. You could tell she had a difficult relationship with
food from the way she held the pan: carelessly, as though
it had nothing to do with her.

'Bye, see you later,' she said offhandedly.

Not even a second glance to take in her generous employer's extraordinary transformation from housewife – she *would* use the word – to fantastically elegant creature en route to a *dîner en ville*. It wouldn't hurt her, would it, just to say something along the lines of 'You look great', after all the bolstering that Laura had given *her* in her interminable journey towards renewed self-esteem.

'Don't wait up, we'll be late,' she said shortly, before stepping out of her small, domestic arena to join the big wide world. She slammed the door and pressed the button to summon the cranky old lift.

Laura parked the car close to Notre Dame cathedral and walked the short distance across the bridge to the Ile Saint Louis. Even after three years in this city she still got a thrill from its charm, its sense of history. Every time she turned a corner to go down another dimly lit street with unfeasibly quaint shops, she expected to see a cast member from *Les Misérables* come swashbuckling up to her in baggy white shirtsleeves. It was a look that the French intellectual Bernard-Henri Levy had adopted for a good few years in the nineties, and Laura had always made a point of watching the telly when he was on.

She found Francine's building, which was so ancient it seemed to be leaning forwards in a Disneyish take on the seventeenth century. The code worked, and the heavy door clicked open, releasing her into an inner courtyard with a stone staircase leading up to the Duvalls' apartment.

One interesting fact that Laura had noticed about the French was their fondness for rather nasty reproduction

Louis XV furniture. Naturally the eighteenth century was France's heyday – they'd done nothing as glamorous since, and who *wouldn't* have wanted to live at the court of Versailles? But those gilt bow-legged chairs looked quite wrong in the modern world, which didn't stop the French from stuffing their apartments full of them as a reminder of the grandeur that was once theirs. Even a spanking new apartment bought off-plan from a developer could be home to a fake escritoire.

Francine ushered Laura into her salon, which was a triumphant piece of retro glory, bright tapestry seats on extremely shiny gold legs, as thin and bent as any inbred aristocrat's. She was the first guest to arrive, which didn't surprise her. She was usually first – there was nothing to detain her, after all, no last-minute emails to reply to or preparations to make for the following day's meetings. And since Asa could just about muster the energy to do the children's tea and baths, she liked to set out nice and early: it made her feel she was getting her money's worth.

While they waited for the others, Francine treated her to a private viewing of her latest pottery collection, which was decorated with a few vague blue and green lines.

'I took my inspiration from Matisse's chapel in Vence. Less is more, you know – it's all a question of what you leave out.'

It seemed to Laura that quite a lot had been left out, but luckily the doorbell rang before she could respond.

It was the guest of honour, Sylvie Marceau, former rock chick, now transmogrified into all-purpose legendary French celebrity. She might be way beyond the peak of her career, but she was still famous enough to bring a flush of excitement to Francine's cheeks as she made the introductions.

'Laura, can I introduce you to Sylvie. You're almost neighbours, you know, over there in the bourgeois sixteenth. And this is her husband, Antoine. Clever woman, she married her doctor. And not just any old doctor, but an anti-ageing specialist if you please! Can you imagine anything more perfect? It's no wonder she looks so wonderful!'

They must be good friends, thought Laura, if she can make jokes like that. Sylvie didn't look the type to enjoy a good laugh about her appearance.

'*Enchantée,*' she said, though she was never sure if this was an appropriate way for a woman to salute another woman, or whether instant enchantment was considered a gallantry reserved for men.

Sylvie Marceau still had her girlish shape and trademark blonde fringe, but her face was curiously bland. Stretched smooth of lines, it had that agelessness that is only associated with the surgically enhanced, where the normal range of emotions is supplanted by a permanent look of mild surprise. As Laura shook her lifeless, chilly hand, she made a discreet inspection of her temples and thought she could just make out the giveaway silver lines, a tiny hair's breadth, set back beyond the outer edges of her eyes. The anti-ageing specialist clearly wasn't averse to referring his celebrity wife on to his colleagues at the sharp end of the business.

In contrast to his wife, Dr Antoine Bouchard exuded vitality. His face was tanned, almost orange in fact, but apparently free of surgery scars. His hair curled energetically close to his finely shaped head, and his dark eyes

were lively as he took Laura's hand in his and pressed it
warmly before raising it to his lips. It was a strangely old-
fashioned gesture, and reminded Laura that he was probably older than he looked. How old would he be, she
wondered? Forty something? Maybe fifty? She felt the
energy from the touch of his hand, and instinctively knew
that this was a passionate man.

Passion was a word the French used loosely and without fear. They could be passionate about Vacherin cheese
and Rodin's sculptures and equally passionate about new
motorways and income tax. Strong feelings were approved
of, not regarded with suspicion as they were amongst the
British. And Laura had a feeling that Antoine Bouchard
was a man of many and varied passions. He was quite
classically beautiful, almost Michelangelo's David, though
obviously a more mature version. And probably better with
his clothes on, she thought, stopping her imagination short
of picturing him mounted in naked glory on a marble
plinth.

'Pleased to meet you,' she said, lapsing into English in
her embarrassment.

'*Moi aussi*,' he replied, and made no attempt to release
her hand.

She tried to wriggle her fingers free. It wasn't that she
wanted to snatch her hand back, but she was aware of
Sylvie watching them from the fragile sofa, where she was
perched like a bird observing the spectacle of this gauche
English girl being taken in by the debonair seduction of
her husband. He did it all the time, of course, but French
women were a little more elegant in their handling of his
attention.

Sylvie reached forward for a handful of canapés which she offered to the two pint-sized dogs that had accompanied her into the room.

'Ah, Laura, Francine has told me so much about her little English friend. I believe you live just off the avenue Paul Doumer? Tell me, do you know the Canicoiff salon? I always take my girls there.'

Antoine finally let go of Laura's hand and she turned with relief to answer his wife.

'No, I'm afraid I don't have any dogs, only children. Do you always bring them with you?'

'Of course. They are perfectly behaved. But you English are so brutal about your animals, always leaving them stranded. And with your ridiculous rabies quarantine laws. Do you know, when we lived in London I had to leave them for six months in these horrible kennels in Southampton. I used to travel down twice a week to bring them prime steak from my butcher in Chelsea.'

'Did you like London?' asked Laura, although the question was redundant. All chic Parisians adored London, and to admit otherwise was tantamount to being a provincial.

'Of course. But I had to move back. The men in London do not look at you. I don't know why, perhaps it is because of your boarding schools.'

Francine's husband Dominique made a theatrical entrance at the doorway, bearing a tray of champagne glasses. He had been fussing about in his cellar for the past hour, inspecting his collection of fine wine, a passion he shared with Jean-Laurent and which usually formed the basis of lengthy discussions on evenings such as this.

'Englishmen only want women to be their friends,' he

said, as he made his way towards them. 'They like them to wear rugby shirts or to dress like gardeners. Whereas we French know how to look at a beautiful woman, to drink in her elegance with our eyes.' He handed her a glass of champagne, making his point with a smouldering gaze.

'But we hate that,' said Laura. 'It gives us the creeps, being stared at. We find it aggressive.'

She was aware of Antoine smiling at her, his head on one side, challenging her.

'There is no harm in looking, surely,' he said. 'Only a barbarian culture would outlaw the appreciation of beauty.' Laura noticed his voice was low and soothing. She knew what to call it in French – *une voix d'alcôve*. She had read it in a romantic novel one rainy afternoon. An alcove voice, a voice made for soft exchanges in secret places, and Paris was full of hidden alcoves where you could be lulled into oblivion by this man's words.

Sylvie, of course, was long past being taken in by Antoine's sweet nothings.

'Let me just say that I am happy to be back in civilisation,' she said. 'I could never feel properly at home in a country where the men do not look at the women. That, after all, is the whole point of our existence, don't you agree?'

She gave a coquettish shrug.

'So, Laura, you must be happy to live in Paris, and I think you chose well to live near us in the sixteenth. We have the Bois de Boulogne to walk our dogs and to stage our romantic trysts. I don't know why Francine is so scornful about it. She thinks she is so central, to live here on the Ile Saint Louis, but you know this used to be the dustbin of Paris? People would bring their stinking rubbish here – it was crawling with diseases.'

Francine smiled indulgently. She could afford to, living in a plush apartment in the city's most enviable location, a stone's throw from Notre Dame but a world away from the busloads of tourists whose itinerary never included the understated charms of the small island adjacent.

The front doorbell rang and Francine left the four of them to continue their eulogy of the sixteenth arrondissement while she welcomed the new arrivals. When she ushered them into the room, Laura felt a familiar twinge of panic, for Hugues and Marie-Françoise were one of those intimidating Parisian couples whose clothes and demeanour smelled of old money and effortless achievement.

The wife was from a famous champagne producing family and now ran the business empire, which included a bank and a clutch of exclusive hotels. Like many successful French career women who had been born to inherit, she assumed the mantle with regal nonchalance, untroubled by the glass ceiling that kept her less well-connected fellow women firmly in the lower ranks.

As she recounted her day with aristocratic *ennui*, Laura withdrew into a quagmire of inadequacy. She hoped to God she would not be quizzed about her own professional activity this evening; she could already envisage the embarrassed silence and swift change of topic that would entail.

Francine cast her hostess smile around her assembled guests.

'So, now we are just waiting for Laura's husband.'

'I'm sorry he's late – hopeless at time. You know, typical French,' joked Laura.

'Ah, the famous English humour', said Dominique. 'I love it – Monty Python, Benny Hill, *Four Weddings and a Funeral.*'

Laura smiled weakly.

Antoine turned to her.

'One would hardly know you were English, you speak French so well,' he murmured, 'though I suppose you do have that sexy little Jane Birkin accent that we find so irresistible.'

Laura could have kissed him. OK, so maybe she was a nothing little housewife with no business empire to run, but at least she had a gorgeous English accent and was fluently bilingual.

'Of course she is English,' boomed Dominique, 'can't you tell from that marvellous rose complexion? You know it is quite true that English women do have the most exquisite skin. There is a freshness to them – you can almost drink the dew off their cheeks.'

'Well, we must remember the words of Coco Chanel,' said Sylvie. '"At the age of thirty, a woman must choose between her face and her behind." And I think you will agree with me, my dear, that you English women mostly choose the face. We French, on the other hand, prefer to know that we can still look stunning in a size thirty-eight, whatever our age.'

'Until you turn round, that is,' retorted Laura, adjusting the flowing contours of her long black skirt and feeling grateful that at least she was sitting down and not offering her hips up for general inspection. 'I mean, not you personally, of course, Sylvie. It's just that sometimes you can be following a fantastic little French bottom down the street and you're thinking, look at that girl, why haven't I got a figure like hers, then suddenly she turns round and it's like a horror movie, there's this ancient face . . . you know, like Bette Davis in *Whatever Happened to Baby Jane* . . . I suppose there's always a price to pay for that tiny figure . . .'

She stopped, realising that she was getting into deep water. Fortunately Sylvie didn't seem to be taking offence, and was clasping her hands together in an actressy gesture of delight.

'Ah, my dear, I do admire your *esprit*, it is always so refreshing to hear a foreign view of how we appear, but that reminds me, too, of something I see in English girls. They very often can have good legs, but then, they have this little pot, *le ventre*, wait, I am trying to think of the English word . . . I have it, a beer belly, yes. Is it because of going to the pub? Do you think that they all drink big glasses of beer with the men? Such a shame, I think, to have this pretty face and then spoil it with a big tummy.'

'I'm more of a champagne person, myself,' said Laura, unwilling to be cast as a hefty beer-swilling Anglo-Saxon sinking the gallon on a Friday night with a marauding band of cavemen.

'Of course you are, Laura,' said Francine hastily. 'Come on, everyone, we will not wait for Jean-Laurent, he can join us at the table.'

She led her guests through to the dining room, which had been transformed into an autumnal woodland glade.

Dead leaves were artfully scattered over the table and the floor, while the candles were supported by twiggy branches. Each place setting was marked by a cluster of pine cones twisted together with a lavish golden ribbon. The dinner plates were painted with tiny squirrels gathering nuts, which produced the required flurry of congratulations. Jean-Laurent was ushered in shortly afterwards by the maid, smiling and apologising for being so late.

How handsome he looks, thought Laura, how unspeakably gorgeous. Even after a long hard day in the office, he still managed to give off the aura of someone who had just leapt out of bed, his hair tousled and shirt coming adrift at the side.

She felt like jumping up from the table and tucking it in for him and smoothing his hair. She remembered how proud she had been of him at London parties, so lithe and sexy and exotically French. The French bit counted for nothing now, of course, *she* had become the enigmatic foreigner, but his youthfulness was even more apparent tonight in contrast to this bunch of old fogeys – that spring in his step as he worked his way round the table, kissing the women on both cheeks, shaking hands with the men with just the right degree of masculine warmth before taking his place next to the hostess.

'So, Jean-Laurent, how is the world of soap powder – all on course to keep us on an upward curve of cleanliness?' asked Dominique. 'Do try this Chablis Premier Cru, it's quite surprising. My *caviste* acquired it especially with me in mind. You can tell how well he knows my tastes.'

'Oh, you know, Dominique, building up the master-brand architecture – I wouldn't dream of boring you with the details . . . mm, yes, I see what you mean, plenty of honey, very well rounded.'

'And yet with a flinty edge that prevents it from being overly feminine. You're not too worried, then, about being out of a job when we get hold of this new washing machine they've invented in Korea that doesn't need detergent?'

'Pie in the sky. Anyway, women will always need to feel that they are making their mark on the family's laundry by choosing the right product. It's a basic emotive need, isn't it, darling?'

He knew perfectly well that Laura couldn't give a monkey's arse what soap powder went into her machine. She gave an ironic little smile.

'Oh, I leave all that to the au pair, as you know, Jean-Laurent.'

'You see how fortunate I am? I have a whole battalion of women to make my life more comfortable!'

Jean-Laurent roared with laughter then held his glass up to the flickering light of the precarious twiggy candlesticks.

'A perfect amber glow with just a hint of green. Lively but elegant. You might get me in a case of this, Dominique.'

Laura picked up her fork to take on the terrine de foie gras. At least while they were on the subject of wine she was safe from interrogation. And at French dinner parties, it was quite possible to stick to one topic all night, unlike in England where it was considered terribly bad form to bang on and on about anything for more than five minutes. She felt a hand on her forearm. Antoine had been seated next to her and was now leaning towards her, his voice intimate and low.

'How sensible of you to leave the boring domestic work to an au pair. I could tell as soon as I met you that you were a dynamic woman of intelligence and style. Tell me, what do you do?'

Oh God. The dreaded question. So soon, and so directly aimed. There would be no wriggling out of it this time, no hasty change of subject, no oblique bouncing the ball back into his court. They all knew what *he* did – Francine had been careful to trumpet that out the moment he walked in the door. So now she would have to give an answer, the pitiful, boring, disappointing answer. She would be dismissed, a makeweight at the table, a poor dull housewife. Why couldn't she just brazen it out, like so many of her American friends? 'I'm a photographer', they might say, or 'I'm a weaver', meaning that they sometimes took a few snaps of the children or did a bit of needlework during the long empty hours. More enigmatically, they might just volunteer a verb: 'I paint', or 'I write', therefore I am. But she was just too British.

'Nothing,' she said. 'That is, I'm not working at the moment. You know, busy with the children.'

He looked disappointed, of course. She wasn't what he had hoped.

'Yes, I understand,' he said politely, 'children can take up a lot of time.'

Laura immediately sprung on to the defensive.

'Expand to fill the time available, you mean? Parkinson's Law?'

'Please, I didn't mean to criticise. I'm just surprised, that's all.'

'Surprised that I choose not to spend my life stuck in

an office pushing forward the frontiers of soap powder or pumping drugs into the corpses of women old enough to know better?'

The voice took on an edge. 'That is a rather harsh view of my profession and of that of your husband. I merely meant that you must surely need some kind of intellectual stimulation.'

'I stimulate my mind at the Louvre and tone my body at the gym. I cook, I read.' Now she was beginning to sound like an American, justifying her existence. 'I enhance my knowledge of French cheeses and the fripperies of the fashion world by spending many hours going round the shops.'

He laughed.

'Well, that's something, I suppose. But judging from your passionate response to my innocent question, it is clear to me that you are not entirely satisfied with your life.'

How dare he. Ten seconds of conversation and here he was telling her she wasn't happy. Well, she would show him she was no intellectual slouch.

'I suppose it all depends,' she said loftily, 'on how much you need to cling to the trappings of professional success to make sense of your life. I have met a great many people who are absolute top brass, what you French like to call *le gratin*, admired and envied by the outside world, yet who are weeping inside, howling like dogs because they are so unfulfilled as individuals.'

He raised his eyebrows in mock concern.

'Oh dear. I hope you don't see me as a howling dog.'

'I don't know yet, do I?'

She scowled at him and saw the amusement in his face.

His eyes were dark and teasing. Come on, they were saying, this is fun, let's have some more.

'Perhaps you would like me to tell you about my life,' he said. 'Then you can decide whether I am an empty shell or a complex, loveable person just like you?'

She was disarmed. It appeared that he had a sense of humour, which was by no means always the case with the French. And he was really rather attractive. She relaxed and took a sip of her wine.

'All right then,' she said, 'talk me through it. A day in the shallow life of an anti-ageing specialist. What made you turn your back on all the useful stuff you could be doing as a doctor to concentrate instead on bolstering human vanity?'

He pretended to wince.

'Ouch! Well, I think you only need to look back through history to understand that the search for the elixir of eternal youth is an obsession as old as mankind itself. Pope Innocent the Third used to help himself to the blood of young men to replace his own when he was panicking about getting old. And that's someone who presumably believed in an afterlife. Then there was the fashion for injecting humans with extracts from bulls' testicles. I am just the latest in a long line of people interested in prolonging life.'

'So what do you do exactly? When you're not siphoning off bulls' balls, that is?'

'I'm an endocrinologist. I make sure people have got the right hormonal balance.'

'How do my hormones seem?'

'Perfect. Very active.'

He held her gaze for a moment before nodding in the

direction of Jean-Laurent, who was engaging Sylvie in intense conversation.

'Just like your lovely young husband, in fact. I can tell just from looking at him that he is bursting with testosterone. And so can my wife – look how she is hanging on his every word.'

Laura shrugged. He had always had charm, why else would she have married him?

'But do you realise,' continued Antoine, slipping his hand across her knee in a way that Laura had to admit wasn't too creepy, 'that in a few years, he will be obliged to visit me for testosterone top-ups, if he is to maintain his current level of performance.'

He looked at her archly.

'Performance? What kind of word is that? He's not an athlete, you know!'

'Oh come now, Laura, we're all athletes, aren't we, within the confines of our own private stadiums?'

Laura pushed his hand off her knee, but not in an unkindly way.

'Let's stick to your job. Apart from the hormones, what do you do? Do you send people off for facelifts?'

'Let's just say I aim to stop the chromosomal clock. In whatever way I can. And sometimes, yes, that will include referral to a cosmetic surgeon.'

Laura's gaze swivelled involuntarily to focus on Sylvie. Antoine saw her trying to work up the nerve to ask about his wife, and deftly moved the conversation on.

'As I was saying about your husband, by the time he reaches fifty, unless he's done something about it, he will have the same level of testosterone as you.'

'No, come off it! I'm a woman!'

'I know, and a very attractive one. But as your testosterone level rises, his will decrease. The difference is that you will avail yourself of hormone replacement therapy, and he will probably be too proud to seek the same treatment. So you see, it is very unfair. My mission is to persuade men to seek help. They need it just as much as women. And that is my life's work. Not too ignominious, I hope? Possibly more worthy than shopping and going to art galleries?'

He saw her rising to the bait again, and quickly came in to smooth things over.

'But of course you have the children. The rest is just well-earned distraction.'

'Yes, of course, the children,' said Laura. 'They make all the difference. When I worked I used to feel so guilty about them, and about Jean-Laurent. I had no time for him. Whereas now I read them stories every night.'

'You read your husband bedtime stories? Lucky man!'

'Of course not! He prefers us to engage in other forms of entertainment. When he's there, that is.'

'Which isn't very often?'

'He works late.'

Come to think of it, she couldn't quite remember the last time they had indulged in 'indoor games', the English expression Jean-Laurent found terribly amusing to describe *les relations intimes*.

'I see.'

'What do you see?'

'I see, Laura, that you should perhaps think of finding someone to love.'

Was he making a pass at her? Is this when she was supposed to give him what they used to call an Old-Fashioned Look? To her irritation, she found she was completely lost for words. Eventually she found her tongue, and gave him her prim reply:

'And I suppose you would like to offer your services? Well, that's very kind, but for your information, I already have somebody to love.'

'You do? Oh, forgive me, I didn't realise the position was filled.'

'I don't think you're following me. I love my husband.'

'Ah, so the position is not filled.'

'Will you stop going on about filling positions and pass me that bottle of wine.'

Antoine refilled her glass, then slipped his hand into his pocket and pulled out a card which he passed stealthily on to her lap.

'If you change your mind, just call me. I find you very appealing. And life can be very disappointing if you do not dare to create opportunities for pleasure. Before it's too late.'

He smiled at her. It was preposterous. But flattering. She curled her fingers around his card and, in spite of herself, tucked it deep into her Kenzo pocket.

At the other end of the table, Francine and Sylvie were on their favourite topic.

'Signature pieces, darling. Lots of printed mousseline. You've got to hand it to him, he's been writing the fashion narrative for years.'

'But Sylvie, Yves Saint Laurent is so conventional, so *"jolie madame"*. Surely you must be more excited by Galliano.'

'Pure spectacle. It's not couture, he's a theatrical costumier. *You* could do it if you had a history book. And then he's English. When you think how English women dress like dogs – no disrespect, Laura – and yet we have brought in these English ragamuffin boys to take charge of our most prestigious fashion houses. Truly, it makes me weep to think about it. Then there are those dreadful American houses. Donna Karan, everything so *huge* to hide those enormous women's hips. I looked at her *rayon* in Printemps, and there was nothing small enough for me, not one thing.'

She sighed and smoothed her hands over her tiny knitted silk two-piece.

'I've got a Donna Karan three-quarter-length jacket that I wear all the time,' volunteered Laura, thereby rather proving the point.

The men had moved on to the Nuits-Saint-Georges.

'Good, powerful body, Dominique, even if it does lack a bit of finesse,' said Jean-Laurent. 'And I'm not sure that the blackcurrant doesn't rather overpower the raspberry and cherry. Sylvie, take it from me, the only interest we men have in what you wear is how fast we can remove it. Anything that unzips in one go and falls from the shoulders is fine in my book.'

Jean-Laurent fondly recalled the moment earlier that evening at Flavia's flat when she had demonstrated that very trick. The grey cashmere dress had slithered to the floor, revealing a lingerie ensemble whose cunning arrangement of bows and peepholes had almost made him pass out with desire.

That's funny, thought Laura. I don't have any dresses with zips.

'Oh, you men, if we dressed to please you we would never get beyond our underwear drawer,' retorted Sylvie, demonstrating an unnerving ability to read his mind. 'No, we women dress to compete with each other, and the older and richer we get, the higher the stakes and the more attention we must pay to our clothes and the *petits soins.*' *Petits soins* in her case, thought Laura, clearly embraced judicious use of the scalpel as well as the mascara.

'Unlike the young and beautiful who can do without,' said Francine, who then went on to recall her dismay on a recent flight to New York when she had found herself surrounded in club class by a herd of tall models in ripped jeans and T-shirts cropped above their achingly young washboard stomachs.

After dinner, the party crunched and rustled their way through the dead foliage back to the gilt splendour of the Louis XV sitting room where Conchita had set out coffee and liqueurs. The autumnal theme was relentlessly continued on the coffee cups which carried childish depictions of trees raining red and orange leaves.

Antoine struck up a seigneurial pose by the window, jangling his keys and coins in his pocket as if in prelude to what might follow for Laura if she was bold enough. He jutted his chin, presenting his best profile, which she had to admit wasn't bad. A roman nose and sensually puckered lips, and a chin that was suspiciously free of excess folds for a man of a certain age. Even Jean-Laurent was just starting to get a tiny bit jowly, but Antoine's lower face presented a crystal-clear outline. Maybe he *had* had a little help. She hadn't noticed any scars, but apparently they were often behind the ears; you would need to push the hair back and have a good look, preferably when he was sleeping. Like Damian in *The Omen* when they find the 666 hidden on his scalp.

Her reverie was interrupted when Antoine suddenly turned to face her and gave her what could be described as a smouldering smile, or a dirty leer, depending on your take on French seduction technique. Go on, he was implying, I dare you. Why not? She blushed, annoyed that he had caught her looking at him. Vain old fool. As if she would be interested in risking her reputation with him when she had legitimate access to the firm, unremodelled flesh of Jean-Laurent, who was now absorbed with Dominique in an in-depth analysis of the twenty-five-year-old Armagnac.

'We must go, Laura,' said Jean-Laurent, once he had had the final word on the in-barrel ageing capacity of his favourite *digestifs*. 'I've got an early flight in the morning.'

He rose from the bandy-legged chair, which looked a great deal more solid once it was free of his powerful weight.

'Francine, that was delicious. Our place next time, Dominique. I've got some interesting '82 Pomerol that I think you'd appreciate.'

The two men exchanged an arm-gripping handshake.

'Sylvie, it was a pleasure to meet you, glad to see you look as delicious in the flesh as you did on the back of my mother's old record sleeve. *Hé hé lollypop*, what a song that was, eh?'

Sylvie looked gratified, even though she realised there was more gallantry than truth in his remark as the photo in question was decades old and even her husband's expertise could not peel back the years to that extent.

'You must call in and see us,' she said. 'We are neighbours, after all. Here, let me give you our number. Antoine, do you have a *carte de visite*?'

Laura guiltily crunched up the card in her pocket as Antoine winked at her and handed Jean-Laurent a fresh copy, man to man, untarnished by the overtures of seduction.

They were shown to the door by Conchita, but then Jean-Laurent realised he had left his phone in the salon and returned to pick it up, which involved another round of lengthy farewells. Before you could say Casanova, Antoine had slipped out of the room and was standing beside Laura in the hallway.

'You didn't say goodbye to me,' he complained softly.

'Didn't I?' said Laura, pulling up her coat collar, eyes wide.

'No. I think you forgot.'

She leaned forward to kiss him on both cheeks.

'Goodnight then.'

He caught hold of her on the second kiss and held his mouth to her ear.

'I want you,' he whispered. 'Please say you'll come and see me.'

Jean-Laurent reappeared with his phone and Antoine sprang back with a deft manoeuvre born of years of practice.

'Ah, Jean-Laurent, I was just saying to your charming wife that I do so hope you will both come soon to have an aperitif with Sylvie and me.'

'Of course,' said Jean-Laurent, 'it would be a great pleasure.'

'Nice evening,' said Jean-Laurent, swaying slightly as they stepped out on to the street and headed for the pont Saint Louis. 'That Sylvie Marceau's showing her age, though, in spite of the best efforts of Doctor Frankenstein.'

'A scary old woman trapped in the body of an eighteen-year-old *chanteuse*.'

'It will impress them at work. Wait till I casually drop in that I had dinner with Sylvie Marceau.'

He thought about his boss, who must be about the same vintage.

'You were quiet tonight, Laura.'

'Uninteresting, you mean. I'm afraid I don't have much to contribute on the subject of wine.'

He ignored the jibe.

'Still, I saw you deep in conversation with Frankenstein.' He laughed suddenly as a ludicious thought occurred to him. 'Hey, he wasn't trying to get off with you, was he.'

'Would it be so surprising if he was?' snapped Laura. 'I'm not quite off the Richter scale of attractiveness yet, you know.'

'No, of course not,' he said hastily, while realising with a shock that it was incomprehensible to him that any man could find his wife desirable. 'Apparently they live in a fantastic house in the Villa Montmorency. It's like Bel Air in there – a guarded estate, wall-to-wall showbusiness and captains of industry. We really should call in on them, take them up on that offer of a drink.'

They continued in silence past Notre Dame until they came to the car. She pulled out her keys.

'Shall I drive?'

'Probably better had.'

She turned on to the left bank and followed the *quai* going west. The book stalls lining the river were packed up for the night, but there were still plenty of people on the streets enjoying the night air. She pointed to a restaurant.

'There's Les Bouquinistes – supposed to be good. We should go there for dinner one night.'

But Jean-Laurent was already asleep, his head lolling away from her. Poor thing, she thought, he's tired.

Four

Ten-thirty on a weekday morning, thought Laura, and here
I am, the envy of my friends, at leisure in my prime-loca-
tion Parisian flat. She unpacked two croissants from a
paper bag and put them on a plate with a generous dollop
of homemade raspberry jam. One thing she had learned
since she had stopped working was the importance of
structuring her day, and her mid-morning breakfast was
an important constant in what could become a loose
stream of aimless activity if you weren't careful.

She poured herself a coffee, milk, two sugars, and sat
down to recover from the morning rush. Jean-Laurent had
gone off at the crack of dawn, rather cross because he
had had too much to drink last night and couldn't find a
clean shirt. Charles-Edouard had been in a panic about
a book that she was supposed to have bought him for
school. She had decided to give the café a miss and enjoy
the peace and quiet of her own kitchen instead. She
wanted to be alone, to think about the dinner party last
night. About Antoine, and exactly what he had said to her.

That last kiss, his urgent insistence that they meet again.

Except that she was not alone. The kitchen door pushed open and in came Asa, steamily fragrant and swathed in three or four freshly laundered towels. She took a fat-free yoghurt from the fridge and sat down opposite Laura, casting a disapproving look at her plate.

'Do you know that there are 250 calories in one croissant? Not counting the jam, that is.'

'So I should hope. I've got to get my strength up after the school run. I daresay if I had only just got out of bed, I too could manage on a yoghurt, but sadly that is not my privilege. Anyway, I'm going to the gym.'

'You'll need to run for fifty minutes at nine kilometres an hour to work off that lot. It's far more sensible to restrain your calorie intake and maintain a steady output of energy.'

And *you* should know about sensible eating patterns, fumed Laura, thinking about the packet of chocolate cereal that had mysteriously disappeared last week, and how she had found the empty packet stuffed down the side of Asa's bed. She changed the subject.

'Were the children OK last night?'

'Oh, fine. They always go to bed sweetly for me, it's only for your benefit they make such a song and dance. How was your dinner party?'

'Sylvie Marceau was there.'

'Oh *really*? What's she like? She has a fantastic figure.'

'Slim and ancient,' said Laura, brushing the crumbs off her lap. 'I'm off to the gym. See you later. If you do get round to ironing those shirts for Jean-Laurent, that would be great.'

Asa watched her go. Fat, lazy cow, she thought, why

don't you iron the shirts yourself? She pulled her chair towards the grocery cupboard, and stood on it on tiptoe so she could reach the top shelf, and helped herself to a large tablet of cooking chocolate.

Oh vanity, oh man, thought Laura crossly, flat on her back on a mat as she heaved her right elbow to touch her upraised left knee for the twenty-ninth time to the tune of a female singer who sounded like she had one of those black, effortlessly supple bodies. 'I'm horny, horny, horny, horny,' went the song, 'oh I'm horny, so horny, horny, horny tonight.' How many of these old French snakes writhing on mats around her even understood the words, never mind the notion of horniness. It made her feel sick just to think of it.

'*Attention, à gauche!*' barked the instructor, a wiry twenty-something who looked as though he lived in a continuous state of horniness that was repeatedly relieved by a bevy of acrobatic partners.

She obediently followed his lead, wincing with each abdominal contraction as they began the same exercise on the other side. The old snakes only made up a third of the class. With the exception of one elderly man who looked as though each thrust could be his last, the others were all youngish women, most of them considerably thinner than Laura.

She had had a bit of a downer on the gym ever since she had mentioned on the phone to a friend in England that she had joined.

'Oh yes,' he had laughed, 'it's something that comes to all housewives at a certain age.'

'But I am not a housewife,' she had protested, 'I'm a professional woman enjoying an extended career break to enhance my quality of life. Cherie Blair goes to the gym, and you wouldn't laugh at her.'

Laura would never have joined had it not been for her Irish friend Lorinda, who was stretched out on the mat next to her. Lorinda had been Laura's best friend since they had met at the *haltegarderie* three years earlier when Laura had just arrived in Paris.

The French didn't do playgroups for pre-school children – that would sound too much like having fun. Instead they had horrible institutions called *haltegarderies* run by hard-faced battleaxes who prepared toddlers for the cruelty of adult life by snatching them from their mothers at the hall gates and making them stand in the corner if they cried.

Laura and Lorinda had both arrived on the first day of term and been so horrified by the sound of mass wailing, reminiscent of a Victorian asylum, that they had turned right round and headed for the café *terrasse* instead, where Pierre-Louis and Victoire played happily amongst the pigeon shit while their mothers exchanged life stories.

Lorinda's life was governed by two contradictory obsessions. The first was saving money, which was why she had agreed to spend a year living rent-free with her French mother-in-law while she and her husband saved up for a new apartment for their *famille nombreuse*. The second obsession was avoiding her mother-in-law, and she had calculated that the opportunities for escape offered by the gym more than justified the hefty membership fee.

'Look, Laura, provided you go four times a week, it's fantastic value for money.'

'And if you go once a fortnight, which is more likely, it's incredibly expensive.'

But Laura had capitulated, and at Lorinda's suggestion they met three times a week for *abdo-fessiers, culture physique* or *body sculpt*, narcissistic, unsmiling exercises in the worship of physical appearance that was the bane of modern urban life.

In six months she had lost one kilo, or half a kilo depending on how you stood on the scales in the changing rooms. By any standards this was disappointing and Laura worried that her agreeing to go to the gym was yet another example of her becoming reactive instead of proactive. She had reactively agreed to follow her husband to France, she reactively let Asa dictate the terms of her employment, she reactively let the kids watch what they wanted on the TV. She was like a giant jellyfish on the beach, pushed around by the sticks of curious children.

The *abdo-fessiers* half-hour was mercifully drawing to a close, finishing with Laura's favourite part which involved sitting with one leg crossed over the other and collapsing, head bowed over the extended leg, for a nice long time. You then had to stand up slowly and unfurl your arms.

Looking in the mirror, Laura was suddenly reminded of a picture from Pierre-Louis's *Babar the Elephant* book of Babar doing his exercises with the Old Lady. There were plenty of Old Lady clones in the room, but Laura felt that as a physical type she was rather closer to Babar. The class applauded themselves briefly, like trained monkeys, and obediently put back their instruments of self-flagellation, thick elastic bands and dumb-bells.

'Thank Christ that's over, I'm starving,' said Laura. 'Lunch? Or have you got to pick up the children?'

'No, they're in the *cantine* today. We get three hundred euros reimbursed from the Mairie on our *carte Paris famille*.'

'Not another bloody handout!'

'Free museum entry, free swimming pool, half-price metro tickets. I keep telling you to have another child. Alexandre saves us eight thousand euros on our tax bill, plus the extra allowance I get for staying at home. And they're giving us back the family allowance.'

'Your protest worked, then.'

Lorinda had joined the ranks of hair-banded bourgeois housewives who had gone on a *manifestation* to protest against the means testing of *allocations familiales*.

'I should think so! I paid my taxes for all those years.'

Lorinda had worked as an air hostess for Air France during her year off before teacher training college. But then she had met Arnaud, and the combination of his Gallic charm and the glamour of international travel meant that the teacher training went on the back burner, and here she was twenty years later with four children and the mother-in-law from hell.

'How about Le Petit Marguéry? They do a great value set lunch including half a carafe of wine.'

'Perfect. I can tell you all about *belle-mère*'s latest outrages. Do you know, she knocked on the bathroom door last night and told me I was taking too long. Apparently, now I've got kids I'm not allowed to spend more than two minutes in the bath.'

The two women made their way down the rue d'Auteuil

past the marketplace, which today was occupied only by pigeons and looked far too small ever to accommodate the density of stalls that would be crammed in there tomorrow. They continued past Le Nôtre, the *nec plus ultra* of cake shops, where a canny beggar was sitting outside the door. You would have to be pretty heartless, thought Laura as she dropped him a coin, *not* to give him something after spending thirty pounds on a smallish cake for afternoon tea.

They reached Le Petit Marguéry and settled down with pleasure on to the worn red-leather *banquettes*.

'I'll have the *travers de porc au miel*, with the *escargots* as entrée,' said Laura, thinking that the *crème brûlée* would slip down quite well after all that.

'And I'll take the *salade frisée au chèvre chaud* and the *daurade*,' said Lorinda, 'and I suppose we'd better have a Kir before the Côtes du Rhône.'

'Well we've certainly earned it.'

Meanwhile, in the Café Marly, Jean-Laurent was pleased to find himself installed at a prime table on the covered *terrasse* which gave a clear view of the glass pyramid at the entrance to the Louvre. From this vantage point he could look down at the long line of tourists queuing for entry through the barrage of uniformed *fonctionnaires* checking out bags for bombs and small penknives of the kind recently used by a thief to cut a small masterpiece out of its frame.

For once, the staff were not on strike. While his French education had taught him to respect every citizen's right to refuse to work, Jean-Laurent had little sympathy for the plight of the ordinary man. He was international business school royalty after all, not some bearded loser in a university faculty who would no doubt be right behind these whingers and their outrageous demands. He honestly couldn't understand what they were complaining about. All they had to do all day was sit on a chair in front of some paintings and watch the totty go by. He wished his working life was that easy, though of course a museum attendant probably only got a fraction of his own package.

The contrast between the anorak-wearing tourists and the chic but cool customers of the Café Marly was a source of satisfaction to him, and so was the fact that this lunch could be charged to his expense account. It really was convenient to have a mistress who was also a bona fide business associate; it made everything so much simpler.

Flavia had just completed a piece of research for him which had involved housewives lying on the floor to the accompaniment of New Age music to recall their first experiences of washing clothes. Flavia had explained to them that washing wasn't just a process, it was a ritual, a spiritual conquest of evil that restored order from chaos. 'I am a woman from another planet,' she had told them, 'and I have come to learn about your experiences of washing.' The women had looked rather baffled, but it was certainly provocative, and, in Jean-Laurent's opinion, well worth the fat fee.

His face brightened as he saw Flavia walking towards him. She took off her coat to reveal a tight jumper that rode up above her belly button, and the kind of dropped-waist trousers that could be so cruel to those with less than perfect hips. She kissed him on both cheeks and he breathed in her perfume. Envy by Gucci, entirely appropriate, for which man could not envy him his lunch date?

She sat down opposite him and smiled. Her blonde hair shone as she screwed up her eyes, dazzled by the sun reflecting on the pyramid, and pulled a pair of sunglasses out of her bag. Trust Flavia to think of carrying sunglasses in November, thought Jean-Laurent in admiration. He was overtaken by a wave of happiness. He was about to spend two hours with her, and tomorrow he would see her again. He was truly blessed, he thought, or, as the German expression went, as happy as God in France.

He turned to the waiter.

'A bottle of Taittinger, please.'

Back in Le Petit Marguéry, the women were on coffee and Lorinda was in full flow.

'And then she had the cheek to say that I couldn't possibly have been that long going round the supermarket. So I took out my receipt and my car park ticket and showed her, look, 95 minutes to buy 120 items, that's 45 seconds per item. You really can't say that's bad!'

'Mad old witch. I don't know how you put up with her,' commiserated Laura, glancing at her watch.

'And then Arnaud was working late last night – who can blame him! – so I had to have dinner with her by myself and she made me prepare this little platter of salad for him to have when he got in, and I was cutting up a tomato and she grabbed the knife off me and said, "No, Lorinda, it must look appetising," and started arranging it on the plate like she was in a bloody cordon bleu contest. So I said, it's not worth it, he'll probably have eaten anyway so he'll end up throwing it in the bin like he did last night, then she started on her old tune about how the kids' room was a tip and I should learn to demand order before it was too late.'

'Never mind,' said Laura. 'A few more years in Paris and you'll become just like her.'

She undid the top button of her trousers. That *crème brûlée* had been a bit of a mistake.

'That's the worst part of it. When I went to spend a week in Ireland with my family, I couldn't stand the chaos, I was desperate to get back to the discipline of Bonne-Maman's home. At least you can always find everything.'

She sighed.

'Anyway, that's enough about her. I come out to get away from her and spend the whole time talking about her. What about you? How was your dinner last night?'

At last, thought Laura, the chance to talk about her little flirtation. She could tell Lorinda about Antoine and how he had come on to her. She had been saving the story up – she knew Lorinda would love it. After all, it wasn't often that a respectable *mère de famille* was subjected to improper advances from someone who was almost famous.

She unwrapped two sugar cubes and stirred them into her coffee, savouring the moment.

'Well, how about this? I was propositioned by Sylvie Marceau's husband.'

Lorinda's eyes widened in delight.

'Get out of here! The anti-ageing guru? What did he do, grope you under the table?'

'Don't be common. He made a very Andrew Marvell point about taking the opportunity for pleasure while one

still had the chance. Not that he mentioned Andrew
Marvell – I don't think poetry is his bag. He's more of a
hormone man.'

'So what did you say?'

'I was suitably indignant and made it clear that I was
in love with my husband.'

'Which you are.'

'Of course.'

'How's his cellar doing?'

Lorinda was the only friend of Laura's who didn't think
that Jean-Laurent was a heaven-sent piece of perfection,
which was doubtless why Laura liked her so much. But
honour obliged her to stick up for her husband before
moving on to discuss her admirer.

'Don't be mean, Lorinda, lots of French men are interested in wine, even if Arnaud isn't.'

'Yes, but he does go on and on, doesn't he?'

'I know you've never made any secret of the fact that
you consider my husband to be a crashing bore.'

'I never said that. He has got beautiful cheekbones.'

'The two aren't mutually exclusive.'

'So what's the deal on the horny doc? Is he attractive?'

Was he attractive? Was the Pope Catholic? She feigned
cool indifference.

'Well, he's older than me. Better preserved than Sylvie,
though. Sort of classical. He has a lovely voice.'

'She really is a freak show, but that's mostly due to him,
isn't it?'

'I really don't know. Strangely enough I didn't get him
to talk me through all the operations he had put his wife
through while we were sitting round the table.'

'So what did you talk about?'

But Laura was not about to share *all* her secrets, even with her best friend. She thought about his hand on her knee, how disinclined she had been to push it away; his arrogant presumption that her life lacked passion and direction; and that he was the one who could answer her maiden's prayer.

'Nothing much.' She said. 'He gave me his card.'

'Which you kept.'

'So?'

'So you must be thinking about it.'

'Don't be ridiculous. It just amused me, that's all.'

'Exactly. Amusement is what it's all about. Laura, haven't you heard about a little French institution known as the *cinq à sept*?'

'Yes, I know all about that old cliché, the love affair which takes place between five and seven o'clock, conveniently slotting in between work and dinner. And how would I manage to absent myself at that difficult time, might I ask, with the boys home from school? Even if I was interested, that is, which I am not.'

'Get that lazy bag Asa to do something for a change. Let her feed the boys, and you can swoop in for the bedtime story fresh from Doctor Sex's love den.'

'I wish you wouldn't be so disgusting. I told you, I'm a faithful wife.'

'Who happens to keep strange men's cards tucked about her person just in case . . .'

'Shall we get the bill? Your turn to pay, I think.'

'Good job we had the *prix fixe* in that case.'

*   *   *

On reflection that second bottle of wine was a bad idea, thought Laura as the rear of her Espace clipped the bumper of a Clio in the course of what should have been a perfectly straightforward piece of parking. She looked round guiltily but none of the passers-by in rue du Commerce seemed remotely interested.

That was one great thing about the French – they weren't precious about their cars the way the British were. She remembered one weekend in Bath when Jean-Laurent had been parking his car in the French style, crashing bumper to bumper, and a horrified crowd of indignant spectators had gathered to watch. Here in Paris, everyone had the odd dent or two; it was *tout à fait normal*.

She got out of the car and walked quickly up towards the avenue Emile Zola. There was just time to pick up some cheese at the Fromagerie du Pays d'Auge before meeting the boys. She opted for the most expensive of the four Roqueforts on offer, and a rich yellow slab of St Nectaire fermier together with a pale St Marcellin, which the shop assistant selected for her after a great deal of prodding and a detailed discussion about when exactly it was to be eaten.

It was one of the miracles of Paris, thought Laura in a happy fog of Côtes du Rhône, that even in a relatively un-chic *quartier* like the fifteenth you could find these little shops that put Harrods' food hall to shame, never mind the bland plastic-wrapped offerings of the average British supermarket.

Her good humour continued as she approached the school gates and the usual crowd of faces – nannies, to whom one did not speak, and other mothers to whom one did, although as a group Laura tended to avoid them. She suspected it was rather like Groucho Marx not wanting to belong to any club that would have him as a member, and the problem with this club of Committed Mothers was that they were always trying to get you to do things. It seemed churlish to say so, but just because she didn't work it didn't mean that she was suddenly possessed by a desire to read stories to classes of other people's children, or to spend her afternoons sorting out the PTA video library. It would be like resigning from the job of company chairman and then volunteering to work as an unpaid filing clerk.

She gave a quick glance round to see if there was anybody she should avoid. There was Ugly Mum, doing herself no favours with a pair of leggings that hugged her droopy bottom, and next to her was PTA Paula, handing out a production schedule for the Christmas show costumes.

In a former life Paula had been a top banker, but her energies were now channelled into developing the human capital of her offspring. While she was entirely credible as a Capable Mother with her short practical haircut, it was hard to imagine how she ever got there, but obviously someone must have once wanted to have sex with her. The sperm could barely have had time to settle before she was leaping up to wipe down surfaces and set the breakfast table.

Further along was Designer Mum, dressed up in a fabulous fur-trimmed green cloak. You wouldn't guess that *she* was just a housewife, although arguably her money and style hoisted her up into the category of Idle Rich or Ladies Who Lunch, neither of which Laura felt she could quite aspire to. It was mostly the American women who masterminded all things extra-curricular. The French mothers, who failed to understand the emotional significance of a bake sale, preferred to go out to work, leaving only a handful of pale-faced *mères de familles nombreuses* to represent them at the school gates. These pious-looking mothers with headbands and sensible coats were usually pushing double buggies containing their latest tax-rebate offspring, and whisking their older children, dressed in smocked dresses and knickerbockers from Cyrillus, off to catechism classes.

The gates opened and the children spilled out on to the narrow pavement. Laura was gratified, as always, to see Pierre-Louis's eyes light up as he saw her, while Charles-Edouard, more serious, just looked relieved. It was pitiful, really, how much importance she attached to these small moments of pleasure. She held Pierre-Louis's hand and put her arm round Charles-Edouard's shoulders as they made their way to the car.

'How was your day? Did you have chips for lunch?'

She was often struck by the banal nature of her conversation with her children. It would be nice to ask more penetrating questions, but she had come to realise that you couldn't expect too much stimulating banter from anyone under the age of eight.

'Mum, do you have a job?' asked Charles-Edouard as she opened the car door for him.

'No. Well, I look after you two.'

'So does that mean you're *au chomage*? Madame Pinault says that people who don't work are called *chomeurs* and they get money to help them.'

'No, Charles-Edouard, I'm not unemployed. I choose not to work, it's quite different.'

'Why's it different?'

'I suppose it's because I don't need to work.'

'Does Daddy pay for everything?'

'Yes.'

'That's nice of him.'

Laura felt her self-esteem ebb another couple of notches as she drove off to spend one more evening awaiting the return of her benefactor.

'Jean-Laurent, does it bother you that I don't work?'

It was Friday night, and they were in the car, crawling west along the A13 in the thick of the weekend traffic and the pouring rain.

'You don't work? But you're always telling me that you're busier now than you've ever been.'

'You know what I mean. Is it embarrassing for you that I don't "work outside the home", if you want to be politically correct about it?'

'We've been through all this. I thought you were happy pottering around with the children? Anyway, you're hardly likely to find anything interesting that you can do part-time, and I thought we agreed that it was important that one of us was there for them after school. It's not as if I've got the kind of nine-to-five job that lets me come rushing home to do tea and homework.'

Research meetings with Flavia, of course, came into the quasi-professional category.

'I know, but do you think I've become more boring since I've been at home?'

Jean-Laurent didn't think it was wise to answer this question too directly.

'You can't look at it like that. Our lives are different now. We've got the boys, things aren't going to be the same as they used to be.'

'So you *do* think I'm more boring?'

'I didn't say that.'

'But you do think so.'

'Look, Laura, now you *are* being boring. If you want to go out and work a sixty-hour week, that's fine by me. I'll stay at home and have a nice time and you can worry about keeping the family in designer trainers and skiing holidays.'

'Would you really like that?'

He thought for a moment about a life without an expense account. No more meetings in which he could look dashing in his Hugo Boss suits and impress pretty young marketing assistants with his mastery of brand architecture. No more off-site think tanks at luxury hotels. No more lunches with Flavia. He would become like his sad, pussy-whipped friend Jean-Michel, bowed over the pushchair, taking the hoover in for repair while his wife swept off to her high-powered job at the Assemblée Nationale. Poor fucker.

'No, not really. I don't think I'd have anything to say for myself.'

'Exactly. That's just how I feel some of the time.'

Jean-Laurent braked violently as a Mercedes sports car overtook him from the inside lane. He swore at him, '*Enfoiré!*', and took his hand off the steering wheel to tap his head in an expression of disbelief. The driver responded by raising an insolent finger in the rear-view mirror. A hot-looking piece beside him had her arm draped across his shoulders. There were no child seats sensibly strapped into the back of this car. No doubt they were off to a little hotel for a weekend of mutual pleasure and self-gratification. Whereas he, Jean-Laurent, could look forward to fixing the dripping tap in the attic bathroom, and possibly digging over the rose beds before sitting down to a tiresome child-orientated lunch with some tedious friends of Laura's and their new baby.

He sighed as they drew up to the *péage* and held his upturned hand out to Laura.

'Got a card?'

She handed him her bank card and he opened his window and fed it into the machine. The barrier lifted and they drove on in silence into the darkness.

Ninety minutes later they scrunched up the gravel drive to their country cottage. It was chocolate-box pretty with its black and white timbers, set in a fairy-tale garden that had seduced them with its mature trees – perfect for the hammock – and whimsical wishing well, now prudently boarded up to prevent disaster.

Unfortunately the house was situated rather a long way from the car parking area, particularly unwelcome on a filthy November night when you arrived with sleeping children and bags of heavy shopping. Jean-Laurent turned off the engine and slumped back in his seat, while Laura pulled up the collar of her coat against the rain and picked her way across the stepping stones that Jean-Laurent had spent the best part of his summer holiday embedding into

the lawn. Laura had wanted him to get someone in to do
it, but he had insisted that physical labour was what he
needed to counteract the stress of his job. His back had
been giving him trouble ever since, though he did not like
to be reminded of it.

Laura pulled the keys out of her pocket, opened the
door and stepped into the cold, damp kitchen, switching
on the lights and the central heating then putting on the
kettle for hot-water bottles in a well-practised routine. She
then hopped back across the stepping stones, which were
really placed too far apart for anyone under six foot two,
and lifted Pierre-Louis from the snug cocoon of his car
seat. Back across the stepping stones she went with him,
into the house and upstairs into bed where he burrowed
under his duvet like a small animal. She did the same
with Charles-Edouard, puffing up the stairs under his
greater weight, then went back to the car to ferry in carrier
bags loaded with the weekend's provisions.

Meanwhile Jean-Laurent was pouring himself a whisky
in the kitchen, unwinding after the journey.

'What's for dinner?' It was so cold that his breath hung
in a visible cloud.

Laura was unpacking the groceries, still wearing her
coat and hat.

'Soup. Warm us up. Then cheese.'

'I think a robust Cahors should see us right in that case.'

After supper they climbed up the spiral staircase and
quickly changed into their out-of-season country weekend
bedwear: pyjamas, socks and sweatshirts that had seen
better days. Laura wrapped herself into Jean-Laurent's
folded back.

"Night, then.'
'Goodnight.'

There were, she thought fleetingly, better ways to spend a Friday night.

Saturday morning brought no improvement in the weather. The children sat at the kitchen table drawing pictures of their favourite cartoon characters, while Laura was concentrating on stuffing three different sorts of cheese under the skin of a chicken.

'It's boring here, why can't we get a telly?' asked Charles-Edouard as he put the finishing touches to his bulbous-nosed Super Mario.

'You watch quite enough in the week. It should brighten up later, then we can go for a bike ride.'

'Oh, boring. Can we get a comic?'

'Maybe this afternoon. Here, take this coffee up for Daddy.'

'He's still asleep.'

'So wake him. It's nearly eleven o'clock.'

But Jean-Laurent was not asleep. He was sitting up in bed cradling the phone.

'Oh, nothing. It's raining. I've got to fix a tap, then we've got some people coming to lunch. How about you? . . . sounds marvellous. I only wish I could come and help you choose . . . Do you think they'd let me into the changing room? . . . Oh, I *see* . . . well, you'll just have to give me a private viewing next week.'

He started as Charles-Edouard came slowly into the room with a bowl of coffee, frowning in concentration as he tried not to spill it.

'Anyway, got to go. I'll call you next week. *Ciao*.'

'Who were you talking to?' asked Charles-Edouard, placing the bowl carefully on the bedside table.

'Just someone from work. *Merci, mon ange*, what a big boy you are. Come and read me a story, let's see how you're getting on with your reading.'

Charles-Edouard climbed into bed with his father and rubbed his unshaven chin.

'You've got spikeys. Why does your beard stink in the mornings?'

'It's not my beard, it's my evil breath. I'm the big bad wolf and I'm going to EAT YOU UP!'

Charles-Edouard shrieked in delight as his father threw him into the air and caught him in a noisy snuffling impersonation of a wild beast with his prey.

By 12.45 Laura had set the table and the cheesy-skinned chickens were beginning to smell appetising. By two o'clock the gratin potatoes had rather shrivelled up. At 2.30 Laura decided to feed the boys as they were getting hungry and bad-tempered.

'Where the fuck are they?' grumbled Jean-Laurent, helping himself to his third glass of pommeau, a potent blend of cider and Calvados that had been devised by depressed Normans as an aperitif to help them get through grey days like this one.

'They rang from Evreux to say they had to stop to feed the baby. They should be here by now.'

'Can we get our comics now?' asked Charles-Edouard, licking the last crumbs of chocolate cake from his plate.

'No, we've got to wait for Harry and Susie.'

Harry was an old school friend of Laura's brother who had been sent to work in the Paris office of his bank three years previously. Laura had never cared for him, but he had been persistent in inviting them to his parties, which were ghastly braying affairs, full of British expats clinging together in the face of Johnny Foreigner. Laura had never invited him back, as she was unable to think of anyone to have with them, and thought that it would be better to have him here in the country, where a cosy foursome looked less like an insult to his presentability.

Harry's wife, Susie, like the wives of many bankers who could afford the luxury, was a Creative Person who had taken a course in Interior Design at Parsons College in Paris. She had done up quite a few apartments for Harry's colleagues, who were too busy making money to be interesting themselves but who compensated by paying Susie to hang up lengths of hand-painted hessian. They especially appreciated the signature chandeliers she made out of old bath taps, which invariably provided a talking point during dinner parties. Susie's most recent creative outlet, however, was a baby called Paris. This child was, to put it mildly, the focus of her life.

'They're here,' announced Pierre-Louis from his vantage point on the window sill above the kitchen radiator, which he had long ago identified as the only warm place in the house. Laura watched through the rain as Harry climbed out of the grey BMW and fussed about in the boot until he came out with a large striped golf umbrella. Opening the passenger door, he held the umbrella over Susie and the baby as though she were a visiting foreign dignitary.

There was not enough room for them both on the stepping stones, so he squelched alongside her on the grass, her confident, Sloaney stride easily taking in the too-wide gaps between the stones.

'Laura, I'm *so* sorry we're late. We had to stop for the baby, and then we found this wonderful pottery in Bernay.' She held out a parcel in the hand that wasn't attached to the baby. 'Here, can you take this? Careful, it's fragile.'

'Oh, thank you, is it for me?' Laura knew the pottery, which used only beautiful natural blue-green dyes.

'No, it's for my study actually, but it's quite delicate and I didn't want to leave it in the car in case we forgot about it and it got broken.'

She gave an appraising glance around the kitchen.

'Well, this is very cosy, I must say. Etruscan Red, Sugar Bag Light and Mole's Back. Don't you think there's something reassuringly nineties about the National Trust paint range? Harry, could you bring in the playpen, please?'

She turned to her husband who was busy ferrying in what seemed to be a disproportionate amount of luggage for an overnight stay.

'Let me take your coats,' said Laura. 'Jean-Laurent, can you organise some drinks?'

'No alcohol for me, thank you, I'm still breastfeeding,' said Susie. 'Do you think we could just move that table a fraction? Then the playpen will fit in.'

Harry obligingly shoved the kitchen table into the corner of the room to make way for a large wooden playpen that took up at least half the floor space.

'I didn't think you could buy those things these days. I thought they were supposed to be damaging to a baby's psyche,' remarked Laura crossly, straightening the plates on the displaced table which was now rammed up against the radiator.

'You probably can't – that was Harry's old one that his mother gave us.'

Even at that age, thought Laura, Harry's bottom must have required giant-sized accommodation. He stood up now in his massive green corduroys and entered into a playful air-punching routine around Charles-Edouard and Pierre-Louis who stared at him coldly. Laura thought he looked like a page from the Johnnie Boden mail order catalogue, the one that used photos of its well-bred customers to promote trousers boasting plenty of room round the seat for gentlemen of traditional build.

Undiscouraged by the boys' stonewalling of his display of camaraderie, Harry turned to their father.

'So, Jean-Laurent, how's fatherhood treating you? Hell at the weekends, isn't it? *Au revoir* golf! Still, wouldn't be without them, would we, little monsters? I always say, it's changed my life, and I wouldn't have it any other way. A sea change for the better, and come hell or high water, that little chap will always mean the world to me. I've already laid down a case of claret for his twenty-first. Bloody marvellous!'

He accepted a glass of pommeau and raised it to the fat toddler who had now been parked in the playpen. Laura remembered how her mother had donated her old playpen to a school fête where it was used to house a baby pig. You had to guess its weight to win a bottle of champagne.

'Cheers! Up your bum! Bottoms up and down the hatch!' roared Harry, downing the pommeau in a single draught.

'He's definitely got my chin. And hung like a donkey, of course – no doubting the paternity of that little fellow, I can tell you!'

He held his glass out for a refill then turned to his hostess.

'What about you, Laura, still keeping the home fires burning?'

Laura ignored the question as she put the charred potatoes and collapsed-looking chickens on the table.

'We can sit down now, lunch is ready. Susie, you'd better go on the end with the baby, and Harry, you go opposite her. Jean-Laurent and I will squeeze in next to the radiator.'

After lunch, Susie retired to her bedroom with the baby, and Jean-Laurent and Harry took the boys off to the local town to pick up some comics. They intended to call in at the farm afterwards to stock up on Calvados for Harry's cellar. You could be sure that none of it would make its way on to his hosts' table. Laura cleared the table, folding away the maps that had been brought out to assist in planning an itinerary for tomorrow morning's drive, and moving with difficulty around the obstructive playpen.

She had just finished washing up when Susie emerged, carrying the baby, who was swaddled up like the Michelin Man.

'Still slaving away, you naughty girl!' she said, as if Laura's single-handed clearing of the kitchen was an act of pure self-indulgence. 'Why don't you come out for a walk with me and Paris? I want to show him his first cows now it has stopped raining. By the way, is there a problem with the heating? The radiator in our bedroom doesn't seem to work.'

'It probably just needs bleeding. I'll have a look.'

'Thanks. I wouldn't normally worry, but Paris has had a bit of a cough. You did say you had a cot for him, didn't you?'

'Oh yes, I need to dig it out of the barn.'

'Are you sure you won't come with us? We're going to walk down the lane so we can meet Daddy on his way back, aren't we, little man?'

'No, I'll take a look at that radiator, then there are some things here I need to get on with.'

'As you like. We'll see you later then.'

She handed Laura a small orange plastic bag that felt slightly warm to the touch.

'I don't know what you want to do with this. I couldn't see a bin in the bedroom. Bye, then. Do let me know if there's anything I can do, won't you?'

She strapped Paris lovingly into his buggy and pushed him out into the garden.

'Look at that, Laura,' she called through the open door. 'Look how he's staring up at the sky – you can just tell he's going to be creative. I can still remember lying in my own pram watching the patterns of the clouds. It starts so early, if you're an artist.'

Selfish bitch, thought Laura, tossing the nappy into the bin. She made up the spare bed, fixed the radiator, got a fire going in the chimney place and washed the salad for supper. She then hunted through the dusty pile of broken pieces of furniture and assorted rubbish in the barn until she came across the cot, dismantled into an alarming number of pieces. It was a major operation to assemble it in the guest bedroom and by the time she had finished the others had returned, the two boys triumphantly waving their comics, trophies from the material world.

Jean-Laurent disappeared upstairs, saying he needed to make a few calls.

'Oh, that was *lovely*,' sighed Susie, dropping into the most comfortable armchair in front of the fire. 'Darling, would you change him, please?'

'Hen-pecked or what?' guffawed Harry happily. 'Lucky Jean-Laurent's not in the room, can't be seen skivvying for the wife in front of a Frenchman, they all think we're pansies as it is!'

He raised his son in the air and pretended he was a red devil stunt aircraft, dive-bombing through the salon.

'Did you get your Calvados?' asked Laura.

'Yup. Bloody good stuff. Can't touch it for ten years, though, got to lay it down. Nee-yeow . . . dagger-dagger-dagger.'

He disappeared upstairs with the child, leaving his wife free to stretch out her legs on the coffee table while she flicked through a copy of *Wallpaper** magazine that Laura had brought down from Paris but had not yet had time to look at. Susie ripped out a few pages on concrete baths that she intended to file away later in the 'good modern' section of her reference folder.

'It must be wonderful having this bolt hole to come to whenever you want,' she said, reaching up to take the proffered cup of tea from Laura. 'If there are any week-ends that you're *not* using it, do let us know, won't you? We'd be very happy to come and house-sit for you. Do you have any sugar – sorry to be a bore.'

Laura returned with the sugar bowl.

'Thank you. Now, is there anything I can do?'

'Well, you could grate these carrots for the salad.'

Susie looked rather surprised – clearly she hadn't expected Laura to take her up on her offer.

'Oh, right. I'll just finish my tea first, if that's all right. It's so cosy in front of the fire.'

Harry made a timely reappearance with the newly fragrant Paris.

'Put him in the playpen, darling, then you might give Laura a hand with the carrots. I just need to go and sort out his pyjamas. Oh, Laura, you don't happen to have a warm pair of socks I could borrow, do you? I have such poor circulation.'

'Yes, of course. Anything else you need?'

But the irony was lost on Susie, already through the door with the magazine tucked under her arm.

They're going tomorrow, thought Laura. Just a few more hours, then we'll never need to see them again.

Harry and Susie left on Sunday afternoon, after lunch but before washing up. Susie was very pleased with herself because she had picked up an unusual cast-iron coal bucket in the local *brocante* that she intended to use as a magazine rack. She had also bought a boudoir chair covered in yellow silk with a shepherdess pattern that reminded of her of Marie-Antoinette, but unfortunately it wouldn't fit in the boot of their car so Harry had got Jean-Laurent to help him strap it on to the roof rack of their Renault Espace.

'Don't mind, do you?' said Harry, securing the tarpau-
lin that he had found on a shelf in the garage. 'You can
drop it round to us sometime next week. Come and have
a drink at the same time, kill two birds with one stone.'

'Thank you *so* much, Laura,' drawled Susie as the last
of their luggage was stowed away, including some cuttings
from the herb garden that Susie had helped herself to and
planted in little terracotta pots that Laura had been saving
for the spring.

'Here, this is for you.'

She handed Laura a small chrysanthemum in a plastic pot that she had hastily picked up at the supermarket.

'And thanks for looking after Paris this morning – it
was marvellous being able to hunt out the bargains without him. You know what it's like when you're stuck with
a baby all the time.'

'Wait until you've got two,' muttered Laura.

'Bye, old girl,' said Harry, looking even more enormous
today in his Norwegian fishing sweater, perhaps on
account of the generous quantity of Sauternes with
which he had just washed down his third helping of
Clafoutis.

'Bye, Harry. Drive safely.'

'*Quelle barbe*! What a bore!' groaned Jean-Laurent as
he shut the door with relief.

'I know. I apologise. We'll never have them again.'

'Did you see how he guzzled his way through that
Chateau Lafitte?'

'I always tell you not to waste decent wine on English
people – they really can't tell the difference. As long as
there's lots of it, they don't care.'

'And now we've got to drive back with that damned chair rattling around on the roof rack.'

'At least they didn't leave the baby as well.'

'I'm going to fix that tap. Do you want to load the car up? I don't want to be too late tonight, I need to pop into the office to finish something.'

'Oh no, not on Sunday night! Can't it wait until the morning?'

'No, I'm off to England tomorrow for an off-site meeting on deodorancy at the Lygon Arms.'

'Lucky you. I wouldn't mind being off-site at the Lygon Arms. Why do you have to go all the way to the Cotswolds to talk about the smell of sweat?'

'It's a neutral, stimulating environment for a think-tank situation.'

'Just another few thousand down the pan, all those executives making their expensive way to a luxury country house hotel. Bloody ridiculous if you ask me.'

'Don't complain, it pays the bills.'

Laura cleared away the lunch things while Jean-Laurent tinkered in the bathroom and the children played in the garden. She then stripped the sheets from the guest bedroom, swept the floor, put out the rubbish and filled up the car with a selection of carrier bags containing left-over food, dirty laundry, children's school bags and the sad chrysanthemum. Finally she strapped in the protesting children, who, now that it was time to go, decided it would be better to stay, and called Jean-Laurent to take his manful place behind the wheel.

They drove off on the all too familiar route, speculating about where they might or might not run into traffic

jams. As they hit the motorway, they both fell silent, lost
in their own thoughts.

Jean-Laurent wondered whether Flavia's shopping trip
would have resulted in any lingerie *aux dentelles raffinées*,
and if she would be modelling it for him when he dropped
by later on. Or maybe she would be saving the silky
surprises for the Lygon Arms. The thought of her *trousseau*
caused him to press harder on the accelerator, but an
alarming flapping noise from the roof rack reminded him
why he was sticking to the slow lane.

Laura was too tired to think about much. The whole
point of having a country cottage was supposed to be rest
and relaxation, but instead it had the reverse effect,
making her feel like a worn-out drudge. She thought about
Antoine, and wondered how he and Sylvie had spent the
weekend. Probably a light sprinkling of celebrity parties,
with plenty of quality time listening to music and making
sure their hormone levels were up to scratch. She couldn't
imagine they would choose to waste time in a dreary round
of wet country walks and home repairs, being exploited
by house guests they didn't like.

And Antoine had seemed to find her so interesting,
even though she didn't have a career. He wanted to know
more, he was intrigued by her, he didn't just see her as a
provider of meals and other people's comfort. I must ring
him next week, she thought. As a friend and neighbour,
nothing more. She would suggest calling in to see him
and Sylvie in a casual, friendly sort of way. Churlish not
to, really.

FIVE

Monday morning is quite possibly my favourite time of the week, thought Laura, worrying that she might be turning into a recluse. Her reasons for liking it were entirely anti-social. The children were back at school, which was always a blessed relief after the weekend. Jean-Laurent, too, had seemed quite pleased to go off to work, if you could call it work – breakfasting on Eurostar first class before being driven off to the Cotswolds, where he had reserved a feature room, to the amusement of his secretary.

'I thought you would be going too,' she had said to Laura. 'It seems such a waste having the four-poster all to himself.'

But Laura was happy just to have her own bed to herself this morning, and was lying fully dressed on the covers as she leafed through a gossip magazine and read about Jacques Chirac's infidelities. His disloyal chauffeur had revealed that he often drove the President to see one particular lady, and that the entire visit lasted three minutes, including the shower afterwards. The disgrace all lay in the three minutes. Laura had lived in France long enough to know that there was no shame in a political leader having a mistress, it was only the gawky Protestant countries like Britain who got their knickers in a twist about that. But three minutes *including* the shower: that could do irreparable damage to the reputation the French fostered of themselves as world-class lovers.

In their more passionate days, she and Jean-Laurent used to play a truth game: 'What would you do if you found out I was cheating on you?' Both had insisted that they wouldn't stand for it, but it was safely academic anyway, since they had been so wrapped up in each other that no one else got a look in.

The occasional frisson of jealousy only served to fan their desire in that short, intense time before they had children. There had been a secretary at Jean-Laurent's office who made no secret of the fact that the new French recruit was the sexiest piece of beefcake she had ever had the pleasure of brushing against on her way to the photo-copier. He had laughed off her infatuation, but Laura had seen the desperation in the girl's eyes at the office party and had gloated that he was hers – the most primitive form of victory.

She had become pregnant that very night, consolidating her triumph, ensuring that it was too late for anyone else to get their claws into what was her own rightful prey. Not that she had seen it in those terms. It was officially defined as an accident, except that educated women in a stable relationship do not become pregnant by accident.

They hadn't discussed infidelity in recent years. Once the children came along, there hadn't been time for that

kind of introsopective conversation, and what with work
and babies, sex in any form was peripheral to the daily
grind. The sharp intimacy of the couple had been replaced
by the amorphous family which swamped everything with
its dull needs and sweet rushes of selfless love.

Laura wondered if Jean-Laurent had shifted his position since living in France. Would he take a civilised view,
for instance, of his wife becoming party to a *cinq à sept*?
And would she be content to play Bernadette Chirac,
regally turning a blind eye, or would she turn into a venge-
ful harridan, lashing out at her husband and the Other
Woman? You probably have no idea until you find yourself in that position, she decided, and thankfully they were
not.

She got up from the bed and went to make herself a
sandwich with the baguette she had brought in earlier. It
was no longer on the kitchen table; perhaps Asa had put
it in the bread bin. Not there either. Laura made her way
down the corridor to Asa's room and knocked on the door.

'Come in!'

Asa was sitting on the floor, legs wide apart, engaged
in her morning workout routine. She wore a face pack
and her UVA tanning machine was wastefully plugged in
beside her.

'Asa, do you know what happened to that baguette I
brought in this morning?'

It was hard to gauge her expression beneath the face
mask.

'Oh, I'm sorry, I thought it was stale. I put it out on
the window sill for the birds – they're so hungry at the
moment.'

'Please don't throw away food without my permission. Particularly not fresh bread.'

She noticed some telltale crumbs on the carpet.

'And switch off that machine if you're not using it. Do you know how much electricity those things use up?'

'Some of us can't afford to go to the gym.'

'I'm not running a bloody health farm here, you know.'

Laura retreated to the kitchen and avenged herself by depleting Asa's supply of rice cakes, which she smothered with a generous layer of taramasalata. That wretched girl. She was the one blot on the horizon, a great ugly blot, and if it wasn't for her, Laura's life would be entirely perfect.

She tried to ring Lorinda to share the outrage of the missing baguette, but it was the mother-in-law who answered and unfortunately recognised Laura's voice, which meant a few minutes of polite conversation before she could disengage.

By this time her anger had wilted, and in its place she felt the familiar weight of boredom settling in. All she had to do today was feel angry about the au pair, and once that had fizzled out she was confronted by a threatening void. The afternoon stretched ominously ahead.

It was, of course, fantastic to be her own person, and she loved her life now more than she had ever loved it – her husband, her children, her beautiful home. A magnificent city, the best in the world, was just outside her front door, waiting for her to explore its every treasure. Each morning she was free to step out and visit some hidden corner of the City of Light, following the recommendations of newspaper cuttings she kept in the desk in a file marked 'Paris – outings'. But just sometimes, like now, she was seized by a kind of blank inertia. Nothing seemed interesting; everything was too much effort.

Her practical side would tell her to find something to do, to pull herself together. She could read an improving book, for instance. In the days when she went out to work, she used to dream of having the time to read properly instead of snatching a few chapters on the tube or late at night when she would fall asleep with the open book dropped on to the bed. But now that she had the oppor-tunity, reading seemed so pointless, like watching daytime television, an unproductive activity that was a pale substi-tute for real life. And so lonely. It was company she wanted, adult company, and not in the form of the infuriating Asa.

She thought about Jean-Laurent, surrounded by colleagues at his luxurious think tank. Work made it so easy – you never had to arrange to meet anyone, they were just there. Whereas she had to make the effort to join things and organise outings. Maybe it was time to take up golf. Or salsa classes. Or have another stab at the painting on porcelain. There were plenty of things you *could* do, it was just that the very idea of any of them simply bored her to death.

There was, however, one idea that didn't bore her to death. In fact, you could say it was not so much an idea as a preoccupation. For reasons she couldn't fathom, she wanted to see Antoine again. She wanted to see if he could still have that effect on her. The way he had made her feel like the most fascinating person in the room. She *would* do it. She would dig out that card and give him a ring. On his home number, of course – it would be too compromising to call the mobile. If she rang now, Antoine would be at work and she could speak to Sylvie, which would be much more suitable, or else, better still, leave a message. After all, they had told her to look them up, and there was no point sitting around feeling sorry for herself.

She opened her wardrobe and pulled out the Kenzo skirt. The card was gone. In its place was a crumpled metro ticket and a cinema ticket from Saturday night when she had been in the country. Damn. Asa had clearly seen fit to help herself to Laura's clothes again, and this time had taken it upon herself to empty the pockets first. Then she remembered, of course, that she had hidden the card in her jewellery box. She took it out, still creased, and dialled the number.

Sylvie answered straight away: she must have been sitting right by the phone. Perhaps she, too, was a desperate housewife, waiting for the phone to ring and wondering how the hell to fill her days. Surely not. Sylvie was a celebrity and it was different for them. And yet she did sound glad to hear her.

'Yes, of course I remember you, we would love to see you. Please come for an aperitif tonight. Around seven-thirty. Your husband is not here? Never mind, come by yourself. Antoine will be so pleased.'

Laura hung up and walked down the corridor to bang on Asa's bathroom door.

'Asa, can you babysit tonight, please? I'm going out.'

It was a clear, cold night, and Laura decided she would walk. She needed to clear her head, having spent most of the afternoon unblocking the hand basin in the bathroom. Poking around with an unfurled coat hanger, she had identified the cause of the blockage, which was a large piece of undigested bread probably regurgitated shortly after the disappearance of the baguette.

She really should speak to Asa about it now that her eating disorder was all out in the open, but it was difficult to see how to broach the subject. 'Asa, please could you vomit in the lavatory pan instead of blocking up the narrow pipes of the hand basin and forcing me to spend my day playing at plumber's mate.' It was rather like asking someone if they would mind awfully not shitting on the carpet.

She walked briskly down the avenue Paul Doumer, pausing to look at the lingerie display in the window of Les Caprices d'Elodie. Even after five years in Paris she was still overawed by the willingness of French women who were not millionaires to spend a hundred pounds on a bra and a pair of knickers. It wasn't as if these were durable investments. A few goes through the washing machine and it would be time to spend another hundred pounds.

But then Laura did not have that innate French feel for *la séduction*, the idea of investing in the pleasure of the moment. For all her European veneer, she still belonged amongst the frumpy British, laughed at by the French for their meanness and lack of aestheticism. Why bother spending an arm and a leg on underwear that no one was going to see (British men, of course, were too busy getting into their flannelette pyjamas to notice), when the money could be saved for a rainy day. Why bother blowing a day's wages on a romantic dinner, every delicious detail of which would be imprinted on your memory for ever, when you could more economically open a packet of sausages at home – for another evening vanished without trace.

Laura crossed the lights at La Muette, the boutiques of rue de Passy stretching away to her left as she continued down the more sedate avenue Mozart with its gracious, swirling nineteenth-century apartment buildings and its succession of small, exquisite shops.

La Comtesse de Barry, purveyors of foie gras to the gastronomic classes. Patisseries with cakes that made you realise you would never eat another British-style Danish pastry, *traiteurs* offering aspic-covered takeaways that looked like works of art, and *primeurs* with their appetising piles of fresh fruit. And, of course, the usual high density of pharmacies, the flashing green crosses reminding the French that their delicate constitutions required constant maintenance, preferably in suppository form. How could Napoleon have described the British as a nation of shopkeepers when it was so clearly the French who were born to display and entice?

At the foot of avenue Mozart, Laura turned right into the rue Poussin where a heavy stream of traffic crawled along towards the Porte d'Auteuil. Here was evidence of encroaching foreign invasion: Domino's Pizza, introducing a vulgar note from America. Less threatening to the French was the Irish store, offering a bizarre mix of rugged Aran woollen sweaters completely unsuitable for overheated Parisian apartments, bacon, Marmite, Guinness, and postcards of Irish beauty spots. The French were terrible snobs about Ireland; a golfing holiday in the Emerald Isle was the epitome of chic.

Halfway down rue Poussin, Laura arrived at the high metal gates of the Villa Montmorency. The gates were open, but an automatic barrier was in place to keep out the cars of the great unwashed, and a uniformed *gardien* was sitting in the lodge to scrutinise would-be visitors. Laura walked straight past him, but he came running out after her.

'Can I help you, *madame?*'

'I'm going to Mme. Marceau's house. I believe it's up there on the right.'

He looked her up and down to satisfy himself that she wasn't a deranged stalker, then nodded grudgingly and went back to his watchtower.

Walking into the Villa Montmorency, Laura had the impression that she was stepping into a secret garden, a super-rich oasis of provincial tranquillity. The leafy street was lined with large, country-style houses of varied architecture with neatly tended gardens. And it was so quiet, a world away from the teeming traffic of Paris, though the faint sounds of distant cars served to remind you of the city that lay just outside this toy-town cocoon.

She turned right into another road that led to a roundabout where a fountain was planted out with hibernating roses and never-say-die winter pansies. Two gardeners were sweeping up some dead leaves that had had the effrontery to fall on to the carefully maintained pavement. It was a Parisian take on Beverly Hills: there was the same sense of nature carefully prinked and manicured into a pleasure ground for the wealthy.

She came to a magnificent bow-fronted Regency villa,

its show-piece first-floor window hung with an extravagant sweep of taupe silk. It was a perverse law of designer
tyranny that the richer you were, the less colour you were
allowed. Perhaps a few cheerful outbursts on your way up
the ladder, but once you reached the pinnacle of wealth
and sophistication, you had to hire the kind of designer
who made you feel like a vulgar parvenu if you suggested
introducing a splash of anything beyond the monochrome.
Laura rang the bell labelled 'S.M. & A.B.' Oh, the delicious intimacy of those initials.

'Yes? It's you, Laura? Come in.'

The door clicked open, revealing a gravel path flanked
by a tidy lawn which was embellished by half a dozen life-
size statues of ornamental sheep.

Sylvie stood at the front door, a tiny figure with two
little dogs snapping round her heels.

'I see you are admiring my sheep. The sculptor is so
talented. He also did some for Mitterand.'

'Can't you make them go "baa", then it would be as
good as the real thing. Your transformation into Marie-
Antoinette would be complete.'

'Ah, you English, always the little joke. Come in, *je t'en
prie.*'

Laura stepped into what was indeed a temple to
moneyed monochrome, depending heavily on grey slate,
dark wood, and neutral furnishings. She looked around
in vain for a small personalising touch, and her eye fell
upon some teak picture frames containing blurred black
and white photographs. It was hard to tell what they represented, but whatever it was seemed to fall into the category of Art, rather than snaps of friends and family.

Sylvie took her coat and led her up the customised walnut staircase and into the drawing room, where Antoine was elegantly draped against a cream sofa which harmonised beautifully with his toast-coloured suit. He looked even more handsome than she remembered, maybe because he was showcased in his own home, the suave seducer of maidens reclining in his lair. He looked unsurprised to see her: his eyes said it all. I knew you'd come, they said, I knew you couldn't resist me. Which made his affectation of astonishment all the more irritating.

'My dear, what a pleasant surprise! I'm so flattered that you bothered to track us down!'

As if she had spent days trying to find out where he lived. Had he forgotten that he had given her his card? And a second one to Jean-Laurent for good measure.

'I said I would, and I always mean what I say,' she replied briskly.

'An admirable quality. And tell me, what do you think of our own private paradise?'

'Very exclusive. It makes me long to be rich.'

Antoine laughed.

'You are very direct – that's refreshing in an English-woman. So often you British disguise what you think, afraid of appearing impolite.'

'Not something you French can be accused of. I'm afraid a lot of English people find it hard to cope with your fondness for saying just what you think.'

'How dull life would be if we did not express our opinions.'

He turned to his wife, who was watching them from the bay window where her black-clad figure stood out, a tiny silhouette against the backdrop of taupe silk curtains.

'Sylvie, I believe there is a bottle of champagne in the fridge. Shall we take it up here?'

Sylvie moved past them, and Laura watched her girlish body sashaying towards the stairs, encased in an expensive-looking sheath made up of lycra bands. Probably Hervé Léger – she had seen them hanging up at Bon Marché whilst in search of something more forgiving to the fuller figure.

Now that she was left alone with Antoine, Laura found herself bashful and tongue-tied. Amused by her discomfort, Antoine let the silence hang heavy for a moment. Then he said, 'You admire my wife, I think.'

'She certainly has a wonderful figure. I wouldn't mind getting away with a dress like that at her age. Or at my age, come to that.'

'Age is not something we discuss in this house,' he said mischievously. 'Yes, she is beautiful. There was very little to do on her body, once I had established she had an underactive thyroid. It was just the face where she needed my partner's expertise. We started with the eyelids, a very simple operation, and then the upper lip – it is so sad for a woman when the lipstick starts to fall into little crevasses. You yourself have not yet encountered that problem, I can see. You have a perfect cupid's bow.'

Laura blushed foolishly. Once again, she could think of nothing to say. Antoine sat forward and lowered his voice.

'I am so glad you came to see me. Looking at Sylvie is like looking out of this beautiful window. Everything is perfect, but so dull. I need movement, excitement, life.

And I know you feel the same. Why else would you have come?'

The urgency with which he now cut to the quick put her swiftly back on the defensive. He saw straight through her pretence, he knew her real motives, but her reply was an indignant denial.

'I came to have a drink with you and your wife, as a friend and neighbour, since you both so kindly invited me to. Please don't embarrass me by talking like this while your wife is out of the room, it makes me feel very uneasy.'

'You are right, we must postpone this conversation to another occasion. I think you will come for lunch near my *cabinet*. Maybe on Thursday?'

Was it always this fast? No wonder it took Jacques Chirac only three minutes.

Before Laura could reply, Sylvie returned with the champagne.

'Welcome to the Villa Montmorency, Laura. What a shame your husband couldn't join us. Does he travel a lot?'

'Quite a bit at the moment. He hates it, of course; he'd rather be at home with us. But he has to move the business on, as he puts it.'

'Move the business on. Yes, that's about the sum of it,' said Antoine with a knowing smile. '*Santé!*'

And he raised his glass to Laura with a wink.

'Can you really be interested in that plump little *lapine*?' asked Sylvie as they waved off their visitor.

'My dear, you should not be so dismissive of women who reproduce. Breeding like a rabbit, as you so charmingly describe it, is the motivational force that drives many women. I find it fascinating that they can choose to surrender everything else to that one banal objective.'

'I'm not sure that there was much else to surrender in that particular case. If you are not suffocated by her folds of flesh, you certainly will be by the domestic quality of her conversation. And whatever you do, don't get her pregnant.'

'It is quite safe, she already has children. You know how careful I am to choose only those who have passed beyond the baby hunger stage. But there is something fascinating to me about that woman. She says one thing and often means quite the opposite. I think she may prove to be quite a challenge. Now, shall we go for dinner?'

In the heart of the Cotswolds, Jean-Laurent was energetically moving the business on beneath the canopy of the fifteenth-century mahogany four-poster that dominated his feature room. It was well worth the supplement, he thought, not to be in one of those modern boxes next to the health club, and anyway they'd been given a special deal by the Lygon Arms, so the extra cost to the company was negligible.

Flavia rolled on top of him and he fumbled tenderly at the strap of her aubergine Aubade bra (worn, naturally, with matching lace G-string). What a campaign that had been: 'Lesson No. 9, tease him a little'. Sometimes he thought it would be fun to work in lingerie, forging hard new marketing plans for those flimsy little pieces of satin. It took thirty-two of them, he had once read, to make up a standard bra – would it be the same for an AA cup as a D cup, or would large sizes require more? But then again, soap powder and deodorancy were much bigger, altogether more global, and he was nothing if not global these days. He carefully removed Flavia's underwear and gave his concentrated attention to a performance worthy of a master of the universe.

'What do you mean, you're not sure? You're obviously gagging for it, or why would you have invited yourself round to see him in the first place?'

Lorinda pushed the speed control of her treadmill up to a brisk 10 km per hour, anticipating an upturn in the tempo of their conversation.

Laura lumbered on at 5.5.

'I do wish you wouldn't debase everything. Though actually, that's exactly what he said, if in a more poetical way. But the point is, I really don't know what I'm getting into. I only went along out of curiosity – Jean-Laurent said I should see where they lived. It is amazing by the way. So that was all. I didn't know he was going to come on with a secret lunch date the minute his wife was out of the room.'

'Oh, come on, it was a fair bet after your last encounter with old Doctor Sex. First he crushes his card, clammy with desire, into your hand under the dining table, next thing he knows you've turned up, without your husband, offering yourself like a sheep upon the altar of his lust.'

'That's hardly fair,' said Laura, wiping the sweat from her forehead to prevent it dripping unappetisingly on to the control panel of the treadmill. 'All right, so maybe I do find him attractive. That doesn't mean I'm going to do anything about it. Nothing wrong with a bit of flirting, is there? And it's quite nice to have a conversation with someone who is not at all interested in children. Or global marketing,' she added.

'Or wine,' said Lorinda, getting into the game, 'or management handbooks. Or competitive advantage.'

'All right,' said Laura. 'Let's not go down that route. Anyway, it was nice to see him. And Sylvie, of course. It was her I rang to arrange the visit, and he just happened to be there.'

Lorinda pulled a lascivious face and leered at Laura from her treadmill.

'Lying in a quiet ferment of desire to pounce on you at the earliest opportunity,' she said.

'Not to pounce,' said Laura. 'Only to arrange a date for possible future pouncing. This Thursday, to be precise. Except that I've decided to cancel. It's all too complicated.'

Which was why she had left Antoine's house in the sure knowledge that she would never meet him privately. He had insisted they should have lunch, but there was no point; it would only end in tears. She knew only too well from the experiences of her friends that what started out as something perfectly simple soon became horribly complicated, with irreparable fall-out all round.

But Lorinda was having none of this defeatist talk.

'Nonsense. Sounds perfectly straightforward to me. I think you should go for it. Nothing to lose.'

It was all right for her to say that, thought Laura, it wasn't *her* home life she was laying on the line.

'Oh no, nothing to lose,' she said. 'Only my happy marriage, in which I have invested so heavily. Not to mention the stable, loving home I've created for my children.'

'Now who's exaggerating?' said Lorinda, raising her hands in comic disbelief as she pounded on. 'He's only invited you to lunch, and I assume he's paying. You don't have to take it any further if you don't want to. Then you can tell me all about it. It will help us through Friday morning's *abdo-fessiers* session.'

You don't understand, thought Laura. You don't understand at all. If I have lunch with the divine Dr Bouchard, there is no way of knowing where it will lead. I might not be responsible for my actions. There was something about him that made her long to throw out all precepts of reasonable behaviour. She pressed the stop button and stepped off her treadmill, puffing after her fifteen minutes of exertion and shaking her head at her friend.

'Lorinda, how empty is your sad life that you have to push me into unwanted adventures just so you can hear about them? Tell you what, why don't you go in my place since you're so keen on the idea?'

'I'm happy to say that my marriage is not in crisis,' retorted Lorinda. 'I'm quite happy with Arnaud, it's just his mother I can't stand.'

'My marriage isn't in crisis! What are you on about? That's my whole point. I love Jean-Laurent and we're perfectly happy.'

Lorinda slowed down her treadmill to a fast walk, then to a standstill. She wiped the sweat from her face with her towel and turned to face her friend.

'In that case, Laura, why are we even having this conversation? Anyway, I'm off, there's a toy promotion in Leclerc today. Spend sixty euros and you get thirty back. I'm getting all my godchildren's Christmas presents.'

'But it's only mid-November.'

'The early bird catches the worm. Talking of which, I'll be interested to hear about Doctor Love's pet worm, once you've had a sighting. You mark my words, it's only a matter of time!'

'You're disgusting. See you on Friday then. And Saturday. You are coming to dinner, aren't you?'

'Of course. I'm hoping you'll line someone up for me, so I can join you on the slippery slope to ruin.'

'Ha ha. Actually, there might be someone, Francine is bringing her brother, recently divorced, *grande école* – sounds rather eligible.'

'Can't wait. Bye then!'

Laura moved on to a cycling machine and pushed the pedals in a desultory way. Maybe Lorinda was right. It was only lunch, after all. Just the once. It was something to do, and perfectly innocent. But in that case, she was going to have to make a big effort to bring down her body-fat ratio before Thursday. She had read that morning that the normal ratio for a woman was 21.4. Even going by her optimistic weight of 68 kg and her height (in low heels) of 1.67 m, her own worked out at 27, which bordered between the 'slightly overweight' and 'obese' categories as defined by *Santé et Fitness* magazine.

She looked down at the dial on the machine, which told her she had been cycling for only three and a half minutes. What a bore it was. She looked through the glass wall at the *culture physique* lesson in progress in the next studio. Really, if that girl in the cropped T-shirt got any closer to the mirror, she'd be having sex with it. The T-shirt had the words Californian Girl printed on it, but that was clearly a lie, as she looked about as cross and French as you can get. And thin, Laura conceded with a sigh, glancing down at the dial of the bike which informed her that she had burned up 27 calories.

Bollocks to this, she thought, it must be time for lunch.

Back at the apartment, Laura turned the key in the lock and stood stock-still in her entrance hall. Like a hunting dog, she pricked her ears and flared her nostrils, sniffing the air for clues. She could always tell whether Asa was in or not, and today she clearly was at home. It wasn't just the smell of recently fried popcorn or the cosmetic-scented steam from the bathroom that told her, it was something more primitive. Someone was on her patch.

She heard the wardrobe door close as Asa stepped casually from Laura's bedroom and gave her a bright smile.

'Hi! I was just putting the laundry away.'

You liar, thought Laura, I know what you were up to. You were trying on my clothes to see what you might wear to your Overeaters Anonymous meeting next time I'm out of town. She really should speak to her about it, but it was hard to know how to start the conversation. Perhaps something caring-sharing like, 'Asa, we need to talk.' Too heavy. Better to drop it in casually. 'By the way, Asa, I'd appreciate it if you wouldn't wear my clothes without asking my permission.' Or just go for pure aggression. 'Wear your own clothes, you sly, inadequate person.'

Instead, Laura said, 'Oh, thanks. Do you want some lunch?'

'No thank you, I've had mine. Devon said it was quite OK to have an earlier lunch, provided you don't eat dinner too late. I'm quite pleased with myself. I managed to eat six Ryvita slices and a tub of cottage cheese with my salad.'

Oh good, thought Laura. Does that mean that I can count on my cauliflower remaining in the vegetable basket until dinner time, rather than being regurgitated down the S-bend? She glanced at the fruit bowl: only two apples left. Clearly the early lunch had been rounded off with a particularly generous bowl of fresh fruit salad.

Asa followed her into the kitchen and poured herself a large glass of mineral water. She threw the empty bottle into the bin.

'That's the last bottle, by the way,' she said, wagging a warning finger at Laura, a particularly annoying gesture that she had picked up from the French.

'I'm going shopping tomorrow,' snapped Laura. 'I dare-say you can last that long. Store it up in your hump, like a camel.'

Asa looked at her uncomprehendingly, then sat down at the kitchen table and began filing her finger nails.

'Jean-Laurent rang. He says he won't be back until Friday.'

Damn, thought Laura. He had promised to be back in time for their usual Thursday evening trip to the cinema.

Asa read her mind.

'Does that mean you won't need me to babysit on Thursday? I was thinking of going to the exhibition at the Musée d'Orsay. It's their late-night opening.'

'I suppose not. But don't think you're going to borrow any of my clothes to wear to your precious bloody exhi-bition.'

At last she'd said it.

But Asa wasn't exactly crushed by her harsh words.

'I don't know what you mean,' she said loftily. 'Anyway, they wouldn't fit me.'

She walked out, flushed with indignation. So what if she did occasionally borrow that Ghost skirt. It was the only thing in Laura's elephant-sized wardrobe that did fit her, provided she wore a belt with it, and why did Laura need so many clothes anyway? It wasn't as if she ever went anywhere – only to school and the gym with her silly friend Lorinda and shopping for more clothes that she didn't need. God, she hoped she never became like Laura. At least she was young and had a life, even if she did have some emotional issues to address through group therapy support groups.

Laura sighed. As usual Asa had stolen the moral high ground and made her feel like a nit-picking old bag. She'd have to apologise and make it up to her yet again, or go through the tedium of finding a replacement.

She dialled Jean-Laurent on his mobile to leave a message, but to her surprise he answered.

'Hallo.' He sounded distracted.

'Hallo, it's me. I didn't think I'd catch you at this time – I thought you'd be bonding with all those international buzzards. It sounds very quiet, though.'

'No, well, I just forgot something in my room. I've got to go back, actually, I'm preparing a presentation.'

'OK, I won't keep you. I got your message – I'll see you on Friday then. By the way, I've invited Lorinda and Arnaud with Francine and Dominique for Saturday night. Francine's brother's coming, he's an eligible bachelor, so I thought you might invite someone from work for him. What about that research girl you used to go on about, that one with a silly Latin name — she's single and gorgeous, isn't she?'

Jean-Laurent hesitated for a fraction of a second.

'Who? Oh yes, Flavia. I don't know, it might not be her thing.'

'What do you mean, not her thing. We're not that dull, are we?'

'No, it's not that . . . she's probably busy.'

'She might not be. Or ask someone else. All my friends are married, so it's up to you to find a dishy dolly for Arthur. Don't want him to think we haven't made an effort.'

'All right, I'll see what I can do. Everything else OK? How are the boys?'

'Fine. Pierre-Louis says he's the smallest in his class, but he doesn't mind because he has lots of friends.'

'Sweet boy. Give them a big kiss from Papa. See you on Friday. Bye!'

Jean-Laurent replaced the phone and Flavia looked up from the bed.

'Did I hear you mention my name?'

He looked at her nervously.

'Laura thought you might like to be the spare female at our dinner party on Saturday.'

'At your apartment? How thrilling!'

'I told her you'd probably be busy.'

'I can't wait. How shall I dress? Virtuous *fille bourgeoise* or *femme fatale*?'

'I'm not sure this is such a good idea.'

'Why ever not? It will be enormous fun. And finally I get to see you on a Saturday!'

Jean-Laurent frowned at the thought of the boundaries

breaking down in his carefully compartmentalised life. On the other hand, Laura had made it clear that he had to invite someone, and wouldn't he rather be opposite Flavia than some other female dredged up for the occasion? The lightly moustachioed Hélène was a fine secretary, but she wouldn't exactly adorn his dinner table.

He lay down beside Flavia and traced his fingers over her smooth flank.

'All right then. But promise me you'll be discreet.'

'How could I not be? I'm hardly going to blow your cover, am I?'

Six

Sometimes Laura found it hard to remember why she had chosen to trade in her proper job for her current position as part-time, unpaid chauffeur. In her past life, *she* had been the one sitting in the back of the car flicking through her papers or gazing out of the window while the company driver negotiated the traffic. Now the tables were turned and she had been demoted to the driver's seat, while her children sat sullen and ungrateful in the back seat, complaining loudly if she dropped them more than a few metres from the school gates.

On Wednesdays, she was particularly sensitive to the pressures of her role as chauffeur, since the children spent only half a day at school. It was a clever idea that the French had come up with. Rather than incorporate sport and art into the week's curriculum, the schools came to an abrupt halt at midday on Wednesday, so that the roads were jammed with children's chauffeurs – mothers and nannies, including one or two proper, professional ones in uniform – rushing them home for lunch before driving them on to their fencing or dance classes.

Of course, no parent of any ambition would be content with a one-dimensional child. There was no point in having a crack tennis player if he was inadequate in musical skills or '*les arts plastiques*'. So mid-afternoon, it was all change again as pinched-faced women viciously competed with each other for parking places outside the Conservatoire (for young Mozarts) and the Louvre (for young Michelangelos).

All that wasted energy, thought Laura, all that educated manpower, and all those car exhaust fumes going into ferrying around little Henri and ensuring his proper *épanouissement*. This was a favourite word among the French. It described the condition of flowering fulfilment which all this education was supposed to bring about, although you certainly didn't see much evidence of it amongst the adult population; at least not in Paris where dissatisfaction and snarling resentment seemed to flourish at the expense of all else.

Laura's own Wednesday routine was less frenetic since she had opted for the expatriate solution. This came in the form of an out-of-town British country club where ladies of leisure like herself could congregate while their children beefed up on outdoor games in grounds that would put the finest English public school to shame.

Every Wednesday at midday, she picked up Charles-Edouard and Pierre-Louis and drove out into the leafy western suburbs, deep into a forest until she reached this little piece of France that would be forever England, and which prided itself on possessing the country's only full-size cricket pitch. Here they would take lunch, then the boys would be despatched to their sporting and artistic activities, leaving

Laura free to join the other mothers – and the odd, eagerly received father – to sit around eating Swiss roll from Marks & Spencer beneath a portrait of the Queen and complain about the French. Mostly the complaining was done by those who had married French partners and thereby consigned themselves to a lifetime of exile, but there was also a fair sprinkling of short-term expats, proper house-wives waiting around in pale tracksuits for a couple of years until their husbands were posted back to Surrey.

Laura ordered three plates of ham and chips in the bar, and prepared for a long wait. It was astonishing how the club bar, though staffed entirely by French people, managed to completely bypass the brisk professionalism that characterised even the humblest café in France. Instead it seemed to take pride in importing the sham-bling service and indifferent food of a British transport café, but without any of the warmth and atmosphere. The food eventually arrived, on cardboard plates. Laura helped the boys to ketchup.

'Yoo-hoo! Laura! Over here!'

Laura looked across the bar and saw Flo Knightley beaming at her, a lovely full-blown English rose in exile. She was exactly the kind of wholesome, blonde, large-hipped beauty who could make you feel homesick for the Shires, except that Flo was a long-term resident of Paris who had been a mainstay of the club for nineteen years. She once told Laura that she had got rid of her dining chairs because men didn't feel comfortable in them: 'Men can't relax unless they're sitting in a proper chair, dear.' She must surely have been talking about wide-bottomed, Johnnie Boden-style English men, because French men only seemed to look right when perched nervily on the edge of a fragile piece of repro.

Laura set her tray down at Flo's table, where two women in cardigans were already installed.

'Hallo, Laura, do you know Hilda and Rosemary? We met at the Laura Ashley fashion show. We were just saying, isn't it ridiculous that they're spending all that money resurfacing tennis courts that can't be used in winter? I think we should all go to the AGM to make that point. And you know they've managed to sack that new groundsman? They just put some money in his path, then hid and pounced on him, caught him red-handed!'

The cardigans nodded. It was just so English-village-hall – you expected the verger to appear at any moment, flanked by choir boys and peddling raffle tickets.

Flo pushed a plate of biscuits in Laura's direction.

'Here, have an M&S biscuit – back on sale at the bar, I'm glad to say. You know they've been banned for three months for being too expensive! When you think how much you pay for a *pain aux raisins* in any old *boulangerie* in this country. And Hilda brings them over from England in her Volvo, so there's no delivery charge.'

Laura helped herself to a chocolate wafer and took a greedy bite.

'Delicious,' she said. 'Just the kind of thing I can't keep at home unless protected under lock and key from my supposedly anorexic au pair.'

'Anorexics?' said Flo.' Don't touch them with a barge-pole, darling! Reformed drug addicts are what you want – they really are super. Thoroughly honest, God's own!'

And the women were back on their second favourite

topic of conversation (their very favourite being How Awful The French Are), which came under the broad category of Help. Help was the modern term for what a previous generation of expats used to call the Servant Problem. Help was what you needed when you lived abroad. It was all right to do your own dirty work when you lived in your own country, but there was no point in giving up a perfectly good job in London to come to Paris if it meant spending your days ironing vests and wiping floors.

'My Australian girl was the best,' said Hilda, who turned out to be a senior civil servant on an extended career break as a trailing spouse. 'No problem mucking in. She had such a big appetite, though – cost me a fortune in cornflakes. That's the great thing about Filipinos – they never seem to eat anything.'

'No, they just help themselves to your jewellery instead', said Rosemary, a former human resources manager who had sacrificed her career for the sake of her husband's advancement in the world of toothpaste. 'I've had the lot, believe me. I do it all myself now, it's easier in the long run. By the time you've explained everything, you might as well just make the beds, wipe down the surfaces, load the dishwasher . . .'

Mercifully the inventory of her domestic chores was interrupted by Flo.

'Your boys are doing tennis, aren't they, Laura?'

'Yes, two o'clock, then theatre at three, then art class at four-thirty – the whole damn show.'

'Yes, well, I just wanted to warn you about bad language. There's a little boy called Jerome in the tennis class who called my Philip a '*conard*' last week.

How very perspicacious of him, thought Laura. She laughed.

'I'm glad you're not sitting in my car on the morning run, Flo, you would blush. But I'm glad to say my boys are too well bred to follow my example.'

After lunch, Laura accompanied the children outside to find their tennis teacher. The foul-mouthed Jerome was already knocking balls over the net and scowled at Philip as he arrived, clean and portly in his all-whites and side-parted blonde hair. Even though he was only six, you could see exactly the adult he would become – white shorts straining over broad backside, the mainstay of the tennis club. As physical types, her own boys were more like Jerome, weasely and scruffily dressed, and Laura was grateful for it.

She sat down on a bench and pulled out her book, thinking how infinitely preferable it was to read alone down here rather than rejoin the company upstairs. Few things were more depressing than the conversation of women with time on their hands. She opened *La Maladie de Sachs*, the tale of a country doctor putting up with the rantings of his hypochondriac patients. No wonder it had been a bestseller in France.

And tomorrow she would be taking lunch with her very own French doctor. Well, it had to be better than ham and chips on paper plates and Flo's tales of the AGM. Although she couldn't say she wasn't nervous. Not to say terrified. She had picked up the phone twice to ring him to cancel, but on both occasions had told herself to stiffen her sinews and stop being a wimp. It was no big deal. It was just lunch. Think of all those men she had lunched with before when she was a career luncher. In fact, 'Lunch' used to be Jean-Laurent's affectionate and slightly bitter nickname for her when he was still a student. While he would have to put up with a chicken tikka sandwich and apple trellis from some unspeakable café, she would be picking over her rocket and parmesan salad and anchovies and red peppers (she always ordered two starters and no main course) in front of the huge plate-glass windows at Kensington Place. Usually there would be a crowd of them, but quite often it might be just her and a client, often a man. So what? That didn't send her into a flutter of girlish butterflies, so why should she be making such a fuss now about a simple lunch appointment with an ageing anti-ageing specialist? She should just treat it as a one-off, a piece of fun, and that would be that.

She looked up and caught Charles-Edouard's eye as he raced around the court picking up tennis balls and putting them into a basket. He smiled and waved at her happily. She waved back. Perhaps, she thought, the life of an unpaid chauffeur was not so bad after all.

The morning of Laura's lunch date dawned grey and resentful. It was the kind of weather that doubled your journey time in the rush hour; a few drops of rain was enough to bring the traffic to a standstill for reasons Laura couldn't fathom, and the Parisians became even nervier, making furious gestures to each other through their car windows.

'School is boring,' said Charles-Edouard as they crawled over the pont d'Iéna. 'Every day the same: French, recreation, Maths. I wish Charlemagne had never existed, then schools would not have been invented.'

Laura gazed ahead at the Eiffel Tower, shrouded in grey clouds. Groups of tourists were already huddled round each of its four feet. God knows why anyone would want to pay to go up it today: there would be nothing to see. She looked at Charles-Edouard in her rear-view mirror.

'Charlemagne only invented schools in France. Someone else invented them in England, so you could have gone to school there instead.'

'Who invented schools in England?'

'How do I know.'

'You don't know anything.'

'I expect I knew once, but you forget things.'

They continued in silence, turning right on to the left bank.

'It's all right for you,' said Charles-Edouard, 'you don't *have* to know anything. You don't even work, not like Dad.'

Pierre-Louis leap indignantly to her defence.

'But mummies don't work, Charles-Edouard!'

'All my friends' mummies work,' said Charles-Edouard, 'except for Olivier's, but she's got a baby and she's on *congé parentale*.'

Laura pulled up outside the school behind a large Mercedes driven by a woman who was clearly dressed for something more dynamic than sorting out the sock drawer, which was Laura's vague project for the morning ahead.

'Look, some mummies work, and some don't, it just depends. It doesn't mean that one is better than the other.'

'But you're always telling us to work, then you just do nothing yourself. Very fair I call that!'

Laura jumped out of the car and opened the back door.

'Here we are, out you get. See you later.'

She waved them off with a sigh. How could it be that her elder son showed her so little respect? Did he not understand that it was for him and his brother that she had decided to sacrifice her career? He should be grateful to have his mother meet him out of school each day and not some hired hand, instead of which he slagged her off for being lazy and not doing anything. She would have to have a little chat with him.

It was at moments like this that Laura sometimes entertained creeping doubts about the path she had chosen. She imagined a high-spirited Australian nanny (gap year, nice and bright) taking the boys to school, all enthusiastic and asking them interesting questions, while she, Laura, went her separate way, back to the agency, maybe working on a pitch for a new piece of business.

She had always enjoyed that: the late nights, working to a deadline, the adrenaline rush of the presentation, engaging with prospective clients, fielding their questions off the top of her head, thinking quickly. Then the excitement when you won the account, five million pounds' worth, which she, Laura, had directly helped to bring in to the business. There would be champagne in the office and the kind of massively extravagant blow-out in a restaurant that advertising people were so good at.

She had none of that now, no feeling of achievement, unless you counted her progress in cooking and her contribution to the stylish — or would you call it pretentious? — furnishing of their apartment. Why couldn't she be like Jackie Kennedy, who used to come back to the White House from her daily morning ride and brief her thirty-strong household whilst still wearing her jodhpurs? Jackie was a model career housewife. Running the house for her meant directing a team of interior designers and museum experts to spend a vast budget acquiring major works of art, whereas Laura had only the useless Asa to do her bidding, and had to rely on her own judgement when nervously selecting suitable framed prints from one of the more affordable galleries in rue de Seine.

Disgruntled by these thoughts, she turned her mind to her forthcoming date. Less than four hours to go. At least having lunch with the smooth Dr Bouchard was a bit more Jackie Kennedy than her usual Thursday routine of cupboard sorting and the Carrefour supermarket trip. She had already picked out her outfit, a dove-grey woollen dress; she had laid it out on the bed this morning.

Jean-Laurent was still away at the Lygon Arms, which was convenient, as she hadn't yet decided whether to tell him about all this. It rather depended on how it went. Obviously it wouldn't do to mention it if Antoine made any improper advances. In fact, it was probably better not to mention it at all – there was no point and he might get the wrong idea. He might think she was turning into a sad, Madame Bovary-type figure – which would cast him as the poor, stolid old cuckolded husband. He wouldn't like that at all.

So absorbed was she in her reverie that she turned right instead of left after the pont de Bir-Hakeim and found herself wedged in the traffic jam heading into the city centre. Cursing her stupidity, she sat smouldering behind the wheel until she arrived at the pont d'Alma and was able to peel off and head back against the traffic.

By the time she got back to the apartment it was nearly

ten o'clock. Asa was grating apples into a bowl containing carefully chopped nuts and raisins from a packet that
Laura had bought in London and had been saving for the
Christmas pudding. Damn, she had hoped to spend the
morning alone preparing for her lunch, and now she would
be forced to subject herself to Asa's cool, appraising eye.

'Haven't you got a class this morning?' she asked. Like
many au pairs, Asa was enrolled at the Institut Français.

'I thought I'd catch up with some revision at home. It's
so horrid out this morning.'

Home, thought Laura, *my* home that you so casually
refer to as 'home'. She remembered a consumer guide to
childcare that she had read from cover to cover in her
anxious pregnant days. 'Be careful,' it had warned under
the 'live-in' section. 'Her home will be your home.' How
right they had been, though they could have been more
explicit and added, 'She will be hogging the bathroom,
burning up the electricity with the sunray lamp and empty-
ing your cupboards of fresh and packaged food, much of
which will never get as far as her digestive tract.

'Very wise,' said Laura. 'Look, I'm sorry about our little
misunderstanding yesterday. I didn't mean to upset you.'

'That's OK,' said Asa. 'I know you are crossing a difficult period in your life, which makes it hard for you to
be in contact with younger, more desirable women.'

'What *are* you on about? I'm not quite at the menopause
yet, you know!'

'No, but you are resentful of your waning powers of
seduction, and wistful for the life you led before you gave
everything up for the children.'

She really had to go. Just who did she think she was???

'Oh, is that right? Tell me, is that your own opinion, or do I hear the sinister overtones of group therapy speak!'

'Devon tells me it was the same with his wife, before she became reconciled to her role shifting from seducer to nurturer. In fact, she has written a book about it called *Fullness at Forty*.'

'Asa, I'm nowhere near forty!'

'It's an attitude, not an age.'

'Oh, do spare me your ludicrous psychobabble. And watch out for that Devon. Now his wife has gone over to nurturing, he's obviously desperate to take advantage of feeble-minded young girls with eating disorders.'

Asa looked at Laura in disgust over the brim of her tall glass of freshly squeezed orange juice and left the kitchen.

What on earth had possessed her to employ Asa? It wasn't as though she had been short of options – her ad on the bulletin board of the American church had brought in quite a few calls.

She could have had a lovely Philippine lady who said she only liked working for English families because they were kinder than the French, so she was obviously a sound woman. Or that German living in Saint-Germain-en-Laye who was desperate to leave the suburbs for a nice city job like this one. She would have been brilliant – you could tell from the way she looked round the kitchen that she couldn't wait to get the mop out. But she was just a little bit too good-looking; there was no point in inviting trouble into your house.

Asa had seemed like a good compromise: hopefully she'd have a bit of Nordic efficiency without looking too Wagnerian. And she had said she was vegetarian so would do her own food and not eat with them. That was appealing. The last thing Laura had wanted was a silent gooseberry sitting down with her and Jean-Laurent every night; the spectre at the feast intruding in their intimate conversation.

Unfortunately, 'vegetarian' had turned out to be a euphemism for 'bonkers' when it came to Asa's eating habits. Laura had obligingly stocked up on pulses, cauliflower, chickpeas, enough roughage to feed an army of horses, then realised that this was only camouflage to conceal the real damage inflicted on her food bill by the newcomer's weakness for sweet carbohydrates. Within three weeks of her arrival, Laura was praying for the day when Asa would gather up her beauty aids and self-help guides and just leave.

The prayer had been running for two years now, and in her imagination Laura had already enacted the scene of repossessing the bedroom. She would open all the cupboard doors, brush out every last trace, and throw open the windows to blow away all evidence of Asa. It was the human equivalent of cocking a leg and urinating in each corner of the room, staking out her territory once again.

Two hours later, Laura pushed open the door of the Brasserie Stella, a traditional neighbourhood haunt for the well-heeled inhabitants of the *seizième nord*, and a stone's throw from Dr Bouchard's practice. No sign of Antoine, though there were plenty like him: dapper men with neat salt and pepper hair enjoying the consolation of life's small pleasures as they fastidiously sucked at oysters or sipped their aperitifs while consulting the menus. Perhaps he had stood her up. She felt a wave of relief and thought about leaving, but the maître d' was already approaching.

'Bonjour, madame.'

'Yes, I'm meeting Dr Bouchard. I don't think he's here yet.'

She tried to sound as though she met men for lunch all the time. Men who weren't her husband, whom she didn't know very well, and whom she had no particular reason to have lunch with.

'Ah yes, Dr Bouchard, of course. Here is his table. *Vous désirez an apéritif?*'

How could one possibly *desire* an aperitif? Really, the French language was preposterously overblown.

She ordered a glass of champagne and hoped he would be paying. He was surely too old to suggest going Dutch.

Two women at the next table were holding an animated conversation, their hard blonde hair sprayed into rigid helmets that nodded emphatically. That was the other hairstyle you got in Paris if you didn't go for the cropped bob that Laura wore. She wouldn't mind changing, but at least she knew how to ask for a *carré*, and although she invariably came out of the hairdressers looking like a blue stocking, she could always ruffle it up a bit afterwards, like she was doing now. She looked at herself in the mirror that disconcertingly ran along the entire breadth of the opposite wall. Not bad for someone teetering on the brink of middle age. Bloody Asa. At least she looked more shaggable than the blonde helmets. Or presumably Antoine thought she did if he had invited her here?

'Bonjour, Docteur Bouchard!'

He had arrived. Oh God, he was wearing one of those awful green woollen loden coats that fell into an A-line from the shoulders. Catholic mafia coats, as someone had once described them. Luckily the maître d' was taking it from him, carrying it off to the cloakroom where doubtless many other identical ones were already steaming quietly. He'd have to make sure he didn't take the wrong one home.

Under the coat he was wearing an immaculate grey suit. He was coming towards her, smiling – an elegant mover, you had to say that for him.

'Ah, Docteur Bouchard!' One of the blonde helmets had intercepted him. In a flurry of smiles and handshakes she introduced him to her friend. Basking in his attention, the women grew animated to an extent that had not been necessary before the arrival of a man at their table. After a few moments he excused himself, and the blonde helmets settled back into the restrained demeanour of Ladies Who Lunch.

'So', he said, leaning over to kiss Laura on both cheeks, 'I am glad you are here. Champagne, an excellent idea, I shall order the same.'

'They looked happy to see you,' said Laura.

'She is a patient of mine, and now I suspect her friend will become one. Women are always grateful for the company of a man during the day, don't you agree?'

'Look at me. Dripping with gratitude.'

'Now you are being sarcastic, but it is true. Women who do not work become lonely, and tire of the company of other women.'

'There you go again, boosting my ego.'

'But you are intelligent enough to arrange diversions for yourself.'

'Is that what you are, a diversion?'

'That depends on you.'

Laura blushed. This wasn't turning out the way she had hoped. They hadn't even looked at the menu yet, and already things were getting a bit heavy. It seemed that there was indeed no such thing as a free lunch. She tried to change the subject.

'What shall we have? Oysters for me I think, then the *pavé*.'

'Oysters, yes,' he said. 'Well known for their aphrodisiac qualities.'

'Although they used to be the cheapest food of all. Do you know that line from Chaucer? "He didn't give an oyster for that text that said that . . ." Oyster used in that context to mean something entirely worthless.'

'I am dazzled by your learning. But I shall order oysters as aphrodisiacs, not as worthless objects.'

He was laughing at her. She sighed.

'Look, Antoine, I'll be frank with you. I really don't know why I agreed to have lunch with you. I should tell you that I am very happily married and have no intention of cheating on my husband. As far as I'm concerned, this is just . . . a social occasion.'

He shrugged.

'Of course it is a social occasion. I too am happily married, so you see, we are in the same position. I would not dream of taking you from your husband. But there is no crime in adding to our happiness, is there? And I think you are happy, are you not, to be having lunch with me today?'

Laura laughed.

'I suppose so. At least it gets me out of the house.'

'Thank you for the compliment. Now I shall pay you one. You look ravishing. The first time I saw you I thought to myself, now there is someone I should like to take to lunch. For a social occasion. And here we are.'

He raised his glass.

'To us.'

She raised her glass. Out of the corner of her eye she could see one of the blonde helmets looking at her with a mixture of envy and disapproval. It was really rather gratifying.

'To us.'

In fact, she enjoyed the lunch so much that she was mildly disappointed when they stood on the pavement outside and Antoine merely kissed her hand.

'*Au revoir*. You have my work number. Ring me when you want us to share another social occasion.'

She watched him as he walked off in his green loden coat, and fought the impulse to run after him with her diary to pencil in the next date. She really wasn't used to this.

SEVEN

As their plane touched down at Roissy airport, Flavia looked across to Jean-Laurent dozing in the next seat. She was still entranced by the novelty of seeing him sleep, and was struck by the beauty of his long dark eyelashes. He was dribbling slightly, but four days of intense love-making enabled her to overlook his imperfections. It had been so relaxing to wake up with him every morning, and she was sure it wouldn't be long before they were together every single day. He must realise soon that she was indispensable to him, and that they couldn't carry on this charade for much longer. She had already seen some bunk beds that would fit nicely into her spare bedroom for when his children came to stay. She would be good as a part-time step-mother, and the boys would understand that you can't stand in the way of love. What else was there, after all?

She stroked his cheek, and he opened his eyes.

'We're here.'

Jean-Laurent stretched his long legs and squeezed her hand.

'God I'm tired. You've worn me out.'

'I didn't notice you complaining.'

He yawned and pulled her towards him, kissing her sleepily.

'No complaints, that's true. What time is it?'

'Three o'clock. Not worth going back to the office. Why don't we bunk off, see an exhibition. Or we could go shopping.'

She was envisaging a romantic stroll down the boulevard Saint-Germain, maybe taking him into Verbel to show him the bunk beds. They were specially designed for boys, with trains and cars painted on the sides.

He looked evasive.

'That would be nice, but I was thinking of surprising the boys, going to pick them up from school.'

'Oh.' She felt a faint chill of rejection. Still, no point in nagging, that was Laura's department.

'You *are* a good daddy. But won't Laura be going to get them?'

He shrugged.

'Of course, but they like it when we're both there.'

This was not encouraging.

'I'm looking forward to meeting them tomorrow. Are they as handsome as their father?'

Oh God, thought Jean-Laurent, he'd forgotten about that damned dinner. This was in danger of getting out of hand.

'Look, are you sure you want to go through with this. You can easily cry off sick.'

'Don't be silly. I'll have to meet them sooner or later, and this will break them in gently.'

Break them in gently? To what? Jean-Laurent had an ominous sense that Flavia was getting the wrong idea.

'Flavia, I think perhaps we need to discuss this . . .'

'Sshh . . .' She kissed him. 'There's nothing to discuss. I'm coming to dinner with you and your wife, we're colleagues, it's perfectly normal. Don't worry, I won't let you down.'

He smiled in relief. That was more like it. Everything was perfectly well balanced as it was. There was no sense in moving the goalposts, Flavia must understand that. They made their way off the plane, past the glazed smiles of the cabin crew who had obediently lined up at the door to wish them a *bonne journée*. There was a delay at the baggage reclaim area, which irritated Jean-Laurent. Normally he took only hand luggage, which meant he was spared contact with the ordinary traveller. He could sit in the first-class lounge sipping complimentary coffee until the last possible moment, and then stroll casually on to the plane, turning left through the curtain, leaving the little people to pig it in economy (and hopefully absorb the shock in the event of an accident – although Jean-Laurent worried that it might be the other way round).

Once you got off the plane, however, this class segregation fell woefully to pieces if you had baggage to collect. He and Flavia stood and watched the conveyor belt offering up a dismal procession of lookalike suitcases and scruffy holdalls. Eventually his Mandarina Duck suitcase came into view, sealed within a protective polythene sheet which he always insisted upon to prevent its aristocratic corners from being sullied by contact with less prestigious luggage. Flavia's Louis Vuitton was tucked in beside it, and Jean-Laurent lifted them both on to his trolley.

'At last, let's go,' he said, pushing the trolley in a disdainful way that suggested that trolley-pushing was not something he was used to. 'My car should be waiting. Shall I drop you off on the way?'

But when they got outside, the car was not waiting. Jean-Laurent irritably punched numbers into his phone to find out what the hell was going on, while Flavia took the opportunity to disappear to the ladies and repair her make-up. From the tone he took with the taxi company, you might have thought that this minor inconvenience was of earth-shattering importance, but it paled into insignificance beside the huge embarrassment that was heading his way.

For by a cruel coincidence, this happened to be the day that his wife's best friend Lorinda had met up for a girly lunch at the airport with her ex-colleagues. She was on her way to take the Air France bus back to town when she spotted Jean-Laurent shouting angrily into his phone. She could have ignored him – he didn't look in the mood for agreeable conversation – but he was obviously waiting for a taxi, and Lorinda was certainly not about to turn down a free ride.

She came up behind him and gave his bottom a playful squeeze. His reaction was not what she had expected. Without interrupting his conversation, he placed a hand over hers and pressed it slowly against his buttock, gently stroking his forefinger over the back of her hand. It wasn't until he had come off the phone and turned round to confront his assailant that he realised his mistake. His conspiratorial smile was replaced by a look of frank horror.

'Lorinda!'

'So it seems. Were you expecting someone else?'

'No, of course not! What are you doing here?'

'Having lunch with the girls. I must say I wasn't expect-ing such a warm welcome. We must do this more often.'

Jean-Laurent looked nervously over her shoulder.

'I'm waiting for my car. I thought I might go and meet the children from school.'

'Good, I'll share your taxi. Promise you won't get fresh with me on the back seat?'

She glanced at his trolley.

'You've got a lot of luggage. I suppose you have to dress for dinner at the Lygon Arms.'

'Not all mine,' he confessed miserably as he saw Flavia heading towards them, wearing fresh lipstick and an expression of amused curiosity.

The two women nodded at each other as a flustered Jean-Laurent made the introductions.

'Um, this is Flavia, she's been doing some research for us. Flavia, this is Lorinda, a friend of Laura's.'

'And of yours, Jean-Laurent, or so I like to think.'

Lorinda took in the blonde hair, the little-girl figure, the insolently pretty face. You bastard, she thought.

'Hallo, Flavia,' she said. 'Pleased to meet you. How did the research go?'

'Pretty conclusive, I'm glad to say.'

Brazen hussy. She didn't look the slightest bit embar-rassed.

'Lorinda's going to share our car,' said Jean-Laurent. 'She's just had lunch with some friends at Air France — she used to work there.'

'Oh, did you know Christian Blanc when he was chairman?' asked Flavia sweetly. 'He's absolutely charming, isn't he? What did you do, were you in marketing?'

'Nothing so grand, I'm afraid. I was a hostess.'

'Oh.'

Trust Laura to be friends with a dimwit trolley-dolly.

A white Mercedes pulled up in front of them. Jean-Laurent quickly appropriated the front seat and set about giving the driver the full benefit of his opinions on efficiency and standards of service. Lorinda and Flavia sat in the back. Flavia struck up a conversation; after all, she was well trained in talking to housewives – she knew how to make them feel at ease.

'So, Lorinda, your children are at school with Jean-Laurent's?'

'Yes, two of them are, anyway – the others are too young. Do you have children, Flavia?'

'Not yet. Too busy, I'm afraid. But there is plenty of time,' she replied, drawing attention simultaneously to her youth and her professional success.

'Are you married?' She might as well get as much information as possible for Laura.

'No. I don't think marriage is relevant today for women who are financially independent. Although of course I respect the opinions of those who think otherwise.' She gave Lorinda a patronising smile.

'Like Jean-Laurent and Laura, you mean?'

'Yes, of course.'

'And how did you find the Lygon Arms. Comfortable beds?'

'I travel a great deal for my work, so I'm always happy

to get back to my own bed, but, yes, it was a comfortable hotel.'

Jean-Laurent had finished with the driver and turned round to the back seat.

'Where shall we drop you, Flavia?'

'Just let me out at Etoile. I don't want to make you late.'

The taxi pulled in by the Arc de Triomphe to let Flavia out, and Jean-Laurent ensured that he was fully engaged on his mobile for the rest of the journey to avoid the need for further conversation with Lorinda.

The children were already spilling out on to the pavement when they arrived at the school. Jean-Laurent saw Laura, and was surprised to see she was looking rather good, wearing a coat he didn't remember. She caught sight of him and smiled her surprise. A father at the school gates was still a comparative rarity, and Jean-Laurent cut quite a dash in his suit. She felt a rush of guilty affection and made her way over to him.

'Hallo, this is an unexpected treat. They're just coming out now – they will be pleased.'

Charles-Edouard waved shyly at his father while Pierre-Louis hurled himself into his arms.

'Dad, I'm up to level thirteen on Super Mario.'

Jean-Laurent hugged them both, filled with paternal pride while at the same time enjoying the public spectacle he was presenting of himself as the devoted father. Some of these mothers weren't bad looking – quite a good place to pick up a bit of bored totty if you weren't already doing quite well in that department.

Lorinda came up with her children.

'Did Jean-Laurent tell you he gave me a ride in his taxi? Met his gorgeous researcher, Flavia.'

'Oh really?' said Laura. 'You'll be seeing her again tomorrow – she's coming to dinner, I think. Is that right, Jean-Laurent?'

'Er, yes. She just happened to be free, luckily.'

'Free as air,' sniffed Lorinda, trying unsuccessfully to make Jean-Laurent meet her gaze.

'I'll see you tomorrow, then. Thanks for the lift, Jean-Laurent.'

'Pleasure.' He smiled down at her.

You dirty dog, she thought. Still, at least it would add a bit of zest to the dinner party. And there was every reason now for Laura to pay him back with a retaliatory dalliance with Antoine.

Much later, in bed, Laura lay in the darkness listening to the steady breathing of her husband. He had seemed pleased to be back home, appreciative of the intimate little dinner she had prepared, more out of guilt than from any desire to eat boeuf bourguignon, which her cookbook had assured her was 'every man's favourite dish'.

When they went to bed, she had heard him rummaging in the bathroom cabinet and discreetly opening the drawer of his bedside table, so she wasn't surprised when he reached for her under the covers and initiated their well-practised love-making routine. It had seemed to her that they were both just going through the motions. Married sex. It was her fault – she just couldn't work up any enthusiasm. Maybe Antoine was right, maybe you did need the sparkle of adventure, as he put it. 'You Anglo-Saxons,' he had said, as though referring to Beowulf-hunting savages living in mud huts, 'you Anglo-Saxons insist upon the misery of serial monogamy. You destroy your families for the thrill of the new, and then the same thing happens all over again. It is futile. We Latins know that love does not destroy, it enhances.' He had made it sound so simple.

Was that what they needed, she and Jean-Laurent, a bit of enhancement at the hands of the suave Dr Bouchard? It was tempting, but she couldn't do it. She couldn't deceive Jean-Laurent. It would be so unfair.

'Do you have to wear that apron?' asked Jean-Laurent crossly.

It was half past seven and Laura was busy shelling *langoustines* over the kitchen sink. Her dress was protected by a jokey pink plastic apron which had enormous breasts printed on it. It had been a present from an ex-boyfriend who believed it was their shared sense of humour that made their relationship work. Jean-Laurent found it inappropriate.

'Don't worry,' she said, 'I'll take it off before the guests arrive. Have you set the table?'

'Almost. I just need to find two more underplates.'

'Not those things! They serve no purpose and they don't fit in the dishwasher.'

'So what? Asa can wash them up tomorrow – that's what she's there for, isn't it?'

Jean-Laurent held the French view that au pair girls should be used as cut-price servants.

'It's Sunday tomorrow. And it's not one of her duties.'

'I keep telling you to get rid of her and find yourself a Sri Lankan houseboy. They wait at table too, you know.'

'For the pittance we pay Asa? I don't think so. Anyway, who are we trying to impress? We're not diplomats, are we? I hardly see the need for white-gloved manservants hovering round the table.'

Jean Laurent sighed.

'Laura, I do wish you wouldn't be so *practical* all the time. If you had your way, we'd all be pigging it in the kitchen so everyone could put their own plate straight into the dishwasher. You seem to have no aesthetic sense of how a dinner party should be presented.'

He opened a cupboard and brought out a pair of massive frosted-glass underplates which he carried huffily through to the *triple living*. Decorating the table was his contribution to their entertaining effort, and he had to admit the results were pleasing. The table was groaning with glass and crockery, conforming with the Parisian idea that a dinner at home should as far as possible resemble a night out in a stuffy restaurant.

He looked across at the salon, where two angular sofas were aggressively parked opposite each other in readiness for confrontational conversation. Bookcases made from recycled industrial steel were sprinkled with a careful mix of English and French texts. It was, he thought with satisfaction, an appropriate setting for interesting, contemporary people.

Laura had done well, once he had educated her out of her homely preference for Osborne & Little chintz and introduced her to the Conran Shop in rue du Bac, where third-world chic was elevated beyond the reach of the vulgar masses by reassuringly first-world prices. His real decorating triumph, though, had been his solution to the television problem. Some people got round this by installing a cabinet with sliding doors to hide the offending object, but this was too petty bourgeois. Instead Jean-Laurent had hit upon the creative idea of a cast-iron screen with a hand-painted panel that flipped up to expose the telly when required. In practice, though, the television was on almost continuously, so the screen remained propped up against the wall like a heavy white elephant. He dragged it now across the parquet, completing the tableau. There: now they were ready for their guests.

Laura called him from the kitchen.

'Jean-Laurent, could you get the boys to bed, please, I've still got to finish the pudding.'

'Whatever you say. You know me, New Man *extraordinaire*.'

She came in carrying a large platter of *langoustine* salad.

'I would hardly say that putting your children to bed once a week and fussing about with table decorations qualifies you as a New Man.'

'And I would hardly say that patiently hanging around all week like a good housewife waiting for your husband to come home qualifies you as a New Woman, so we're well matched.'

He squeezed her bottom playfully.

'Get off. Anyway, how do you know I've been hanging around waiting for you. I might have been seeing my lover.'

Jean-Laurent snorted. 'I hardly think so – you know when you're already getting the best. Now, if you had married an Englishman, that would be different. Lucky for you you had the sense to marry me.'

He thought back to last night, reassured by the memory

of her undemanding behaviour in bed. It had been quite a relief, after the acrobatic performance he had felt obliged to put in all week at the Lygon Arms, to be safely back in the marital bed with the mother of his children.

'Ah, the great French lover-man, another modern myth. Tell me, Jean-Laurent, is there anything you French don't believe you're best in the world at?'

Jean-Laurent frowned as he pondered the question, then his face cleared.

'Yes, I've got it. Cricket.'

He wandered into the boys' bedroom where they were waiting for their bedtime story. He enjoyed reading to them – he acted out all the voices and they loved it because of its rarity value. Laura was always much more brisk and businesslike. Tonight they wanted Babar, one of Jean-Laurent's favourites which reminded him of his own childhood. He lay especial emphasis on the last line, with its relevance to his own role as paterfamilias:

'"Truly," said Babar, "it is not easy to bring up children, but aren't they worth it?"'

The long-suffering father closed the book and kissed Pierre-Louis on the soft hair that spiralled out from the crown of his head.

'Goodnight, my angels.'

From the other bed, Charles-Edouard looked up from his book.

'Dad, can we go to La Tête dans les Nuages tomorrow?'

La Tête dans les Nuages was a cavernous inferno of video game machines, and therefore a paradise for boys.

'Oh, I should think so.'

'Yes!' Charles-Edouard punched the air in delight.

It was so gratifyingly easy to please them, thought Jean-Laurent as he made his way into the salon to see to the drinks. Oddly enough, he felt quite relaxed about the evening ahead. Flavia was right: it was perfectly normal that they should appear to be on friendly terms. They were colleagues, after all, and when Lorinda had seen them at the airport they were only doing the normal thing – sharing a taxi back from the airport. It was a bit embarrassing the way he'd squeezed her hand against his bum, but he felt he'd done a good job of laughing it off. It wasn't as if she had run into them in a restaurant when he had told Laura he was working late; that would have been more difficult to explain.

He had just put the champagne into the ice bucket when the door bell rang.

'I'll get it,' called Laura, whipping off her larky apron.

His carefully rehearsed calm fell to pieces when he saw Flavia walk through the door. Why was she so early? He had told her not to come before nine.

'Hi,' said Laura, smiling. 'You must be Flavia, unless Jean-Laurent has invited some other pretty stranger he hasn't told me about.'

'Pleased to meet you,' said Flavia, kissing Laura on both cheeks. She was wearing a straight, knee-length skirt, which was very 'in' this season. Laura had tried one on herself, but it had made her look like a policewoman.

Flavia did not look like a policewoman. A soft cream jumper hugged her upper contours, straight blonde hair streamed down her back and she carried a cutie-pie handbag with little handles instead of a shoulder strap. She looked like an upmarket Barbie, one of the special collectors' models that gay men pay five hundred pounds for. Laura's father would have described her as top totty.

'I'm sorry I'm early. I rather hoped I might have a chance to meet the children before they went to bed.'

'Too late, I'm afraid,' said Laura, 'but they're probably still awake. Jean-Laurent will take you down if you want.'

Jean-Laurent stepped forward.

'Flavia, we meet again,' he said, a touch too heartily. He went to kiss her but they both went for the wrong cheek and their lips brushed clumsily.

Flavia reached into her toy handbag and pulled out a package.

'Laura, this is for you. It's from Frères Mariages.'

'How kind!' said Laura, ripping off the black paper to discover a hexagonal jar. 'Tea-flavoured jam – what an original idea. Thank you, Flavia. Jean-Laurent, why don't you take Flavia down to say goodnight to the children, then we can have a drink.'

'Yes, of course. Come and meet the little terrors.'

He led her down the corridor. As soon as they were out of Laura's sight, Flavia took Jean-Laurent's hand and gave it a conspiratorial squeeze. He shook free angrily.

'Why are you so early?' he whispered.

'I simply couldn't wait – I was bursting with curiosity.' She giggled. 'Laura's quite . . . matronly, isn't she?'

Jean-Laurent felt a surge of defensive indignation. That was his wife she was talking about.

'Be quiet, they'll hear us.'

They arrived at the children's bedroom.

'Charles-Edouard, Pierre-Louis, this is Flavia, who works with me.'

Charles-Edouard looked up from his computer magazine. 'Hallo', he said shyly. Pierre-Louis dived under his
duvet and refused to come out.

Flavia sat down on Charles-Edouard's bed.

'My word, Charles-Edouard, that's a grown-up magazine. Would you like to work with computers when you
grow up?'

'Not really,' he said, shrugging.

'What would you like to be then?'

What was this, a job interview? thought Jean-Laurent.
She'd be asking him where he saw himself in five years'
time next.

'Nothing,' said Charles-Edouard. 'I'd like to do nothing, like Mum.'

Flavia laughed. 'I don't think you'd find that very interesting.'

She herself would present a far more acceptable role
model for these children. You really couldn't expect them
to become high-fliers if you set the kind of example that
Laura did. A plump homely figure sacrificing her career
for the comfort of her family – what kind of message was
that sending out to the next generation?

Jean-Laurent ruffled Charles-Edouard's hair affectionately.

'He's got plenty of time to worry about all that. Right
now, he's more interested in beating me at FIFA 2002
. . . On the Nintendo,' he added in explanation, seeing
that Flavia hadn't a clue what he was talking about.

'Oh, I see. What fun!' she said, with a bright smile.

Jean-Laurent was suddenly reminded of a scene in *The
Sound of Music* which he and Laura had watched with the

children last weekend – the bit where dowdy Julie Andrews has run back to the convent, and the haughty baroness is left trying to play ball with the disconsolate children. Flavia had no business being in his children's bedroom. She belonged in a different compartment altogether.

'Come on,' he said impatiently, 'let's go and have a drink.'

'Goodbye, boys, it was nice to meet you,' said Flavia.

In the salon Laura was serving champagne to the other guests, who had arrived together. Francine and Dominique sat on one sofa, nibbling at radishes. Lorinda and Arnaud faced them across the coffee table, a macho slab of oak which had been specially commissioned by Jean-Laurent. He justified the expense on the grounds that an interesting table created a focal talking point, and had got the interiors architect to drive him and a carpenter deep into the forest so he could choose the tree for himself. It was a tale that Jean-Laurent took pleasure in recounting to his guests over the aperitif, though Laura was often anxious that they might all have heard it before.

Francine's brother, Etienne, sat stiffly in an art deco occasional chair. Laura did not hold out much hope for him as an entertaining guest. He had what she now recognised as the Boring Frenchman look, which was found mostly in émigrés from provincial towns. Neat hair and glasses were the key features – why did so many French men wear glasses? – together with a wan complexion and a locked-in expression. The French had a word for it: *coincé* – squeezed in, repressed. The opposite was *branché* – plugged in and vibrant, cool and free-wheeling, which is how all French people wished they were.

'Where's Jean-Laurent?' asked Lorinda.

'Oh, he's in the bedroom with Flavia,' Laura replied.

'Already?' said Lorinda archly.

'Seeing the children, you fool.'

Lorinda watched her critically as she splashed champagne into the glasses.

'Laura, give me the bottle – I'll show you how to do that properly. I was serving a French captain of industry on a plane once, and he was so shocked at my lack of savvy that he snatched it off me and gave me a lesson on the spot. Watch this. You hold the bottle underneath and stick your thumb into the hole, making sure you show off the label so the *gratin* in first class can check you're not fobbing them off with any old sparkling wine.'

'So you're an air hostess!' said Dominique admiringly. He was old enough to belong to the generation that considered this a proper occupation for a woman.

'Now put out to grass, luckily,' said Lorinda, handing him a glass. She looked up and saw Jean-Laurent and Flavia. 'Ah, here comes our host and his lovely assistant.'

'Hardly my assistant,' smiled Jean-Laurent. 'I couldn't justify paying Flavia to type my letters. She's a Jungian psychologist and top-drawer research professional. And she speaks five languages.'

Bully for Flavia, thought Laura.

'Most of the Air France staff have three or four languages,' said Lorinda. 'But strangely enough they have nothing of interest to say in any of them.'

Flavia smiled at her patronisingly and shook hands around the coffee table, bending over conspicuously to show off her faultless haunches. She made a particular fuss of Etienne, who blushed at the attention, miserably aware of his shortcomings as a dinner partner for such a creature. She reminded him of the girl in the advertisement for an Internet dating service. He had spent many a lonely journey in the metro staring at the poster and wondering whether he would ever find himself within lungeing distance of such a pouting beauty. And now he was. She didn't seem to be repulsed by him, but he suspected, quite correctly, that she was just being polite.

'You're an engineer?' she was saying, 'At the Ponts et Chaussées?'

Hard to believe that this dull little man had followed the most prestigious career route known to the over-achieving French school child – a degree at Polytechnique followed by a post as a high-flying *haut fonctionnaire* spending public money on roads and bridges. Not the kind of thing that would turn an Englishwoman's head, but in French women's eyes it was enough to turn an insignificant toad into a very marriageable prince.

'No wonder you're still single,' she breathed in genuine admiration. 'No time for matters of the heart when you're on that kind of fast-track career.'

Etienne smiled gratefully, feeling that his stock was rising. Jean-Laurent frowned. He liked to think that he, too, was a high achiever, but in France the marketing of fast-moving consumer goods was considered the poor relation to public service. And unlike Etienne, he had found the time along the way to lumber himself with an overweight wife and two children.

'Shall we go through?' he said. 'Flavia, I've put you next

to Etienne, so he can talk you through his meteoric rise at the Home Office.'

Flavia gave him a look of such flagrant complicity that Lorinda checked to see if Laura had noticed, but the hostess was on her way into the kitchen.

Dominique murmured into Jean-Laurent's ear as they made their way into the dining room.

'God, she's a hot little piece, old chap. I'm clearly in the wrong business.'

'Luckily for you, Dominique, I've put you on her other side. Now, if you'll excuse me, I'll just give Laura a hand with the *entrées*.'

Laura helped herself to the last slice of creamy Rigadon. It was a shame to waste it, and no one else seemed to want seconds. The evening was quite a success so far, she thought, and Flavia was proving to be an excellent guest – lively and easy on the eye. The kind of catalyst you needed to enliven dinner parties made up of couples. She watched her across the table, pushing a spoonful of dessert around her plate while holding forth amusingly about cultural and national stereotypes. Etienne and Dominique were both enraptured by her, but Jean-Laurent looked rather irritated. Perhaps he had heard it all before.

Flavia was reaching the climax of her set piece: 'And of course, the Austrians, well, they are just like the Germans, but without the sense of humour!'

The table erupted in appreciative laughter. 'Oh, very good, yes!' said Dominique. '*Heil Hitler!* He was an Austrian, of course!'

'And tell me, Flavia,' said Lorinda, annoyed at being

kicked off centre stage, 'how do you define a Franco-Brazilian-Italian – that's your own parentage, I believe?'

'Absolutely,' smiled Flavia. 'Well, I suppose I'm just perfect – a potent mix of French cleverness, Brazilian sexiness and Italian *joie de vivre*! Always supposing that I don't turn into a frumpy spaghetti-stuffed mama the moment I hit thirty, of course!'

'Oh, I don't think there's much risk of that,' said Etienne, emboldened by several glasses of Pomerol.

'In fact,' said Dominique, 'if you were a wine, Flavia, I would say you were definitely vintage champagne. Sparkly, aristocratic, strictly for special occasions.'

'Oh really,' said Francine. 'And what does that make me? Cheap old *vin de table*, I suppose.'

Dominique looked at her affectionately.

'Of course not, my dear. You are a high quality Bordeaux – from the Right Bank or its satellites. And Lorinda is, let's see, a spicy Côtes du Rhône – a funky animal, definitely Shiraz. Laura, too, is not what you would term a classic Bordeaux. No, she is more of an earthy burgundy peasant wine – full-bodied, well rounded in the barrel.'

'Well, thanks a lot, Dominique,' said Laura. 'Excuse me while I slip into my smock and clogs.'

'Which is why Flavia has such perfect potential as a trophy wife!' continued Dominique, now well into his stride. 'Let's face it, when you've spent thirty years grinding up the ladder on a diet of *vin ordinaire*, you feel you deserve something better at the end. Yes, a nice refreshing bottle of vintage champagne, that's what you want!'

He turned and grinned leerily at Flavia, who laughed prettily.

'And what makes you think,' asked Lorinda, dangerously, 'that a classy champagne would be interested in an old bottle of stout like you? No offence, Francine, but don't you think she might prefer something more potent, someone more virile, like Jean-Laurent, for instance?'

'Why thank you, Lorinda. I never realised I was the object of your secret fantasies,' said Jean-Laurent, bluffing over his discomfort.

'Oh, I wasn't putting myself up for a trophy wife, no thank you,' blustered Dominique. 'I'm perfectly happy with the old model, aren't I, Francine? I know when I'm well off – I was only talking theoretically.'

'Talking theoretically?' scoffed Lorinda. 'When did you ever catch a French person *not* talking theoretically? We all know the joke about the Frenchman dissenting in the meeting – that is fine in practice, gentlemen, but how does it work in theory? Now, in theory I would say that when a fine bottle of champagne is going cheap amidst a shelf-load of supermarket plonk, it's a recipe for disaster.'

Laura had caught the edge in Lorinda's voice, and wondered why she seemed determined to play the bitch tonight. Of course, it was always galling to share a table with a younger, prettier woman, but it was terribly bad form to show it. She would have to have a word with her later about the need for graciousness. There was nothing to be gained by turning spiteful.

'Take no notice of Dominquie and his nonsense,' said Francine. 'It's just the sad hallucinations of a menopausal man. He's stuck with me and he knows it. But it may not be too late for us, girls, to score a young trophy husband. Look at Sylvie Marceau. Her husband is years younger than her — it's not just men who can earn the right to firm young flesh. Have you seen them, by the way, Laura?'

Laura quickly swallowed the last of her Rigadon and faked nonchalance.

'Funny you should ask. As a matter of fact I dropped in for an aperitif last week.'

Jean-Laurent looked up from his plate. 'Oh really? You didn't tell me.'

To her annoyance, Laura felt herself blush. 'I forget to mention it. Yes I did actually. You know, they live just down the road from us. You couldn't describe her husband as firm young flesh, though, could you? Fifty if he's a day.'

'Firm enough when she married him,' said Francine, 'and she must be pushing sixty now. It's all relative.'

Laura stood up. 'Would you like some coffee? Let's move into the salon. I know Jean-Laurent is anxious to ply you all with cognac.'

It was after two o'clock when they finally shut the door on their guests. Jean-Laurent put his arms round his wife, comforted by her familiar curves, relieved to be free of Flavia and away from Lorinda's accusing stare.

'Well done, darling. That was quite an evening.'

Laura gently detached herself from his embrace.

'Your friend Flavia created quite a stir. Dominique practically had his tongue hanging out, and poor little Etienne couldn't believe his luck. I don't suppose he meets girls like that at the Ponts et Chaussées.'

Jean-Laurent laughed non-committally.

'He should move into a sexy business like mine. Gorgeous girls by the score.'

Laura looked at him.

'Lucky I'm not the jealous type, or I might start worrying about you. Lorinda seemed to have it in for her. I don't know why – I thought she was perfectly pleasant.'

'She's just bitter. It can't be easy being a jaded ex-air hostess approaching middle age. Every time you see a pretty girl it reminds you of what you used to be.'

'What about jaded ex-ad-women approaching middle age? Isn't it just as bad for them?'

'Darling, you have a brain and a distinguished career behind you – it's quite different. Inner resources. The life of the mind. That's why I love you.'

He drew her to him and realised, with a jolt of surprise, that it was true. He led her to the bedroom and began to make love to her gratefully. His wife was a sensible woman, she took a balanced view of things. She even liked his mistress. Everything was going to be all right.

But Laura had other ideas. Even as Jean-Laurent was giving attentive physical expression to his love of her mind, she was thinking about the doctor. Healing hands that would run over her body in a reverential ecstasy of discovery. Practised hands that would delight her in a way that, to be honest, her husband's hadn't for a very long time. She would call him. Soon.

EIGHT

'Good morning, could I speak to Doctor Bouchard, please?'

'His line is busy. Will you hold or can I take a message?'

'Oh no,' said Laura, 'no message. I'll hold, thank you.'

She paced nervously up and down the salon, trying to focus her attention on the vase of yellow roses standing on the Interesting Oak coffee table. They had been delivered this morning with a card from Francine and Dominique thanking her for a *soirée exceptionelle*.

'He's still busy. Would you like to try later?'

'Oh yes, good idea,' said Laura in relief. 'I'll try again later.'

'Shall I tell him who called?'

'Oh, no, no, really, it doesn't matter. I'll call again. Thank you.'

Laura hung up and gazed out of the window across the Seine. That was a lucky escape. What did she think she was doing, chasing Antoine like some kind of desperate frustrated housewife. She remembered how her mother used to disapprove of her phoning boyfriends when she was

a teenager. 'Let them call *you*, dear,' she would say, banging round the kitchen in tight-lipped disappointment that
her daughter should be reduced to making the first move.

She sat down on the sofa and picked up the style section
of last Sunday's English newspaper. There was a photo of
an It Girl in a tiny pair of white trousers posing with two
celebrities outside a nightclub. She didn't suppose an It
Girl would ever need to stoop so low as to call a middle-
aged endocrinologist to add zest to her life.

'Oh good, you're off the phone.'

Asa had appeared from nowhere. At least Laura
supposed it was Asa – it was hard to tell beneath the thick
layer of pale grey plaster that was hardening over her face.

'I need to call Devon to sort out the arrangements for
tonight.'

'You've got a date with that old pervert? Watch out with
that face mask, it just dripped over the sofa.'

'Of course not, he's like a father to me. Don't you
remember? It's the Thanksgiving party tonight.'

Like many self-centred people, Asa presumed that
everyone took a detailed interest in her plans.

'What Thanksgiving party?' said Laura. 'Why aren't I
invited?'

'It's a joint party for the OA and the AA. At the American
Church.'

Laura snorted with laughter.

'Oh my God, Overeaters and Alcoholics! What a brilliant combination – like Jack Sprat and his wife. I suppose
the fatties have to drink all the wine and the drunks stuff
themselves on pumpkin pie! All beneath the watchful gaze
of Higher Power, or whatever you call him. Oh, please,

can I come? I could qualify on both counts. I eat too much *and* I'm a hopeless old boozer.'

Asa stared at her coldly, her eyes mottled and discoloured against the white of the mask.

'I don't find it funny', she said. 'I happen to think it is brave of people to face up to their problems and try to resolve them in a positive environment. If you don't mind, I think I'll make my call from my bedroom.'

She picked up the phone and swept out.

Laura dabbed at the sofa with a tissue to remove the face mask stain, then settled back with the newspaper to find out what she should be wearing to this year's Christmas parties. Not that she had been invited to any. The French had a tedious approach to Christmas, which was limited to a family dinner on Christmas Eve where everyone ate foie gras and behaved with dignity. There were no opportunities for pulling crackers or wearing paper hats. And you never saw anyone being sick on the metro after getting drunk and embarrassing themselves at the office party.

She succumbed to a wave of nostalgia for the tinselly, bad-taste, London Christmas season. In Paris, all the decorations were so aesthetically correct that you longed to install a flashing Santa Claus in your apartment window to jar against the perfect Christmas bouquets of silver twigs, mistletoe and clementines on sticks that people bought from the florist. You couldn't even get a bog-standard mangy Christmas tree that festively dropped its needles the moment you got it home. Instead you had to pay fifty pounds for a Nordman grey-green thing that left your parquet floor pristine.

'Laura! It's for you!'

Asa came in with bad grace and passed the phone to Laura.

'It's a man,' she said helpfully.

'Hallo?'

'Is this Laura?'

'Yes.'

Oh my God, it was Antoine. Asa was staring at her. Laura stood up and took the phone into her bedroom, closing the door behind her.

'Hallo, I'm sorry, I'm just retreating from my au pair – you know how it is, no privacy, well, no, you probably don't know, I don't suppose you need one for the dogs. What a coincidence, I just tried to ring you.'

She was gibbering hopelessly.

'I know. My secretary told me that someone with an English accent had called, and I guessed it was you.'

'Really? How did you know it wasn't Jane Birkin ringing up to get her thyroid checked? No, you're right, she wouldn't need to. But there are other English women in Paris, you know.'

'I was expecting your call. I was hoping you might suggest that we meet again.'

'That would be nice.'

Oh for God's sake, how gauche could you get?

'How about Friday. One o'clock at the Ritz. I have a free afternoon.'

A free afternoon. In a hotel. This was it then. She was to be ruined.

'All right,' she said faintly.

'Good. I'll see you there. *Au revoir.*'

'Ciao.'

She hung up. *Ciao?* When did she ever say *ciao?* What was she, some teenage piece of Eurotrash? She walked into the kitchen to be confronted by Asa sitting down to a monster bowl of fat-free yoghurt.

'Who was that?' asked Asa. 'You look quite flushed.'

'Oh, a friend. And at my age, you tend to flush. The Change, you know.'

'You are a little young for that,' said Asa kindly. 'But there is someone at the group who runs a seminar on Approaching the Menopause. I can give you her number if you want.'

'No thanks,' said Laura. 'I was only joking. Though I don't suppose that translates into Finnish.'

At ten to two, Laura was standing beneath the glass pyramid of the Louvre looking out for Lorinda and her other cronies amongst the crowds of tourists. She was honouring one of the non-essential engagements that punctuated her uneventful days. The Louvre, after all, was the cultural epicentre of Paris, and what was the point of living in the city if you didn't take advantage of all it had to offer?

Amongst her circle of Parisian women who preferred not to work, it was universally agreed that living in the suburbs was out of the question. They had not given up their careers to vegetate in a no-man's-land where you had to get the car out to buy your baguette. So they chose to sacrifice the chance of a large comfortable house in favour of a city apartment that just begged you to leave it to enjoy the attractions of the outside world. And while the shops and the hairdressers and the beauticians clearly held the most appeal for these *femmes inactives*, they also attached great importance to Culture. Which is why Laura and Lorinda, together with ten other women, met once a month at the Louvre to enjoy a guided tour of its works of art. On this particular Monday, it was the turn of Jean-Baptiste Pigalle to come under scrutiny from the Ladies Who Lunched.

The guide led them through a hall of marble to arrive at their destination, a sculpture of an unfortunate-looking woman. 'As you can see,' she said critically, 'this poor lady has not been spoilt by Mother Nature.' The ladies laughed appreciatively, nothing being more enjoyable than the spectacle of an ugly woman. They then moved on to ponder the aesthetic decline of Madame de Pompadour, captured in full blowsiness by Pigalle.

'Madame de Pompadour preferred *amitié* to *amour physique*, so she was glad when her affair with the king dwindled after years into a non-physical relationship,' explained the guide disapprovingly. 'She started to put on weight, as this statue shows.'

'Christ,' whispered Lorinda, 'even in the bloody art gallery they still have to go on about how fat women are. What is it with the French?'

'You're just jealous,' murmured Laura. 'At least, that's what Jean-Laurent thinks. He says that's why you didn't like Flavia.'

'What? Damned cheek!' Lorinda's voice was raised in indignation and several members of the group turned to look at her.

'Sshh,' said Laura. 'Save it for later. Feast your eyes on our artistic heritage.'

'The reason I don't like Flavia,' whispered Lorinda, 'is that she's a hard-faced whore who's after your husband!'

'Now you're being melodramatic! Just because you saw them together at the airport.'

'Laura, believe me, Jean-Laurent squeezed my hand against his bum thinking it was hers.'

'Sshh! Keep your voice down.'

'I'm warning you about your husband and that trollop, and all you're worried about is disturbing a boring spiel on a misogynistic old sod of a sculptor.'

'Not only misogynistic, he's horrid to men, too. Look, now she's showing us his statue of Voltaire. There's a sad, skinny old man if ever I saw one.'

'Laura! Listen to me!'

'All right, let's go for a coffee afterwards. Now, can we shut up?'

An hour later the ladies of the Louvre kissed each other goodbye, Pigalle vaguely lodged in their consciousness until later that afternoon when he would be displaced by the more pressing demands of small children. Laura and Lorinda made their way along the underground shopping mall that led from the inverted glass pyramid. They sat down at a café on a table next to a party of bored-looking teenagers who seemed committed to smoking their way to recovery from an afternoon of unmitigated culture.

Laura carefully unwrapped her sugar and stirred both halves into her dark espresso.

'So,' she said reasonably, 'you think Flavia's after Jean-Laurent. I suppose it's possible. She is the classic golden career girl starting to panic about going home to her empty flat. And he is very attractive, that's why I married him.

But he is also my husband, and I happen to trust him. We are happy together. What kind of marriage would it be if I got twitchy and suspicious every time he intro-duced me to a good-looking colleague?'

Lorinda sighed in exasperation.

'Laura, listen to me. When I saw Jean-Laurent at the airport, he obviously thought I was her. I came up from behind and pinched his bum, for a laugh. I thought I would surprise him! Instead of which he just carried on talking on the phone and grabbed hold of my hand and started sort of massaging it against his bum. Then when he turned round and saw it was me, he was devastated! Guilty as hell!'

'Of course he was shocked! I would be if some mad woman assaulted me while I was trying to make a phone call!'

'But you wouldn't start stroking her hand, would you? Come on, Laura, don't play the ostrich. Think about all those business trips, all those Sunday nights in the office – no one goes to the office on Sundays!'

'Stop it, Lorinda. This is so cheap, I can't believe you're talking this way to me. I just know that Jean-Laurent would never cheat on me – we've always been totally honest with each other.'

She picked up the sugar paper from her saucer and began tearing it into tiny strips. What Lorinda was telling her was shocking and unwelcome. But it was not entirely unexpected. She really couldn't put her hand on her heart and say it had never crossed her mind that Jean-Laurent might be looking elsewhere.

'So if your relationship with Jean-Laurent is so honest,'

Lorinda said gently, 'how come you never told him about your little lunch with Antoine?'

Laura blushed.

'It wasn't relevant. There was nothing in it, and he might have got the wrong idea. Lorinda, I appreciate your concern, but quite honestly this has nothing to do with you.'

'Except that I'm your friend and I don't want you weeping on my shoulder later on saying you feel such a fool, you were the last one to know. He's French, Laura, and we all know that French men are never averse to a bit of extra-curricular. I should have told you earlier, only I didn't want to upset you.'

Laura stood up abruptly. 'I've heard enough. My marriage is my concern, not yours. Go and pick on someone else with your dirty, suspicious mind.'

Lorinda watched her go, storming angrily through a crowd of bemused Japanese tourists neatly lined up behind their leader's fluorescent orange flag.

'Laura!' she shouted, 'Don't get mad, get even! Think of Doctor Bouchard!'

But Laura was already out of earshot. The teenagers looked across at her from their table. A bit of human drama was worth all the art treasures of the Louvre when it came to arousing their interest.

While Laura was angrily defending her husband in the underbelly of the Louvre, he was just the other side of the Tuileries gardens happily cruising his Porsche down the rue de Rivoli. The radio was tuned to Radio Nostalgie, and he was singing along to an old classic. '*The only way is up, baaby, for you and me girl,'* he crooned as he skilfully cut up a wide-bottomed Mercedes and veered left round the place de la Concorde.

He was feeling pleased with himself after the morning's meeting, in which he had successfully demolished the strategy of the advertising agency's proposed new campaign. He had followed the guiding principle of his hero and mentor, the general von Clausewitz, that you should 'attack the enemy at the weakest point and outnumber him'.

By lining up seven colleagues to pick holes in the feeble reasoning of two hapless admen, he had pulled off a proper routing, sending them off cowering behind their storyboards. That would mean more work for Flavia to get them back on strategy. She would no doubt find a creative way in which to express her gratitude to him at their next rendezvous.

Not that Flavia was his priority this afternoon. That was for a future occasion. To celebrate the morning's victory, he had decided to spend the afternoon working at home. He wanted to be there to surprise Laura and the boys when they got in from school. A man's family life, after all, was the rock on which he built his success.

He turned right on to the *quai*, drove through the first tunnel and then pulled off the embankment just before the pont d'Alma, where he drew up outside a flower shop. To add the final flourish to his role of Caring Husband, he needed to arrive home with a lavish bouquet, so he jumped out of the Porsche, engine running and warning lights flashing, and hurried in to make his selection. As the assistant carefully arranged the lilies and wrapped them with two sheets of toning tissue paper, he glanced out of the window at the monument of the golden flame, where the usual cluster of tourists were reading the tributes to Diana. Years after the tragedy, the loyal herds still continued to leave flowers and embarrassing poems pasted on to the flame above the tunnel where she died. Most of them believed the statue had been erected in her honour, though of course any educated Parisian could tell you that it was a gift from the Americans that long predated the death of the Princess of Wales.

Jean-Laurent drove off and indulged himself in a fantasy of his own tragic road death, his grieving widow and children standing heads bowed at his graveside, while Flavia loitered at a discreet distance, half hidden by a tree – although he supposed she could legitimately join the main throng since they were colleagues and she had once had dinner at his home.

A business book he had just read suggested writing your own obituary to see if your life was going the way you wanted. He tried it out. 'He courageously pushed his brands forward, and was a devoted father and husband.' Perhaps slightly lacking in grandeur. 'The youngest ever chairman of a multinational company, he was as charismatic in his personal relationships as he was in the professional arena.' That was better. Perhaps he might even father a secret child along the way, like President Mitterand. But right now, he was more intent on consolidating his family life.

He parked his car in the underground car park beneath their apartment building. They rented only one space. Laura agreed that there was no point in paying to park her car since she was out in it so much and, anyway, it was the Porsche that needed protecting. He took the lift to the third floor and opened the front door. His good mood was immediately soured by the sight that greeted him. Asa, that pain-in-the-arse Finn, was standing in the hall admiring herself in the full-length mirror. She was wearing a blue suit of Laura's that Jean-Laurent recognised from her office days. She spun round guiltily as he came in.

'I recognise that suit,' he said. 'Did Laura pass it on to you?'

Asa shrugged casually.

'It doesn't fit her any more. And this style is coming back in. I thought I might get some wear out of it. I can't afford to buy any new clothes.'

She disappeared huffily to her bedroom. Jean-Laurent watched her go, irritated that this ungrateful intruder should have carte blanche to go prowling round his home. Why on earth didn't Laura get rid of her and hire an Asian, or a high-cheekboned refugee from the former Yugoslavia?

He moved into the dining room and spread his files over the table, planning to work for an hour until the family came home. His mind drifted back to the obituary. Was it the done thing to mention servants? Perhaps just a discreet line towards the end. 'He was much respected by the many loyal staff who ran his homes.' He would only hire good-looking ones and he'd make them all wear black and white. Certainly not electric blue like that horrible suit of Laura's that had always reminded him of Mrs Thatcher.

Laura angrily crunched her gears as she drove out of the Carrousel du Louvre car park and on to the rue de Rivoli. How dare Lorinda speak to her like that! She really should get a life instead of drumming up malicious ideas and sticking her nose in everywhere. It was pitiful that she had so little to think about – just that mother-in-law that Laura was sick to death of hearing about, to be honest, and her petty little economies.

She rounded the place de la Concorde and headed down towards the pont d'Alma, trying to get the image of Lorinda's concerned face out of her head. I'm your friend, she had said, I didn't want to upset you. Then why did you, thought Laura, why couldn't you keep your suspicions to yourself instead of turning my life upside down with your vile allegations.

She swerved to avoid a silver Porsche, badly parked outside a flower shop, that was forcing the traffic heading over the bridge into a single lane. French drivers were just the pits, egomaniacs with no sense of decency, not like in England where people parked where they were supposed to – or at least they did in her rose-tinted memory. She stopped at the lights and glanced in her rear-view mirror at the offending car: its driver had returned, his arms full of flowers, smooth bastard. Oh my God. It was Jean-Laurent.

Where was he going at this time in the afternoon? Oh sweet Jesus, Lorinda was right, he was off to a silk-draped love-nest, a voluptuous *garçonnerie*, where that skinny cow would be waiting for him. She could see her now, reclining on the crimson sheets, holding out a glass of champagne for her ardent lover. Tears of rage pricked her eyes as she watched him jump into his car and speed off up the avenue George V, while she, good old Laura, true to her dull routine, prepared dutifully to head off for the school gates. On her way across the bridge, she saw a young woman attaching a message to the Statue of Liberty torch, while people in anoraks took photographs. Poor Diana, she thought, her self-pity overflowing into sentimentality – you and me both, betrayed and humiliated in our dream of the perfect marriage.

She parked outside the school and remained in the car trying to compose herself before the children came out. Through the window she could see the mothers locked in small groups, talking and laughing amongst themselves. PTA Paula was looking particularly unattractive in a maroon jogging suit, nodding earnestly to one of the Catholic mafia mums dressed Versailles-style (modern suburban version as opposed to eighteenth-century courtier) in a green padded anorak, her grey hair restrained by a navy blue velvet headband.

Why aren't their husbands cheating on them? thought Laura. You couldn't blame *them*, coming home to that every night. Whereas she, Laura, dynamic retired account director and sophisticated woman around town, who went out of her way to provide her husband with every reason to find her adorable, surely deserved better than to be cast upon the junk heap of unwanted old bags. She waved through the window to Charles-Edouard and Pierre-Louis, who came running happily towards her, blissfully unaware that they were soon to become the innocent victims of a broken marriage, pawns in the cruel game of marital chess.

She drove home in silence. Pierre-Louis, sensing her mood, pulled a drawing out of his satchel and, in the hope of cheering her up, leaned forward to shove it under her nose.

'Look, Mum. We had to do a drawing of our family.'

'Not when I'm driving, Pierre-Louis, we might have an accident.'

She waited until she had stopped at the lights and glanced down at the picture.

'That's lovely,' she replied automatically in her usual tone of unqualified admiration. 'There's you and Charles-Edouard playing football, and Daddy carrying his brief-case. What am I doing?' She could make out a stout female figure crouched on the floor over a box.

'You're cleaning everyone's shoes,' replied Pierre-Louis.

'So I am. Well, I suppose someone's got to do it.'

Jean-Laurent was clearly not the only one who saw her as a dumb stooge. Good old Laura, the faithful retainer, her pinny stained with boot polish as she lovingly prepared her family for the outside world from which she had so willingly resigned.

They arrived home, the boys running ahead into the lift while Mrs Danvers staggered behind with the satchels. No doubt her third child, that stroppy post-adolescent Scandinavian, would be lounging around the apartment. Laura should ask her if she had any shoes she needed cleaning – after all, she might as well service the whole damn bunch of them.

But it was Jean-Laurent, not Asa, who opened the door to them.

'Papa!' Charles-Edouard jumped into his father's arms and Pierre-Louis trotted after him, pressing his face into the soft cashmere of Jean-Laurent's suit.

'Surprise!' said Jean-Laurent, looking at her in amusement.

'You're here!' she said, the weight of her misery suddenly lifting from her. 'I saw you parked by the pont d'Alma. I saw you drive off. I couldn't think where you would be going.'

'Home to my lovely family, of course, where else?'

Not to the silken love den then, not to a place of betrayal and iniquity. How could she have had so little faith in him? She kissed him lightly, giddy with relief.

He produced the bunch of lilies from behind his back.

'Here – for you.'

Of course the flowers were for her. Her mind had been warped by Lorinda's preposterous ideas. Everything was at it should be.

By the time they were in bed, Laura's euphoria had given way to a more reasonable level of equanimity, which in turn gave rise to reasonable doubts which she mulled over as she stared up at the dark ceiling while Jean-Laurent's body rose and fell in the gentle rhythm of untroubled sleep. Why would Lorinda lie to her? She wouldn't. Perhaps she just misinterpreted the scene at the airport and leapt to wild conclusions. And anyway, Jean-Laurent would never have agreed to Flavia coming to the house if she was anything more than a colleague. The office on Sunday nights? Well, why not, it was the best time – it was calm, with nobody around. There was really nothing wrong with that. She certainly wasn't going to rock the boat with a direct confrontation based on such flimsy evidence. Keep things as they were, that was best.

But just supposing it was true? She knew, of course, that it wasn't, but just supposing it was – what then? She leaned towards Jean-Laurent and placed her hand in the small of his warm, sleeping back. It was impossible for her to imagine this body that belonged to her arched in passion over someone else. The idea was preposterous.

And yet, if she was honest, she couldn't say that their love-making these days was anything like the way it used to be. Uxorious. Friendly. Accomplished and perfectly satisfactory, but with none of that animal, gut-wrenching hunger that now seemed to belong to the past. The kind of hunger that drove men and women beyond the confines of marriage into the arms of someone new. The hunger that had prompted her, she now remembered with a shock, to agree to meet Antoine in what promised to be very compromising circumstances.

The next morning, Jean-Laurent took the children to school as part of his new campaign to be an all-functioning family man. He would be back late, he said – he was having dinner with François. Dinner with François again, Laura had said. Are you sure he doesn't fancy you? Hey baby, do I look like a *pédé*'s delight? he had asked, striking up a macho pose. Not really, she had laughed as she waved them off, but now she knew, she had a plan.

It was low, she admitted, it was pretty damned humiliating, but she had to know. There was no point in tormenting herself with guilt over an innocent lunch with an admirer if her husband was up to much worse. She would follow him. She would become her own private eye. And if she discovered that what Lorinda had intimated was true, she might consider her flirtation in a quite different light.

Still wearing her dressing gown, she took a packet of

luxury cereal from its hiding place in her underwear drawer and poured herself a large bowlful. She should have time to finish it before Asa emerged from the shower. At the age of thirty-seven, it should surely be possible to leave her food supplies openly in her own kitchen cupboard, but first she would have to get rid of that compulsive overeater who at this very minute was busy ensuring there would be no hot water left for Laura's bath.

She turned on the radio, but that bad-tempered man on the *Today* programme was preventing his guest from finishing his sentence. Irritated, she tuned into a French station on which a marriage guidance counsellor was explaining why one in two Parisian marriages ended in divorce. Love, she said, was not enough to ensure a successful marriage. You needed a common goal, an ongoing project that you shared.

Well, we have a common project, thought Laura, we have the children. And the country cottage, though that was perhaps more of a common millstone. And then they had their common *bête noire*, Asa the bogeyman, the one they whispered about together in bed as they listened to her rustling through the kitchen cupboards in search of a late-night snack.

And what about infidelity? asked the interviewer. Was that what brought most couples to see the counsellor? Not at all. It seemed that lack of communication was the main problem in marriages today. Did that mean it was OK to go to bed with your lover as long as you talked about it over dinner with your spouse? How was your day, dear? Oh, not too bad, but my girlfriend gave me a hard time because I forgot her birthday. Oh, poor you. Tell you what,

I'll put it in my diary, then next year I'll be able to remind you.

Asa came into the kitchen with the post that had just been slipped under the front door by the *gardienne*. She tossed an electricity bill across the table to Laura, and put down her own pile of handwritten letters while she helped herself to four large oranges which she began squeezing into a tall glass.

'There's a carton of orange juice in the fridge,' said Laura. 'Save you going to all that trouble.'

Asa pulled a face.

'It's not the same. You only get the vitamins when you squeeze them yourself. And I need to restore my chemical balance after the party last night.'

'Did you get shit-faced then?'

Laura was saved from Asa's contemptuous stare by the phone. She went into the hall to answer it.

'Laura? It's Lorinda.'

Lorinda. The bringer of bad tidings. Or the underemployed rumour-monger. Laura would know soon enough and judge her friend accordingly.

'Oh, hi,' she said in a neutral tone; not too chilly but with less than her usual warmth.

'Do you hate me? Say you don't hate me.'

'Why should I hate you? You were only trying to do your duty as a friend. Now it's up to me to draw my own conclusions.'

'That sounds terribly mature. I'm glad you see it that way. I thought afterwards, though, that perhaps I shouldn't have said anything . . .'

'Well, you did, but as far as I'm concerned, the subject

is now closed. At least between us. For the time being. I'm not alone here, by the way.'

'You're not? Is Jean-Laurent there?'

'Think again. Think Northern Lights, think regurgitating geysers, think humourless Norsewomen.'

She can't be that furious, thought Lorinda, she's making jokes.

'Oh, her! Well, if you ask for a Scandinavian you get what you deserve, in my opinion. How did her party go?'

'I'm just about to find out. I'll get all the horrible details once you're off the phone.'

'OK. So I'm glad you don't hate me, anyway. Are you going to the gym today?'

'No. I've got other fish to fry.'

'How intriguing. What fish might that be? The duplicitous cod flesh of your husband? Or the exotic deep-sea red snapper of your ardent suitor?'

'I need to get things clear in my own mind. I'll speak to you again once I have. Goodbye Lorinda.'

'All right then, don't tell me. I know you will in the end. Bye!'

Laura hung up and went back into the kitchen where Asa was stirring her fresh fruit cocktail.

'It was fantastic, actually,' said Asa, wiping the juice from her upper lip with a freshly laundered linen napkin that Laura normally reserved for dinner parties. 'Devon brought his guitar and led us all in a sing-song. He really made us feel that we were united in a common purpose.'

'How touching. Did he bring his wife?'

'No, she feels it is important for them to be able to grow in their own separate spaces.'

'I can imagine which space he would like to grow in.'

'What do you mean?'

'Never mind.'

Asa looked at Laura critically.

'I know it's none of my business, but I think you could learn a lot from Devon. You should try to be strong and separate rather than always hanging around waiting for Jean-Laurent to come home. He'd respect you more for it.'

Laura's hackles rose.

'Well, thank you for your advice, but I think that my relationship with my husband is my business.'

Asa drained her glass and slowly crossed the kitchen to open a cupboard door. With infuriating nonchalance she helped herself to a new packet of rice cakes.

'Devon read us this wonderful passage from *The Prophet*, where it talks about marriage and how both partners should grow like trees, not overshadowing each other.'

'Oh, please! I can't remember a wedding where that hasn't been used as a reading!'

Asa shrugged. 'I thought it was beautiful. But I suppose one day I'll become as jaded and cynical as you.'

'In fact,' said Laura, 'I'm going out tonight. By myself, like a strong and separate tree, you'll be pleased to hear. I'd like you to babysit, please.'

Laura pulled her coat collar up around her ears and clapped her gloved hands together. She glanced at her watch. It was seven-thirty, and she had been sitting in her parked car for an hour now, her eyes trained on the entrance of Jean-Laurent's offices. Ahead of her she saw the curved alcoves of the pont Neuf, made for lovers, suspended over the darkness of the river. She had seen a few people she recognised coming out of the office, hurrying down to the metro, going home or off in search of the city's distractions.

Then she saw him, tall and striking in his long overcoat. He didn't look hurried. He was alone – François was nowhere in sight. She watched him walk past the car park. He wasn't taking the car, then; she would have to follow him on foot. She locked the car and followed him up the dark road until he turned right on to the rue de Rivoli. What was the optimum distance if you were shadowing someone? Ten metres maybe? She hoped to God she didn't bump into anyone she knew; she couldn't afford any delay or she would lose sight of him.

He continued down the rue de Rivoli, walking against the traffic, until he turned left up another side street. She followed him through the narrow maze of seventeenth-century streets that made up the Marais, now the favoured meeting place for gays in Paris. Maybe he was off for a secret tryst with another man? Maybe he was calling her bluff?

They eventually came to the place des Vosges. He walked slowly down the western arcade, glancing casually in the shop windows. He paused outside an antiques store, glanced at his watch and stepped inside. From a careful distance, she saw him pointing to a small jewellery box. Oh my God, he was buying her a present, the bastard. The assistant took it to the desk and carefully wrapped it, embellishing it with a swirl of golden ribbon. He smiled at her, handing over his card, then walked towards the door.

Laura quickly retreated into the shadows as he stepped out and continued walking under the romantic arcades until he reached what she supposed must be his destination: L'Ambroisie, a restaurant that Laura had read about in one of her greedy browsings through the *Food Lover's Guide to Paris*. She remembered it was supposed to glow with antique, upper-class French charm. She had suggested to Jean-Laurent that they go there, but he had obviously preferred to keep it for a different dining companion.

She watched the waiter showing him to his table by the window. Flavia was already there. She stood up to kiss Jean-Laurent, who handed over the present. Laura felt sick. She sat down on a bench, unable to take her eyes off them. She felt as if she were attending her own funeral. Above all, she felt horribly lonely.

So that's it then, she thought. Her husband was a cheat and liar, and she was just another deceived wife. She leaned over and vomited on to the venerable paving stones, within spitting distance of where her husband and his strumpet were already raising their glasses of champagne in a toast, she supposed, to their own cleverness in managing to dupe his stupid English wife.

NINE

'Go on, say it,' sobbed Laura. 'Say "I told you so", why don't you?'

Lorinda sighed and reached across the table for her friend's hand. Laura had abandoned all pretence of anger with Lorinda after last night and had summonsed her for an emergency morning meeting in their favourite café.

'You knew too, Laura. You just didn't want to face up to it. And now you know for sure, which is good. Come on, it's not the end of the world. You should see this as an opportunity.'

Laura glared at her, wiping the tears off her blotchy cheeks.

'Are you mad? An opportunity to realise that I've been a stupid docile cow who has driven her husband into the arms of someone thin and gorgeous with far more to say for herself than his fat wreck of a wife whose only conversation is homework and paintings at the bloody Louvre!'

'Two perfectly good topics, I'd have said. And let's face it, Jean-Laurent isn't exactly overburdened with interesting things to say, unless you're looking for a human wine compendium, that is.'

'Of course he's interesting! Why else would I have married him? I know you've never liked him, but I won't hear you slagging him off – he's my husband and I love him, and it's my fault that I've bored him into adultery!'

'Laura, you're suffering from poor self-esteem. It's very common when people discover they've been cheated on.'

'Stop it! You sound like Asa spouting all that loony psycho rubbish! I'm sure she knows. You should have seen the way she was looking at me this morning – a horrible mixture of pity and triumph, as though she couldn't wait to enrol me in one of her damned classes!'

Their coffee was brought to the table and Laura stirred six cubes of sugar into her large *crème*. She was struck as usual by the pallor of the waiter's skin. She now knew, of course, that Parisians were pale because they spent all their time indoors having sex with people they weren't married to. Silly of her not to have realised earlier.

'The thing is, Laura, you need to decide what you're going to do about it,' continued Lorinda.

'You mean, like cutting off his dick then throwing myself off the top of the Eiffel Tower?'

'That's one option. Or you could go for a more controlled form of revenge.'

Laura's face crumpled once again.

'I don't want revenge, I want him all to myself! I'm going to tell him I'm sorry, I understand why he did it and that I'm going to improve myself – lose weight, get a job, do anything he wants, so he won't be forced to seek his thrills with that . . . bitch-face.'

'Laura, stop making out it's your fault! He's the one who lied to you, remember. And there's no point in grovelling after him – what good will that do? As I see it you have two options. Assuming you're not prepared to leave him, that is.'

Laura shook her head.

'Right, so you want to stick with him, though God knows why. Option one is, you do nothing. You put up and shut up, like a good French wife. He'll never leave you unless you push him into a corner with your weeping and mewling, in which case he'll find you so depressing he'll be forced to go off with her – which is what she's after, of course.'

'Bloody bitch-face,' whispered Laura. 'She's not breaking up my family.'

'That's the spirit. Which brings us to option two. Very proactive, and much more fun for you. You beat him at his own game.'

'What do you mean?'

'He's cheated on you. Now it's your turn to cheat on him.'

Laura sniffed back her tears and took a slow sip of coffee, trying to take in what Lorinda was suggesting.

'Antoine Bouchard,' she said slowly, pronouncing his name carefully. Her admirer. Could he become the instrument of her revenge?

'Exactly!' said Lorinda. 'The timing is absolutely perfect. Bring in Doctor Bouchard on his pure white charger and let the show commence!'

'As a matter of fact,' said Laura, 'I'm supposed to be having lunch with him on Friday at the Ritz.'

'Well there you are, the stage is set!'

'But I can't! It's all very well having a flirtatious lunch with him, but I couldn't possibly let him see me naked! I haven't taken my clothes off in front of anyone for years!'

'Poor Jean-Laurent, no wonder he's had to look elsewhere!'

'I'm not counting him, of course.' Laura fought back the image of Flavia undressing slowly in front of her husband. 'I can't, Lorinda, it's just so embarrassing!'

'But you do find him attractive – you said so.'

'Yes, but . . .'

'And you can no longer have any objection on the grounds of betraying Jean-Laurent?'

'No . . . I suppose not.'

How naïve she had been to worry about an innocent lunch when all the time Jean-Laurent had been having it off with that little tart. How long had he been seeing her? A few weeks, months? Years, even? How could he come home to their bed after that? How dare he humiliate her by telling those lies, by letting her live out alone the fantasy of their perfect family life?

'So there you are,' Lorinda continued. 'It's the perfect way for a woman of character to respond to her husband's infidelity. Fantastically upbeat and ingenious. Turning a problem into an opportunity.'

Laura pulled a face.

'Sounds like you've been reading one of the man formerly known as my husband's business books.'

But why not, she was wondering as grief hardened to anger and she thought of the contempt he had shown her. Why the hell not? She was damned if she would continue to play Laura the loyal, the good old homebody, sure and dependable, keeping the family going, while he flitted off to first-class hotels with his mistress whenever he fancied it. Well, screw you, Jean-Laurent, she thought, I'm going to go for it. I am going to have a love affair with Dr Antoine Bouchard.

'I've always told you Jean-Laurent is boring,' Lorinda continued, 'and now you've found out he's a love rat as well. I tell you, you'll have a much better time with Doctor Bouchard. He can treat you to all the gossip on his famous patients' secret lives . . .'

'I think perhaps you're right,' said Laura. 'Do you know, Lorinda – I think I might be really on for it!'

'Good girl!' said Lorinda. 'Very good girl!'

She picked up the bill and whipped out a ten-euro note. Good God, thought Laura, she must be feeling sorry for me.

'What's more,' said Lorinda, 'I'm going to take you shopping now for a full set of sexy black underwear!'

'I have to say, darling,' said Jean-Laurent, pushing his plate away from him in displeasure, 'that was slightly below your usual standard.'

He and Laura had just finished dinner, which had consisted of a watery cabbage soup unenlivened by fat or flavour in any form.

'It's not supposed to taste nice. It's a diet. Joanna Lumley does it once a year. You eat nothing else for three days and lose half a stone.' She watched him fill his glass. 'Unless you wash it down with a bottle of wine at every sitting, that is.'

She was looking at her husband through new eyes tonight. His smug smile, his slightly spreading stomach, the way he sucked the wine through his teeth, everything about him filled her with disgust.

'Anyway, I daresay you got a good bellyful last night. With François.'

He shifted in his chair.

'Mmm, let's say it was slightly more appetising than this. What's for dessert?'

'More cabbage soup. How was the restaurant?'

Jean-Laurent picked up his newspaper.

'What restaurant?'

'The restaurant you went to with François. How was it?'

'Oh, you know. The usual.'

'The usual?'

'Yes, the usual! What is this, Laura, the Spanish bloody Inquisition? It's always the same with you when you go on a diet, you get so irritable! It really doesn't suit you.'

'So what does suit me? Bouncing around the kitchen like one of the Two Fat Ladies, ladling cream on to everything?'

'Yes, actually.' He saw her face darken as she left the table. 'Hey, come on, I was only joking.'

But Laura had stormed off to the bedroom, slamming the door behind her. She took a sheet of paper from her bedside cabinet on which she had drawn two columns. The left-hand column was entitled 'Reasons why I shouldn't sleep with Antoine Bouchard' and had just one line underneath it which rather lamely read, 'I am married to somebody else.' The right-hand column, under 'Reasons why I should sleep with Antoine Bouchard', extended right down the page, but there was just enough space for her to scratch one more furious line: 'My husband thinks of me as a Fat Lady.'

She read back over the list:

My husband is screwing bitch-face.
My husband is a cheat and a liar.
My husband is a deceitful Frenchman.
Antoine is an attractive man who finds me seductive.
I need to focus my life away from the home (that sounded as if it had been written by Asa).
Lorinda thinks it's a good idea (pathetic, that one).
I need to broaden my sexual experience while I have the chance.
And, finally, the apocalyptic:
Vengeance is Mine.

It rather looks as if I don't have much choice, thought Laura, trying to think of something else to add to the 'Why I shouldn't' column. She heard Jean-Laurent banging around the kitchen, opening and closing the cupboard doors. He shouted down the corridor after her: 'Laura! Where did you put those chocolates that Francine and Dominique brought?'

'Ask Asa!'

A moment's silence, and then, 'I'm just going down to the cellar!'

Laura guided her pen towards the right-hand column to add a final nail to the coffin of her too-long-preserved fidelity. She wrote, 'My *husband* is a wine bore who should be banged up Edgar Allen Poe-style in his own damned *cave.*'

Jean-Laurent sat at his desk and gazed out over the Seine. It reassured him that his office boasted this breathtaking view over the Conciergerie and the Ile de la Cité. Plenty of his contemporaries had to make do with a window over-looking the ventilation shaft. Admittedly the ventilation shaft had been refurbished in the form of a Japanese garden, but a few lines of gravel and an occasional stiff little plant hardly matched up to the sweeping panorama that had been offered to him, Jean-Laurent de Saint Léger, as a token of the esteem in which he was held by the company. He was marked for greatness, it was clear, which is why he had been among the few clients chosen to meet the new global chairman of their advertising agency.

The agency had pulled out all the stops with a lavish menu constructed around truffles, but the Chairman had flexed his American muscles by refusing everything and demanding an undressed green salad and a piece of grilled fish. Jean-Laurent had found him deeply impressive. He spoke in that low whisper that Americans acquire when they get seriously powerful, just like the Godfather. When you had really made it, you left the shouting to the second rank and simply sat there quietly, exuding success.

And his clothes said it all. Whilst his henchmen were dressed up nervously in smart suits, the Godfather had worn a grey T-shirt beneath his jacket. OK, his sixty-year-old neck looked a bit scrawny sticking out of it, but still, it was fabulously fuck-off. Jean-Laurent wondered how he could incorporate T-shirts into his own office uniform. He had a well-built neck, and it should be shown to advantage. He jotted down on his pad: 'Buy T-shirts, white, grey, black'.

The Chairman's wife had been at the lunch, and she, too, had given Jean-Laurent food for thought. Young and thin, of course, but that wasn't enough these days. Anyone could get a bimbo, and there was no kudos attached to marrying the first pretty secretary who came along.

The Chairman's wife had been a senior figure in the organisation before she married him, and now she had added the ultimate sexual partner to her portfolio of achievements. She was so confident, she had been wearing training shoes to the lunch. Training shoes! The impudence of the woman! Jean-Laurent could quite see himself as a whispering magnate in a T-shirt – he was on the right track for that – but if he was honest he couldn't imagine Laura as a suitable consort. Flavia, yes. But Laura? Even in her best earrings and squeezed into one of her new Kenzo suits, she just wouldn't do.

He sighed and thought back to Laura as she had been before the children. Tough and edgy, she had been a hotshot in the advertising agency she worked for in London. He had been flattered that she had agreed to give it all up to follow him to Paris. He had seen her as a feather in his cap. But now she seemed to be standing still while he was on the way up. Flavia seemed far more in tune with his ambitions – she was hungry, like him, and that hunger brought an electric charge to all their secret rendezvous.

He shifted in his chair as he thought back to their last dinner at L'Ambroisie, and the love-making that had followed at her apartment. She had put the jewellery box he had given her next to the bed. That way, she said, she would think of him every time she went to sleep; every night she would dream that he was with her. But afterwards he had suffered his usual pangs of remorse and found himself thinking about his children, already regretting that he hadn't been there to see them before they went to bed. He couldn't imagine how it would be if he only saw them every other weekend.

And Laura, the focus of his home life, a warm, safe place that was his anchor, he couldn't possibly pass it all up in spite of the increasing pressure from Flavia. Every time he saw her now, she would make casual reference to their future together, and it was becoming increasingly difficult to dodge the subject. Let the future take care of itself, he had said, we are together now, why can't we just enjoy it? She had gone all sulky and said that only animals lived for the present and the future didn't take care of itself, it needed to be worked out.

He doodled on the pad in front of him and stared back out over the Seine. Poor me, he thought, poor, wonderful me, everything is going my way, yet I find myself in an intolerable position.

Laura parked the car on the champs de Mars and flipped down the vanity mirror to reapply her lipstick. What I really need now, she thought, with the future of my marriage lying in the balance and adultery beckoning me into its dark abyss, is a wine-tasting soirée *chez* Harry Bullock.

She had completely forgotten about it until that

morning when the invitation had fallen out of her hand-bag. 'Oenophiles one and all!' it read. 'Our next degusta-tory encounter takes us to the south-west of France. Prepare yourselves for some muscular Madirans and some gay Gaillacs! It had become a matter of pride for Harry to provide alliterative descriptions of the wine communes that were presented at his monthly tastings. Last time it had been mellifluous Margaux and spirited Saint Estèphes.

As usual with Harry, though, nothing came free and there was a reminder to bring along thirty euros and a contribution to the 'pot luck supper' that meant their stom-achs were lined so they could safely swallow everything in their glasses instead of wastefully ejecting it into the copper spitoon provided. On Laura's invitation, Harry had scrawled at the bottom, 'I've put you down for three dozen foie gras tartlets and a couple of cheeses.' What infuri-ated Laura was that there was always far too much food, which was subsequently ferreted away in the Bullocks' fridge. No doubt the leftovers kept them going for a week.

Jean-Laurent was already installed at the table when Harry ushered her in. He liked these occasions as they gave him the opportunity to display his superior nose. He was usually the only French person present, which made him feel a cut above, and he liked to think he gave the English teacher a run for his money. 'Of course, you know why French people have all got big hooters?' Harry had guffawed towards the end of the last evening. 'So they can absorb all that bloody vanilla and *sous bois* and apri-cot overtones. As far as the rest of us are concerned, it's all just damned good alcohol!'

Laura nodded to the others round the table. Some she

recognised from the last occasion, like Chester the square-jawed American banker, wearing his off-duty uniform of sky-blue shirt and beige slacks. He was accompanied by his wife Janice who loyally shared her spouse's eagerness for European culture, affecting French elegance with a scarf that did little to enliven her dull skirt and jumper.

As at most gatherings of expats in Paris, there was a small representation from the OECD, fusty academics given a faint sheen of international glamour by their diplomatic car number plates. Laura remembered one of them from last time. Her name was Josephine, a blue-stocking psychologist with a haircut from hell who apparently specialised in Deprivation. 'Not tonight, though, Josephine,' Laura had joked, watching her face flush behind her specs as she filled her glass from a fifteen-year-old bottle of something very expensive.

Harry's wife Susie came out of the kitchen with a trayful of thimble-sized dollops of mashed potato, each one crowned with an erect mini-banger, Dennis the Menace-style. Susie acknowledged the appreciative murmurs about her creativity and relieved Laura of her tartlets and cheese. 'Oh, good girl, Ossau-Iraty, perfect for the region. I'll just cut it up.' She disappeared into the kitchen and returned with a considerably reduced quantity of the cheese, cut into small pieces on sticks and spread thinly around the plate. Laura made a mental note to sneak a look in the fridge later to see if she could find the rest of it.

'Shall we begin?'

The teacher hung his tweed jacket on the back of his chair and launched into the historical background of the wines of south-west France. Laura retreated into her own thoughts, swerving her gaze occasionally to avoid eye contact with the American Banker sitting opposite her, who nodded assertively every so often to show he was following the oenologist's thrust.

'Can I ask a stupid question?' asked the American Banker's wife at one point.

'Hey!' said her husband, running a patronising arm around the back of her chair, 'there are no stupid questions.' Everyone nodded in agreement and looked so supportively at the banker's wife that she became covered with confusion and couldn't remember what her question was, so the oenologist continued uninterrupted.

He produced the first bottle, which was dressed in a chainmail sheath to conceal its label from cheats, and passed it solemnly around the table. Everyone had to write down what it tasted of.

'Janice,' said the teacher, once everyone had finished making their notes, 'would you like to lead the commentary?'

'Oh no, I'm not working tonight!' she twittered. 'Ask Chester!'

The teacher turned to the American banker.

'Chester?'

Chester looked pleased. He clearly felt it was his kind of wine from the description he gave. Masculine, angular, structural, with plenty of fresh liquorice and tobacco, a long finish. He would hazard a guess that is was an Irouléguy.

Laura was aware of the vibes of irritation coming from Jean-Laurent beside her.

'Very good,' said the teacher. 'What year?'

It was fair enough, thought Laura, being able to identify the regional origin of a particular wine, but how in
God's name were you supposed to know what *year* it came
from?

'1992,' said Chester confidently.

'No, it's much younger,' chipped in Jean-Laurent, '1996,
maybe even 1997.'

The teacher unsheathed the bottle.

'Spot on, Chester. 1992 it is!'

A murmur of admiration ran around the table. Only
Jean-Laurent remained tight-lipped.

'Watch out, Jean-Laurent old boy,' said Harry Bullock.
'You've got a bit of competition there from our Yankee
friend!'

'There's no need to sulk,' said Laura later as she drove
them home, 'just because you were burnt off by an
American stiff.'

'I'm not sulking. But I hate these evenings. It is so arti-
ficial to sit around like that eating those stupid little bits
of sausage and mash, horrible English food, no wonder it
put me off.'

'There were my foie gras tartlets. Though not as many
as there should have been. They really are cheap, those
Bullocks.'

'And just because I didn't get the year of the Irouléguy
right, Harry felt he had to go on about how useless the
French are. How our failing knowledge about our own wine
was only another part of the general decline that also encom-
passes our "shortfall in military grandeur since 1815".'

'He was only joking. Anyway, he borrowed that expression from a French historian. François Furet, I believe.'

'And then that stupid joke about why were Parisian boulevards planted with trees.'

'So the Germans could march in the shade? I thought that was quite funny.'

'Well I didn't. I felt I was the victim of a racist attack in my own country.'

Laura couldn't help feeling rather pleased at her husband's discomfort. There's worse to come for you, she thought to herself, and tomorrow is the day. She felt a cold clamp in the pit of her stomach.

On her second lap around the place Vendôme, Laura paused outside the Boucheron window and tried to calm herself by concentrating on her breathing. She gazed at a diamond-encrusted watch in the shape of a terrapin, on sale for thirty-five thousand pounds. Thirty-five thousand pounds! And it was horrible, a nasty shiny bauble, real magpie's nest material.

Who bought this stuff, she wondered. Nouveau-riche Russians, perhaps, the ones who dressed like prostitutes, clipping around the city in their high heels and heavy make-up, their post-Perestroika purses stuffed with crisp new banknotes. She glanced at her watch. Five to one. Just a couple more minutes of window shopping and she wouldn't be too shamefully early for her date with destiny.

She was glad she had decided against the red dress — that would have been just too corny. Far better in her safe black, in mourning for her life of virtue. She had run her bath in a spirit of solemn self-sacrifice that morning, stepping into the foaming water as if to baptise herself into her new life as an adulteress. A born-again cheat, that was her. When lovely woman stoops to folly, she had murmured as she ran her fingers first over her armpits to check for stubble and then over her Caesarean scar.

It had been a long while since she had offered the imperfections of her body up for fresh scrutiny. The last time had been for Jean-Laurent and there had been a lot less to apologise about in those days. Beneath the black dress she was wearing the expensive new *parure* that Lorinda had helped her to choose. Forty pounds for a pair of knickers! It was scandalous, but she couldn't risk humiliation at the final hurdle, and she didn't want Antoine's ardour to be dampened at the sight of her greying sports bra and fraying briefs.

She crossed the square and tried to look nonchalant as she headed towards the doors of the Ritz. She wished she had arrived by car instead of metro, but she had been worried about parking, not realising that one of the flunkies hanging around the entrance was there for the sole purpose of relieving you of your limo. But that would have presented the dilemma of how and when to tip him, and she would have embarrassed herself by handing over too much and then worrying about him getting biscuit crumbs and bits of old tissue stuck to his smart uniform. A lived-in Renault Espace was not the ideal carriage to convey an international Woman of Mystery to her dangerous liaison.

She smiled nervously at the doorman and headed down the long gilded corridor, where members of staff graciously acknowledged her at every five paces. There was something repugnant, she thought, about people being paid to be nice to you. No wonder the rich became paranoid and suspicious about the motives of everyone who gave them the time of day.

Antoine was already at the table. While Laura felt gauche and out of place in this archaically sumptuous dining room, he looked perfectly at ease. Expensive and elegant. If a man's appeal always depended on how he fitted his environment, then this was the ideal showcase for Dr Bouchard. He wouldn't look so good on a desert island, she thought, suddenly struck by the ludicrous image of him as Tarzan stripped to a loincloth, his soft hands ill adapted to fighting beasts and constructing a rude shelter. But here in the epicentre of old European luxury, he looked exactly like what she wanted.

He kissed her lightly on both cheeks and ordered her a glass of champagne. She sat back, relaxed in the knowledge that she could be guided by him through the minefield of the menu without risk of a long discussion with the *sommelier* essential to any outing to a grand restaurant with Jean-Laurent, who usually enjoyed throwing his weight around by sending a bottle back once he had tasted it.

'You look different today,' said Antoine. 'More assured.'

'Do I?' she replied. 'I don't feel it. To have lunch with you once could be overlooked, but twice in a week is a bit compromising, isn't it?'

'Eight days,' he said, stroking the stem of his champagne glass.

'Sorry?'

'Eight days since I saw you, not one week. Eight days during which I have thought about you every single moment. Have you been thinking about me?' He leaned forward, his dark eyes searching hers for reassurance of a reciprocal passion.

It was a far cry from the light and civilised tone of their last meeting.

'Yes. Yes, I have. Of course I have . . .'

'Good. That is all I ask. That you should keep me in your thoughts, your most secret thoughts.'

Was that all he asked? Was their affair to remain on a strictly thought only basis? She had better put her cards on the table right now – he might have been misled by her previous coyness.

'As a matter of fact,' she said quickly, 'I think you should know that I have reached a decision. That is to say, I accept your proposition. You know what you said at the dinner party about taking opportunities for happiness? Before it's too late? The fact is I no longer have any objections to deceiving my husband, since he turns out to be a grubby cheat and a liar who has been screwing a . . . colleague . . . behind . . . my back.'

Her voice grew tight and she felt tears rising. Damn, this wasn't how she had planned it. She had come here to get away from all that pain.

Antoine was looking concerned. He raised his hand and stroked her cheek. His touch was warm and soft, a doctor's healing touch.

'Don't judge him, Laura,' he said gently. 'You don't know how things are for him. He didn't mean to hurt you, and if you hadn't found out you would never have been harmed by his little affair. He is a Frenchman, as I am, and we believe in the creation and enhancement of pleasure. And so do you, clearly, else why would you have come here today and told me what you just have?'

How comforting he was: he could just dismiss the cause of her suffering so lightly, whilst reminding her that she was about to do the same herself. He was right, of course.

He continued in that lovely low voice, stroking her cheek.

'Let me be clear, Laura. I am certainly not interested in being party to any form of revenge. Your husband is your business; it does not concern me at all. All that concerns me is the potential for the most elevated form of human happiness that we can share in the hours that we have together.'

Doctor Love, I love you, thought Laura, sipping gratefully at the glass of champagne that a waiter had just brought to the table. Everything was going to be all right. She would put Jean-Laurent out of her mind and concentrate only on this, her new venture, her married woman's love affair, creating a cocoon of joy away from the turmoil and confusion of the outside world.

'I'll drink to that,' she said boldly.

Antoine took his hand from her face and raised his glass, and Laura noticed his perfectly manicured nails resting lightly on the stem.

'Let us drink a toast to love, as it was perceived by Voltaire,' he smiled. 'He defined it as the stuff of nature, embroidered by the imagination.'

'How very concise of him,' replied Laura. She would not be the passive victim, the betrayed wife. She would be the active protagonist of a wonderful love affair, she would be healed by her infidelity. And it was so poetic to slip into adultery under the auspices of a venerable French

philosopher. It made her feel almost as self-righteous as
her cultural tours of the Louvre.

'I also rather like Chamfort's definitions of love,'
Antoine continued, carefully steering the conversation
away from husbands and heartache. That really wasn't
what he had in mind; it was so boring to ruin a tender
moment with tears and recriminations. 'Rather more cyni-
cally, Chamfort said it was nothing more than the
exchanging of two fantasies and the contact of two epider-
mises. But to my mind, those can be two very powerful
forces.'

'Hitting skin,' said Laura.

'I beg your pardon?'

'Hitting skin. That's how American teenagers describe
having sex, apparently.'

He looked affronted.

'That suggests the crudeness of raw youth. Believe me,
my dear, I am utterly incapable of any such brutality. And
a skin as soft as yours can only deserve the most attentive of caresses.'

To reinforce the point, he laid his hand lightly on her
shoulder and ran his forefinger along the hairline at the
back of her neck.

'Now,' he said, 'shall we order? I rather thought I might
have the lobster.'

As a practised seducer, Antoine made a point of letting
Laura know early in the lunch that he had reserved a
room upstairs. It was better to have that knowledge
simmering below the surface so there was no awkward-
ness or sudden lunging over coffee and petits fours.
Instead they just left the table and went up to their room

as though it were the most natural thing in the world.

Disarmed by the talk of poetry, and wholehearted in her commitment to adultery, Laura soon forgot her reservations about exposing her body to a stranger. Their bodies were almost irrelevant – it was the fantasy that drove them, that locked them in excitement as the delicious intimacy deepened between them. Afterwards, Laura stretched out luxuriously in the bed, feeling the cool Egyptian cotton of the pillow beneath her fingers as Antoine slowly dressed before her.

'I love hotels,' she said. 'I love these crisp sheets and having fifteen fluffy towels in the bathroom. It's so decadent.'

Antoine slipped on his Rolex and smiled at her.

'I am glad the accommodation is to your liking. But I hope you also appreciated the entertainment.'

'I can think of worse ways to fill my time. Beats shopping any day.'

He looked at her in amusement.

'Shopping is the consolation of the loveless. But surely that's not all you do?'

'Of course not. I run the house, the children, this and that, you know. Barely a moment to call my own – that's the myth we non-working women like to promote. But I am more than happy to find you a regular window in my crowded diary. Unless you've lost interest in me, now you've had me. Isn't that what happens in these cases? I'm sorry, I'm a bit out of my territory here.'

Antoine slipped into his rather too pointy shoes. It was funny, thought Laura, how otherwise impeccably dressed French men always fell down on their shoes, which were too insubstantial and made them look like Italian car sales-men.

He sat down beside her on the bed and ran his fingers down her spine.

'First of all, I have no interest in one-night stands, or even one-afternoon stands. Secondly, you are far too desir-able not to become my mistress. I have every intention of meeting you as often as we can both arrange it. I can see that we have many hours of pleasure ahead of us, which we must enjoy as regularly as we can.'

He kissed her and stood up to leave.

'Shall we say next Friday? In this room? We can have lunch brought up.'

Laura nodded happily as he slipped out of the room, like a panther leaving his lair. A grey panther, as Jean-Laurent would no doubt categorise him, a lush, mature target for the marketing men. She stepped out of her adul-terous bed and walked into the bathroom, running herself a bath into which she poured the contents of all five miniature bottles provided. She sank into the foaming water.

Lorinda was right, this was a million times better than crumpling into a tearful heap of self-pity as the wronged wife. The boot, she felt, was now well and truly on the other foot. *La botte est sur l'autre pied*, she smirked to herself, and lifted her right foot out of the bubbles to turn on more hot water. Good God, she thought, my toenails are like claws. How on earth did I miss that in my rigor-ous beauty routine? Luckily, Antoine hadn't seemed to notice, and somehow she didn't think it would have mattered if he had.

TEN

The weekend that followed Laura's fall from virtue was not to be spent in the country, a decision that suited both Laura and Jean-Laurent, who were absorbed in their separate preoccupations.

When Jean-Laurent announced after breakfast that he was going into the office, Laura was relieved, not disappointed as she would have been until recent events had turned her life around. She didn't even bother to speculate whether he had a rendezvous with Flavia: frankly, she couldn't care less. She was struck by the fragility of relationships, the complicit bond with her husband had been pared down to a thin thread that either of them could snap at any moment. Was it the end of love when the noise of the cherished one eating his muesli was enough to invoke cold revulsion and the need to leave the room immediately?

Asa, on the other hand, was not pleased to find the family still installed on Saturday morning. She considered that the apartment belonged to her at weekends, and she had planned to spend the day sifting through Laura's wardrobe for something to wear that evening as she had invited a few friends from the group round to watch *Friends* on video and eat popcorn. Devon had even said he might drop in later on.

She sighed as she slumped down on the sofa next to the children, frowning at the noise of the cartoons they were watching and pulling a nail file out of her dressing-gown pocket. Now she would need to ring round and cancel everyone. She stood up and picked up the phone and was just retreating to the privacy of her bedroom when Laura intercepted her.

'Asa, are you in this morning? I thought I might get my hair cut if you don't mind looking after the boys. It looks as though you'll be busy on the phone anyway.'

Asa shrugged with a bad grace.

'And if I'm not back by twelve, you can give them lunch.'

Laura could feel the wave of resentment as she pulled the door shut behind her. Asa had better get used to it, because from now on she was going to do what she was told. No more pussyfooting around. Laura was in charge and that was that.

The rue de Passy was vibrant with the anticipation of pleasure that distinguishes Saturday mornings in Paris. Baskets on wheels – strictly the preserve of old ladies in England – were towed by men and women alike in their manic search for the best possible ingredients for that evening's dinner party. In the covered market, Parisians became almost convivial in their exchanges with stall holders, their usual cold formality relaxed in the knowledge that today they were indulging their particular talent for *l'art de vivre* that set them apart from the rest of humanity.

Laura hurried past, glad that today she didn't have to lay on a show-off dinner where every course would be discussed and analysed. The merits of *cèpes* versus *pieds de moutons* mushrooms would not be a topic around her dining table this evening, thank goodness.

She thought of all that time she had spent preparing elegant dinners for Jean-Laurent's friends – 'friends' was pushing it a bit; 'business acquaintances' would be more accurate – evenings when she had sat back listening to her husband holding forth about where to buy the best smoked salmon, or the influence of Lacan on French psychology or how the Cac 40 was holding up against the Dow-Jones Index; enjoying the novelty of hearing him speak his own language, seeing him in a new light.

When they moved to Paris, he was no longer the foreigner to be smiled at and helped along in conversation – he had turned from listener to shouter, and she had loved to see him in a more dominant role.

But all along he had been deceiving her. While she was spending her afternoons alone, filling meringue nests to create a successful evening for him and his important associates, while she was pushing aside all thoughts of herself, fighting back the niggles of self-doubt to further his career – all that time he had been knocking off that pretty blonde, laughing behind Laura's back, making a mockery of her life's purpose.

Since her discovery of his betrayal, she had said nothing to him. She knew that to broach the subject would open the floodgates of resentment and create a scene she didn't think she was ready to cope with. Instead she had frozen him out, trying to have as little to do with him as possible.

She arrived at La Muette and continued her journey down the avenue Mozart where the other Parisian obsession apart from food, that of Keeping Up Appearances, was equally well catered for. Here were beauty salons and shoe shops interspersed with poodle parlours, *bon chic, bon genre* children's boutiques, and even a lavish mink coat emporium, the French having no truck with the limp-wristed notion that fur was morally unacceptable.

Laura went into one of the hair salons where a row of hard-faced women was being teased and prinked into elegance, as if one last *brushing*, as the French quaintly called a blow-dry, could really haul you back from the brink of ugliness. Someone should tell these women, thought Laura, that you can't make a silk purse out of a sow's ear. And yet wasn't that, after all, the point of elegance – making the most of the raw materials, whatever their quality?

One thing anyone could do was turn into a blonde. It was unusual to find a woman over forty in Paris who wasn't a blonde, and most of the young ones were too. Never mind the Latin genes and angry dark eyebrows; they could be tamed and plucked into submission. Blonde was it for Parisiennes. Laura had always thought that her skin colour wouldn't allow her to take the peroxide route, but she was rethinking a lot of her ideas at the moment, and the decision to change her hair colour came to her in a flash when she noticed a woman sitting by the door. She had the complexion of a Greek olive, dark and wrinkled, yet was carrying a bob of dazzling pale straw.

212 ~~~ *Sarah Long*

This is the most spontaneous thing I've ever done, she thought as she slipped into a geisha-girl gown and smiled into the mirror at the reflection of her coiffeur, who had started brushing her hair as though she were a dog in need of grooming. He looked at her enquiringly. What would Madame like today – the usual two to three centimetres?

'Actually, André, I think I'll have some colour today. I'd like to be blonde. Not old-lady silver-blonde – I want young sex-chick blonde, with dark roots showing through, like Gwyneth Paltrow, please.'

André looked at her with a respect he'd never shown her in the five years of their relationship.

'*Oui, madame, ça serait beaucoup plus joli,*' he nodded enthusiastically, 'but you have always refused to let me colour your hair. What has happened? Have you taken a lover, perhaps?' He laughed to show that the remark was made within the bantering context of customer relations, then pulled out a book of blonde hair samples so she could select her devastating new look.

Jean-Laurent gazed out of the window of Flavia's apartment, watching a line of tourists in anoraks make their way up to the *funiculaire*, the cable car that would transport them up the hill to visit the *Sacré Coeur*. Flavia lived in Montmartre, at the heart of this oddly provincial part of Paris with its steep and narrow cobbled streets and dilapidated houses that showed no interest in undergoing any form of gentrification.

Jean-Laurent liked the artistic ambience, the expectation of bumping into members of haute Bohemia at the corner café. He had wanted to live here when they first moved back to Paris, but Laura had complained that there were no parks or suitable schools for the children, and anyway, there wouldn't have been anywhere to park the Porsche. Montmartre wasn't what you'd call *grand standing*. It was, however, the perfect place to visit your mistress.

Flavia called to him to come through for lunch, which was an Italian salad involving baby artichokes and figs, far more conducive to pleasure than the makeshift sandwiches that were all Jean-Laurent could have expected at home on a Saturday morning. She opened the fridge to take out a bottle of Sancerre, and Jean-Laurent noticed with pleasure the contrast between her sparse provisions – a bottle of champagne, two lemons, a packet of smoked salmon – and the heavy load of Laura's giant fridge, which was always filled to bursting with nuggets and family packs of yoghurt. He sat down amidst the elegant minimalism of Flavia's child-free haven where your eye was never offended by the discordant colours of nasty plastic toys.

'This is a treat,' said Flavia, filling his glass. 'What have I done to deserve a weekend visit?'

'Oh, you know, Laura didn't seem to mind when I said I had some work to do. She seems to have relaxed a bit, thank God. I haven't had the Inquisition bit recently.'

'Good. Maybe she knows about us, and she's preparing herself for the inevitable.'

'No, no, nothing like that,' Jean-Laurent said quickly. 'Nice wine, lots of flint. Aren't you drinking?'

He looked at her empty glass.

'No . . . not today. So you don't think she's got any idea, then?'

214 —w— *Sarah Long*

'No. Look, can we not talk about Laura, please? That's not what I came here for, you know.'

Flavia looked at him provocatively over the table. Jean-Laurent noticed her breasts were gently spilling over her décolleté lace blouse.

'Oh really? So what did you come for then?'

He sipped his wine.

'A free lunch, of course,' he teased. 'And conversation. And anything else that might crop up between friends.'

'Friends? Is that what we are?'

'Special friends, I'd say.'

'How special?'

'I'll show you after lunch. If you've got time.'

'Oh, I've got plenty of time, Jean-Laurent. I've got all the time in the world. Time is usually your problem.'

She picked over her salad and gave him a look that excited him yet at the same time set off a warning bell somewhere in the boring, rational part of his brain. He chose to ignore the dull voice of reason – it was the weekend, after all, and it wouldn't do to ruin the pleasures of the moment with unspecified worries about the future. He had enough of that as it was, and every man deserved to live a little.

He speared a forkful of carpaccio, air-dried almost to transparency.

'You look nice in that blouse. Have you got a new bra, or are your breasts even more voluptuous than in my fondest imaginings?'

'You'll just have to see for yourself.' She adjusted her neckline to offer him an even more advantageous view.

He took a mouthful of salad.

'You know, if these figs weren't quite so succulent, I

would say forget the lunch and go straight to the main course, if you know what I mean. It's just too bad you can't do both at the same time.'

'Who says you can't?'

She stood up and walked over to him and bent down to kiss the top of his head. Her breasts swung against his mouth, still full.

'Now just you carry on eating. Don't worry about me.'

She turned him on his chair to face her and kissed his face, then his chest, unbuttoning his shirt as she went and lowering herself until she was kneeling at his feet. She pulled at the buckle of his belt, releasing him into her power. His hands gripped her hair, and she pulled away to look up at him.

'Go on, finish your salad. Take no notice of me.'

He bit into a baby artichoke and leant back in his chair, closing his eyes against the overwhelming rush of pleasure.

'Oh, Flavia . . .'

'Mmmm?'

'You must invite me for lunch more often.' He took a sip of Sancerre, slipping his hips forward on the seat and arching his back.

Flavia knew better than to talk with her mouth full. But just you remember, Jean-Laurent, she thought to herself, there is no such thing as a free lunch.

'What has happened to you?'

Asa opened the front door and stared aghast at Laura's dazzling blonde bob.

'I've gone native, Asa,' said Laura. 'As you know, Parisian

women are all blonde, and I'm fed up with being the English frump. What do you think?'

Asa shrugged.

'In Finland, everyone is blonde, it is nothing special. Anyway, you can see your dark roots, you can tell it's not natural.'

'That's the whole point. You need to show that you are a blonde from choice. I am in control of my life. I don't have to stick with the colour I was born with.'

'I think it must be the start of your menopause – you really should go to that class Devon's wife is running.'

Pierre-Louis came running out of the sitting room.

'Mummy, I saw a—' He stopped dead in his tracks.

'Charles-Edouard! Look, Mummy's got yellow hair like Madame Bertrand!'

Madame Bertrand was their headmistress, who was well into her fifties.

'Charles-Edouard came out to take a look.

'Oh yes . . . funny!'

'But nice, though, Charles-Edouard?' said Laura. 'Wouldn't you say it looks nice?'

'It looks OK.'

Jean-Laurent seemed to think it looked OK, too, when he returned from Montmartre. He found himself in an inexplicably good mood as he poured a glass of champagne for Laura and himself in anticipation of their married couple's video evening in.

Things really could be a lot worse, he thought. He had been overreacting, worrying too much about problems that didn't exist. He was in fact experiencing the living truth of one of his favourite business-book maxims: 'There are no problems, there are only solutions.' Perceived problem: his wife was rather lacking in the glamour department. Solution: she had suddenly got a sexy new blonde hair cut. Perceived problem: his mistress was getting too serious. Solution: he managed to placate her with a weekend visit, and got a reassuring blow-job. Everything was falling nicely into place, with no particular effort on his part. And now he was going to spend a cosy night in at home with the wife, in front of the video.

'Here you are, blondie,' he called to his wife, and watched her in amusement as she flicked her new hair behind her ears. There was a neat symmetry to having wife and mistress with the same coiffure – less chance of him being embarrassed by the discovery of a blonde hair on his collar. And neither of them natural, as he alone could vouchsafe.

Laura took the proffered glass but returned directly to the bedroom. She could hardly bear to be in the same room as her husband right now, and told Jean-Laurent he could watch what he wanted – she preferred to read her book.

Jean-Laurent failed to interpret this as a snub and noted instead that his wife seemed to have acquired a Parisian sense of dissatisfaction which he found rather sexy. A nervousness, a tension that he put down to her continuing with the cabbage soup diet. Luckily, he felt he could dispense with that. He had a fabulous physique that kept two women – two blonde women – gagging for it, so he felt more than justified in taking a jar of foie gras and a packet of hazelnuts to prepare a luxury TV platter for one.

Asa came into the kitchen, her combat trousers hanging

shapelessly round her hips, while a child-sized T-shirt stopped just short of her belly-button. She clearly needed to have the danger zone exposed to remind her of the terrible price to pay for succumbing to the easy lure of empty calories. She winced at the sight of Jean-Laurent's plate, and virtuously filled a bowl from the casserole of evil-smelling vegetable stew, which she loaded on to a tray together with a two-litre bottle of Evian, and disappeared into her bedroom.

Jean-Laurent was just getting into *Die Hard II* when there was a ring at the front doorbell. He waited to see whether Laura or Asa might answer, but the bedroom doors remained closed, so he put the cassette on pause and got up, mildly irritated, to open the door.

A middle-aged man with a grey ponytail stood in front of him, a guitar in one hand, and a bunch of flowers in the other. He looked rather embarrassed.

'What is this, are you a busker or what?' said Jean-Laurent.

'I am sorry to disturb you,' said the man in an American accent. 'There's clearly been a misunderstanding. I came to see Asa – she invited me. I think she thought you wouldn't be here . . .'

'Well, obviously I am allowed sometimes to spend Saturday night in my own home. Is this what happens when we go away – the au pair organises hippy singa-longs?'

He raised his voice, 'Asa! Someone to see you!'

'I am her sponsor, you see. We occasionally hold these informal evenings . . .'

'Hi, Devon!'

Asa kissed him warmly on the cheek. It was probably

the first time Jean-Laurent had ever seen her smile.

'I tried to reach you to cancel – I told everyone else, but you weren't answering.'

'Everyone else?' Jean-Laurent interjected. 'How many old blokes with guitars do you know, exactly?'

Devon looked wounded.

'I hear your aggression, Mr de Saint Léger, and I appreciate your concern for Asa, but surely she has the right to enjoy the company of caring friends?'

'It's not Asa I'm concerned about, it's me,' said Jean-Laurent. 'I'm trying to watch *Die Hard II*. And I don't like the idea that every time we go away for the weekend, Asa turns the place over to some kind of Bob Dylan revival.'

Laura had emerged from her bedroom. 'Devon, we meet at last. I'm Laura, and you'll be pleased to know I managed to eat three rice cakes with my cabbage soup tonight. And not a trigger-food in sight!'

She laughed to show she was joking, but Devon looked uneasy.

'It's OK, Devon, Laura is following my progress,' said Asa.

'Come in, Devon,' said Laura. 'It's a shame you couldn't bring your wife – I'd love to hear about her book on the menopause. Asa thinks it could be just what I need.'

The three of them moved into the kitchen. Jean-Laurent returned to the salon and switched the video back on, but the evening was ruined as far as he was concerned. Clearly Devon had a libidinous interest in that charmless Scandinavian, though he couldn't see it himself. He supposed you had to take what you could get when you looked like him. How low could you stoop, though, hanging around vulnerable girls young enough to be your daughter? Was this the future of adultery? When he was fifty, would he be reduced to knocking on doors, guitar in hand, to crave favours from the domestic staff of people younger and more successful than himself?

He dismissed the idea, and tried to concentrate on Bruce Willis committing acts of effortless brutality. Bruce Willis must be around fifty, and Jean-Laurent was far more likely to look like him at that age than that sad old caring sharing American has-been.

'You did it! I'm so proud of you, I really didn't think you would!'

Lorinda leaned across the table and helped herself to the remaining oysters on Laura's plate.

'Sure you don't want these?'

'Go ahead.'

'So was it fantastic?'

'Yes, in a word. High quality. You can tell he's older, though. Everything sort of sags.'

'Everything?'

'Don't be arch. I'm referring to the force of gravity on skin that has lost the taut elasticity of youth.'

'Hasn't bothered to take his own medicine then?'

'Oh, I think a few hormones. At least that's what he prescribes for all his patients over the age of forty, so he must do. And he's very keen on trace elements. I imagine he's knocking back a bit of melatonin.'

'You're very knowledgeable.'

'He talked about it over lunch.'

'No surgery though?'

'Only the eyelids, apparently. He got a friend to do it, said it was the only place he showed his age, though I'm not sure I'd agree. But seriously, Lorinda, it was wonderful. And the best thing about it is that it made me feel so good about myself. I always thought I'd feel guilty and sneaky afterwards, but I didn't. I felt great. I still do. I really feel as if I don't care about Jean-Laurent and Flavia – I've freed myself from all that misery.'

She chewed reflectively on a piece of bread. 'I suppose I might feel differently if Jean-Laurent hadn't turned out to be such a pig. If he was still my nice, decent husband, I *would* feel bad. But he's not, so I don't.'

'When's the next date?' asked Lorinda, slipping the final oyster into her mouth.

'Friday. Same place, same time.'

'Lucky you – free lunch at the Ritz. Can I come? What if he doesn't recognise you with your new hair?'

'It's OK, we're meeting in the room.'

'So you'll need to come to the gym with me to limber up, then.'

'No, I've finished with the gym. Too damned narcissistic. I've decided to take a practical view of my future. I'm thinking of going to see a life coach.'

'Laura, you're not! You hate therapists!'

'Life coaches aren't therapists – they don't care about your relationship with your father or whether you were abused as a child. They just try to help you achieve your personal goals.'

'Which are?'

'I don't know, that's why I need a life coach.'

'Marny Simpson had a life coach who told her that as

a housewife she needed to treat her domestic chores and bringing up the children as a small business with its own mission. Is that what you want to hear?'

'I don't know, but I don't have to do what he says, anyway.'

'I don't know why you need a life coach when you've got love in the afternoon lined up with Dr Bouchard. You don't need to pay him, *and* you get a free lunch.'

'And so do you today,' said Laura, calling for the bill. 'I believe it's my turn, isn't it?'

Jean-Laurent didn't know quite what had got into his wife, but whatever it was, he liked it. He might not have been so keen had he realised that what had got into his wife was Dr Bouchard, but being spared this detail he appreciated the new coolness in her attitude. He had noticed this morning that she had left a list of tasks for Asa to do, which was a welcome change from her usual method of suppressing her irritation and not daring to ask her to lift a manicured finger. It was, he thought approvingly, the way a French woman treated her domestics.

Then there was her new hair, that resolute blonde crop that made her look tougher, more self-contained. It seemed to coincide with a greater detachment towards himself. Laura hadn't seemed the slightest bit interested in what time he was coming home tonight, which was just as well as he had promised to take Flavia out to dinner.

But at the same time, he found her apparent indifference towards him made him desire her more strongly than he had for some time. Seeing her zip herself into a new dress this morning, he had been overcome by a sudden impulse to cancel all his appointments and throw her on to the bed for a day of carnal pleasures.

He settled back into the deep plush banquette and sipped his champagne. He was waiting for Flavia in Le Vieux Bistro, just across from Notre Dame. It was reassuringly traditional, perfect for a rainy winter night, with masculine pieces of meat spread across the plate instead of nancy morsels piled up high in a fragile tower, which was what too many restaurants were now committed to serving. Vertical food that collapsed as soon as you took a knife and fork to it. In London, they liked to call it Pacific Rim. They could keep it. It would be a sorry day, thought Jean-Laurent patriotically, when traditional restaurants like this one ripped down their burgundy awnings and gutted their dark insides to replace them with cool open spaces and pretty boy waiters.

The door opened and Flavia came in, shaking the rain from her umbrella and handing it to the maître d' as he took her coat. She looked small and vulnerable, her hair – now the same colour as Laura's – falling in damp tendrils over her shoulders. For reasons he could not identify, Jean-Laurent felt a sense of foreboding as she approached the table. He stood up to kiss her and noticed she seemed a little too grateful to see him.

'How was your day?' he asked heartily.

She shrugged. 'It was OK. How about you?'

'All right. Except that I hate the British. Always giggling among themselves about some joke that nobody else understands.'

'But you are practically British yourself. You speak perfect English.'

'Not like an Englishman. We were in a meeting today with lots of English people talking about focus groups. For some reason, every time a French person spoke they were laughing quietly to themselves; then I found out why. They had agreed before the meeting that they would get the French people to say "focus" as often as possible. With our accent, of course – "Ferr-cus" . . . like "fuck us", you see? And they think that is funny.'

Flavia smiled. 'Well, you can see it could be funny if you were in on the joke. If you had a sense of humour, that is.'

'Flavia, please, nobody could doubt that I have a sense of humour.'

'Everybody believes they have a sense of humour, the same way that everyone thinks they have good taste. But yes, of course, darling, you have a wonderful sense of humour. That is one of the reasons I chose you.'

'Chose me? You make me sound like the prize truffle in a box of chocolates. I thought the point about us was that it just happened, neither of us *chose* it.'

Flavia chose to ignore this remark.

'That and your fabulous body, of course,' she continued, 'not to mention your mind. I really couldn't have done any better.'

She looked at him complacently across the table.

Jean-Laurent suddenly felt claustrophobic.

'I really don't know why I booked this restaurant. You feel so hemmed in somehow in these ridiculous booths. Shall we just have a drink and then move on somewhere else?'

'No, it's adorable here, so cosy. Anyway, you told me

it was one of your favourite restaurants.'

'All right, we'll stay. Champagne?'

'No, I'll have a Perrier.'

'You really are virtuous these days,' said Jean-Laurent petulantly. 'What happened to that wild South American spirit that used to drink me under the table? Come on, let's enjoy ourselves, that's what this is all about, surely?'

'Jean-Laurent, of course that's what you and me are about, enjoying life to the full, in every possible way.'

'Good, so let's get a bottle of champagne in. God, at this rate you'll be telling me you've got a headache next.'

'Never. I promise I'll never have a headache for you.'

Her eyes were shining as she gazed at him.

'It's just . . . Oh, I wasn't going to say anything yet, but I can't help it, it's just so exciting. Jean-Laurent, I'm going to have a baby!'

Jean-Laurent felt his stomach lurch as his life fell gently into ruins around him. He tried to put back the clock; he wasn't in this restaurant, he wasn't having this conversation. Flavia continued to stare at him, locked up in her own happiness, unaware of the devastation she was creating.

'What did you say?' he said weakly.

'I'm going to have a baby. Isn't it wonderful?'

'No! No, Flavia, it's a disaster, it would be a disaster. Thank God you've told me before it's too late.'

She frowned.

'What do you mean, too late. I've just told you, I'm pregnant, I'm going to have a baby!'

She had raised her voice and the couple at the next table turned around to take a look.

'All right, sshh, please keep your voice down. Let's talk about this sensibly.'

His mind was racing, trying to keep hold of the situation.

'Now, Flavia, you have to realise that this would be a terrible mistake. Your career . . .'

'Oh for God's sake, Jean-Laurent! Just because Laura couldn't wait to give up work to become a fat little *hausfrau*, you needn't worry that I'm going to throw away my business the moment a baby comes along!'

'Yes, but you're young, this isn't the right time, you've got years ahead of you for all that!'

'This *is* the right time. All right, so it wasn't planned, but the best things in life arrive when you least expect them. And I've met the man who is right for me – you're the one I want to father my children, so what is the point in waiting until my eggs go off?'

'But what about me? You didn't think you should ask me what *I* want?'

'It's a well-known fact that men always need to be pushed into fatherhood. It is the woman who must decide. I didn't force you to make love to me, by the way.'

Jean-Laurent sank into his seat like a trapped animal.

'But you seem to be forgetting, Flavia, that I already have children. I don't need any more. Dear God, it's the last thing I need.'

'Jean-Laurent, look at the successful men you know – they all have second families. You can't seriously think you are going to stay with Laura? You know you deserve better than that!'

'Shut up about Laura!'

Flavia picked up her serviette and twisted it in her hands. Tears welled up in her eyes.

'I thought you'd be pleased! Shocked, perhaps, but then happy!'

Jean-Laurent looked coldly at her. This was not the Flavia he knew – this weeping, needy woman was worlds apart from the independent, sexy release from the everyday that she had represented for him.

'When did you find out? How many weeks is it?'

She sniffed. 'Five. I only just did the test.'

Good, thought Jean-Laurent. At least that means I have time to pray for an accident. Or to persuade her to think again.

Charles-Edouard and Pierre-Louis were sitting pink and warm from their bath in their pyjamas on the sofa when Jean-Laurent returned from the office the following day. He gathered them up in his arms and squeezed their delicious firm flesh, enjoying the particular sensual pleasure that is reserved for parents of young children.

'Your beard stinks, Papa,' said Pierre-Louis, rubbing his father's stubbly chin.

'I haven't got a beard, sweetheart.'

'Your spikeys, then.'

'Is Mummy here?'

'She's gone to get some flowers. Asa is looking after us because you are going out.'

'Yes, I know.'

'Dad, look!'

Charles-Edouard rummaged in his satchel and brought out an exercise book to show his father.

'Eight and a half out of ten. Philippe only got seven!'

'That's my boy, you beat him!' said Jean-Laurent, thinking how marvellous the French education system was in the way it fostered ruthless competitiveness. Not so good for those who were deemed '*echecs scolaires*', or scholastic failures, but that was hardly likely to affect *his* children.

Laura came in with a bouquet of purple flowers immaculately wrapped in a swirl of crimson paper and a golden bow of curling ribbon. She was wearing a cropped jacket over a pair of close-fitting trousers that showed off a waist a good deal trimmer than Jean-Laurent remembered. He pushed aside a sudden image of Flavia with a belly distended by pregnancy. How could he have got himself into this?

'You look nice,' he said, taking in her new blonde hair that had been brushed back to reveal a pair of gold earrings.

Laura looked at him as though she couldn't remember who he was. How could he appear so unaffected by her new coldness? How dare he patronise her with his little compliments when all the time he was at it with Flavia?

'Let's go, shall we?'

They had been invited to a cocktail party at a friend of Laura's that she had met years ago at the 'Bloom where you are planted' seminar organised by expatriate women for newcomers to Paris. It was something she had attended in a panic attack of loneliness when she had first arrived in France, and she was still embarrassed by the name, suggesting as it did that women were fragile hothouse plants dug out of friendly soil by cruel careerist husbands and then transplanted into alien territory.

What else were they supposed to do if not bloom? Wither and die like feeble seedlings? Presumably this fate awaited those who failed to sign up for any of the courses offered by the zealous band of wives.

Laura had become friendly with one woman there, an American called Sonia who had been distraught, on learning to speak French, to find that her husband was not the glamorous intellectual she had believed him to be. 'I used to watch him talking with his brothers and thought they were talking about Descartes,' she wailed. 'Now I realise it's only rugby and football. My husband is a bore and I've only just found out!'

Laura and Jean-Laurent drove in silence to the party. Laura tried to think about Antoine, about Friday when she would be alone with him, when she could leave this mess behind and join him in his wonderfully simple take on love and pleasure. But instead her thoughts were clouded by resentment at her husband sitting beside her, his fine, muscular hands gripping the wheel, his strong, beautiful thighs loosely encased in fine grey wool.

She, that woman, Flavia, must have sat in this very seat watching her lover drive them away to a place of stolen happiness, an intimate restaurant, perhaps, or a bar where he could show her off, or, just back to her place for the evening. Maybe even a whole night if he had managed to come up with some excuse. Easy enough – Laura was never suspicious, it never crossed her mind. It didn't when you were in a trusting relationship. Flavia might have admired his profile as she glanced across to watch him concentrating, looking up at the lights, waiting for them to change. She might have reached across to lay a small hand on Laura's husband's thigh, the thigh of the man who had lied to Laura and loved another.

Jean-Laurent stared through the windscreen and tried to see a path ahead. Only a week ago, it had all been so simple. He had his wife and his family, his job and his mistress, all hanging together as a cohesive unity formed of separate parts. He had even been congratulating himself on how well it was working out, how he had achieved the perfect balance, handling each element with his own uniquely insightful managerial skills.

And now Flavia had stepped right out of line. It was clearly a trap, but if she thought she could catch him that way, then she was underestimating the formidable force that was Jean-Laurent de Saint Léger, MBA. She had made a bad error of judgement, and it remained to be seen how the issue would be resolved.

They arrived at the party and Sonia's husband opened the door. Laura was intrigued to meet him after hearing Sonia complain about him for the last five years. He didn't look *that* boring, she thought, but then Sonia had a tendency to be disappointed by life, and few disappointments can match up to the realisation that you have married someone who is less than you had hoped.

Sonia came forward to greet them wearing an exotic silk combination that blended well with the harem-style décor that she had incongruously imposed on their modern high-rise apartment overlooking the Seine. They lived in the area close to the Hotel Nikko in the fifteenth arrondissement, favoured by Japanese because it was the one part of Paris with nondescript tower blocks to remind them of Tokyo.

Laura recognised a couple of women from the school. They were both members of an organisation called AAWE, which stood for the Association of American Wives of Europeans. This had always sounded rather sinister to Laura, with its overtones of racist exclusion. What if you were an Asian or even a European wife of a European, or not even a wife at all – would you be allowed to join? She had never bothered to ask. As far as she could make out, they spent most of their time making giant patchwork quilts and swapping packets of instant cookie mix.

One of the women made a beeline for her and started to solicit her opinion on the security arrangements for an upcoming school trip to the country. With precise French logic this was known as a *classe rousse* since it took place in autumn when the leaves were red. When they went in spring, it was called a *classe verte*.

'I really think we should insist on having a night monitor,' said the anxious mother. 'Someone to patrol the dormitories. After all, you never know who might break in.'

'Prowling paedophiles, you mean?' said Laura. 'The problem is, how do you know your night monitor won't turn out to be the worst paedophile of all? All those angelic sleeping children to choose from – it could push anyone with the slightest tendency over the edge.'

'Oh my God, you're so right, I hadn't thought of that. In that case I think the only thing we can do is organise a rota of mothers. We'll take it in turns to go down and spend the night.'

'Count me out,' said Laura. 'I'm not ruining a week off from my son by having to drive all that way for a sleepless night.'

The woman looked bewildered.

'You British,' she said. 'I just don't get it. I suppose it's that boarding-school system you have.'

'That's it,' said Laura cheerfully. 'We've all been buggered senseless by the age of ten, so we find it perfectly normal. Oh look, there's a man in a white coat with a tray of champagne. Do excuse me.'

Jean-Laurent followed her admiringly towards the refreshments.

'Laura, I am so happy I didn't marry an American woman. Please remember that.'

But Laura was not in the mood for his compliments. She was sick of this charade, of the pretence that everything was just fine, that he could smooth-talk his way out of his despicable behaviour.

'Why's that then?' she retorted. 'Is it because they have high moral standards and won't stand for any hanky-panky on the side?'

Jean-Laurent decided to play it light.

'Hanky-panky – I love that word.'

'It's not just the word you love, though, is it Jean-Laurent?'

Her hurt had hardened into pure anger. It was odd how she could dismiss her own adultery so easily and stand there, a pillar of righteous indignation. She was the wronged party, and he was a low-down cheat and home-wrecker who had forced her to retaliate.

Jean-Laurent saw the fury in her face and realised that he had been found out. She knew. It was time for him to fall on his knees and beg for forgiveness and she would understand and they would make a fresh start. If only it were that simple. If only it *were* just a bit of hanky-panky he knew he could make it all right – there would be tears and recriminations, but they would get through it. A week ago it would have been so easy, but now Flavia's pregnancy had changed everything. It was all getting horribly out of control.

A cocktail party, however, was not the ideal forum for the bitter slanging match that promised to ensue. Mercifully, they were interrupted by a tap on Laura's shoulder. She turned round to see her friend Emma, a statuesque English beauty, accompanied by her Napoleonic husband who barely came up to her breasts but who held himself as though he were the ruler of the universe.

'Laura, meet Pierre-Marie. I'm just trying to persuade him that we really don't need to live in an enormously wide boulevard to maintain our status. I have seen a lovely house for sale but it's in a narrow one-way street and he won't consider it.'

Laura and Jean-Laurent shook hands with the minuscule husband.

'You will understand,' he said with a smile, 'that when you live in a grand apartment in a *pierre de taille* building on avenue Bosquet, you are not in a hurry to rush off to an undistinguished dark alley where the buildings are nothing but *crépi*.'

'Excuse my ignorance,' said Laura, relieved to slip back into small talk, 'but what is *pierre de taille* and what is *crépi*?'

This was a mistake, and she realised too late that she had involuntarily launched him on a monologue that looked set to last all evening in that peculiarly French way. Whereas the English would knock you off the subject within minutes, the French would all join in, taking turns to throw in their own half-hour contribution to the dissertation. No doubt it came from the higher education system where philosophy majors were expected to spend seven hours writing about one tiny point. It seemed that *pierre de taille* referred to noble blocks of stone whereas *crépi* was a plebeian rough plaster used to cover up inferior masonry.

'And so I have explained to Emma that *crépi* is out of the question,' said Pierre-Marie. 'Avenue Bosquet is an address, rue Erlanger is not an address. People from London do not understand, as London is a very ugly city because there is so little noble stone. *Crépi* everywhere, which is why I could never live there.'

'Right, that's sorted that out, then,' said Emma.

Laura decided to go for a diversionary tactic.

'Your name is rather intriguing, Pierre-Marie. Terribly transsexual. Did you ever find it confusing during your formative years?'

Pierre-Marie drew himself up to his full diminutive height.

'Excuse me, madame, but you speak with the ignorance of a foreigner. Pierre-Marie is an unquestionably masculine name, just as Marie-Pierre is an entirely feminine one.'

'Oh yes, of course, Marie-Pierre! I'm afraid that had you gone to English school, you would definitely have been known as Marie-Pierre – you know how we can't resist nicknames, especially anything that might imply sexual ambivalence.'

Pierre-Marie judged this remark to be unworthy of a reply and turned to Jean-Laurent, reverting seamlessly to his theme.

'But for real, wonderful *pierre de taille*, you must go to Bordeaux,' he enthused. 'Building after building of beautiful stone. You must know it, Jean Laurent – it is a jewel in our country's *patrimoine*.'

Laura and Emma slipped away, leaving the men to continue the eulogy of aristocratic French architecture.

'God, they go on, don't they?' said Emma. 'Don't you wonder why you married a Frenchman? But at least yours is tall, doesn't have so much to prove.'

'I don't know, you should hear him on wine.'

'Oh well, that's them gone for the evening, then. I like your hair, by the way. Does the new look mean you've taken a lover?'

Laura was spared the need to reply by the arrival of Sonia, who came rustling up in her silks, waving a book.

'Girls, look, here is something you must read.'

The book was entitled *Women Who Do Too Much*. The author was an American woman who evidently did too little, since she had found the time to write it.

'It's no wonder we are always exhausted,' said Sonia. 'It's all right for men just going off to work and leaving us to cope with everything. Really, you must read it – you realise we are just wearing ourselves out? It's scandalous.'

'But Sonia, we really don't do anything, I don't know what you mean,' said Emma. 'None of us does our own housework and the children are at school all day.'

Sonia looked put out.

'Well I don't know whose side you're on. We have all the worry, the organisation . . .'

'Oh come on, Sonia!' said Laura. 'You know that's a load of bollocks. Let's be honest, now, what exactly are these onerous responsibilities? Getting the kids to school and meeting them, and that's about all isn't it? Oh, and fixing up the odd play date. It's damned cushy compared with the lives of women who work.'

'You mean work outside the home,' Sonia corrected her.

'Yes, OK, work outside the home. Which we don't choose to do, so we should count ourselves lucky.'

'But it's the emotional stress, Laura, surely you must feel that? The burden you carry for the wellbeing of the entire family?'

'That's a self-inflicted anxiety. Our kids are privileged little things – they want for nothing, so we beat ourselves up trying to dream up problems for them. I tell you, if we went out to work we wouldn't have the time to feel hard done by.'

As she spoke, Laura realised with a sudden flash of enlightenment that she had had enough of being on the other side. She didn't want to spend her life worrying about her husband, fixating on the au pair, doing nice dinners and building her life around her children's social engagements. She wanted to leave this coterie of spoilt wives with not enough to think about.

'Well, I can see I'm wasting my time here,' said Sonia. 'You British, you're so damned long-suffering.'

She laughed to show she meant no malice, then headed off to the other side of the room in search of women more prepared to see themselves as victims.

Emma raised an eyebrow. 'Of course, I didn't tell her the very best thing about being free in the day. Which is the chance of a bit of extra-marital.'

Laura choked on her champagne.

'I hope you haven't told Pierre-Marie.'

'Oh, he knows. He's got someone as well. That's one thing about the French – they're quite sensible about marriage. No point in frightening the horses just because of a little dalliance here and there.'

Laura twirled her glass non-commitally.

'I'm right, aren't I?' said Emma, 'You have got someone?'

'No comment,' said Laura.

The atmosphere was tense as Laura and Jean-Laurent drove home from the party. Neither of them alluded to Laura's half-formed accusation, and she concentrated on her driving, staring coldly ahead as Jean-Laurent reached across for her knee.

'Laura,' he began, 'there is something I need to tell you.'

'Not now, please. Can't you see I'm driving.'

He cowed back in his seat, staring miserably out of the window.

'The thing is, I seem to have got myself into a rather awful situation.'

'That's really not my problem.'

'How can it not be your problem? We are married, you are my wife, my problem is your problem, isn't it? I love you, Laura!'

'Jean-Laurent, I don't want to hear about it. Please, let's just get home, shall we? It's too late to be having this conversation.'

Before going to bed, Laura checked on her sleeping sons, tucking them up under their duvets. A light showed under Asa's door, and the perfume of aromatic oils over-laid with the lingering smell of fried popcorn suggested that she had spent the evening indulging her twin passions for bingeing and beauty treatments.

Laura checked the lavatory and saw the telltale flecks underneath the seat. Asa was clearly not making quite the progress she claimed with the Overeaters Anonymous programme.

She climbed into bed, where Jean-Laurent was already curled up on his side, and picked up her new bedtime reading. It was called *Be Your Own Life Coach*. In the end she had thought it easier to buy the book than go to the bother of seeing someone. But there was nothing in it that she didn't already know – just the usual anodyne brew of common sense dressed up in new clothes.

She dropped the book and turned her mind to her approaching rendezvous with Antoine. For her, it was pure pleasure, a secret world that presented an escape from what had so rapidly become the tangled mess of her home life. She closed her eyes serenely and drifted off to sleep.

Jean-Laurent, for his part, stared wakefully into the darkness. He had to break with Flavia, that was clear. Baby or no baby, there was no way forward for them now.

ELEVEN

Laura lay beside Antoine in the luxuriously appointed bed at the Ritz and stroked his upper arm. His skin was slack, the muscles underneath soft and unused.

'Isn't it strange,' she murmured, 'that my husband has what can only be described as a *corps magnifique*, and yet I so much prefer yours.'

'It's normal,' he replied. 'We are at the discovery stage. I too have a beautiful wife, but to me your stretch marks and little pot belly are more delicious at this moment than her perfect figure.'

'Pot belly! That's rather insulting. You'll be sending me off for liposuction soon.'

'Never. I love you because you are happy with your body. All the women who come to see me are miserable because they see the difference between what they are and what they think they should be.'

'And afterwards, are they happy?'

He shrugged. 'For a few months, maybe, then they will come back for something else.' He ran his hand, white and manicured, over her soft belly. 'But you do not care. For me, that is freedom.'

'And for me, this is freedom. Away from all the rest of the stuff, my cheating husband – you know he is trying to confess to me now, but I won't let him.'

'You are right. Marriages need secrets. And the joy of marriage is the opportunity it presents for deception. If we were not married, this tryst would lose all its charm. More champagne?'

He stepped out of bed towards the damask-draped trolley bearing the remains of their lunch and lifted the bottle out of its silver bucket. Laura contemplated his naked body: the imperfect body of a man beyond his prime. He advanced towards the bed with the bottle and topped up the glass standing on her bedside table.

'You know that in this vale of tears we must seize the moments of pleasure that are offered to us.'

Laura sat up happily, prudishly pulling the sheet up to conceal her breasts.

'You're quite a philosopher for a medical man,' she laughed. 'So how can we multiply our opportunities for happiness? Once a week seems rather miserly.'

'I agree. I wonder, have you ever been to Thailand?'

'Thailand! Well, yes – as a matter of fact I went there years ago with Jean-Laurent. We went trekking near Chang Mai and rode on an elephant. We slept nine to a hut. I was so exhausted I thought I was going to die.'

'That is not what I had in mind. I go once a month to perform operations in a clinic in Bangkok. I always stay at the Sukhothai Hotel. I think you would like it.'

Laura remembered she had seen the Sukhothai featured

in a recent copy of *Elle Décoration* – bathrooms the size of a studio apartment, all teak and slate with doors leading off to an obscene number of cubicles and giant his-and-hers washbasins.

'You surely can't expect me to come with you! I'd love to, of course – in fact I can't think of anything nicer – but I couldn't possibly get away with it. What on earth would I say to Jean-Laurent?'

'You'll think of something. There is no limit to a woman's ingenuity, especially a cunning blonde like you.' He flicked her hair playfully. 'I thought we could spend two nights in Bangkok and then fly to Phuket for a weekend at Amanpuri.'

Laura's head was spinning. Amanpuri, the ultimate fuck-off resort. That flat black swimming pool that seemed to pour straight into the deep turquoise sea – she had seen that, too, in one of the aspirational magazines she liked to indulge in. She could hide away there with her lover while Jean-Laurent remained in wintry grey Paris wrestling with his conscience. It would give her the distance she needed from him; she would see everything more clearly. And Antoine was such a darling. He wanted nothing from her except the pleasure – sensual and intellectual – of her company. A mini-break with no strings attached. How perfect.

'I really don't know, Antoine,' she said. 'It would require a lot of planning, and a lot of lying which I can't bring myself to think about. Though actually, there is one thing that might work . . .'

Her mind was busily scheming. She was thinking of that hen party she was supposed to go to in Barcelona.

Her old school friend Marion had finally got engaged and was celebrating by inviting her best women friends to a weekend of feckless celebration in the city she now called home. Laura had already mentioned it to Jean-Laurent, warned him that he might be left in sole charge of the boys for a couple of days.

Antoine smiled down at her.

'Of course. You just let me know when you are ready. I am at your service, as you know.'

He replaced the champagne bottle and slid under the sheet to join her.

While Laura was dreaming of a luxurious Asian escapade with her lover, Jean-Laurent was having an altogether more pedestrian lunch with his mistress.

She had turned up unannounced at his office, and he had taken her, with bad grace, to the Panorama café down the road on the *quai*. 'Panorama' referred to the view of the medieval strongholds of the Ile de la Cité, but unfortunately this was obscured by five lanes of thunderous traffic. Flavia was aware of the slight. This was not a place Jean-Laurent would have dreamt of taking her to before she had made the greatest declaration of love that a woman can make to a man; before she had told him that she was carrying his child.

Of all her many potential impregnators – and God knows she could have taken her pick: they had always been queuing up for gorgeous, clever, cosmopolitan Flavia, South American but above all a citizen of the world, at home all over the globe – of all those men she could have had, she had chosen Jean-Laurent, who was now insulting her by bringing her to a two-a-penny café with grimy city-polluted windows.

She pushed her *salade Niçoise* around her plate while Jean-Laurent mournfully shovelled in the rabbit with mustard, the *plat du jour*, good value at ten euros. He could have been eating for nothing in the Directors' Dining Room had Flavia not arrived, pale and vindictive, and demanded he take her somewhere. He looked at her eyes, puffy and unmade-up, her hair unwashed beneath her woolly hat.

'Well you're not exactly dressed for the Tour d'Argent, are you?' he said, defensively.

'I'm so tired. Tired, and worried, and very disappointed in you.'

Jean-Laurent looked away and caught sight of his reflection in the mirror. He was wearing the grey T-shirt today beneath his suit jacket. It was a look that sat well on him. He might abandon conventional shirts completely, except for formal meetings.

'Look at it from my point of view, Flavia. You suddenly move the goalposts, you say nothing to me, and wham-bam here I am, the innocent victim suddenly being cast as the heartless villain.'

'Please don't talk about moving the goalposts – this isn't a game of football. Why do you use all those dreadful English sporting metaphors?'

'All right, you rewrote the rules . . .'

'What rules? What are you talking about? This isn't a game, this is my life, *our* life!'

'No, Flavia, it's not our life, it is *your* life, it has nothing to do with me. I wasn't consulted. Nothing was agreed between us. You used me like a sperm bank and now you want me to leave my family and trot after you like a tame dog, but I won't do it! I can't leave Laura and the boys.'

'A sperm bank! Is that all you are! Is that all it was between us! How can you say that? Don't you love me?'

'Look, we had a great time, it was . . . great, all right? But that was then and this is now and everything is different.'

He slumped gloomily into his seat. Flavia took his hand.

'You're not thinking straight, you just need time to get used to it, that's all. You know as I do that there is no pleasure without responsibility. You already have responsibilities, of course – you will continue to be a good father to your boys – but I know that you will also be a wonderful father to our child . . .'

'Don't say that! We don't have a child! You are not my wife!'

She withdrew her hand crossly.

'No, I'm not your wife, I'm not a sad sack of potatoes who sponges off her husband while dreaming of the career I left behind . . .'

'Don't talk about Laura like that!'

'Who said I was talking about Laura? But obviously that's how you see her. Hardly a suitable consort for someone as ambitious as you are. And she's too old for you now.'

The young and gorgeous Flavia had played her trump card.

Damned if I do damned if I don't, thought Jean-Laurent. If he stayed with Laura, he would be hounded by Flavia and forced to acknowledge his paternity of a child who would be a lifelong reminder of his marriage-wrecking *folie à deux*. If he left Laura—. But that was unthinkable. He had never seriously considered leaving her for Flavia. The game had turned into reality and he no longer wanted to play.

Why couldn't it be like in the old days, when a pregnant mistress would obligingly melt out of sight, leaving the sire with no burden beyond the occasional wistful thought for the secret child he never knew. That was before DNA testing, which spelt the end to all freedom.

What about poor old Yves Montand, dug out of his grave to see whether or not he was the father of some money-grabbing little bitch? He wasn't, as it turned out, but Jean-Laurent had no hope of a similar exoneration. Unless, of course, Flavia had been seeing someone else? But that was out of the question – she knew when she was already getting the best. Miserably he called for the bill and they left the Panorama café, the last poisoned gasp of their love drifting off into the traffic fumes of the *quai de la mégisserie*.

Laura cleared the breakfast things and opened a bottle of cheap red wine to marinade the *rosbif* for supper. Like all responsible mothers, she had avoided beef for a year or so, but now quite honestly she was bored to death with the alternatives, and what *could* you eat these days that wouldn't kill you? She salved her conscience by jumping on the bourgeois bandwagon and paying twice as much for organic meat.

The neurosis about tainted foodstuffs had reached

epidemic proportions – the luxury of a society with not enough to worry about. Not like the good old days, when every mealtime was a celebration that there was enough to eat, that another day had passed and here everyone was, happy and alive. Why couldn't people just be grateful and get on with it?

Her enthusiasm for cooking had entirely evaporated. It was hard to imagine that just a few weeks ago the act of preparing food for her family could have brought her such pleasure. Poor, sad woman, whose days had revolved around waiting for her loved ones to return from their active lives to the nest she so willingly created.

Now she was still playing the waiting game, but of a new variety. She waited for Antoine's phone calls, the summons to her new, secret life, where children had no place and each moment was savoured like the *amuse-gueules* that invariably accompanied their bottle of champagne. They met every Friday, and whenever else Antoine could fit her in between patients. Every time her mobile vibrated in her pocket, her stomach churned in excitement, hoping it would be him.

That was the short-term waiting. There was also the medium-term waiting – the promised trip to Thailand which might happen soon if she felt able to lie about that weekend in Barcelona. This required a level of deception that she wasn't yet up to. It would mean getting a step ahead of Jean-Laurent, and she preferred to consider herself still the injured party; her transgression was less than his – he started it. Not that he seemed to be reaping much happiness from his infidelity. He looked preoccupied much of the time and she sensed that he was dying to confess and seek forgiveness. But she rebuffed him, ignoring the searching looks, the hand reaching for her under the bedcovers. Let him suffer. He had brought it on himself.

She finished the marinade and went through to the study and sat at the computer. 'Amanpuri, Phuket's luxury resort' floated up before her. She felt as if she had already been on her adulterer's trip to Thailand, so thoroughly had she researched the promised venues.

She scrolled down the home page: 'Amanpuri, a Sanskrit word meaning "place of peace".' Peace came at a price here, with room rates starting at $575. Each pavilion had its own sun-deck and dining area; she was rather hoping that Antoine would see fit to go for pavilion 105 at $1,400, as it had the best sea view.

She had thought that Buddhism was all about giving everything away and living in a cave while draped in an orange toga, but there didn't seem too much evidence of that at Amanpuri.com. Perhaps they could take a day trip to see some bald-headed monks before returning to dine on Thai and European specialities at The Terrace.

She suddenly really fancied tucking into a plate of glass noodles studded with prawns and hot peppers, like the ones she had eaten with Jean-Laurent on holiday all those years ago. But it was all pie in the sky, anyway, this trip to Thailand. She just couldn't see a way of making it happen, couldn't imagine herself capable of the barefaced lying it would involve. That was her husband's department, he could tell lies for England, he was so accomplished at it, or rather for France, his native and deceitful land. He was a world class liar.

She went offline, hoping that Jean-Laurent wouldn't nosily try and check out the websites she had been visiting. Though it was very unlikely he suspected anything. He had made it quite clear that he no longer considered her the type of woman that other men might covet. If only he knew, she thought. The idea of his ignorance gave her a small sense of triumph.

Adultery might occur in random patterns, but nothing interrupted the ruthless routine of the school year. The Christmas party was a high point for the Organiser Mums, who filled many an empty diary page with pre-planning meetings. The Final Run-Through for the International Christmas Buffet was scheduled for Tuesday morning at the home of PTA Paula. Laura and Lorinda rolled in late and helped themselves to a cup of something indescribable from a thermos at the table at the back of the room.

'I'm gonna teach you some Yiddish, Laura,' whispered Lisa from New York, watching Laura wince as she sipped the cinnamon-flavoured coffee. '*Pisch-wasser.* That's what you're drinking!'

PTA Paula took the floor to address the motley gathering of multinational Full-Time Mothers. It was like a menopausal Miss World in which the dolly birds were replaced by older, plainer contestants.

'Welcome, everybody, and thank you all for coming. *Bienvenue à tous, et merci d'être venu.* As you know, the international buffet is going to be the high point of the Christmas party. Fifty-seven nationalities represented by their native cuisine, and I want this to be the most spectacular event ever realised by our school. First of all, I'd like to go round the room and hear what you've managed to secure for your respective tables. *D'abord, je voudrais demander à tout le monde ce que vous avez pu obtenir pour vos tables.'*

'What is this, the bloody Eurovision Song Contest?' muttered Lorinda to Laura. She put up her hand.

'Paula, if you're going to say everything in two languages, it'll take twice as long. Can't you stick to one or the other?'

Paula was proud of her linguistic skills, and might have had a career as an interpreter had she not decided to put family first. She did not appreciate the interruption.

'Let's put it to the test. *Mettons-le à la teste,'* she said, her French slipping slightly under stress. Is there anyone here who doesn't understand English? *Est-ce qu'il y a quelqu'un ici qui ne comprend pas l'anglais?'*

A handful of French women raised their hands.

'*Et, quelqu'un qui ne comprend pas le français?* Any non-French speakers? Yes, there, our Japanese ladies. I'm afraid that's your answer, Lorinda! I'll have to continue in both. Right, let's start with the US. Lisa?'

Lisa stood up.

'I've got Maryland chicken for 150, eight apple pies, six dozen brownies and ten tubs of Haagen-Dazs ice cream.'

'That's terrific Lisa, well over target.' PTA Paula led the applause and Lisa punched the air before taking her seat.

'Now, how about Eastern Europe. Anya?'

Anya jumped up, a diminutive Russian in a fringed jacket and make-up applied with a trowel.

'Well, in fact a lot of the Russian mothers don't know too much about cooking the Russian food, so we have decided to take a money collection and we have hired a caterer to provide stroganoff for sixty.'

'That's maybe not quite in the home-made spirit, Anya, but if that's what you are happy with, then let's go with it. Well done. Laura, how are we doing on the British table?'

Laura felt like the under-performing rep humiliated at the regional sales meeting. She squirmed in her chair and cleared her throat.

'Well, the good news is that Trudy Yeoman has promised to make a dozen mince pies.'

Silence.

'And I'm getting my husband to bring back a few packets of sausage rolls from M&S on his next trip to London. They are easy to eat so we won't need forks,' she added lamely.

PTA Paula looked grievously disappointed.

'Laura, we are expecting two thousand people at this event. For the first time ever, we have a Brit heading up the PTA and I want to see a Big British Presence. I can't believe you're seriously trying to fob me off with a handful of sausage rolls and mince pies – this isn't just a mid-morning snack for the Christmas postboy! I shouldn't need to be saying this. It should be self-evident that two thousand people are going to need a lot of feeding.'

Laura wondered if she could pull off a Jesus-style stunt and break the sausage rolls and mince pies into five thousand pieces. She shrugged.

'I'll see what I can do.'

She wasn't going to apologise to horrible, ugly PTA Paula who was now shaking her head in despair.

'See me afterwards, Laura, and I'll give you a list of

numbers of contact. People want to do this, you know, they want to contribute – it's just a question of harnessing their energy.'

Laura stared angrily at the floor. I don't need this, she thought. I'm a professional graduate career woman, not some sad little double-glazing sales person. What was the matter with these women that they chose to devote so much energy to something that nobody really wanted anyway? How desperate could you be to fill your time?

She sat silently through the rest of the meeting, thinking of Antoine. His voice, his delicate white hands with their perfect fingernails, their afternoons spent in voluptuous oblivion in the suite at the Ritz. These women should get themselves a lover, she thought – it was an infinitely richer way to fill the empty hours. Then they wouldn't feel the need to draw up charts and schedules in a fury of pointless organisation.

Her thoughts turned to Antoine's proposal to take her to Thailand. He mentioned it every time they met, urging her to make her decision, gently chipping away at her reasons for not going, which were beginning to sound tired and feeble. She imagined herself boarding the plane with him, sitting side by side like giant babies, their highchair trays of food before them. Then arriving in Bangkok with her lover, exploring the floating markets and filling their arms with fresh flowers and rolls of richly coloured silk. Instead of which, she was stuck in this room with a boring crowd of women making arrangements for a school function. She ought, perhaps, to give Antoine's offer her serious consideration.

*   *   *

'Daddy, how long till my birthday?'

Pierre-Louis was lying on the sofa watching cartoons in a bored, half-focused way that infuriated his father. If he were a proper parent, he should leap up and switch off the television, engaging his son in a more suitable form of entertainment. Instead of which he was sitting next to him, trying to blank out the sound of the TV while rereading *The 7 Habits of Highly Effective People.*

'A few months. Two hundred days,' he added, remembering that his son didn't understand months.

'Two hundred! It's not fair! I want my party now. I want the clown to come and everyone to give me presents.'

Pierre-Louis twisted himself in a convulsion of misery.

Waiting, we are always waiting, thought Jean-Laurent.

'It'll come soon. Why don't you do something else instead of just watching television?'

The author of *7 Habits* allowed only seven hours' television a week in his home, a decision taken after a family council devoted to studying the data on TV-dependent sickness.

'Like what? There's nothing to do. I'm bored. I want to have my party *now*. I want *presents*.'

Jean-Laurent frowned at the realisation that his son was Possession and Pleasure Centred, which meant he would have only negligible power in later life.

'Go and do some Play-doh or something. Where's Mummy?'

'She's gone out. She's taken Charles-Edouard to a party. You're the one in charge.'

Jean-Laurent sighed. It was clearly time for him to make a deposit in the Emotional Bank Account of the father-son relationship, but it was so much more satisfying to read about it than actually to do it.

'OK, go and get Pictionary Junior.'

Pierre-Louis ran off happily to his bedroom and Jean-Laurent flicked back to Stephen R. Covey's advice on marriage. 'Proactive people make love a verb. Reactive people make it a feeling. Proactive people subordinate feelings to values. Love is a value that is actualised by loving actions.'

That was all very well, he thought, but what happened when those unsubordinated feelings resulted in a mistress carrying your child? Where did that put you and your wretched values and responsibilities? He wished that he was like Stephen Covey: clean-living, church-going, goal-achieving and, to boot, damned rich. Instead of which he was a useless reactive wreck who was being pissed over by his so-called girlfriend. Now there was someone really proactive. Flavia had her circle of influence well in control of her circle of concern, and her personal mission statement was clearly going just the way she wanted.

Pierre-Louis ran back in, clutching the game, his eyes shining with excitement. Jean-Laurent hugged him.

'I love you, Pierre-Louis, do you know that? Now go and bring me that bottle of wine from the fridge, and a glass and the corkscrew.'

After all, when you made a deposit you could surely make a small withdrawal, couldn't you?

Laura had taken special care with her appearance before delivering Charles-Edouard to the party that afternoon. By chance, the seven-year-old host lived in the Villa

Montmorency, and Antoine had been delighted by her suggestion that she call in to see him. Sylvie was away, and three to six was as good a time frame for adult indoor games as it was for a children's party.

She drew up outside the party boy's house, a dilapidated old hunting lodge that sat scruffily between its nouveau-riche neighbours, and escorted her son up the path. The door was opened by the father, a scion of the wealthy aristocrat who had once owned the entire estate until he had sold the land to developers. He bore all the trademarks of the last cry of European aristocracy – a booming voice, negligible chin and cavalier disregard for fashionable clothes. It was what the French termed *fin de race*, enough to turn the mildest citizen into a class warrior. There was no more powerful advertisement for the benefits of racial integration than the sight of this product of centuries of inbreeding.

'Come in, *je vous en prie*. I'm afraid Alexandre's rather upset, he's just sat on his guinea pig.'

Laura and Charles-Edouard looked on aghast as the maid removed the flattened animal in a dustpan.

'He was so excited – it was a present from his uncle. He put it on a chair, and next thing you know, he'd forgotten all about it and sat down – and there you are.'

A chubby, red-eyed child came forward and took Charles-Edouard's present, which he tossed on the pile on the hall table. An adult dressed as a harlequin was applying festive make-up to a solemn ring of children sitting on the floor.

Parisians didn't do musical bumps and pass the parcel. They rang agencies to send in clowns or fairies with puppet shows and fishing lines for *pêche à la ligne* so the children could reel in their own presents at the end of the party. You couldn't expect much change from three hundred euros, but then your child would recoup at least that in gifts from his guests, since video and computer games had supplanted the ladybird book or six coloured pencils that were expected in Laura's own childhood.

She said goodbye and drove round the corner, past Antoine's Regency villa, and parked her car discreetly a few doors up. She didn't know anybody else who lived here in the Villa, but you couldn't be too careful. The gate buzzed open and she made her way past the sheep statues up to the front door, where her ardent lover stood waiting.

He was dressed in leisurewear, which was slightly disappointing. She had only ever seen him – clothed – in a suit before, and she had to admit this was the better option for men of a certain age. Whereas Jean-Laurent looked rugged in joggers or jeans, Antoine looked somehow wrong in his pressed casual trousers and lemon cashmere sweater. His voice, though, was as irresistible as ever.

'You look beautiful,' he said. 'And as Stendhal said, beauty is the promise of happiness.'

Laura returned his kiss and followed him upstairs into the neutral elegance of his child-free salon. A three-tiered silver platter bearing sandwiches the size of postage stamps was placed on the coffee table. He served her coffee in a tiny porcelain cup.

'Welcome to my home. I am so pleased you could come. And so much has changed since you were last here,' he said.

Laura blushed at the memory of her first visit to the

house. It must have been so obvious why she had casually arranged to drop by, although she had so strenuously
denied it at the time.

'I'd like to introduce you to my library,' he continued.
'Here, what shall I read to you?'

He showed her the bookcases which ran from floor to
ceiling across one wall of the room.

'I had to fight for this, you know. Sylvie's designer
insisted there was no place for unmatching book spines
in his concept, but I couldn't live without them. Thornton
Wilder said literature was nothing more than the orches-
tration of platitudes, but I believe that books are the
second greatest source of happiness. Do you like the work
of Abel Bonnard?'

'I'm afraid I've never heard of him. How come you are
so well read? In England all our doctors are terrible
philistines.'

'I believe that is because all your cleverest students turn
their back on the sciences. In France, it is only the intel-
lectually ungifted who sit for the literature *bac* at school.
The able students follow the scientific route, which means
there are plenty of unfulfilled poets following careers as
doctors and engineers. Here, let me read to you from
Bonnard's *Savoir Aimer.*'

Laura couldn't help noticing the book looked rather
well thumbed. Perhaps he made a habit of reading to
his mistresses from an all-time top ten of literary
favourites.

He read aloud in his rich low voice, and it struck her
yet again how French was the only language for love.

'To love is to grow as you forget yourself. It is to escape

through one soul being the mediocrity of all the rest. It is to be more alone through trying to be less so. It is to become like everybody else while imagining that you are like no one else. It is to give a rendezvous to happiness in the palace of fate.'

Antoine looked up and saw his words were having the hoped-for effect. Laura opened her eyes.

'You're right, that is very beautiful.'

'Do you know any Shakespeare by heart?'

'By heart? Of course not. The only lines I can remember are from pop songs.'

'Such as?'

'Oh, I don't know, they hardly bear repeating.'

'Don't you love the line from Romeo and Juliet, "love is a smoke raised with the fume of sighs"?'

'Yes.'

'Or Lamartine's "The Lake" from his *First Meditations*. Such a pressing sense of urgency.'

'Go on then, recite it for me.'

Antoine knelt beside Laura.

'Let us love then. / Let us love then. / Let us hurry from the fugitive hour, let us rejoice: / Man has no point of port, time has no river bank. / It is running, and we are slipping away.'

He wrapped his arms around her legs.

'I believe it was your own Oscar Wilde who said that love was a sacrament that must be taken on one's knees.'

He pushed up her skirt, his voice becoming muffled as he continued his theme.

'He also said that the sex of a fascinating woman is a challenge, not a defence.'

So ends my lesson in European literature, thought Laura as she closed her eyes once more and leant back into the neutral harmony of the plushly upholstered *meridienne*.

Asa cast her eye around the bathroom to make sure she hadn't forgotten anything. Her toilet bag, the size of a medium suitcase, lay open on the floor, exposing a neatly packed battery of beauty products.

Real beauty, of course, came from inside, which is why she was so careful about what she allowed to arrive in her stomach. Vegetables make you beautiful, that was her mantra, and these could be welcomed in any form. It was Empty Calories and Bad Cholesterol that had to be ejected from her system before they took their evil toll.

In time, she knew that she would be able to resist them altogether, but for now she still needed to feel the sweet rush of chocolate and candy bars, which she strictly disposed of shortly after swallowing. Otherwise she would become a 'beautiful person' in the fat sense of the word, the disparaging false compliment that was often attributed to the overweight, as though shining hair and a caring concern for others was any substitute for the lissom thighs and waif-like self-absorption of the truly beautiful.

So as Asa fuelled her interior beauty with vegetables, she spared no expense on maintaining an exterior to match. Exfoliating face scrubs, anti-wrinkle creams, cellulite removers, purchased at a cost out of all proportion to her modest income, lay in obedient rows in the case alongside the tanning machine.

She added one or two jars that she had helped herself to from Laura's dressing table – a perk of the job, really, like using office envelopes – then fastened the beauty bag and carried it into the hall, where her clothes were already packed up into two larger suitcases along with a few towels and pillowcases that she thought might come in useful for her new life with Devon.

It had been fortuitous, his *chambre de bonne* falling vacant at just the moment when she felt she could not carry on at Laura's. In exchange for her room, she would do a few hours' housework; there were no children, of course, which would leave her free to concentrate on planning her future. And she would also help Devon with his research, for which he would pay her a small salary. It would be wonderful to have him close at hand to continue monitoring her progress.

She had just sat down in the kitchen to write her letter of farewell when she heard a key in the lock. Laura came in and looked in surprise at the bags in the hall and at Asa sitting in her coat at the kitchen table.

'Oh Laura, it's you,' said Asa. 'I was just writing you a note.'

'Obviously.'

'I hope you don't mind, I wasn't planning to say goodbye – I thought it would be easier if I just left. I hope you are not angry with me.'

'No, I'm not angry,' said Laura. She couldn't be less angry. In fact, she was absolutely bloody delighted. At last the cuckoo was leaving, and she hadn't even needed to deliver her often-researched speech about Asa being a Beautiful Person but them all needing their Own Space.

'I quite understand,' she said, taking Asa by the shoulders and hugging her warmly. 'I think it's absolutely the right decision.'

'You do?' Asa looked disappointed. She had rather hoped that her departure would drop Laura well and truly in the shit.

'But you don't even know where I'm going.'

And I couldn't care less, thought Laura.

'Whatever you have decided,' she said, 'is bound to be the right decision.'

Asa was not about to be put off by Laura's lack of curiosity.

'I'm going to live with Devon,' she explained. 'And his wife, of course. They are letting me stay in their *chambre de bonne*. Devon will be able to keep a closer eye on me. I think it's what I need.'

'Well, that all sounds very cosy,' said Laura. 'I hope the three of you will be very happy.'

Asa stared at her blankly. That dreadful Scandinavian dullness, thought Laura. Thank God I won't have to put up with that any more.

'I was going to ask you to send on my salary,' said Asa, 'but as you're here . . .'

'Absolutely.' Laura couldn't open her purse fast enough. She pulled out a handful of notes. 'Here, with my blessing. Have a happy life.'

She eagerly opened the front door.

'Do you need a hand with your bags?'

'No, I can manage. Goodbye.'

The farewell hung in the air as Asa negotiated her cases through the swing doors of the lift and nodded a final

goodbye. This is the last time, thought Laura, that I will
ever have to meet that cold grey look.

She watched as the coffin-lift carried away its heavy
load, then turned back to reclaim her territory. Asa's
bedroom still carried her smell, a heady confection of
unguents overlaid by the faintest trace of vomit. The
wardrobe doors hung open to reveal a satisfying row of
empty coat hangers. The shelves were free of self-help
books, the blank bed wondrously unoccupied.

In the kitchen, she took a bin liner and opened the
fridge. In went the zero-fat yoghurts, low-fat spreads, slim-
line meals for one and cans of Diet Coke. Out of their
hiding places came the packets of biscuits, cereals, sweets,
all the satanic temptations that with the cunning of a
fallen angel she had kept out of the reach of the pillag-
ing Finn.

Laura made herself a cup of creamy hot chocolate,
went through to the *triple living*, kicked off her shoes and
stretched out on the sofa, luxuriously alone. She made a
mental list of all the things she couldn't stand about Asa
and thought how much richer her life would be without
her. The inconvenience of having no babysitter was negligible compared with the freedom she would now enjoy.
That was the thing about domestic help – it was supposed
to free you up, but all it did was create chains to tie you
into a tense interdependent relationship with someone
you invariably came to hate.

She was still there half an hour later when Jean-Laurent
let himself in. Hearing his key in the lock, Laura thought
for a horrible moment that Asa had changed her mind
until she remembered that her keys had been handed over

and safely relegated to the kitchen drawer. She smiled brightly at her husband as he walked in.

'She's gone!' she announced, forgetting the crisis in their marriage in the euphoria of the moment.

Jean-Laurent took in her happy face and thought for a second that she was referring to Flavia. Flavia and the foetus, disappeared in a puff of smoke. If only.

'Asa has gone,' Laura explained. 'Packed up her troubles in her old kitbag and gone to seek redemption in the arms of Devon, or at least in his *chambre de bonne*. Isn't that fantastic?'

'I suppose. Yes. *Bon débarras*. Good riddance.'

He sat down beside her on the sofa, his shoulders tensed, his head between his hands. He was clearly preparing to launch into the difficult conversation she had been dreading.

'Oh Laura, what has happened to us?'

But she didn't want to go along with it, this heavy unburdening of his guilty secrets that she already knew. She was determined to keep things light.

'Come on,' she said, 'remember the motto on your office mug: "Cheer up, it may never happen".'

It used to be a private joke between them, mugs with jokey messages. Jean-Laurent had found it a peculiar trait of British office life, colleagues forever brewing each other tea and coffee – it all tasted the same – served up in mugs saying things like 'You don't have to be crazy to work here – but it helps!' Those damned mugs, you couldn't go into anyone's office without seeing them steaming offensively on the desk. 'My mate went to Skegness and all I got was this useless cup.' He had read in the British press that five million cups of tea a week were spilled at work because of the wires sticking out of people's computers. Five million cups! Damn the Brits, why couldn't they have their coffee before they got to work, like civilised Europeans.

But bad British jokes were the last thing on his mind right now.

'It's no good, Laura. I need to talk to you. There's something I need to tell you.'

So this was it, then — he had decided it was confession time. Laura felt strangely calm. She even felt sorry for him. In fact she felt so sorry for him that she decided to let him off the hook.

'It's all right, I know.'

He looked up at her in surprise. A glimmer of hope appeared before him.

'You know?'

Laura, good old Laura, his helpmate, his companion. She would sort it out for him. She would know what to do.

'You and Flavia. I know,' she said.

He laughed.

'Oh Laura, you don't know what a relief that is to me. You know. Thank God.'

He buried his face in her lap.

'But how? And why aren't you angry? I thought you'd be furious, I thought you'd throw me out.'

'I was angry. I was devastated. I still am, I suppose. But I'm not the first wife that this has happened to. It goes on all the time, doesn't it? In fact, it's really rather banal. Sex in the workplace. In the old days it would have been with your secretary; now that's too infra dig, so you go a notch higher and bed the hoity-toity research consultant, though I do think you might have had the imagination to look a bit further. But then you always were lazy. You married your landlady because it saved the effort of going elsewhere, and now you've shagged the first little hot ticket that made eyes at you across the meeting room. I can't say I'm not disappointed in you, Jean-Laurent.'

The shamed adulterer hung his head. Banal? Disappointing? How swiftly his glorious affair was reduced to a pedestrian bit of after-hours jiggy-jiggy.

'Laura, I am so sorry. I have been such a fool.'

Laura shrugged.

'Shit happens, Jean-Laurent, and you let it happen.'

She was surprised at her cool self-control. If she hadn't had her own delicious secret to draw on, she would now be flailing around in a scene of wild sexual jealousy. Instead of which, she could enjoy the spectacle of her husband squirming like a butterfly under the pin of her noble forgiveness. How wise she had been to follow Lorinda's advice.

Then Jean-Laurent dropped his bombshell.

'If it wasn't for the baby, it would be so simple now. I could just walk away and we could be like before. You'd forgive me and we could pretend it never happened.'

Laura's carefully constructed shell shattered around her so loudly she could hear it crashing in her ears.

'Say that again,' she said faintly.

'I said, if it wasn't for the baby—'

'She's having a baby,' whispered Laura.

'You didn't know? No, of course you didn't know, how

could you? It's just that when you said you knew, I thought you meant you *knew.*'

'She's having a baby,' said Laura again.

'Not if I have anything to do with it,' said Jean-Laurent. 'It's still very early, and I'm hoping she'll come to her senses.'

'A baby,' said Laura. Babies were what she and Jean-Laurent did. Babies were years and years of dull and cosy commitment. Babies were a thing apart – they had nothing to do with affairs, nothing to do with Antoine, and certainly nothing to do with that narrow-hipped scheming blonde. She had thought she knew his game, she had thought she was playing by the same rules – but this changed everything.

'*You stupid, stupid man,*' she wept, entirely out of control and ugly in her pain as she picked up a cushion and repeatedly pushed it into Jean-Laurent's face. Her tears were hot and raw as she berated him. 'You just let her walk all over you. Well don't come crying to me about it, You got yourself into this – it's *your* problem. *Démerde-toi!*'

TWELVE

'Oh my God, that *is* tricky.'

Lorinda nodded sympathetically at Laura as she took a slice of baguette from the basket and spread it thickly with butter. They were sitting in a local boulangerie that had diversified into lunches by cramming six tables into an unfeasibly small space between the door and the counter. It was not the ideal location for an intimate confessional, but at least they were speaking English, which gave them an illusion of privacy.

'Old Barbie-face has used the oldest trick in the book to reel in her man,' Lorinda continued. 'That girl is *so* unoriginal. I can't think what Jean-Laurent sees in her.'

'What he sees in her now is a tiny seed of himself, doubling in size every day until he can persuade her to have an abortion.' Laura took a savage swig of her wine. 'He says he doesn't want it, Lorinda, but if she does go ahead, he's bound to love it, how could he not? And what if it's a girl? The daughter he never had, the daughter *I* never had, for God's sake. It's just not fair!'

Two old ladies who were seated about eighteen inches away looked up from their cassoulet. Lorinda smiled at them and patted Laura's hand reassuringly.

'Now calm down, Laura, let's think clearly about this and not get things out of proportion.'

'But that's what's so unfair,' cried Laura. 'I thought I *had* got things in proportion. I was all ready for his great confession. I'd been through all that angst so that when he was finally ready to come clean, I was prepared. And then he tells me she's pregnant. A little half-sister for my lovely boys. Can't you just see the photo? The two of them cradling the newborn. Jean-Laurent will probably have it made into a Christmas card!'

She took her head in her hands.

'Or half-brother,' said Lorinda.

'What?'

'Or half-brother. It might be a boy.'

'Well thanks very much,' said Laura, glaring at her friend, 'for that small consolation.'

Their lunch arrived and they both leaned back to make room for two plates of steaming rich beans, aromatic with bacon and sausage.

'Chicken soup for the soul,' said Lorinda in her best American accent.

'I bet Flavia only eats lettuce,' said Laura, tucking in and feeling slightly better. 'You can just tell by looking at her. She doesn't love food, does she, not like us?'

'No, she's a picky cow,' said Lorinda, gesturing to the waitress to bring more bread. 'A bloody nightmare, in fact – worse than Asa. Didn't you notice her at your dinner, chasing that tiny bit of fish around her plate?'

'No, I was too busy being the anxious hostess . . .'

Laura's voice tightened and Lorinda quickly intervened to reassure her.

'Now come on, Laura, let's get this straight. Things could be a lot worse. It's obvious that Jean-Laurent wants to stay with you, so the ball is entirely in your court. Though I must say if it was me, I'd want him out of that door faster than shit off a shovel.'

Laura frowned.

'No, Lorinda, you must understand that he's in a terrible state about this. Much worse than me. He's so sorry, he's just so terribly sorry . . .'

'It's a shame he wasn't terribly sorry earlier on. How long has it been going on, anyway?'

Laura shrugged. 'I don't know. Over a year, maybe two, it makes no difference. I just feel so confused . . .'

'Do you still want him or not?'

'Yes, he's the father of my children. I don't want to be a single mother. I love him. Or I did, until this.'

'And what about Antoine in all this? You haven't forgotten that you, too, are engaged in an adulterous affair?'

Laura smiled at the mention of his name.

'Lovely Antoine. But I can honestly say that has nothing to do with my marriage. We neither of us lay any claim on the other.'

'Which is exactly what Jean-Laurent would have said about Flavia before she ensnared him with her fertile womb.'

'No, the vile Flavia is obviously looking for a life partner. Antoine is not, and neither am I, since I already have one, or so I thought.'

They ate their cassoulet in silence for a moment, then Lorinda spoke.

'I think what you need right now, Laura, is to take a break from it all. Leave Jean-Laurent to sort things out with Barbie-face while you relax in the arms of your lover. Why don't you take him up on that offer of a trip to Thailand? You've already told me that you've got the perfect excuse. Pretend you're going to the hen party in Barcelona.' Laura sighed.

'You know, I had already decided to do just that. But I can't. I feel that Jean-Laurent needs me.'

'Oh yeah, like he's needed you for the last two years while he's been screwing that stick insect! Buck up, Laura! Do something for yourself for once in your life!'

'But what about the children? Don't forget I haven't got Asa any more.'

'As if that would have made any difference. I'll take them after school and your lovely husband can play caring repentant Dad all weekend. It'll be fine.'

'But I'd have to lie some more. I'm sick of it, the lying—'

'It's a little white lie. He need never know – and you would never have been in this position were it not for Jean-Laurent's staggering capacity for lying. He started it – never forget that.'

'Well . . .'

'Go on. Do it. You should.'

And so it was that Laura found herself in a taxi on her way to the airport. The road signs called it the Charles de Gaulle airport, but perversely all Parisians knew it as

Roissy. Another plot to confuse the hapless visitor. The organisation that had gone into getting Laura this far had been so exhausting that she felt that any resulting pleasure was unlikely to outweigh the cost. She felt crushed by the weight of her own dishonesty.

Jean-Laurent had seemed almost relieved when she told him she was going away for the weekend. He was hoping she would relent and forgive him, and she had popped the question one evening when he was particularly intent on pleasing her. He had just put the children to bed and done all the washing up while she sat alone reading Sylvia Plath in the salon, the lofty injured party. He had come in with a cup of coffee for her which he had put on the Interesting Oak table.

'Believe me, Laura,' he had said, his hand covering hers, 'I would do anything to make it up to you. You can't know how much I regret this whole situation.'

He had just read a book on rebuilding trust, and sincere expression of intent was apparently the best starting point.

It was now or never, Laura had thought at the time. She would never get a better opportunity than this.

'Well actually, Jean-Laurent, I do think it would be helpful for me to take some time away from all this. You remember I told you that Marion was organising that weekend in Barcelona? Obviously I'm hardly in the mood for partying, but I think perhaps it would help us all if I took a few days away. If you felt you could cope with the children, that is.'

He had fallen for it hook line and sinker, the damn fool. So overwhelming was his sense of guilt that he couldn't wait to help her find a way to forgive him. She even managed to build in the idea that she would need a few sessions on the sunbed to get rid of her betrayed wife's pallor, thereby ruling out any suspicions when she returned with a winter suntan. It was all so laughably easy – the way Jean-Laurent must have found it so easy lying to her when she never saw any reason to disbelieve his glib excuses.

Laura had unearthed her summer wardrobe, grimaced at the sight of her pale winter body in her bikini and taken care to pack three pareos, those lifelines of the lumpen beach goddess. She had left everything organised at home and in a guilty high of excess adrenaline had even sent out all the Christmas cards. Penny Porter's was enclosed with the vests for Thaddeus and contained a slightly barbed message congratulating her on her latest little achievement, which she hoped would be received in the correct spirit.

Jean-Laurent had kissed her a tender goodbye, wishing her a good trip and hoping that on her return they could work things out. If you only knew, she had thought, if you only knew what I am up to, and felt a small rush of triumphant excitement. She had left him the household record book that her mother had given her last Christmas, filled in with all the numbers he could possibly need. Except for the Barcelona hotel, naturally. She would call him regularly to touch base; there was no point in even giving it to him.

It had all been incredibly straightforward. She had always been amazed by those stories of men who maintained two separate families for twenty years without either wife ever getting wind of the other. Now she realised it couldn't be easier. But it didn't prevent her from feeling entirely wretched. Holidays were what she did with Jean-Laurent and the children, yet here she was sloping off like Bathsheba. She deserved to be stoned to death in a long black robe at the fringes of a biblical village.

She paid off the taxi and took her small holdall – one of Jean-Laurent's lesser Mandarina Ducks – into the terminal, shivering slightly in her linen jacket. Antoine had given her her ticket and told her to check in without him, in case he was late. There was no danger of Laura missing the plane. Being unfamiliar with the world of glamorous international travel, she had allowed an absurdly huge margin for error and the girl at the check-in was suitably patronising. Most people travelling club class didn't arrive at the airport three hours before take off.

Laura called Lorinda on her mobile: yes, the children were fine, no, they didn't want to talk to her, no, of course she shouldn't feel guilty, just think of how Jean-Laurent had treated her.

'But two wrongs don't make a right, do they?' Laura insisted.

'Why don't you just forget it and come home then?'

'I can't do that, it's all arranged.'

'Well just shut up and enjoy it, in that case. Goodbye.'

Laura drifted through the duty-free shops and decided she probably didn't need a model of the Eiffel Tower or a Hermès scarf.

She went through to the Air France lounge – her club-class ticket granted her access – and sat down to read her book, an academic study comparing the work of Rimbaud with that of Jim Morrison. It seemed that the lead singer of The Doors was quite in the debt of the French poet, and had even written to the book's author to thank him for his translation of the poems. What lovely manners, thought Laura. You couldn't imagine Eminem doing something like that.

She peered at the photo of Jim Morrison, wild-eyed rock star, printed alongside the portrait of Rimbaud, wild-eyed romantic poet. On balance, she would probably prefer to go to bed with Jim Morrison. Antoine was more like Rimbaud, or at least an older, less wild-eyed version. More like Charles Aznavour, really. She was going on a dirty weekend with a Charles Aznavour lookalike.

That was not to say that she wasn't excited. Now that everything was in place, she could take a deep breath and anticipate the pleasure that lay ahead. It was wonderful to be sitting here in the Air France lounge, helping herself to free snacks and relishing the luxury of being alone.

She had done a few long-haul flights with the children, and had always emerged crushed and humiliated by her failure to keep them quiet for eleven hours, only to spend the fortnight's holiday dreading the flight home. Jean-Laurent had usually managed to engineer things so he travelled on a separate plane; it was hard to know now whether that was for Flavia-related reasons, or simply to avoid the horror of flying with the under-fives.

How very different, then, to be sitting here in splendid isolation, dreaming of the forthcoming few days with her lover, who – to be fair – was really much more Sacha Distel than Charles Aznavour.

Once Laura was seated on the plane she began to worry seriously about whether she might be spending her adulterous weekend on her own. The thought was not unpleasant, except that she would have to pay her own hotel bill, which might look incriminating on the joint bank statement. A man with a large collection of spreadsheets settled into the seat next to her and took off his shoes, slipping his podgy feet into the complimentary cabin slippers provided.

There was no avoiding the ghastly intimacy of aeroplanes, even when you travelled club class, and the thought of sharing the lavatory with him and others like him for the next twelve hours made Laura feel quite queasy. No wonder wealthy frequent travellers bought themselves Lear jets – it was the only way they could get to crap in comfort.

It was while she was entertaining this thought that Antoine appeared in the aisle, hair immaculate, wearing a light suit that shouted Gentleman In The Tropics. He leaned across Laura's slippered neighbour to kiss her on both cheeks. Slippers immediately volunteered to change places to allow them to sit together, but to Laura's surprise Antoine declined.

'No, thank you, actually I'm sitting up in first class. I need to sleep, you see. You don't mind, do you, Laura, only some of us need to work in the morning!'

He then dropped his voice to a whisper in her ear.

'It's actually written into my contract with the clinic: first-class travel for me, club class for my assistant, which is the ticket you are on.'

'No, you go ahead,' said Laura out loud, glossing over her humiliation.

So she was being charged up as Dr Bouchard's assistant. Would she have to dress up in a green surgeon's gown and hand him his implements as he squeezed the prostates of his patients? Her neighbour with the spreadsheets would be in no doubt now that she was some kind of floozy, unworthy of occupying a seat that turns into a bed alongside her fancy-man. Instead she could expect a night of being dribbled over by a stranger in cabin slippers.

'I'm just grateful to have a cloth serviette and proper cutlery,' she added. 'What do they give you up there, nectar and ambrosia?'

'There's usually caviar. And vintage champagne.'

'Served in lead crystal? After all, if you only get ordinary old champagne glasses, you might as well pig it back here in club.'

She smiled to show she didn't mean it; that she was grateful not to be in economy.

'Sleep tight. See you in Thailand.'

He disappeared through the curtain to the realm beyond, with its luxuriously low person-to-toilet ratio.

Slippers turned to Laura.

'Isn't it fascinating how life in an aeroplane is a microcosm of the real world? Here we are, the comfortable bourgeoisie, envied by the common herds behind us, but envious in turn of the Happy Few in first. Too bad your friend couldn't get you an upgrade.'

He turned out to be in forecasting; his job was to predict what the next trends would be. A sort of prophet for our times. He was quite entertaining and hardly dribbled at all when he dozed off during the film.

As Laura slept her way halfway across the world, Jean-Laurent was grumpily getting out of bed to fix breakfast for his small sons.

'When's Mummy coming back?' asked Pierre-Louis, his short legs swinging from the kitchen stool as he took a spoonful of Coco Krispies.

'Give her a chance, she's only just gone,' said his father.

'Three more days,' said Charles-Edouard, 'then she'll bring us back some presents. Won't she, Papa?'

'I expect so. For you, anyway. I don't think she'll bring anything for me.'

'Why not?'

'She's rather cross with me.'

'Why?'

'Never mind. *C'est compliqué.* Do you want some toast?'

Charles-Edouard watched him critically as he cut a slice in half diagonally.

'Not like *that*! Mummy always does it in soldiers!'

He took the knife from his father and cut the remaining slice into four neat strips.

'That's better,' he said, lining them up carefully on his plate, the way he used to organise his toy cars into neat rows.

Christ, these kids should loosen up, thought Jean-Laurent, wondering which of his business books would be appropriate to the task. One of his fears was that he would have a child with mental problems – he knew he wouldn't be able to handle it. A friend of his had a son who had chewed his way through his father's entire tie collection. They all had to go along to a family therapy session where a Nosy Parker shrink had asked everyone to give their assessment of the family dynamics. The thought of it made him shudder; it was one thing to read psychology books in private, and quite another to sit around with a stranger and talk about What Makes You Tick.

Jean-Laurent was afraid of quite a lot of things these days. He had the usual French fears, of course: the taxman breaking down the door at six in the morning for a dawn raid; the prospect of a bankrupt old age, his pension fund all having been spent on *fonctionnaires'* salaries, and the country peopled by old people like himself living to a hundred and fighting over what little was left in the kitty; the worry about contracting a serious illness – like all the French, he made frequent visits to the dermatologist in pursuit of rogue moles and was a regular at the high-street laboratory where they took blood tests in search of some abnormality. These were a normal part of life, the *petits soucis* that gave Parisians their pinched, stressed-out look.

The antidote to this worry had been his rock-solid home life; his marriage to Laura and the daily joy of watching his children grow, nature's way of instilling optimism into even the most committed misanthrope. But now he had a fear that dwarfed all others – the fear that this would be snatched away by Flavia, triumphant in her fecundity, as she claimed her trophy, the father of her unborn child.

How big was it now, her foetus? Two, three centimetres? A writhing piece of tissue – nothing that couldn't be sucked away and nobody be any the wiser. Women got pregnant all the time; often they didn't realise – it just self-aborted, nature's way of washing out a being that wasn't meant to be. Well, this child wasn't meant to be: it had only one consenting parent, and one unwittingly duped poor sod who had only been fooling around. A friend had once told him that when a woman tells you she is pregnant, your reaction isn't 'Do I want this child?' but 'Do I want to stay with this woman?' And he, decidedly, did not.

Laura closed her eyes against the tropical sun and laid back on her lounger. She felt the heat soaking into her, a heavy, moist heat that you never got in Europe. Before her an empty swimming pool stretched out, and beside it stood a table stacked with large white towels. A boy had escorted her to her chair and prepared her bed of self-indulgence, spreading out one towel for her to lie on and placing another one, still folded, on the table for her to dry herself with after her swim.

He was returning to her now, bearing a tray with a fruity cocktail which he placed on the table. The elegance of his buttoned-up white coat and his graceful, silent manner made her feel crude and brash in her lumpen near-nudity. What did they make of their customers, these hotel employees, as they smiled and averted their gaze from the wisps of pubic hair escaping from bikini bottoms to lie in dark contrast to white flabby thighs?

He glided away from her, past the glass wall of the gym, where a solitary middle-aged man was puffing away on a treadmill. There was a pile of towels in there, too, endless fresh laundry waiting to absorb the sweat of bodies ill suited to this enervating climate. If you took into account the towels and dressing gowns in the bathroom, you could probably get through your bodyweight in linen in one day.

To be idle in a working world was the most decadent luxury. Everybody else, including Antoine, had business to attend to this morning, which meant that the leisure facilities of the Sukhothai hotel were for Laura alone. It was, therefore, ungrateful to feel slightly bored.

She picked up the book that Antoine had given her last night, a polemic extolling the wonders of anti-ageing medicine that he had written with a colleague. His photo – rather flattering, probably taken ten years ago – decorated the back flap, together with a brief career resumé which mentioned his marriage to the 'incontestably ageless' singing star Sylvie Marceau.

Laura was still stuck on the introductory chapter, which talked a lot about Promethean fire, and how our body cells were good for at least a hundred and twenty years provided we didn't abuse them. What with drugs to combat the free radicals and cosmetic surgery to nip and tuck the droopy bits, there was no reason not to live on as a century-old hard body. It was a repulsive thought. Dry old bodies jigging around until the cells finally gave up at a hundred and twenty, and then what? Did they just disappear into a pile of dust? And how old was Antoine exactly? She had always supposed him to be about fifty, but maybe he was really ninety-five and the living proof of his medical theories?

He was a wonderful companion, though, and their first night at the hotel had fully lived up to her expectations. They had checked into their enormous suite and Laura had rather shyly unpacked her suitcase, hanging up her few clothes in the giant wardrobe, tucking her skimpy pieces of underwear into the corner of a vast, empty drawer. Her intimacy with Antoine until now had been based on short, passionate meetings, and the prospect of a few days together moved it on to a different, domestic footing.

When she was deciding what to wear down to dinner, he sat on one of the two sofas of the suite facility and offered his opinion: no, the other shirt was better with those trousers, and she should go for the gold earrings rather than the silver. It was a husbandly service he was providing, making a contribution to her appearance, whereas before he only performed the lover's role, which was to behold and admire the finished article.

They had dined at the hotel's Celadon restaurant, on a fairy-lit terrace overlooking the gardens. The conversation was discursive and relaxed, for now they were free of all time constraints – the loss of urgency moved things away from their favourite subjects of poetry and philosophy and towards practical plans for the days to come. Laura had even brought her guidebook down to the table so they could decide how to plan their time, but Antoine had pushed it aside, suddenly leaning over the table towards her.

'Laura, we are lovers,' he had said. 'We do not need to look at guidebooks. Look at those people over there.'

He nodded towards a retired-looking couple poring over a map they had spread out on the table.

'They are very clearly married, so they must have their guidebook to get them through the evening. But we are quite different. We need only each other. And if you want to know about Bangkok, I can tell you all you need to know.'

Laura had laughed and apologised and looked only at Antoine, listening to his lively accounts of the bars he had visited in Bangkok where you think the girls are nearly naked but they turn out to be wearing tights beneath their

G-strings; of the snake farm where you can't buy a drink except from the crone living at the adjoining shack who takes your money through a hole in the fence and pushes a can of Coke back in return; of the canal trips he had taken off the Thonburi river, where rich men's comfortable villas with gates opening on to the water give way to shanty huts housing chickens and children who left their chaotic homes to hop into boats in their smart school uniforms.

He spoke of the smells and the crowds of Chinatown, the fluttering shimmering colours of their ribbons, their fortune cookies. Laura was glad to be there, glad to have escaped her husband, happy to laugh at Antoine's stories and know that they would spend the night together, and the next night and the next.

After dinner they had gone to the bar for one last drink before returning to the bedroom, a little drunk but not too late since Antoine had to work the following day. Laura had hung up her clothes and joined him in bed. 'Only ever in hotels,' she said as she rolled on top of him. 'You are my hotel husband. I think you would disappear in a puff of smoke if ever we tried to do it somewhere else.'

'Not true,' he said. 'There was one time at my house, you remember?'

'Not in the bedroom, though, only hotel bedrooms for us. Top-class hotels, of course.'

He had left her in bed this morning, deliciously free to get up and take a long bath before making it down to the dining room in time for a late breakfast. Which meant that she wasn't hungry for lunch, just the fruity cocktail she was sipping now that would take her through until dinner tonight. She rubbed some oil into her stomach and thought about taking a dip. To do so would attract the attention of the pool attendant and the puffing man in the gym. But it was too hot not to.

She lowered herself down the steps – no splashy dive for her – and took a few sedate strokes down the pool. Up and down she went. How boring swimming was. If only she had company perhaps she could work out a formation swimming sequence like in the comic-strip books of her childhood where women in frilly swimming caps simultaneously raised a shapely leg out of the water to create the stamens of a giant flower.

She almost wished she had accompanied Antoine to his clinic; she could have made herself useful, done a bit of filing for him, or Meeting and Greeting of his patients. The life of a medical receptionist suddenly seemed rather appealing, much better than swimming up and down an empty pool with no-one to talk to.

After four lengths she climbed out, modestly pulling down the legs of her bikini bottom which had ridden up during the exercise. She flopped down on the chair again and thought about her children.

They would be sleeping now, dreaming of whatever they did, their arms and legs flung out of their beds in their usual dramatic poses, while she, their mother, was lying here anointing her limbs with the oil of the adulteress, tanning her skin the better to please her lover.

She wished she was at home; she wished she could walk down the familiar corridor to the children's bedroom and stroke their smooth, sleeping flesh. But they were halfway round the world – the distance that separated them made her feel giddy. Imagine if aeroplanes stopped working, if she was abandoned here with only the illicit enjoyment of Antoine, her older man, to comfort her. It was no substitute. She didn't care how much fierce Promethean fire was burning beneath that carefully pampered exterior, she realised with a shock – that she was betraying her lover with dreams of escape. For, if she could, she would leave right now, go home to breathe in the sweet smell of her delicious sons.

Then she could slip back into the marital bed. Jean-Laurent would be waiting for her. She could wallow in the joy of their rekindled love; his broad bulk would comfort and protect her the way it used to when she had been so happy to leave the stresses of her working life for the long slide to happiness that he had promised – and delivered – to her.

They would laugh off the troubles of recent weeks, and tomorrow they would get up late and go to the park together with the children. They would drive up to the Pré Catalan in the Bois de Boulogne. The boys would take their scooters, those funny little silver *trottinettes*, and race ahead along the path while their parents followed, Jean-Laurent's arm round Laura's waist. They would stop by the Shakespeare garden and peer in, as they always did, complaining that it never seemed to be open, and trying to make out the Macbeth heather bed, the Tempest collection of aromatic thymes and lavenders.

Except that she was here in Thailand and Jean-Laurent was in Paris. Probably lying next to Flavia. She bet he would have waited for the children to go to sleep and then invited her round to keep him company in Laura's bed. Flavia, his chosen companion, the partner of his glory years, carefully growing the baby that was to push Laura firmly into touch. Laura, the dignified rejected wife, would selflessly raise her sons in obscurity while Jean-Laurent scaled the heights of professional and personal happiness.

The boys would look forward to their weekend visits, they would delight in their baby sister – she knew it would be a girl – and enjoy the treats their part-time father showered upon them. A divorced friend had told her how it felt when the children went off to stay with their father. 'You can't imagine what it's like,' she said, 'when the door closes behind them and you are left alone. You can't imagine that silence.'

Laura raised her hand to attract the attention of the pool attendant. She ordered another Sukhothai Sling to dull the pain. It shouldn't be like this, she thought. I am living the ultimate escapist housewife dream, a luxury slice of tropical paradise with my clever, attentive French lover, and all I can think about is the everyday reality I meant to leave behind. It was time to stiffen her sinews. I am in Paradise, she told herself firmly, I am in Paradise and I am bloody well going to enjoy it.

'So, you are happy you came with me, are you not?'

Antoine wandered out of the studio-sized bathroom into the bedroom where Laura was lying in bed contemplating the arrangement of fresh flowers whose petals had been neatly folded in on themselves. Origami on lotus blossoms – that really was taking sophistication a bit far. How long did it take someone to fold up a vase of flowers? It would have taken her the best part of an afternoon, but no doubt a deft-fingered smiling Thai had knocked it up in ten minutes.

She looked up at Antoine, who was wearing a white cotton bathrobe provided by the hotel. His thin legs protruded beneath it and were encased by Sukhothai monogrammed slippers. In his hand he held a cotton-wool puff which he was using to clean his face. She had found the Helena Rubinstein cleansing milk earlier when she had been snooping through his toilet bag, and had been mildly shocked by the range of cosmetics it contained.

The arsenal of suppositories was less surprising – she had been married to Frenchman for long enough to know they liked to take their medicine up the shooter – but the anti-wrinkle eye cream and exfoliating facial foam had been a bit of a turn-off. It was one thing to look after your appearance, but for a man to equip himself with a beauty kit worthy of Elizabeth Taylor was a bit too Danny La Rue for her taste. Such were the surprises reserved for those who accompanied their occasional lover on an extended mini-break.

'Yes, of course I'm happy. I'm in Paradise. The Land of Smiles.' She smiled to reinforce the point.

Antoine took the cue to impart a little knowledge.

'You know that Sukhothai means "dawn of happiness"? The hotel was named after the capital of the first Siamese kingdom.'

He disappeared back into the bathroom to complete his *toilette*. Laura heard the jars being opened and closed, and the discreet spray of what she guessed was the anti-baldness potion. He re-emerged, coiffed and scented like a tart's boudoir, she thought disapprovingly.

'I hope you were not bored by yourself all day. When we get to Amanpuri, I shall be one hundred per cent at your disposal.' He raised a suggestive eyebrow and Laura had a surge of mild panic.

'No, I had a great time,' she said quickly. 'I went to Jim Thompson's house.'

The teak house of the British silk merchant who had mysteriously disappeared was a favoured destination of Western visitors to Bangkok. After all, see one temple and squat Buddha and you'd seen the lot. Shopping and Jim Thompson's house, that was all you needed to do here.

'Did you go down the river?'

'I took a short ride. But I've seen the sights before – I just wanted to relax by the pool really.'

Laura didn't add that she had also sought out the guest house where she had stayed with Jean-Laurent years ago, before they had the children.

It was still there, in the street of budget hotels recommended by the Lonely Planet guide. She had taken tea in one of the cafés and noticed how young World Travellers were still as boring now as they were then, with their banal conversations about train journeys and poor sanitation. They might just as well have been in Starbucks on the Charing Cross Road complaining about how long it had taken them to get in from Streatham.

She and Jean-Laurent had laughed at them then, those latter-day hippies in their uniform of wild-coloured cottons and backpacks. How conventional they were, how dogged in their determination to complete their 'year off'. 'Vietnam, yeah, great. You know when I was sitting on the toilet in this hill village, you could actually see the pig with his mouth open underneath the hut, just waiting for it!'

Laura had only known Jean-Laurent a few months when

they decided to go to Thailand for Christmas. It was the first time in her life that she hadn't spent it at home with her parents, and she could sense her mother's disappointment, even though she had said she thought it was a marvellous idea and that Laura was so right to take these opportunities while she could.

When she woke up next to Jean-Laurent in their fan-cooled room on the Khao San road, unburdened by the giving and receiving of presents, then went out in a sundress to take coffee and watermelon for Christmas lunch, she knew that this was freedom. With Jean-Laurent she learned that you didn't have to stuff yourself with turkey and all the trimmings and watch reruns of the *Morecambe and Wise Christmas Special*. You could do whatever you wanted, whenever you wanted. He truly did believe that you made your own happiness.

It was his youthfulness that was so appealing. While her friends were beginning to settle comfortably into the deep groove of premature middle age, saddling themselves with houses to renovate and school-fee plans, she was stuffing a sarong into a rucksack and roughing it on the student trail. True, it was only for three weeks – she had her job to think of and Jean-Laurent his course to complete – but it made her feel so light-hearted. She and her delicious toy boy: not for them a New Year spent sanding floorboards, but rather an evening getting drunk in a seedy dive in Patpong before heading north to ride elephants through the jungle.

She remembered shivering in the doorway of a jungle shelter in the early morning mist, listening to the sounds of the approaching elephant crashing through the trees and stopping every now and then to wrap its trunk round a young sapling which was casually uprooted and eaten, and the fear with which she stepped into the basket on its back, praying it wouldn't slip down and drop her under those heavy feet. Jean-Laurent sat on the beast's head, of course, cross-legged and confident. The guide led them to a different hut that night and cooked them dinner while they and their fellow travellers – all younger than Laura, and all without jobs – smoked opium through a primitive pipe and felt like Samuel T. Coleridge as they each conjured up their personal crystal gorges of the Khubla Khan.

Then it was on to Koh Samui to recuperate on the beach. They slept in a bamboo hut, on a stained mattress beneath a mosquito net, and laughed at the muscled Australian next door. A creature of habit, he performed his full workout outside their door and greeted them the same way every morning – 'Good Exercise!' – though they were never sure if this was a comment on his own perform-ance, or an exhortation to them to follow suit.

After breakfast they would walk down to the beach, bathing in the warm turquoise water, before throwing themselves down on the sand and sneering at the middle-aged guests of the upmarket resort hotel next door who sunbathed on adjustable plastic sun-loungers. 'We will never be like that,' said Laura and Jean-Laurent, lying together on a shared towel, their limbs carelessly inter-twined, sand in their mouths and hair. 'We will never sit on vile his-and-hers plastic sun-chairs.'

On the flight back to London, Laura had held Jean-Laurent's hand and whispered to him of her plans to take a year off after he had finished his course. They could do the whole of Asia, maybe South America too. Perhaps they should drive overland to India, keep a diary, make a documentary.

They could front a new travel series on TV, the camera would just *love* Jean-Laurent with his razor-sharp cheekbones and sleek floppy hair. Laura might stay behind the camera. She would take the year as a sabbatical from the agency, but if the TV idea worked out, they could go into business together: she would produce, he would present – that sexy French accent would be perfect for a travel programme.

She had wrapped both her arms around him then, leaning awkwardly across the arm rest, kissing the soft skin behind his ear. 'I love you, Jean-Laurent. I just really, really love you.'

Back in London, their dizzy plans were diffused by the grey British winter and they settled back into routine: the account director and the MBA student, two career people on the right track.

They had secretly already given up on the 'year-off-let's-travel-and-possibly-become-famous-documentary-makers' fantasy by the time Laura discovered she was pregnant. There was a brief moment of mourning for the exciting new lifestyle challenge that now had to be laid to rest. Then they got enthusiastic about the baby. After all, what could be more creative than forging a gorgeous little new life? Especially when it was conceived with the real passion of a relationship in its early stages, rather than the dutiful in-and-out of those who waited until parenthood was supposed to be the next logical step.

They didn't entirely write off exotic adventures abroad.

As soon as the baby was old enough to be left behind, they promised themselves they would return to Bangkok. Only this time it would not be in some scumbag hotel on the Khao San road, but rather a piece of five-star luxury, possibly the Oriental. If it was good enough for Somerset Maugham, it would be good enough for them.

And eight years on, here she was, just as they had predicted. Just two details were different: the Oriental hotel had been supplanted by the Sukhothai, and instead of Jean-Laurent she had Dr Antoine Bouchard. Where once she had had her hot young boyfriend, strong and ardent in his creased Indian shirt, she now had Antoine, creamed and coiffed in his luxury hotel dressing gown, climbing into a bed she and Jean-Laurent would have killed for all those years ago. It went some way to redressing the balance, usually weighted in favour of the young, that beds most conducive to love-making could only be afforded by those least troubled by the desires of the flesh.

Except that you could not accuse Antoine of loss of libido, whatever his age was. Unfortunately, Laura had read so much about hormone replacement in his book that she could think only of how many testosterone supplements must be fuelling his performance. Not to mention selenium and all those other elixirs that surely he must be taking. It was like going to bed with a bag of pharmaceuticals. She closed her eyes and surrendered herself to physical pleasure, while weeping inside for her husband.

Breakfast was the whole point of hotels. Instead of grilling a bit of stale bread or pouring milk over a Weetabix, you could really go to town. Especially at the Sukhothai, where the buffet was as rich in smoked salmon and tropical fruit as it was in the usual international 'full English'. Laura was holding a large plate and hovering around the silver tureens in that indecisive way of hotel guests who can't decide whether to be reasonable and go continental with a bit of muesli, or say to hell with it and pile on the sausages and fried bread. In the end she exercised restraint, thinking about her bikini, but she did allow herself a croissant alongside the lychees and mango.

She carried her plate back to their table where Antoine was sitting in his tropical leisurewear. Pale trousers with sharply ironed creases and one of those short-sleeved polo shirts that made her think of sales reps dressing down for the informal evening coach excursion. On his feet he was wearing a pair of dandyish cream shoes that made her long for Jean-Laurent's scruffy trainers. He was drinking a large glass of carrot juice, and Laura wondered whether this might be the secret of his rather orange complexion, or whether that was due to the generous platter of salmon that was his personal breakfast choice.

'Urrgh, raw fish in the morning, I don't know how you can!' she said, sitting down opposite him with a shudder that was brought on partly by the salmon, but also by the sight of her lover in his neat, unattractive clothes. Mornings could be very cruel. Breakfast should be taken alone and without conversation, yet here she was obliged to make small talk with a man she felt she barely knew, who happened to be sharing her bed.

'Rich in unsaturated oils,' replied Antoine. 'The Japanese have the lowest rate of heart disease in the world on account of their diet of raw fish.'

He swallowed a mouthful of salmon and raised a folded napkin to dab at his mouth. For some reason this fastidious gesture irritated Laura. It was funny how once you had gone off someone, everything they did started to get on your nerves.

Antoine failed to pick up on her disenchantment and looked to see what she had on her plate.

'Are you sure you've got enough there?'

He leaned towards her and added in a conspiratorial whisper, 'I would have thought you needed to replace your lost energy. After last night.'

She raised a weary smile. She was little versed in the etiquette of extra-marital affairs, but guessed that basic good manners obliged both partners to congratulate each other on their sterling performance.

'Yes. Very good, thank you,' she said.

Antoine moved the conversation briskly on: time for him to cast more priceless nuggets of information in the direction of his charming young mistress.

'I see you are remaining loyal to your adopted home country.'

Laura looked confused. What was he on about now?

He gestured towards her plate.

'The croissant, a symbol of France. But did you know that in fact they come from Austria?' He was wagging his finger at her in that infuriating French way.

'I do now,' she replied.

'Siege of Vienna. They couldn't get bread, so the Poles fashioned croissants in the crescent emblem of the Turks they were fighting. Fascinating, isn't it?'

She shrugged, fighting off the image of him as a

middle-aged history teacher, parading his knowledge before her, a sulky sixteen-year-old.

'I think perhaps you are right,' she said as she slipped down the last piece of mango. 'I think I could manage a bit more to eat.' She returned to the buffet and loaded her plate high with creamy eggs and crunchy strips of bacon, backed up with French toast and maple syrup.

He smiled at her as she returned.

'Good girl, get your strength up. We have a full weekend ahead of us after all! And tonight we shall be at Amanpuri. We will have cocktails on the terrace, then after dinner I will lead you down the steep stairs to the beach and we will walk barefoot along the shore beneath the moonlight.'

Laura imagined him taking off those cream shoes and socks and carefully rolling up his trousers. Like an indulgent, lascivious uncle. What the hell did she think she was doing? It was unfair to say that she had gone off him. It was just that what appeared sexy and sophisticated and elegant in two-hour bursts just didn't when you had it all the time. It would be like eating chocolate truffles for breakfast, lunch and dinner. You'd get sick of them.

THIRTEEN

Beneath the drizzle of a grey Parisian sky, Jean-Laurent glanced at his watch and found, to his weary surprise, that it was only ten-thirty. He was sitting on a bench in the Ranelagh Gardens, huddled into his raincoat while Charles-Edouard and Pierre-Louis were astride wooden horses on a *belle époque* merry-go-round. Armed with wooden batons, they were competing to see who could collect the largest number of metal rings that hung from a wooden panel masterminded by a patient man with kind eyes.

How he could remain so good-humoured was a mystery to Jean-Laurent. Day in, day out, he slotted in those damned rings, one at a time, and at the end of each session counted out every child's takings to see who would win the extra free go. It would drive Jean-Laurent nuts after half a morning, but this guy knew no other way – it was his entire working life.

Charles-Edouard was clearly his father's son, standing up in the stirrups, eyes narrowed, as he approached the target, his first raised triumphantly each time he succeeded.

Pierre-Louis was less successful; he had scored only the two rings that the kind man had put on to his baton so he didn't feel like a complete loser. Jean-Laurent changed the expression on his face as each of his sons turned to him for approval; a smug, good-on-you-my-boy for the elder, and a baleful, never-mind-old-chap for little Pierre-Louis.

He hoped his second son wouldn't grow up with an inferiority complex. He knew only too well how that felt, having suffered from a brilliant elder brother who took his *bac* at sixteen and graduated fifth in his year from the Ecole Nationale d'Administration. That was why Jean-Laurent had decided to finish his studies in England – nobody in his family could judge his performance there; and he had come back with a successful, refreshingly natural English wife who knocked his brother's boring bourgeois blonde into a cocked hat.

He had been so proud of Laura when he took her home to France to meet the family. His parents hadn't been too pleased to hear that their son had shacked up with his landlady. He was supposed to be concentrating on his studies, not wasting his time with a non-Catholic Englishwoman who was approaching the age of thirty and should have known better than to set her sights on an impressionable young boy.

'You'll understand when you meet her,' Jean-Laurent had reassured them on the phone. 'You will love her like I do.'

And they did. In their heads they had conjured up a middle-aged concierge wearing an old dressing gown and hair rollers and jangling a big bunch of room keys, eyeing up her tenants lasciviously before deciding which one should service her tonight. So when Jean-Laurent stepped off the train at Saint-Germain-en-Laye with a pretty young brunette in a camel cashmere coat and expensive-looking boots, they were mightily reassured. Particularly when they realised how well she spoke French, and how successful she was at her job.

His brother Vincent had been jealous of him for the first time in his life: his own wife had never worked, having married him straight out of college to start a family, and Vincent couldn't fail to appreciate the charm of this *petite anglaise* who was a bit of a babe *and* brought home the bacon.

Jean-Laurent's supremacy in the wife stakes was short-lived, however, Vincent's boring bourgeois wife had retrained after the children and now had a thriving career in the *bourse*, while Laura had never really got herself back together after the birth of Pierre-Louis. It was once she had stopped work that the rot really set in.

If only Laura had remained as she was then, when he first knew her. He wouldn't have dreamed of taking up with Flavia or anyone else. Nobody could touch Laura in those days – she was entirely perfect. He remembered coming out of the tube at Stockwell, looking round fearfully; for a boy raised in Saint Germain-en-Laye it was rather terrifying.

He had looked at the map and cut through a housing estate to get to Laura's street, keeping his head down, expecting a hooded killer to knife him at every step. He had already decided against taking the room by the time he reached her house; he wasn't going to risk *that* every night. But then she had opened the door and it was too late.

She was wearing an Agnès B two-piece, with a short skirt that he had followed up the stairs and into the bedroom she was offering for rent. Afterwards he couldn't remember a thing about the room, only the way she looked, the way her legs joined on to her body, the way she had spoken, so seriously, about how he might not like living there, how he should think about it and call her back. And him panicking that she might give the room to someone else and he might never see her again.

When he moved in with her they maintained a pretence of him having his own room, but they both knew it wouldn't be for long and soon he used it only as a study. In those early, magical days, he would go off to his classes every morning and think about Laura, imagining her at work chairing the kinds of meetings he was looking forward to holding himself as soon as he got that MBA under his belt. And every evening they spent together, sometimes alone, sometimes with Laura's friends, who helped him with his English and flattered him with their attention.

And then they had the boys, the fruit of their love, the boys he adored unconditionally but who seemed somehow to have transformed Laura into someone he wasn't sure he knew. Everyone evolved all the time, of course, but when he looked back he found it hard to equate the Laura he loved then with the Laura she was today.

The roundabout was stopping now; the patient man's assistant was turning the handle more slowly. It was mechanically operated: there were no vulgar electric motors in the Ranelagh Gardens, which replicated the nineteenth century right down to the mid-calf corduroy trousers favoured by most of the children who played there. *Les enfants du seizième*, with the side partings for boys, Alice bands for girls, sensible children in burgundy and olive-green clothes purchased by their head-banded mothers so they could grow up looking exactly like their dull-as-ditchwater parents. It wasn't like that in Montmartre – but Jean-Laurent didn't want to think about Montmartre and lovers and a different way of life.

As the antique roundabout drew to a standstill, Charles-Edouard was already petitioning for another go, pointing to his overloaded baton to show that only the under-achieving Pierre-Louis would have to be paid for, he the super-hero would once again be awarded the free turn. Jean-Laurent shook his head.

'No, come on Charles-Edouard, it's raining, keep it for another time. Let's go to the museum now – that's what we agreed.'

He lifted Pierre-Louis off his horse and led them across the road to the musée Marmottan. The trip to the park had been negotiated alongside a more adult-interest visit to see Monet's paintings, which were displayed in the basement of an agreeable townhouse. They joined a modest queue of visitors – the museum was sufficiently small and obscure to keep away the hordes – and Jean-Laurent enjoyed feeling virtuous as he introduced his small sons to the treasures of their country's *patrimoine*.

'Claude Monet,' Pierre-Louis piped up unprompted as he pointed at one large canvas of water lilies, now the stuff of place mats and greetings cards the world over.

'Well done, good boy,' said his father, enjoying the

approving glances of an attractive leggy American girl whose bottom he had been admiring on the way in.

'We did it at school, with the bridge,' explained Pierre-Louis.

'So you did!'

Jean-Laurent remembered the school open afternoon, a wall covered with four-year-old interpretations of the garden at Giverny. The French idea of artistic creativity was to look backwards and offer faithful reproductions of past glories. It was the same at the Louvre school of art: adults were taught not to produce their own work, but rather to see how precisely they could imitate master-pieces of the seventeenth century.

'They all look the same,' complained Charles-Edouard as they moved on to another room with more swirling blues and lilacs and green. 'Can we go back to the round-about now?'

'No, the sandpit, pleeasse!' begged Pierre-Louis.

How does Laura do it, thought Jean-Laurent as he sat on another damp park bench and watched Pierre-Louis climbing up the slide for the umpteenth time. How does she do this stuff every day and not turn into a total cabbage-head? It was true that she wasn't as sharp as she used to be – that was part of their problem – but if he had to do this every day he would become a total zombie. Small children were deeply boring, that was the unspo-ken truth, and should be left strictly to those who were ill educated enough not to care.

He glanced over to the nanny corner, where a happy crowd of Filipinos were chatting to each other while their charges dug sand into buckets and raked tracks for their plastic cars. A bloody nanny, that was what they should have had, instead of that pain-in-the-arse Asa. Then Laura could have worked and remained in the land of the professional-thinking person and he wouldn't have been obliged to look elsewhere.

Charles-Edouard sat beside him. He was too grand for the sandpit now and kept an aloof distance, engrossed in his GameBoy. At least, thought Jean-Laurent, his boys were now entering the age of reason. The sandpit could soon become a distant memory – there would be more museums now, and football matches and computer game arcades, the proper fields of recreation for functional human beings.

Except, of course, that he was to become a father again. More years in the sandpit. The buggy, the car seat, the whole damn paraphernalia. And if he were to leave Laura and go with Flavia, he wouldn't be allowed the nonchalance of those who have done it all before. Flavia would be the starry-eyed new mother, he could just see it. For her it would be the mircale it had been for Laura, and for him, too – the feeling that no one had ever done this before, brought such a precious being into the world.

They had neither of them slept a wink that first night at home with Charles-Edouard. They had taken turns to sit by his carrycot and make sure he was still breathing. Jean-Laurent had put his finger by his mouth to try to feel the tiny breath, had watched the little chest rise and fall beneath the white blanket. And when the baby lay there too still, not moving at all, he would quickly touch his forehead, making sure he was still warm. He couldn't believe a living thing could stay so still.

Then when he started walking, he took his first steps on Clapham Common. Jean-Laurent had taken him there one Saturday morning when Laura had some work to catch up on. An old lady had been sitting next to him on the bench as he coaxed Charles-Edouard towards him. Eight tottering steps in his tiny doll-like shoes. Jean-Laurent had turned to the old lady in excitement and told her, 'That's the first time he's walked,' and she had been excited, too, for this charming young Frenchman so proud of his son.

And now Flavia would want him to go through all that again, all that angst and wonder and emotional draining. She didn't seem to appreciate that he had already been there. Twice. It had all been just as wonderful and bewildering with Pierre-Louis. He didn't want it all over again. He wouldn't have it. He had been abused and taken advantage of. She would have to go it alone.

What did you buy for your husband when returning from an adulterous love-fest in the East? A pirate Rolex? A jar of deep heat Tiger Balm? A silk suit, purchased in the fervour of the moment and destined never to be worn under grey European skies?

Laura wandered through the enormous shopping mall of Bangkok airport feeling happier than she could remember. She was blissfully alone. Free to stare at the miniature Buddhas without Antoine holding forth on their cultural significance and explaining the difference between the Theravada and the Mahayana branches of Buddhism. The Theravada, he had said in the course of his monologue that morning, was the conservative branch: it meant 'the way of the elders'. 'Oh,' she had said, 'that must be for you then. I, on the other hand, would see myself more on the liberal Mahayana side.'

He had got rather prickly and said that in view of the new life expectancy of 120, he was barely into early middle age. To which she had retorted that on that basis she had not even reached adolescence, which made him a child abuser.

This conversation, the nearest they had come to an argument, had taken place after breakfast in their hotel bedroom. They had been packing their bags, getting ready to move on to Phuket for the full-on relaxation part of the holiday. Antoine had checked his watch: the flight wasn't for another three hours. He felt he had time to go to the gym for a quick pound on the treadmill before they checked out.

Laura had been relieved to have a few moments on her own. The prospect of two days and nights of non-stop Antoine Bouchard was making her feel weary. When he wasn't giving practical demonstrations of the art of love, he would be stuffing her head with fragments from the vast compendium that was his Mind. Frankly it was getting to be a bit of a bore.

It didn't take her long to pack – her modest collection of toiletries was quickly returned to the toothpaste-stained sponge bag that was a fraction of the size of Antoine's. She had toyed with the idea of helping herself to a bathrobe, but decided the Sukhothai logo would be too much of a giveaway in the marital bathroom, and anyway she wasn't sure that she really wanted a memento of what was fast becoming in her eyes a shabby little escapade rather than a daring romantic adventure.

After fastening the Mandarina Duck, she had laid back on the unmade bed and wondered who would be using it next. Perhaps a corpulent, sandy-haired businessman and his ill-matched beautiful Thai companion, like the couple she had seen coming into the bar last night: a fat, bulging Western wallet on legs, his freckled arm around the slim waist of a girl who sat politely smiling while he downed a last drink before leading her off to the final pleasure of the night. A business transaction; there was no shame. He wouldn't dream of doing this back home in Woking – she knew it was Woking from his country club polo shirt – but in Bangkok it was part of the scene, along with the compulsory tour of the gilded wats and the shopping arcades.

But then, who was she to judge? Why was she any better? She might not actually have been paid for her services, but she certainly wouldn't be here unless Antoine was footing the bill. His suitcase stood ready by the foot of the bed, and on top of it was his male handbag – or document carrier if you wanted to be charitable. It was unzipped, and Laura could see his wallet lying inside. She looked at her watch – he would be at least another ten minutes. Plenty of time for her to have a satisfying little snoop.

With a frisson of shame, she reached across and drew out the wallet. She fingered the aubergine leather – not a colour she would ever choose herself – and opened it carefully to inspect the contents: Thai and French banknotes neatly stacked behind a line of credit cards, a driving licence, a photo of Sylvie taken several decades ago, some business cards, taxi receipts. All rather disappointing, really. She stuck a finger into the pocket running behind the credit cards and brought out a tightly folded piece of paper, thin and yellow with age. She unfolded it on the bed, and saw it was a handwritten list, with numbers running down the left-hand side and girls' names on the right. And there, right at the bottom, was Number 73: Laura.

Which was why she had decided to make a run for it. Quickly, before he returned from the gym, she had written a brief note: 'Sorry, got to go home. Thanks for everything. Number 73.'

She had hurried down to the lobby where the doorman had helped her into a Mercedes taxi to take her to the international airport. On the way she had stared out of the window and tried to imagine Antoine's rage when he returned from the gym to find her gone. She shouldn't have left that note – he would realise she had been snooping through his wallet. She should have just made an excuse, pretended something had cropped up at home. Would he still go to Phuket without her? She guessed he probably would; the hotel was booked after all. And who could say? He might even bump into Number 74 round that black swimming pool.

And now she was heading home. Laura de Saint Léger, the seventy-third person to have had the pleasure of Dr Antoine Bouchard, was handing over two jade elephants and a suspiciously cheap Quiksilver sports shirt to the girl in the airport shop. It could have been worse, thought Laura as she brought out her credit card. At least he hadn't awarded marks out of ten on a personal score sheet or used a star system depending on what acts had been performed, which was something boys apparently often put in their diaries. And of course it had given her what she had been looking for – a pretext to escape from a weekend of illicit and unwanted sexual activity with a lover she no longer desired.

As she fastened herself into the seat of the aeroplane, Laura prepared herself for the void of the flight ahead. Her feelings of euphoria and relief were waning as she started to think about the reality to which she was returning. Her two lovely boys – the very thought of them made her heart leap with joy. She could feel their small arms around her as she envisaged her homecoming. She would drop her suitcase in the hall and they would all be so happy it would make her realise it was worth the separation just for that moment of reunion.

But then there would be Jean-Laurent waiting nervously in the background, unsure how she would greet him. Jean-Laurent, who had been occupying her thoughts so fully since she had been away. Being in Thailand had brought back memories of how things used to be between them, how much in love they had been. It was hard to believe that this was the same Jean-Laurent, her husband – who had been carefully deceiving her for so long, and who had now engineered a brand-new baby to bring suffering upon her.

She had barely spoken to him since his revelation that Flavia was pregnant. He pretended he didn't want the child, but she knew he would change his mind. She knew with a bitter twist in her heart because, if she was honest, he hadn't exactly been over the moon when Laura first told him *she* was expecting a baby. He hadn't exactly hung the flags out, had he? He never sank quite so low as to ask 'who's the father?', but certainly there was shock, disbelief and a fair dose of panic before he came round to the idea.

But when Charles-Edouard was born, no father could have been more ecstatic. She saw him now, tears streaming down his face as he held his son, awkwardly, like a delicate and precious object he was terrified of breaking. And two years later, when Pierre-Louis was handed to him by the midwife, she saw it again: the joy, the unfettered weeping as he took his baby boy in his arms, more confident this time, instinctively supporting the tiny dark head with his strong, tanned fingers.

So why should it be any different this time? It might well be an unplanned pregnancy, but it was hardly the product of a one-night stand. It would be a beautiful baby girl, conceived in passion by people who made love to each other because they needed to, not because they happened to be married to each other. And this baby would be the stake that drove Jean-Laurent and Laura apart – there would be no avoiding that.

What had she been thinking of, buying her husband a fake Quiksilver shirt? Did she really think the handing over of cheap airport souvenirs was going to win him back from the beautiful mother of his unborn child?

Laura let herself into her apartment stealthily, like a burglar. She had telephoned from the airport to say that she was back early, but the answering machine was on; clearly Jean-Laurent had taken the boys to the café for breakfast. She breathed in the familiar air of home and made a tour of the bedrooms. Their bed was unmade but with no sign of dual occupancy, which was a relief. Although when it came to it she would have been surprised if Jean-Laurent had stooped so low as to bring That Woman into the family home.

The boys' bedroom, with its litter of Lego and small discarded socks, made her hungry to hold them. She picked up Pierre-Louis's Rupert pyjama top and smelt it – the perfume of his body was something she would like to bottle up and take with her were she ever to be abandoned on a desert island. An island paradise in Thailand, with only Antoine as a companion.

She shuddered at the thought of her happy release. How much rather she would be here, in the dull, quiet chaos of her home than in a blue-skied nirvana with her lover. How exotic the ordinary became when you had been deprived of it for a short time.

She went into the kitchen where two cereal bowls bore the hardening traces of Weetabix; they must have had breakfast at home after all. The coffee machine was still on and she drank the bitter-tasting remains of the jug as she flicked through the post. *Elle* magazine for her and, from England, the mini Boden catalogue of clothes for middle-class kids.

There were the usual nauseating captions beneath the photos of Sloaney children: 'Hugo, drummer,' who looked more as though his future would lie in the stock market. 'Helena, mummy': that was a more likely prognosis. She had never – God forbid! – ordered anything from them, but the catalogues kept arriving with all the thick-skinned self-assurance of the upper middle classes that sooner or later she would crack for a pair of man-child cords and a sweater as photographed on the beach at Rock.

Where had they gone? Would they be missing her? She hadn't yet come up with her excuse for her early return from the fictional girls' party in Barcelona – she would make it something emotive, something along the lines of not being able to stand the hysteria of all those women together. Though when it came to girly cosmetics, the contents of an entire hen party's toilet bags couldn't match up to Antoine's bulging vanity case. Would they have gone to the park? Perhaps she could walk along and look for them.

I'm rather like the protagonist of that Maupassant story, she thought as she stepped out into the crisp wintry sunshine. Or was it by Zola? The one where the man falls into a catatonic trance and is nailed into his coffin, attends his own funeral, and then miraculously digs his way out of the grave and goes back home. It doesn't end well, though – he finds his wife being comforted by a handsome neighbour and realises he is no longer required, so wanders off into the world of the living dead.

Would this be her fate? Would she find Jean-Laurent cuddling up to Flavia while the boys scampered around them in loving acceptance of their new mother? Laura would be relegated to the role of Birth Mother, a physical vessel who had served her purpose in bringing them into the world and now, like a used-up breeding cow, would be put out to grass. She would go on cultural tours of European cities with other discarded single women, while Jean-Laurent would take holidays at Club Med. He would lie next to Flavia on a sun-lounger and watch his three children joyfully ensconced in kids' clubs under the care of *gentils organisateurs*. They would epitomise the happy functionality of the new, re-formed family.

Over her bloody dead body they would. With a blinding flash, Laura suddenly realised that she was thinking like a defeatist. In a crushing attack of low self-esteem, she was casting herself as the betrayed, discarded wife, condemned to a life of tragic loneliness. But wait a minute. Who was just returning from a holiday with her secret lover? She was. Hardly the behaviour you'd expect from a doormat wifey. Who had prostated himself before her with grief and remorse, begging her to forgive him? Jean-Laurent. Did she still love him? Of course. And was she prepared to hand him on a plate to someone else? Absolutely not.

By the time she reached the park, Laura had made up her mind. She was not going to lie down like a dog and let Flavia take away her husband. The idea was preposterous. Flavia, that jumped-up self-serving egomaniac claimed to be a research consultant. So let her research a solution to her impending single parenthood. There was no way she was going to break up Laura's family.

I am empowered, thought Laura, delighted that she could now count herself the embodiment of one of the leitmotifs of Jean-Laurent's bullshitting business books. I have freed myself from jealousy and anxiety, and now I have a fixed purpose. She strode into the sandpit and saw Pierre-Louis standing at the top of the slide, snugly wrapped in his balaclava; Jean-Laurent was taking no chances against the weather. Then she saw her husband on the bench, smiling, his eyes feasting on his younger son. And it wasn't Flavia sitting next to him, it was Charles-Edouard, head down, engrossed in his GameBoy. She paused, wanting to savour the moment, to remain a spectator of this tableau of family life. But Pierre-Louis had seen her.

'Mummy!'

He pointed at her, dramatically, from his vantage point.

Jean-Laurent turned towards her. She saw him register surprise and then delight. He was glad she was there – he was getting up now, coming to greet her. How tall he was, how athletically he moved, how different from the carefully mannered gait of her erstwhile lover.

'You're back,' he said as she folded into his embrace. 'I'm so glad. Why are you back so early?'

She shrugged. 'Oh, you know, I just thought it would be more interesting to spend the weekend in the sandpit. I didn't see why you should have all the fun.'

'You still haven't told me why you came back early.'

Jean-Laurent was scraping the debris of fishfingers and rice into the swing-top bin. A few grains of rice missed their target and fell to the floor, joining the sprinkling of coffee grounds and miscellaneous smears that no one had bothered to clear up since Asa's departure. I suppose I could get a cloth and clean that up, thought Laura, but I don't think I will. She took a swig of her Chablis instead.

'I told you. I was missing home too much. What are you making me for dinner?'

'I thought I would be alone, so I just bought one steak.'

'Bloke's food.'

'Which I was planning to prepare with a *sauce aux*

échalotes and a simple rocket salad. With a bottle of St Joseph.'

'French bloke's food,' laughed Laura. 'If you were English, you'd be washing it down with a crate of lager and chips. Tell you what, let's share the steak and get some cheese in and it will do perfectly for two.'

'I have some Roquefort and some eighteen-month-old Comté. And we could start with foie gras.'

He was so eager to please it could have been pitiful had she not been enjoying it so much. He had refused her offer to help, and made her lie down with a magazine while he saw to the boys' tea. If only you knew, Laura had thought as she flicked through *Elle*, if only you knew that I have come hot from my lover's bed, albeit carefully cleansed by the full panoply of the Sukhothai's bathroom toiletries. She hugged her secret and rejoiced in his attempts to win her forgiveness. The anxious eyes, the hunger, the panic at the thought of what he stood to lose.

He was washing the pans now, stooping over the sink, too tall for the woman-sized kitchen. She took in the length of his thighs, the firm curve of his buttocks in his loose jeans. His shirt had come untucked and she could see his smooth, summer-brown skin above the waistband of his underpants. She came up behind him and lowered her face to kiss it, this skin she loved, to drink in its indefinable smell. She felt him stiffen with surprise, and then desire, as she ran her hands under his shirt around his tummy, and up to his chest.

'Laura . . .'

He reached behind him and cupped her face with his hands, still soapy from the water, pressing her into the small of his back. He pushed his hands down further, found her breasts, turned round and seized her roughly, pulling up her T-shirt.

'Do what you did to her,' whispered Laura.

He was pushing her against the wall now, his hand between her legs, his strong thighs locked around her. They slid to the floor.

This is madness, she thought, the boys could come in at any moment. But she couldn't stop. They were sliding now on the greasy kitchen tiles, his mouth biting into her neck as they climaxed beside the open dishwasher.

'You're mine,' she whispered into his ear as he crumpled into her. Sex was power and ownership and she now knew she was invincible.

Later, when the steak and Roquefort had been despatched and the boys tucked up, Laura and Jean-Laurent held hands in the re-ignited marital bed and talked about the Enemy. Every relationship needed an enemy, thought Laura – there was nothing more conducive to complicity. And when the enemy was until very recently a rival to one partner and a lover to the other, the taste was even sweeter.

'She'll just have to manage on her own,' said Laura. 'After all, you weren't consulted. She's just a victim of her own lust and connivance.'

She ran her free hand over her husband's loins. 'I can understand her wanting to have sex with you – who wouldn't? But to trick you into fathering a child is the depths of deceit. She knew you were married.'

She didn't add the logical follow-on, that *he* knew he

was married, too. Sexual satisfaction had made her generous, and anyway she had her own little secret in that
department.

Jean-Laurent was aware that he was being absolved
beyond what he deserved, but thought it prudent to bolster
his case while the hearing was sympathetic.

'We never talked about a future together, believe me.
She used to make hints, but I never encouraged her. She
should have known I would never leave you.'

How easy this was – how true it was that a problem
shared was a problem halved. He should have told Laura
sooner, but good God, if she had come on to him earlier
the way she had today in the kitchen he wouldn't even
have looked at another woman. She was responsible too.
If she hadn't become so mumsy and domesticated, he
wouldn't have fallen into Flavia's man trap.

He nuzzled up to Laura.

'I was a fool. I love you and I will never leave you.'

FOURTEEN

On the day of the school Christmas party, tensions were running high among the Full-Time Mothers. Busy, busy, busy was the message they sent out as they ferried cardboard boxes into the school hall, rolling their eyes at each other and exchanging grim little smiles. Look at us, they were saying, martyrs to the cause.

At the de Saint Légers' apartment, Laura and Lorinda were sitting at the dining table putting the final touches on their home-made decorations for the British stand. Discarded tubes of glitter-glue littered the parquet, along with scraps of green and red paper, the fall-out from their decorative holly frieze. Lorinda was grumbling about the ruthlessly secular approach the school took towards Christmas.

'How can you have Christmas without a Christ child? Mary and Joseph and that little baby, that's what it's all about. It's so barren seeing those kids singing "Jingle Bells" instead of proper Christmas carols.'

'You know why – it's out of respect for all the different

religions. If you wanted a Christian school you should have chosen one,' said Laura.

'I don't want a Christian school, I just want to see a nativity play. I want that heart-stopping moment of seeing my little Mathilde dressed up as the Virgin Mary cuddling a swaddled doll.'

'She probably would have been just a shepherd, and you would have been bitter and twisted. At least this way you won't think she has been slighted – there are no star roles in singing "Jingle Bells". But I know what you mean.'

Laura, too, would have loved to see her children immersed in a proper Christmas play, in a little village hall, on a rickety stage, watched by young and old, and followed by sherry and mince pies. It was part of the nostalgic fantasy of the life in England she had renounced when she agreed to follow Jean-Laurent to Paris.

'We should have married Englishmen and retired to the country to make jam,' she said, entering one of Lorinda's and her favourite games.

'And grow prize-winning chrysanthemums.'

'Raise money for the Church roof.'

'Make home-made chocolate cakes in the Aga.'

'Wear size sixteen floral dresses.'

'And put on all the jewellery we own for our annual trip to town with our old padded-shoulder suits from our glory days as career girls.'

'Instead of which we are city housewives – edgy, sassy, sophisticated.'

'Sad. Except for you, of course, with your glamorous lover and trips to exotic hotels.'

'Lorinda, please don't remind me. I'm trying to put that

dismal little episode behind me. Number 73. How humiliating is that!'

'Not at all humiliating – it served its purpose. Look at you and Jean-Laurent – you're happier now than you've ever been.'

It was true, of course. They had never had such good sex, and Laura knew this was because it was spiced with the danger of betrayal and deception. It was hard to get excited about an old pair of slippers that nobody else would want to wear, and her new enjoyment of her husband's body was interlaced with images of him with Flavia. It was also enhanced by her own short-lived adultery; a secret that gave her an added thrill, a power over her unknowing husband.

She had seen Antoine just once since their return from Thailand. He had been regretful, slightly offended, but had suffered only a light scratch to his self-esteem. They had lunched at the Ritz, though the room upstairs had remained unused. There had been no poetry recitals – she had forfeited the right to hear his wonderful voice delivering words of love from Marivaux. He understood her decision to end the affair, although he felt she was giving into the pedestrian side of her that wanted to stamp out anything beautiful and life-enhancing and plod on in the dreary furrow of normal married life. But that was how she was. He had always felt that her love-making was overlaid – please don't take this as a criticism, Laura – with a rather unappealing grey Protestantism.

Laura had choked on her *truite chablisienne* at the idea of herself lying in bed wearing a Lutheran dog collar. Was it his experience, then, that Catholics were better in the sack? How many other proddy dogs did he count amongst those seventy-two lucky women? He had winced at the crudity of the question as though that just about proved his point, and said that she was lacking a certain willingness to abandon practical considerations to the realms of fantasy, and he didn't know if this was to do with religion or was more simply *une question d'éducation et de sensibilité*. It had been tempting to ask where he would rate her in his list of seventy-three, but luckily for her dignity she had managed to keep her silence.

'Time to go, then,' said Laura. 'We don't want PTA Paula getting her knickers in a twist.'

They packed up the holly frieze into a cardboard box, together with the Santa Claus poster and a couple of rolls of red and green crêpe paper, and took the coffin lift down to the ground floor.

'I feel almost festive,' said Lorinda as they climbed into the Renault Espace. 'Have you got the sherry?'

'Chin Chin,' said Laura, waving a bottle. 'Croft's Original, since we're sophisticated types. And that enormous Christmas cake, which is bound to hang fire, don't you think? I for one will be straight over to the Japanese table. I'd much rather get stuck into sushi than a great heavy slab of cold fruit cake.'

'Handy for climbing mountains, though. A slice of that could keep you going through the nastiest blizzard.'

'Unlikely in Paris.'

The weather was in fact remarkably clement. The sun was shining down on the river as they drove over the bridge – they could see tourists on the decks of the *bateaux mouches*. With the blind faith of the five-year-old,

Pierre-Louis was convinced it would snow on Christmas day, but Laura didn't hold out too much hope for him.

When they arrived at the school, they found PTA Paula standing on the street, fuming into her mobile phone.

'At last you're here. Where were you? I was just trying to call you. I really had to fight to keep the pitch for the British table – we're next to Scandinavia and they arrived hours ago!'

'Don't say the British territory has been overtaken by Viking marauders?' said Laura, irritated into levity.

'It's not funny, Laura, this event has been a nightmare to organise, and it's not fair to let everyone down by rolling up late.'

'Paula, it's three o'clock,' said Laura, 'You can't think it's going to take us three hours to hang up a few sad decorations?'

'They'd better not be sad! You're through the main hall, first room on the left, as long as no one has pinched your table.'

She flounced off, muttering darkly into her walkie-talkie.

'Can you believe it?' said Lorinda. 'She's mental.'

'The whole point of not working, as I see it,' said Laura, 'is that you free yourself from stress. But they can't stand it, these women, they can't stand not having stuff to worry about, so they create stressful situations. When you think of all that energy in there, all those capable women now engrossed in decorating tables and organising who's going to bring what. This is supposed to be fun, for God's sake, for the kids, and it always turns into a hysterical female hormone crisis!'

Lorinda was laughing now. 'Come on, Laura, you're becoming as bad as them. Let's go in and cut you a nice slice of Christmas cake, that'll calm you down.'

'I mean it, Lorinda, they are all mad. They should get a life. Get a job, do something.'

'They *do* do something – they're bringing up their kids. Like you and me.'

'But all this PTA nonsense hasn't got anything to do with bringing up their children, it's just something to keep them busy, to make them feel needed.'

'Hey,' said Lorinda in her faux American accent, 'we all need to feel needed, honey.'

'Well I don't. Not in that way. I just can't stand the idea that I'm "filling my time".'

'So why don't you fill it properly if that's how you feel? Why don't you go back to work?'

'It's funny you should say that,' said Laura, 'because that's exactly what I've been thinking. I've had enough of being a little Homebody.'

How did you get rid of a mistress you no longer required? The question was uppermost in Jean-Laurent's mind as he parked the Porsche behind the marché Saint Pierre and began the slow climb up the slopes of Montmartre.

Under normal circumstances he would have gone for the cold shoulder treatment – don't return the calls, suddenly become unavailable. She knew the rules; she would have got the message. But getting rid of an unwanted mistress who was carrying your child was an entirely different matter. Suddenly you became the complete bastard, the heartless seducer of hapless maidens, even though anyone could tell that *he* was the victim here, the stooge taken advantage of by a cunning and fecund courtesan.

In his dreams he had imagined a trap door opening up on a stage and swallowing Flavia as she stood holding her dolly-sized infant, its face mercifully hidden from sight. If only it could be like that. A puff of smoke and – whoosh! – the problem swooping out of his life for ever.

Then he had had other, darker fantasies: Flavia slipping under an oncoming train in the metro, or plunging to her death in a suicidal leap from her apartment window (unlikely as she was only on the first floor), or dying from an infection after visiting a back-street abortionist, though this obviously belonged to the pre-feminist era.

In reality, she had simply called him to suggest they meet to discuss matters, and he had agreed. Laura knew about it, of course – the last whiff of secrecy had been dusted off the affair, stripping it of all mystique. No longer the light-footed lover, he was now a man burdened by his responsibilities, facing up to the consequences of his actions. No wonder his steps were heavy as he turned into her street and rang the intercom.

Flavia was polite and cool. She sat him down and explained her position. She had loved him, she had genuinely believed they had a future together and there had been nothing in his behaviour to suggest the contrary. When she had come to that dinner party at his home, she had seen it as a subconscious desire on his part to bring her into the intimate focus of his home life, to see how her stellar presence would cast a shadow on his nice, but let's face it rather uninspiring, wife. She had conceived a child because she thought it was the natural evolution of their relationship, the affirmation of their shared future.

'But I realise now, Jean-Laurent, that I have made a mistake. I have overestimated you.'

She was standing by the window, her mood well this side of suicidal, he was relieved to see.

'You are not quite what I had hoped, and my disappointment in your reaction to news of my pregnancy – our pregnancy, if I may put it that way – only confirms my suspicions. You are more ordinary than I had hoped, and I think that on reflection you probably only deserve the wife you already have. I have therefore decided to absolve you from all responsibility for my baby. I intend to move to New York and raise my child as an American. I will be a successful single parent. There are plenty of role models – Liz Hurley, Jodie Foster, Calista Flockhart. And now Flavia Fernandez.'

As easy as that? Jean-Laurent could hardly believe his luck. He restrained the impulse to whoop loudly and punch the air, and nodded gravely instead.

'I respect your decision, Flavia. I am sorry you feel I have disappointed you. I never pretended to be anything other than what you saw, but maybe you hoped there was more there than there was.'

She smiled ruefully. 'I loved you, Jean-Laurent. But I realise now that I was loving you *reactively*. That book you gave me, *The 7 Habits of Highly Effective People*, explains it so clearly. Reactive people make love a *feeling*, they think they have no control over it. That is so feeble. Proactive people make love a *verb*. I am proactive, and I have decided not to love you. I will find someone else to love, someone more deserving of me.'

Good old Stephen Covey! How could he ever have doubted his pet guru! And what unexpected good luck that he should have bought a copy for Flavia at the height of their affair, when sex was often preceded by a warm-up session of reading pornographic snippets from business books.

He stood up. Quit while you're ahead – he was sure that was the route to take.

'You'll be a great success in New York. I really do wish you all the best.'

He awkwardly reached across and kissed her on the cheek. She held his arm briefly then released it and gazed out of he window, out into her golden future, entranced by the vision of herself as a young, beautiful, successful woman with her perfect baby. She need not worry about turning thirty now; the baby thing would have been done and dusted.

'Goodbye then.'

He almost skipped back to the Porsche.

Drained and depressed after the Christmas party, Laura had seen the light. The departure of Asa had thrown her headlong into the horror of 24/7 childcare, and the sight of her kitchen with its greasy litter of yoghurt pots and biscuit wrappers was enough to convince her. If she wished to remain sane she had only one option, and that was to get back to work.

Her desk was covered with copies of her CV, rewritten several times in increasingly glowing terms. The final version was, she felt, irresistible. How could anyone not want to employ this person whose rich life experience was

equalled only by her faultless qualifications and professional success? True, there had been a bit of a hiatus on
the professional front, which was where the life experience section came in, in an attempt to fudge the fact that
she hadn't done anything for years except for go to the
gym and attend too many school functions. And change
her hair colour and have sex with an endocrinologist. But
overall her achievements over the past five years could
best be summarised as a profit and loss sheet. On the
plus side, she had gained two stone, and in the minus
column, she had undergone a substantial loss of mental
agility. Credit and debit – it balanced up nicely.

On the CV, of course, it had to be phrased rather differently, and she was pleased at how well she had succeeded
in dressing up these idle years as a rich period of cultural
study, of broadening her horizons, extending her fields of
knowledge. She had, after all, realised the busy working
person's dream in achieving the freedom to move abroad,
go to museums, read extensively, live life to the full instead
of being chained to a desk.

Except it didn't feel that way. She had once read that
no one died wishing they had spent more time in the
office. Not true. If she was run over tomorrow she would
regret having missed out on so much of the camaraderie
and rivalry that made up office life. She wanted a jokey
mug of coffee on her desk and people to have lunch with.
She wanted long days when the only sighting she had of
her children was via a silver-framed photo of the little
darlings, smiling up at her adoringly. All that lovely adult-
only time.

She would miss them, of course, and look forward to

seeing them when she got in, and spending every minute of the weekend with them. It wasn't like she was packing them off to boarding school for weeks at a stretch. True, she had enjoyed the luxury of time spent with them over the last five years. Hours and hours of slow-moving solitude. The deadening routine, the lack of adult stimulation. How much time did you need to spend with them anyway? And how interesting could you be to other people when your conversation was centred on small children and the shadowy world of those women who surround them?

She remembered an off-the-cuff remark of a friend who had said she would never give up work because she would be terrified of having nothing to say for herself. The friend had realised her gaff immediately and set about backtracking, saying how in Laura's case it was quite untrue, but the damage was done and they hadn't been in touch since.

Laura printed out ten more copies of the story of her life, edited version. At least she was the right side of forty. Bad enough to be climbing off the scrap heap at her age, but a few more years down the line and it would be out of the question. After the menopause it seemed you put on two pounds with every year, which would soon leave you permanently beached. You wouldn't have the agility to hop off the old bag waste pile.

Should she attach a photo to show how un-old-bag-like she was? Probably not; she wasn't applying to be a call girl, after all. An interesting signature together with her wide-ranging list of hobbies should be enough to show how she had a bit more personality than your average unemployed ad executive.

She sealed the envelopes and swept them into her hand-bag. Soon she would be joining the real world. She would be able to complain about her journey to work, lament the lack of consideration for working mothers, smugly read articles about women performing miraculous juggling feats of home and office and children. She would be born again. *Arbeit macht frei*, work sets you free, that maligned Nazi slogan, would become her mantra.

FIFTEEN

'Hallo, my darling; I love you.'

Jean-Laurent had his feet up on his desk and was on the phone to his wife. He could be forgiven for feeling rather pleased with himself. To be let off the hook by the mistress and readmitted so amorously into the richness of married life was more than he deserved. Well, maybe not, he was pretty special – no wonder Laura would want to keep him at any cost – but he really couldn't believe that things were turning out so well for him. And now he was being summoned for a meeting with the European chairman, which was why he had called Laura, to share with her his excitement about what this could mean.

'James wants to see me at three o'clock. I thought I should just ring to check there was champagne in the fridge. I've got a feeling this could be good news.'

'Don't count your chickens,' said Laura, hating herself for sounding like her mother. 'Maybe he's going to fire you.'

'Oh Laura, my little prophet of doom, come on, be excited for me! I've been waiting for this!'

'OK, I'm excited for you. But ring me afterwards when you've got the details. I'll need some stimulating news from the real world after my team lunch with the Full-Time Mothers.'

'Oh is that today? Don't worry, you'll be back in the rat race soon enough, then you'll wonder why you bothered. *Au revoir, chérie,* I love you. Bye-bye.'

He hung up and doodled on his pad. It could mean a move, of course. London, maybe even New York. Best not to mention that to Laura until it was sure. She would be on for it, anyway.

That was the advantage of an Anglo-Saxon wife: they transplanted well. Not like the French, who complained and clung tenaciously to their roots – he had seen it before amongst his colleagues, passed over for promotion because their wives refused to abandon the home country.

Vincent Bernard's wife had tried to explain it to him once. *'Tu comprends, Jean-Laurent, Paris, c'est comme ma maison!'* Jean-Laurent had felt this was a pretty weak excuse for standing in a man's way. After all, if Paris could be your home, why not any other city, particularly as it usually meant another rung up the ladder and a more sumptuous *maison* to boot. And look at poor old Vincent now, sidelined in the domestic market with no hope of promotion. He hoped his wife realised what she had done.

He went into his emails and saw he had a reply from the human resources director in New York. Good, that would be about the payment of a bonus owing to him from last year; he had been chasing it up for weeks. The message was actually addressed to the financial director, with Jean-Laurent copied in for information. He read it, then read it again. It must be a mistake. They had got the wrong person. He checked his name. Jean-Laurent de Saint Léger. It was written in English; maybe he had misunderstood.

He reached up for his dictionary. There must be another meaning of 'severance'. Perhaps it was a coded Anglo-Saxon term for massive promotion or extremely big job. But the only translations *Larousse* offered were *rupture* and *cessation*. He stared back at the screen. There it was, that bald sentence. 'Perhaps this could be included as part of the severance package.' It must be a joke.

He quickly typed in his reply – 'What does this mean? Please explain more clearly.' – then waited for the embarrassed disclaimer. It wouldn't come immediately, of course; it was only 6 a.m. in New York. By the time they got into the office, he would have had his meeting with James.

He walked to the window and gazed across the Seine. That fabulous view – not something you would waste on someone you intended to fire. They would have fobbed him off with the ventilation shaft if that were the plan. Or given him no window at all. Plenty of people had windowless offices – the administration staff, condemned to a lifetime in the netherworld, keeping the wheels of the organisation running below a barrage of strip lighting. Not for them the sight of the sun setting over the Conciergerie, unless they managed a sideways glimpse as they went scurrying off to the metro on the way home to their shoebox apartments or their *pavillons de banlieue*. The little people. The ones who would never make it. The ones who would never be fired.

A girl with a neat shiny bob put her head round the door. 'Jean-Laurent, James will see you now if you are free.'

Did she know? He couldn't detect any pity in her face. Had she thought about him when she washed her hair this morning with the *schadenfreude* of those who comfortably witness the downfall of others without ever having to deliver the cruel blow themselves?

He followed her down the corridor and noticed her black bra showing through her thin blouse. She probably chose it especially as a mark of respect for his imminent demise. They arrived at James's office, twice the size of Jean-Laurent's, with two windows and a pair of leather sofas.

James stood up to greet Jean-Laurent and shut the door behind them.

'Sit down, please,' he said, gesturing towards one of the sofas while taking a seat on the other one himself. He gave only the smallest imitation of a smile, so Jean-Laurent knew it was bad news. He sat back and waited for the blow to fall.

James took a deep breath and left a pause just long enough to spare his victim any hope of a last-minute reprieve. Then he spoke.

'I'm afraid this isn't going to be an easy conversation.'

He's taking the British approach, thought Jean-Laurent. Softly, softly, the iron fist in the velvet glove. He remembered a friend who had been fired by an American manager, all tough talk, straight to the point, we're terminating your contract. This wasn't James's style. Instead there was a lot of general stuff about restructuring, pressure from the holding company, the need to reduce costs by twenty per cent, accompanied by arm gestures and sympathetic nodding.

'The good news for you, Jean-Louis, is that we are prepared to be generous,' he said finally.

'It's Jean-Laurent, actually.'

'I'm sorry, I really hate to do this, you know.'

'So are you firing me, or what?'

'Firing is not at all the appropriate term, Jean-Laurent, not for someone as valuable to the company as you are . . . as you were . . .'

'But you are, as you British like to say, going to have to let me go.'

James smiled in relief. The penny had dropped, the worst was over.

'Yes, I'm afraid that's just about it.' His eyes were beseeching, like a dog's. Please don't hate me, they said.

Then why couldn't you just come out and say so, you coward, thought Jean-Laurent.

He said nothing.

'We will, of course, do everything we can to help you. Legal advice and so on.'

You can shove it up your arse, thought Jean-Laurent.

Humiliation comes in many forms. While Jean-Laurent was being gently pushed off the corporate ladder, Laura was engaged in her own preferred form of self-torment. Crouched at the computer, she was logged on to google.com, following the glorious careers of her friends and contemporaries.

She usually began with a few ex-boyfriends. This was a mild build-up, since there was a certain vindication of her own judgement to be found in the success of an ex. Her university friends might have thought that Stephen Peters was a moronic rugby-playing waste of time, but she now learned through the search engine that he was one of only

three surgeons capable of performing a certain hip operation. She could be forgiven for feeling a little vicarious
pride. Then there was the entirely useless and aristocratic
Humphrey Redesdale. During their brief romance he rarely
found the energy to leave the bed, and was pretty lacklus-
tre even there; yet here he was, the author of an acclaimed
book about a bunch of toffs failing to reach the South Pole.

After limbering up on the men she used to know, Laura
would then move closer to the knuckle by entering the
names of some of the girls she used to call her friends.

Mercifully, there were plenty who didn't show anything,
their illustrious beginnings faded into obscurity. She imagined them leading uneventful lives, bringing up their families, doing dead-end – she hoped! – jobs while shuffling
towards middle age.

This comfort was short-lived, however, because sooner
or later she would have to check on the progress of the
Big Ones. Her best friend from college, for instance, who
was now a High Court Judge, for crying out loud. Laura
always had to take a deep breath before entering her name.

Then there was the dazzlingly beautiful English student
who had shaken off her tragic aura to ensnare a filthy
rich ageing rock star and bear him four children while
winning status and renown for what was frankly a very
slight and pedestrian little volume of poems.

She switched off the computer and went through to lie
down on the sofa to recover. She was still slightly drunk
after the post-Christmas party lunch held by the PTA to
thank themselves for all their hard work.

A long narrow table occupying the length of the restaurant, peopled entirely by women. Women whose only topics

of conversation related to their children. True, they might branch out on to holidays, as in, where are you taking your children for the winter holidays; or politics, as in, don't you think it's scandalous that the tax credit for children has been reduced; or environment issues, like, should we really be allowing our children to eat meat? But mostly it was centred on their own children, in minute detail. 'He only got a seven in spelling and I really feel he could do better.' And this was when the mothers were away from their children, God knows how the conversation went when they were *en famille*.

'Please, for pity's sake talk about something else!' Laura had wanted to scream at them. Though preferably not your step class or painting on porcelain. And certainly not the summer fête: she had already been allocated responsibility for tying ribbons on to the medals on that day, but she hoped she would have crossed to the other side by then, to the world of the living-brained – the rational, stimulating, child-free paradise that was the workplace.

The phone started to ring and she pulled herself up from the sofa to answer it. It was probably Jean-Laurent, she hoped it was good news. But it wasn't Jean-Laurent at all, it was a voice from the past, the confident tone of school prefect overlaid with career sophistication.

'Laura, is that you? It's Penny. Penny Porter.'

Penny Porter, her *bête noire*, the got-it-all monster of ambition.

'Penny, what a surprise,' she said. 'Did you get my card?'

'Certainly did. Impressively early, too. And thanks for the vests.'

Laura winced. It had been a bit mean and she wished

she'd gone the Bonpoint route now. But Penny sounded genuinely touched.

'How did you know about the baby, anyway?' Penny asked, 'I haven't sent the cards out yet, I decided to wait and do it with the Christmas list.'

'I saw you in the *Daily Mail*,' said Laura, before she could stop herself.

Damn, why did she let that slip? Revealing herself as a tabloid-reading housewife reduced to living vicariously through the achievements of her contemporaries.

'Oh yes, terribly embarrassing, awful photo.'

But she was obviously glad that Laura had seen it.

'And are you at home now? On maternity leave?'

'No, I went straight back. Couldn't hack the mother and baby group. Do you know there was one woman there who introduced herself as Rub.'

'Rub? Something sexual?'

'Afraid not. It seems that when she was a girl, she was nicknamed Rub because she always talked such rubbish. That was it for me. I cancelled my maternity leave and came right back to work, only way to keep sane as far as I can see. Look, Laura, I'll come straight to the point. Our agency in Paris is looking for someone to work on their international accounts. Exactly your profile, blue-chip and all that – I thought it might suit you. You can't hang around at home all your life, you know; got to keep the old brain ticking over. If you agree, I'll get them to call you to fix up an interview. What do you think?'

Laura couldn't believe it. Penny Porter, the most unlikely guardian angel, was swooping in to save her life.

'Penny, that's fantastic. You won't believe this, but I

have just this week put my CV together. I've finally come to the conclusion that a life without working is no life at all.'

'You've changed your tune, then. I almost didn't bother to call you – you always seemed such an advocate of the stay-at-home life.'

'I was, but things are different now. I've changed, I suppose.'

'Glad to hear it. Can't have all that education going down the pan. Expect a call, then. I've got to go now, I've got a meeting. We'll speak soon.'

'Yes, right. Goodbye, Penny.'

Jean-Laurent couldn't face calling Laura. He put on his coat and walked quickly past his colleagues' offices to the lift. The receptionist smiled at him, as she always did. Next time she saw him, her smile would no doubt be filled with pity. If there was a next time. He would need to return to clear his desk, but perhaps he could do that at the weekend, when there wouldn't be anyone around to witness his humiliation.

He made his way across the rue de Rivoli towards Les Halles, and took the escalator down into the bowels of the shopping precinct. He was heading for his mecca, FNAC, the media emporium that had long been his spiritual sanctuary. Many an hour had been spent in its business book section, plotting his rise amongst those macho volumes.

He walked through the cartoon book department, where the usual handful of young men were settling down on the floor for an afternoon of flagrant browsing. He was free to join them now, of course, but he would look out of place with his business suit; he would need to go home first and change into an unemployed person's leisurewear. He arrived at the management section. The familiar titles leapt out to greet him. *Power Shift, Brand Leadership, Positioning: the Battle for Your Mind*. Square-jawed, focused, hard-bodied volumes speaking of dominance and beating the enemy.

He searched in vain for something on coping with redundancy; flicked through the indices for references to losing your job, being unwanted, facing up to failure. Nothing. He asked an assistant, 'Do you have anything on dealing with redundancy?' She looked up at him, bored, dismissive. 'You're in the wrong section. You don't need management, you need self-help. *Guides pratiques.*'

Self-help. Him, Jean-Laurent, a future ruler of the universe, reduced to rifling through books for losers. Books for little people down on their luck. He reminded himself of his pet guru Stephen Covey's advice that proactive people carry their own weather with them, but all he could see was a black cloud raining down on him, a discarded piece of reactive old junk.

He pulled a book down from the shelf and learned that redundancy was like a bereavement and that there were four distinct stages. Shock, anger, grief and acceptance. He was in shock, then, and could look forward to anger and grief. It was time to go home to Laura.

At the school gates, Lorinda was unconvinced by Laura's Paul-on-the-road-to-Damascus conversion.

'Laura, I know you're excited about this interview, but let's keep things in proportion. Think about what you'd be missing out on. All those long holidays. Meeting the children out of school. You won't be able to do this any more, you know.'

'Thank God! Look at those women, Lorinda, look how depressing they are. Crumbling into middle age behind their pushchairs. Laying down their lives for the comfort of their children. No wonder Jean-Laurent had to take up with Barbie-face. I'd have shagged her myself if the alternative was someone like me.'

'But you always used to say how lucky you were not to be stuck in an office. The luxury of choice, I seem to remember, was a favourite phrase of yours.'

'Yes, I've had the luxury of choosing to stay at home, and that was fine for a bit,' said Laura. 'But now I want the luxury of choosing to resume my career. That's all right, isn't it? I'm not obliged to remain a Housewife for the rest of my life, am I?'

'Like me, you mean?' said Lorinda, pulling her scarf over her hair and tying it under her chin in a parody of a homely drudge.

Laura laughed.

'No, not like you,' she said. 'You're the bolshiest, most opinionated person I know. You're *thrilled* about not having to work. But it just makes me feel inadequate and dull. And I don't want the boys to grow up with a bitter mother who thinks she gave it all up for them. I don't want them to carry that burden.'

She watched a conversation going on between two women which seemed to involve some complicated dropping off and picking up between judo and music classes. As the plan materialised, the headbands nodded in agreement, deal concluded. Beside them two flashier mums were comparing their preparations for the Christmas holidays, rolling their eyes at the thought of everything that needed to be bought before they were safely despatched on their planes for Mauritius and Courchevel respectively.

'I mean just *listen* to them, Lorinda,' Laura whispered. 'They are so *boring!*'

'But people are boring everywhere. I imagine that even the conversation in an international advertising agency can sometimes be, dare I say it, less than deeply fascinating. And even though Penny Porter seems to have suddenly become flavour of the month as far as you are concerned, I seem to remember you used to think she was pretty massive on the scale of boringness.'

'Actually, she was quite all right on the phone. Almost amusing, in fact.'

Lorinda looked at her friend incredulously.

'Penny Porter *amusing*? Since when did amusing people send their friends padded Christmas cards with a printed message and no signature?'

Laura shrugged. 'She's a busy woman. And so shall I be soon.'

They were interrupted by the arrival of PTA Paula, officious with a clipboard and two highlighter pens.

'Girls, I never thanked you properly after the Christmas buffet. I thought you did jolly well in the end, and luckily there was loads left over on the British table for the late arrivals.'

'Don't remind us,' said Lorinda. 'All those French men turning their noses up at the mince pies and stodgy sausage rolls – it confirmed all their worst suspicions about British food, only to be eaten when there is no alternative.'

Paula ignored her and steamed on with her clipboard.

'I'm drawing up the schedule for English story-reading. I've got a slot at 11.30 on Thursdays for the *dixième* class. Laura, could you take that on?'

'No, I don't think I could.'

'In that case, how about the *onzième* at 9.15 on Fridays?'

'No.'

'It's only twenty minutes. Surely that's not too much to ask?'

'I'm afraid it is. Get the teacher to do it, it's her job. I've had enough of busy-bodying around, "filling my time" along with a load of other sad unemployed women – sorry, full-time mothers. Damned stupid term, that; no one ever described themselves as a full-time child, did they, or full-time brother? You either are a mother or you're not; the number of hours you spend hanging around them has nothing to do with it.'

Lorinda tried to restrain her.

'OK, Laura, cool it, she's got the message. She'll get someone else to do the reading.'

But Laura was well into her stride.

'I mean, look at you, Paula. You used to be a driving force at Goldman Sachs and now you spend your days bullying people into making Roman chariots or contributing to bake sales. How can you live with yourself?'

Paula's face turned red behind her spectacles.

'I made a lifestyle choice, Laura. And at least I make a contribution. I play an active role in bringing up my children, and I'm a key player in the parent-teacher liaison that plays a vital role in their education. Unlike you. As far as I can work out, you do nothing at all, except pour scorn on those of us who do pull our weight.'

'You are absolutely right,' replied Laura, 'but I have seen the error of my ways, and I'm glad to say I'm on course to join the real world.'

'She means she's hoping to get a job,' explained Lorinda. 'I'm afraid it's a case of poacher turned gamekeeper, or something.'

'Well I just hope the "real" world doesn't appear too disappointing,' said Paula with heavily ironic emphasis. 'I know that for me, a "real" world where you get in after the kids are asleep and leave before breakfast does not equate with my idea of family life.'

'I think it sounds fantastic,' said Laura. She had some reservations, of course, about returning to work, but it didn't prevent her from playing the devil's advocate to rile Paula. 'Imagine coming home and finding them all tucked up, fed and cleansed. Just pouring yourself a glass of wine before going in to kiss their sleeping heads. And ask yourself one thing, Paula. Is all this really for the kids, or is it for you? I'll tell you what I think. You do it because you've got nothing better to do and you're terrified of admitting it. You might as well just stick a big label on your forehead saying "put out to grass".'

'Oh look, the children are out,' said Lorinda, desperate to put an end to a most unpleasant conversation.

But Paula was already recovering for the counter-attack.

'You know, Laura, you really are quite poisonous. I can see now why that nice husband of yours had to find someone a little more amenable. And thinner, too, I hear.'

Lorinda raised her hands in self-defence.

'It wasn't me, Laura, honestly. I swear I never said a word!'

Laura waved dismissively.

'It's all right, Lorinda, I know that idle gossip is the other time-filler for sad housewives. God knows we have precious little else to talk about over coffee. For your information, Paula, that's all over now. And it wasn't just him. I too was brave enough to inject some spice into the marriage. You should have a bash at adultery yourself – far more entertaining than organising PTA rotas.'

And with that she swept off to collect her children. I hope to God I get this job, she thought, because I think I might have just burnt my bridges with the non-working mothers' network.

Jean-Laurent was sitting on the sofa when Laura and the boys got home. Without taking off their coats, Charles-Edouard and Pierre-Louis threw themselves upon him in an animal display of affection.

'I wish I got that kind of welcome,' said Laura, picking up their satchels. 'I suppose it's just a case of familiarity breeding contempt. I need to make myself scarcer – that's becoming very clear to me now. You know, I think I might have some very exciting news— Jean-Laurent? What's wrong.'

He was staring ahead completely motionless. He turned to face her.

'I'm sorry, Laura. It seems I had the wrong idea . . .'

'What is it? Are you all right?'

'I'm . . . apparently . . . not as indispensable as I liked to think . . .'

Laura felt her stomach lurch.

'Boys, go and take your coats off.'

They obediently disengaged themselves from their father, sensing that this was serious adult business.

Laura waited until they were out of the room.

'It's Flavia, isn't it? You're leaving me.'

Her temples were throbbing and she pressed her fingers against the pressure. But Jean-Laurent was looking at her in confusion.

'No, no, that's all over, you know that . . .'

'Oh, thank God. Oh, Jean-Laurent, you can't imagine how relieved I am. I'm dizzy with relief.'

She looked at him again.

'You're not ill, are you?'

He shrugged. 'I've felt better.'

'But you haven't just found out you've got six weeks to live?'

'No. Laura. That meeting this afternoon wasn't what I imagined . . .'

'Oh, it's just *work*, is it. Well who cares about that.'

'I've been fired. Made redundant.'

He watched her face, looking for her reaction. She was surprised, certainly, but not devastated. Not humiliated, the way he had felt.

'Those bastards!' she said. 'How dare they! Poor you.'

She took him in her arms and rocked him like a baby.

'Honestly, Jean-Laurent, it couldn't matter less. It really couldn't matter less.'

EPILOGUE

Laura picked up her gym mat and replaced it on the pile in the corner. She smiled at the good-looking young man who had been crunching next to her for the six-thirty *abdo-fessiers* class. One of the many benefits of her new lifestyle was the chance to attend an early evening gym class every Thursday where there was a refreshing absence of full-time mothers. They would be doing the tea and homework routine while she was unwinding after a day's work alongside other young and not-so-young professionals.

After her shower she would go home to a *dîner à deux* at an impeccably laid table. Since he had stopped working, Jean-Laurent had been able to indulge his passion for table decoration and took great pride in varying the theme. Tonight he had promised postmodern rococo with the gilt plates he had picked up at the salon des arts de la table. She was cooking tonight, and had emailed him with the shopping list earlier in the day.

The boys were thrilled at the new childcare arrange-ments. The only other fathers who collected their children were actors or restaurateurs with a seedy glamour that was easily eclipsed in their eyes by Jean-Laurent's casual sporty look. The Porsche had gone, of course, but the Renault Espace was far better for taking the three of them to the golf course on Wednesday afternoons. Jean-Laurent played eighteen holes on Fridays, too, and on Mondays and Thursdays he had his oenology classes to up the ante and so be sure of maintaining his position as chief nose of the wine-tasting evenings.

He would probably go back to work one day, but not yet. First he had to complete his book on growing through rejection. His premise was that only the best get fired, and it was the snivelling losers who remained in employment. His publisher was already talking about supplying corporations who would throw in a copy of *Mounting the Scrapheap* (working title) as part of the redundancy package offered to those being terminated.

Laura showered and decided to spend ten minutes in the steam room before going home. She was usually back for homework duty, but on Thursdays she left it to Jean-Laurent and preferred to return just in time for the children's goodnight kiss. She sometimes felt guilty for not telling Jean-Laurent about Antoine, but it would be such a shame to fall off the pedestal that he had created for her. Everyone needed a secret, after all.

And there was also the small matter that the affair with Antoine had not quite been kicked into touch. She had forgiven him for his remarks about her Protestant love-making, and at her suggestion they had agreed to meet just once a month for lunch in the Ritz, followed by a poetry reading in a suite upstairs. It was, he said, the mature apotheosis of a love affair, the *nec plus ultra* of sophistication. Hot young lovers threw themselves at each other as if there were no tomorrow; but their affair was a fine wine, to be tasted with restraint and proper appreciation. There was one particular verse that he liked to quote at her. It was from *Toi et Moi* by Paul Geraldy, a 1930s playwright close to his heart, a kind of Noel Coward with a twirly French moustache:

> 'we must be happy to be what we are;
> intermittent lovers who are crazy about one
>   another . . .
> from time to time.'

What with a part-time lover, a full-time job and a happy home life, she had it all.